Teddy Baire
Copyright © 2020 by United States

Author: Teddy Baire

www.Fiverr.com
Editor: Heather Williams (heatherwealth)
Editor: Vladonee (vladonee)
Cover Artist: Shinta Ayu Dewi (shinayu)

I0582662

ISBN: 978-1-7349516-0-8

READER BEWARE

This book has depictions of sex, assault, murder, blood, gore, and other questionable acts.

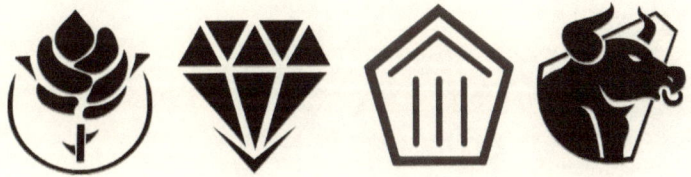

Thank you for visiting this world of magic.

CHAPTER 1

In the late-night hours in the city of Passala, a fire blazed over the mansion of Duke Richards. Its light was so tremendous that it cast an orange glow over the entire city. The residents peered out from their homes to the beacon of flame that shone through the night sky. And from the flames of the manor, soldiers hurriedly escorted the last of the servants out of the burning building. They forced them to their knees only to have them watch and listen to the crackling embers of what was once their home. A bearded soldier in armour walked in front of the servants, glancing them over.

"I am Leonardo Pendra of his majesty's royal guard," the man declared. "We are here at the behest of King Nevander Montavia to arrest Duke Christol Richards on suspicion of treason against the crown. We demand cooperation in capturing the members of his family and household. Now, does anyone here know where little Miss Richards is?"

The servants of the burning manor gazed over each other, wondering who would dare to be the first to speak.

Leonardo sighed at their hesitance. "I am not here to harm any of you. As I said, I have orders to capture and detain all members of the House Richards."

One of the male servants, an older man with grey in his beard, was bold enough to speak. "That... that's not true. There was no detaining. You killed the guards and murdered the Duke and his wife."

Leonardo slowly leaned his head back and pinched his nose, annoyed as the heat of flames roasted the back of his neck. "Why is it always like this?" Turning to his side, he gestured his hand to the burning manor. "This was your Duke's doing. We had orders to capture him alive, you hear me, alive. But he and his wife refused to be detained and started this whole mess. And now thirteen of my men are dead, with many others severely burned all because the Duke and his lunatic pyromancer wife decided it was better to fight the king's army rather than be captured." Leonardo turned facing the kneeling servants and tried to control his anger and tone. "As you can see, none of my men have hurt you lot. Now have they?"

The servants began mumbling to each other as they searched amongst themselves for familiar faces as if gathering stock. Then once again, out of the crowd came the voice of the older manservant. "Well, what have you done with Lady Bridget? I saw her being taken from her bed-chamber."

"The young lady is just fine. She didn't try to fight, unlike her parents, and is being detained over there in the wagon," said Leonardo as he pointed to a wooden carriage a few feet away. "Look, you can see her from here."

Leonardo watched as the manservant squinted his eyes at the wagon, hoping to see into the darkness of the carriage. The manservant smiled and mumbled something under his breath before turning back to him. Leonardo took this gesture as acceptance that his words were valid. "Now, if you're satisfied that I'm not a heartless murderer, will someone inform me as to the whereabouts of Precillia Richards?"

The older manservant started to rub at the skin between his knuckles nervously. "She's, um, she was supposed to be off with young master Daniels of the Brie Estate, bu... but she should have returned before the sun went down. I was going to retrieve her myself, but, well..." The manservant turned his attention back to the smoking remains of Richard's manor. "My guess would be she's still with Mistress Vanessa, if she's not here."

Leonardo frowned at the servant's revelation and turned to another soldier. "Riggs, who is this, Vanessa?"

A young soldier stepped forward. "She's the wife of The Goose Sir, the city's wine distributor. She and the lady of, ahh... well, the late lady of the estate, apparently were close friends. So it would make sense if she were there."

"Right, well, gather some men and go there to try and search for her. If she is there, detain her and bring her down to the barracks."

Riggs saluted, "Yes, Sir. Shall I also request the aid of a tracer?"

"No. Chances are anything we would need to perform a trace was lost in the fire."

Riggs nodded his head and walked over into a crowd of soldiers, barking orders.

Leonardo turned back at the estate as the heat from the flames seemed to be slowly dying out. "Okay, we're done here. Please escort Lady Richards to the barracks." He walked over to the wooden carriage, peering inside at Lady Bridget. "Forgive us, Miss Bridget, but we will be escorting you to the barracks now."

A young blonde-haired blue-eyed woman in a cream dress turned to Leonardo and gave him a satisfied smile. "You know, out of all the roles I've played, I think the role of a noblewoman is what I'm the most suited for. There's a level of selfish smugness that only they have." She placed her hands on her dress, gripping at it near the knees, and began to lift it for Leonardo. She slowly opened her legs for him and made an audible blowing noise from her lips as she leaned back. "Tell me, dear Leonardo, do you find this appearance to your liking?"

Leonardo shook his head in disgust before closing the door to the carriage with such force that it shook from the impact.

"Alright, send her on. I will be down shortly."

The horses clopped forward as the carriage wheels began to creak as it lurched ahead, making its way down the cobblestones, pulled away from the settling flames throughout the estate of Christol Richards. The only thing it would leave behind was the sound of feminine laughter heard in the distance.

From the brush that surrounded the burning building, a young brown-haired girl watched on as the carriage creaked off past the gate of what used to be the large manor. She had heard the bearded man yell, "Where is she?" many times, and out of the fear of being caught, she dared not to reveal herself. So for hours under the crescent moon sky, she'd lay there in the brush, covered in dust and dirt of the soil beneath her body. Even though she felt the small creepy-crawly creatures of the world beneath her crawl upon her body, sliding along her skin, she would remain as still as a stone. And continue to look ahead, focusing on each guard as they walked past her location, unaware of her presence. Because with the area under heavy surveillance, all she could do was watch as the light and warmth from the now slowly burning manor began to fade away into the night.

Finally, after what seemed like hours, she removed herself from the brush, feeling twigs rake across the skin of her body and face. She kept her eyes on the guards that were over by an old well. They seemed distracted as one of them tried pulling up water from a bucket tied to a rope. Creeping in the moonlight, she reached the shadows, placing her back against the wall. She could still feel the remaining heat from the embers left inside of the stones against her skin. Slowly, she inched her way down to the corner of the ruined building. Taking a deep breath, she leaned her head over, peeking around the corner, seeing two guards. They were chatting about something, but she couldn't hear them. Stretching out her arm, she reached forward to pull herself to the next safe area. One step, then another, then, plop!. Her foot had sunk into a small mud puddle. *Dammit, no, not now!*

"Who's there? Hello, who's there?" asked the voice of a guard.

The girl dashed away to hide as she saw a guard face her direction. He called out once again, but no reply came from the shadows in front of him. She observed carefully as he began slowly walking forward, placing one hand on the hilt of his sword in preparation for danger. But at the location where her foot sunk, all he saw was a muddy puddle. He looked down, noticing something in the pool of mud. Crouching, he grabbed the object, pulling out a small slipper. Her slipper.

He lifted the soaking wet slipper to his face, inspecting

it. Frowning at it, he started to look around suspiciously. The guard stood back up again and glanced around the area until he spotted a wagon of hay slumped over on its side with a broken wheel. He walked over and plunged his hand inside, sending the hay scattering about. After moving his hands around, he felt something substantial and grasped it, pulling out a large stick, which he frustratedly slammed to the ground.

"Blasted thing pricked my finger," said the guard.

She watched his frustration as he drove his hand in once again, feeling around for anything but finding nothing inside. The guard glanced around again with his suspicion growing and walked over to the brush of small low-cut trees surrounding the manor. Lifting his torch over the bush, he began to wave it back and forth, trying to get a better view into the darkness between the leaves. Not finding anything, he turned back around, noticing a small animal's den a few steps away and walked over to it. Placing his hand on the roof of the shelter to steady himself, he knelt to peer inside.

The girl saw the flames as the man descended.

"Hey, what are ya doing over there?" asked the voice of another guard from behind the man.

The guard in front of the animal den turned as the man walked up.

"Ahh!" The first guard said. "I found a slipper; might belong to that girl the captain was babbling on about."

The other guard just shrugged his shoulders.

"Figure that little girl might still be around here, so I'm having a look," said the first guard.

"Ahh, we looked everywhere. You heard that servant. She was with The Goose's wife or something," said the other guard.

The first guard then frowned and lowered his torch to peer into the small animal shelter and saw just a short stack of hay that a dog had probably slept on. He then raised back to his feet and jogged back over to where the other guard was standing at the corner of the house.

"Told ya, we gotta get back to report in or we ain't gonna get fed," said the other guard.

Then a man's voice was heard yelling off in the distance. "I think I found something over here. Hey, get back here." The two guards turned to each other before they took off running into the shadows towards the man's voice.

The girl breathed deeply as she watched the guards move from one place to another, relieved to watch them go away. Laying low on the ground curled up in a ball on the muddied ground under the hay cart, she clutched her knees to her chest. She watched as the two guards vanished into the night. Only when the fire from their torches became a glimmer in the distance did she squeeze herself from under the cart. Her nightgown was dirty from laying in the brush beforehand, but now her face and clothing were smeared with mud. The sensation of the cold, muddy water had soaked through her shift and now rested on her body.

She wanted to scream in frustration, but she knew that the guards would hear her. So she slowly closed her eyes for a few seconds while standing still and clenched her fists. Taking a deep breath, she focused on remaining calm and steeling her resolve. *Right, now's not the time to cry.* She crouched and began making her way toward the pond at the bottom of the hill that the manor rested on. But along the way, she noticed three other guards. Two that were by the lake itself and one that seemed to be asleep on the ground next to an old log. She took her time trying not to make a sound as she crept downhill.

She stayed low to the ground while searching for movement in every direction, before making her way to the pond. With the shadows around her deepening the farther she went from the manor, she began to move more freely under the blanket of the ever-growing darkness around her. Only the pale moonlight shining off the pond was clear in her vision. The rest was shrouded under cover of the night.

She could feel the coldness of the night on her skin with every small breeze and through her feet as the moistness of the grass beneath her left its wetness between her toes. But she continued on her way towards the pond with only the thought of escape running through her mind and how to accomplish that goal.

I can do this. I can do this. Just a little more.

"Hey! What are ya doing down there?" a guard bellowed from up the hill.

Her heart stopped. She dropped to her knees, then pressed herself flat against the ground, eyes darting back and forth in a panic. *No, not now, I'm so close, dammit, dammit.* With her eyes closed and her teeth planted into the side of her lip, she dug her toes into the ground beneath, preparing to run.

"Hey, aren't ya fools coming for da meal? They ain't gonna have none left if ya tarry any longer," shouted the guard.

Another guard in a helmet turned around, waving his arms, "Aye Mother, we shall be along shortly, Jims and I just wanted to play a quick game of four Queens." The girl turned her head to the direction of the first guard's voice, only to see him waving his arms back.

"Alright, smart ass, but don't blame me when you get no supper," said the guard up the hill as he turned around and walked back towards the burned estate.

The girl sighed a breath of relief across the grass and lifted her head, checking the position of the two guards still by the pond. With their backs turned, she snuck towards the edge of the pond while trying to keep herself out of viewing distance.

"Aye, why don't we just go up that hill and get some grub? I'm starving here," One guard said to another holding a fishing rod over the water.

"It's one of these rich fart's ponds, so there's bound to be some good fish here," said the guard with the fishing rod.

The other guard laughed. "Well, that'd be great if you could catch anything, but we'll starve before ya get any fish. And where'd ya get that rod from anyway?"

The first guard with the fishing pole shrugged. "I found it out here and figured why not try my hand at it."

While the guards were busy talking about fishing, the girl crawled along the ground, trying her best to be as quiet as possible. As her fingers combed through the grass, she pulled herself forward, inching through the darkness like an animal stalking through the night. She crept closer and closer to the wall and the unnoticing guards until she could feel the cool cold mist of the water flow across her face.

The guards were so close that she could see the Ox sigil across their breastplate. Minutes that seemed like hours passed as she stared at the guards from across the other side of the water, knowing that soon her moment would come. This sensation of hiding in the shadows was starting to feel familiar to her; reminding her of when her father would take her hunting in the woods. She remembered him telling her to always wait for the right moment. And here in the shadows, she would do just that, wait for her precious moment to appear.

"Ahh, come on, you ain't getting no fish, and we won't be getting anything in our bellies if we wait any longer," said the other guard to the first one.

The guard with the fishing pole dropped it by the lake, "Fine, I'll just try again after I eat."

The guards turned their back to her and made their way up towards the ruins of the manor. Only after their bodies had gone off into the shadows did she lift herself back up to a kneeling position. With muscles tensing in the back of her neck, she made her way to the other side of the pond, placing her hand on the stone wall looking down into the water. Dipping her toe into the murky moonlit blueness, she clenched her teeth to prevent them from chattering as the chilling sensation went up her leg and through her body.

She stepped into the cold water's embrace, lowering herself inside of it until only her shoulders were barely above the water. She reached her hands forward under the water, feeling against the stones. Moving her fingers across each one until she found what she was searching for. There it was, a hole between the rocks that let water and fish travel from one side to the other. She reached inside of the hole gripping the other side of the stones, and began tugging until it began to give a bit. She pulled on it harder, again and again until it started a swaying motion under the water until she felt one rock free itself from the rest and sink harmlessly to the ground below.

"What's that?" asked a man's voice.

The girl turned to her side and saw a guard's head peeking above the grass by the water. *Dammit, where'd he come from?*

The guard stood up and yawned.

Why did he have to wake up now?

She soon realized that the man had yet to see her as he glanced over the pond, noticing the ripples from her shaking the stones beneath the water. He lifted himself to his feet, yawning and stretching out his arms, making his way towards her. She turned herself back to the now loose rocks and began to pull at more stones, clawing at them until they began to fall like the first. The man noticed the sounds of splashing ahead and quickened his pace. After another set of stones, the hole finally seemed large enough for her to fit through. Ducking her head under the water, she placed her hands in the hole gripping at the sides of the opening, and pulled herself through the water over to the other side. The guard arrived just in time to see the last ripple of her body as a small fish circled the area above her.

CHAPTER 2

The girl's head emerged from the other side of the pond into a fountain where two frogs were lazily sitting on the top stones of the fountain's bench. One of the frogs croaked at her as if it were in a tizzy after having been awoken from its nap. But after its annoyed croak, it then slowly closed its eyes, and dropped back down in anticipation of another rest.

The girl began to look around suspiciously into the night, but everything seemed quiet amongst the cobbled city streets. The only movement was in the flames of torches lit amongst the doors of people's homes, but she did notice a low hanging fog that persisted into the night. Slowly she swam over to the end of the fountain to lift herself, but into her sight appeared something odd by the stone wall surrounding the manor. It seemed to her as if a part of the wall was moving. The girl stared intensely at the wall's image as it started to bend and morph before her eyes. Then it seemed to shift; slowly, it started making its way closer to her.

"Over here, I think it was this way," said a voice, and soon the sounds of men running could be heard into the night.

The girl quickly resubmerged herself beneath the waters of the fountain as the guards came storming past. And only after she could no longer feel the echo of their footsteps vibrate through the water did she raise her head back into the fresh air above the fountain. Head above water, she once again turned her attention towards where the wall was morphing and stared at it again. After a few seconds, the wall began to change once more, except for this time, the image of the wall shed like silk falling to the ground, and the stone visage was replaced with an old grey-haired man cradling his arm.

The older man gazed around cautiously in the fog-filled streets and limped off over the cobblestones street until he was finally out of sight. She lifted herself from the coldness of the water to the edge of the fountain and hopped down, placing her feet upon the road. Her small body shivered as the night's cold air wrapped around her, nearly freezing her shift.

Gotta find someplace to warm up.

But the problems of the night would only seem to

compound themselves, because not only was she wet, cold, and in a chemise, but somehow she also managed to lose her other slipper under the water somewhere. Wiping her damp hair out of her face, she looked herself over while trying to stop shivering in the cold night air. Eventually, she got her shaking under control and started taking in her surroundings. The night was quiet and dreary, except for the occasional wine of cats that came from someplace unseen.

The frogs had also leaped away. Apparently, they must have run off after the guards came through. She could see lights in some of the houses throughout the streets, but she made a displeased face at the unfamiliar houses. *Right, well, I won't find any help there, So I'd best be on with it.* And with one cold, hard, barefooted step, she began to make her way down the cobblestone street.

While passing the second building, she heard footsteps again. She dashed into a side alley as a guard walked past, heading down the street in the direction of the fountain that she had just previously emerged from. She gripped the corner wall of the cold stone of the building. The guard vanished into the fog. She turned around back into the alley only to see two other children in rags staring at her. One was a brown-haired girl, and the other was a small dirty blonde boy.

"What'd ya steal?" asked the other girl.

She took a step back, "What?"

The other girl stepped closer to her. "You scared of that guard that just passed. And them guards, for the most part, leaves us alone. So if ya looking for 'em not to see ya, then ya musta stole something." The other girl narrowed her eyes, inspecting her. "And why ya all wet anyways, and in ya nighties? Fine nighties, though."

She dropped her head, trying to inspect her state of dress and felt the coldness of her soaking wet hair as it fell back down, smacking her in the face. She then closed her eyes and just sighed.

The other girl stared up to what was left of Richard's manor on the hill. "You steal something from there during the fire?"

"I didn't steal anything, I... I um, I just don't want to be seen, that's all." Then she glanced over the girl and the boy standing behind her. "Then, why are you out here, aren't you hiding too?"

The other girl tilted her head in confusion. "What? We live here," pointing over to a wooden cart with a torn piece of fabric that seemed to be covering a large hole in the wall. She leaned over, looking to where the girl was pointing. Throughout the alley, there was an assortment of old broken pieces of wood and trash scattered across the ground. She shook her head and pointed at the small shanty.

"You live there? Really?"

The other girl placed her hands on her hips. "It's better than what most of us be getting, unless you got a proper sponsor. And only the pretty girls get that." The other girl folded her arms across her chest. "Why? You don't look no better off than us, except for ya nice nighties. And you ain't even got no shoes on." The other girl glanced down at her own feet, which had a hole in one of her shoes. "Okay, well maybe, I ain't that much either."

She lifted her head and rubbed at her nose with her sleeve. "Right well, no need to argue with each other over who's the more ragged. I'm Maggie, and this here's Billy." She turned and pointed to the small boy behind her, who had already lost interest in the new girl. Billy walked back to their shanty house, sitting down on the ground, placing his back against the side of the cart. "He's mute, but he's nice and easy to get along with." Maggie turned back around, stepping forward and pointing her finger at the wet girl. "Well, ya knows ours now, so what's yer name."

The girl jumped up, "Oh, I'm Fa... uhh, I'm Rana."

Maggie raised an eyebrow, "Okay, well, Rana's a good

ah name as any, I spose. So Rana, I never seen ya before. Where ya from?"

Rana took another peek around the corner. "Ahh, No. I'm not from here. I'm from another city." Then she turned back to face Maggie. "Actually is Green Village near here?"

Maggie rubbed the side of her face, thinking. "I've never heard of no Green Village before. There's Crolac's Village; I heard that's nearby."

Rana shook her head, "That's okay; I guess it wouldn't be after all."

Maggie raised an eyebrow, shrugged her shoulders, and turned around, heading back to her shanty house. "Well, ya needn't worry about the guards this time of night, they mostly leave us alone, unless we steal some noble's stuff."

Rana turned back into the alley and noticed Maggie sitting down next to Billy in the shanty. "Can I get to Haggar street from here? It's nighttime, and I'm not used to the streets yet."

Maggie moved some hay aside before placing a blanket back on top of it, then laid down and cuddled up to Billy. "Yeah just turn up there and..." Maggie yawned, "Head up the hill and take another right at that stupid statue, and you'll get to Haggar street."

Rana nodded, "Thank you, I appreciate it," and walked back off towards the corner of the building.

"No worries and goodbye. Hope ya... find..." Maggie yawned again, "Out who ya trying to be."

Rana stopped and turned around only to see that Maggie had pulled the fabric down, covering the entrance to the shanty. She narrowed her eyes while looking at the little hut, then turned to peep out at the other side of the alley before disappearing into the night. On the way, she saw a few other children huddled up in the corners of the buildings, each wearing torn and worn clothing. Some even with holes in their shoes. *What am I supposed to do now? Dammit, this isn't fair.*

After traveling through the foggy streets of the town, she eventually found her way to the statue that Maggie had mentioned. The roads were beginning to seem familiar to her. *I think... I think it's this way.* Turning right, she made her way uphill towards what she thought was the direction of the Goose's manor. On the way, the doors of a nearby tavern opened, and a man strolled out, bouncing a bag in his hand that made a soft jingle every time it landed in his palm.

"Not a bad night, maybe next time I'll bring Jasper so that he can tell the story of a night well made," said the man out loud to himself as he stepped back, looking at the still swinging tavern doors as if waiting for someone to follow him. He then whirled around on his feet and walked straight into Rana, knocking her to the ground.

"Ugh," coughed Rana as she landed on the street.

The man caught his balance from the impact, stopping himself from tripping over Rana and glanced down. "Oh, sorry, little lady, I wasn't watching where I was headed." He hung the bag from his belt, reached down, and grabbed Rana by the arm. As he lifted her to her feet, he patted her down to knock off dust and dirt from her thin shift, although he may have patted her bottom a few times too many.

"Are you okay, dear?" he said, feeling the moisture on his fingers. He then craned his head closer. "Why are ya soaking wet?"

Rana had taken a step back after she felt her bum squeezed with that last pat. "Ahh, yes, Sir, I, I'm sorry." She noticed his short golden hair and green eyes. He was still holding onto her arm.

The man gave a gleeful smile. "Not at all, child, it was my fault, I should have watched where I was going." Then, the door to the tavern opened again, and this time a red-haired woman and an older looking fat round man walked out together.

"Ya done already Jacob, you sure you don't wanna stay

the night? I've got a room upstairs," said the woman, slowly rubbing her fingers across her lips.

The older man walked over to the side of the patio and pulled out a pipe. "Hell, I just want another chance to win my money back, or at the very least buy a man a drink after you rob him blind."

Jacob smiled at the two while still holding on to the arm of Rana. "As much as I'd like to, the daughter of one of my companions has come to fetch me, so I really must be off."

"What? Like that? She's barely dressed, and her hair's all wet," said the red-haired woman.

Jacob stepped behind Rana and placed both hands on her shoulders.

Suddenly she heard the man's voice inside her mind. *Stay still.* And Rana's body locked itself in place. She tried moving again, but it was as if she no longer had control over herself anymore.

"Of course, she's a child of the street; you'd not expect her to dress any better than any other child you'd see around here, would you?" he asked.

Rana heard the voice in her head again. *Smile.* Rana couldn't figure out what was happening, her thoughts started to become jumbled, and it became harder for her to focus. But her lips spread, giving the woman a big smile.

"Her father's started taking care of her just recently, and now he takes her wherever he goes," said Jacob to the lady at the tavern door.

Rana heard his voice once again. *Nod your head.* And Rana's smile vanished as she began to bobble her head up and down.

The lady gave a suspicious look but then shrugged her shoulders. "Alright, guess there's no helping it then," she said as she smiled, leaning forward, exposing a lot more of her bosom. "Well, come back when ya can, and I'll be sure to treat ya to something special."

The man with the pipe grunted while giving a wary eye

towards the lady.

Jacob smiled, "I'll be sure to take you up on that offer the next time I visit," as he moved to the left of Rana, holding her hand.

The voice appeared in her head again, *Walk forward,* it said. And she began waking up the street into the night with Jacob hand in hand.

Soon, the two turned down an empty street, and Jacob released her hand. Slowly Rana felt herself regain control of her body as her thoughts once again became her own. She jerked her hand away and raced from Jacob, hiding behind a large piece of wood that was leaning against the wall of a building. With legs shaking uncontrollably, she glared back at the man who had just recently taken control of her mind.

Jacob raised his hands in the air while smiling. "Sorry about that, but you came in right handy."

"What... what did you do to me?" asked Rana with knees shaking, and her fingers clenched to the side of the board.

"It was just a little trick. I'm not gonna hurt you."

"Stay there, I... I know that was magic. I've seen magic before."

Jacob smirked, lowering his right arm to his side and gesturing with the other. "Oh, and where has the lady seen magic before? Do you dance with the nobles, or fly in the halls of Sceana?" Jacob saw Rana's legs were still shaking and seemed to regret his words. "Ah, well, you seem like a bright girl. The truth of it is, you got me out of a bit of a problem, so I owe you at the least something in return." Jacob reached in his pocket and pulled out a few shiny silver pieces. He then took another closer look at Rana. "What happened to your clothes?"

Rana frowned, "I fell."

Jacob then glanced at her feet. "Your feet have mud on them. Where are your shoes?"

"I lost them."

Jacob then pointed at her body. "And what of the scrapes

over your body?"

Rana looked down, eyeing herself as if retaking stock, and turned back to Jacob, "I fell in mud and in bushes."

Jacob pointed to her wet, tangled head. "And the hair?"

"I washed myself off in the fountain."

Jacob raised a brow and rubbed his chin, "Right... somehow, I now find myself getting quickly frustrated." He then placed the silver coins back into his pocket and reached into the pouch at his side. Pulling out two gold coins, he knelt in front of Rana and extended his hand to her, showing her the shiny pieces. "They're all yours."

Rana's eyes lit up as the gold mirrored in her eyes, but she dared not leave the safety of her wooden board. She then narrowed her eyes at Jacob, not fully trusting him, "What do you want?"

Jacob smiled, "Child, all I'm doing is repaying a debt since you gave me an excuse to run away and leave those two back there. Think of it as an extra bit of generosity from an appreciative fellow." He began moving one of the coins between his fingers.

Slowly removing herself from the wooden board, Rana stepped forward to reach out for the gold coin. Jacob stopped the coin, moving it to his palm with the other and began to make them float in the air above his fingers. Rana quickly pulled her hand back. But, as the coins continued to float spinning in the air in front of her, she reached out once again and snatched them away. She took a few steps back and held the coins against her chest.

Jacob placed one hand over his shoulder and bowed to Rana. "And thus, the debt has been paid." He stood up, "Take care, my muddy princess, I shall leave you with the wonders of the night, for I have other places to be."

Rana watched him turn his back to her and wander back off into the darkness, being swallowed up by the night's fog. When she could no longer hear Jacob's footsteps in the distance, she turned and set off in the opposite direction and soon realized that she was near the street to The Goose's house.

She moved through a few alleys and saw the Goose's house on the other side. Peeking her head out from around a corner, she noticed some guards leaving out the front door. The man Riggs, from the Richard's manor fire earlier that night, had already made his way here.

"Alright, you two stay here and be lookouts tonight," said Riggs. "No one should leave or enter. If the girl shows up, capture her and bring her down to the barracks."

The soldiers saluted, "Yes, Sir."

"The rest of you men with me," said Riggs as he mounted onto a horse and made his way down the street with a few soldiers trailing behind him.

Rana stared at the guards in the entrance for a few seconds before turning back toward the alley. Glancing around, she noticed a wooden cart next to the wall. Walking over, she climbed on top of the cart, lifting herself on top of the wall. From there she could see lights in the house. On the top floor, there was a shadow moving around near the window. The person above was pacing back and forth between the lights on each side of the room.

Oh! Someone's here; I can get them to help me.

She tried to lower herself to the ground on the inside, but she was too short, and her feet wouldn't touch the ground. She let go of the edge anyway, allowing herself to fall. But the landing wasn't smooth, and she slipped, falling back into the mud. Before she could curse herself in frustration, she heard a man's voice.

"No, Nessy, we will not be harboring a fugitive here."

"But Goosey, she needs our help," said a lady's voice.

Rana recognized the voices and saw two shadows in the lights on the windows downstairs. She moved closer to the voices.

"Her parents needed help too," Goosey said, "and look where they are now. I told the Duke this would happen. And now, you want to drag me down the same road. I've got a business to protect."

"Fine, well, I want to help her, and you can just wallow and hide for all I care," said Nessy.

"Oh, for the love of... Nessy, come back here, you'll get us both arrested," said Goosey as the voices slowly moved away.

Rana pulled her thighs to her chest, wrapped her arms around her ankles, and buried her face in her knees, closing her eyes. *Papa... I... I don't know what to do anymore. Why did those people attack us? What am I supposed to do? I don't have anyone to help me. I wish you were here now.* She felt trapped as the one place she had come to for help seemed to be the one place she couldn't hide.

Rana sat on the ground with the light from the Goose's window shining on the ground in front of her. She thought about her father and all the times he used to take her hunting with him or when he'd teach her how to ride his horse, how he used to pick her up, always saying the same thing. *My brave little girl,* every time she did something, he was proud of.

After sitting in the dark shadows of The Goose's Manor for some time and hearing the guards' conversations as they entered the house, she raised her head and took a deep breath. *Right, I gotta keep moving, find someone to help me. This brave girl will find someone to help her.* Rana stood up, walked back over to the wall, and realized the wall was higher than she remembered. She then took a couple of practice jumps, trying to grab the top. She could not reach it, so turning around, she placed her back against the wall looking around.

Rana then spotted some wine crates stacked perfectly to reach the top. Walking over to the containers, she climbed on top of them, one after the other till she was able to see over the wall. On the other side, down a hill, was a whole different town that she had never been to before. Rana stared over the lower city as a thousand lanterns and torches lit up the night before her. After some time, Rana lifted herself over the wall before finally lowering herself and dropping to the ground again, but this time landing properly. After gazing at the city below her one more time, she took a deep breath and began making her way down into its streets.

Rana entered the lower city and instantly noticed that gone were the cobblestone streets of Hightown, replaced instead with the dirt, mud, and grime of a city in disrepair. And whereas the roads of Hightown were mostly empty at night, these streets had a multitude of sleeping beggars and children. But unlike Maggie and Billy, who at least had a little shanty home, these children wore ill-fitted clothes and slept on the cold hard ground. Rana looked into the city, but instead of wandering these uncertain city streets, she decided to stick to its walls, following them wherever they led.

While walking through the cold and silent streets, she began to feel the night's adrenaline wear off, replaced with exhaustion and sleepiness. She tried rubbing at her dreary eyes but only succeeded in smearing mud on her face from her arms. But still, she continued to walk down the dark street alone with her hand sliding along the wall to give her some sense of comfort that something was real about this night. She noticed ahead of her that there was a small tavern near the gates of the city, and to the left of it, she saw stables. And with that sight came the thought of soft hay to lay in for a small rest.

She walked over to the stables, peered inside, and noticed horses in the first two stalls, but no horse in the third. Exhaustion seemed to take control of her mind as she stared at the soft, inviting hay inside the booth. She stumbled forward, falling to her knees, and dropped her face into the soft hay. Just allowing the cold softness of it all to soothe her worn body as the smell of horses reminded her of a much more peaceful time with her father and their horse. Her eyes felt so heavy as she nuzzled her face against the hay.

"Wow, you must be tired. I've never seen someone just drop to their knees like that," said a man's voice from behind her.

Rana's eyes shot open as she lifted her hay-filled head, turning around to see a dark-haired man in a leather vest squatting behind her. "I... ah... I mean." Her words caught in her throat as the surprise of him being before her ripped words from her mind.

The man sucked on his lips while holding an apple in one hand and a long dagger in the other. "Well, maybe I did see a couple of girls drop to their knees before, but I paid them for what came next," said the man as he began peeling the apple with his dagger, placing the cut off piece into his mouth. Rana quickly crawled across the hay, putting her back against the stall and huddled up in the corner. Her eyes focused on the man in the moonlight as he smiled down at her, waving his dagger around. "You know, you're the second little girl to try and steal some sleep from this shed." The man glanced over the shed with a curious look on his face, "I wonder if horse stables are like honey catchers, but for little girls."

Rana slowly stood up. "I... I'm sorry, I thought nobody would mind... I'll leave." Rana took two steps forward, but the man waved his dagger in front of her, rolling it back and forth between his thumb and fingers.

"Oh, you can't be going like that, now. We haven't even gotten to know each other yet," said the man as he stood up, towering over Rana. He leaned forward, reaching down towards her arm. Rana jumped to the other side of the stall, sending hay flying into the air as she searched for a way out. But the only exit was ahead of her with the large man standing between herself and escaping.

"I'm sorry, I... I promise I won't come back."

The man pulled back to his full height, "Oh! Well, aren't

23

we skittish?" He grabbed a small stool from nearby, took a seat in front of Rana, and bit into his apple again. Rana watched as he stared back at her while chewing and sucking on the apple, the dagger in his hand shimmering in the pale moonlight as the apple juices dripped from the blade. He didn't say anything, just continued to eat his apple, never taking his eyes off her. After a few more bites, the sound of a door opening was heard, and Rana saw a brown-haired lady with half her gown hanging off her shoulders come out.

"Broddy, are you out here?" asked the woman.

The man stared down at Rana. "Yeah, I'm here. Come over for a second, will ya?"

The lady walked over, "What's the matter? You said you'd be right back. Did you lose... oh," the woman noticed Rana huddled in the corner as she walked up behind the man, "Oh my, another one. This one's a cutie," she said as she wrapped her arms around the man's neck while rubbing her face against his and sighing, "It's the third one this week. Isn't it?"

The man kept his gaze on Rana. "Second, one was a drunk I threw out, so he don't count."

"Does that mean we can keep her?"

"I had a feeling you'd say that," said the man as he placed the dagger back into his belt, "You always wanna keep 'em, and I end up having to pay till I get 'em trained."

The woman rubbed the stubble of the small beard on the man's chin. "Well, us girls have a way of paying too," she said as she playfully bit the man's ear.

The man smiled while looking at Rana. "Alright, we still got space for another. We'll keep this one. Take her inside and get her cleaned up."

The woman planted a kiss on the man on the cheek. "You spoil me so much." She then reached her hand out to Rana while keeping one arm around the man's neck. "Come, child, we best get you cleaned up." Rana looked at the man the woman was still attached to, and the woman noticed her weariness. "Don't worry about him. As long as we follow the rules here, he won't hurt us none." After a few seconds, Rana moved towards the lady's outstretched hand while staying as close to the stable wall as she could. She grabbed the woman's hand and was escorted past the man on the stool. The man's eyes followed her as she passed by him. The woman led Rana to the steps of the building.

"Girl," said the man, and the lady stopped. Rana slowly turned to him. "If you try to run, I will find you, remember that," he said before she was shuffled through the door by the woman. Inside, Rana found herself standing in the middle of a large kitchen.

"Girls! Come to the kitchen; I got someone I want ya to meet," yelled the woman.

Rana heard footsteps coming from several directions, and soon several young girls made their way into the kitchen. They all began peering at Rana and asking questions.

"Oh! Did Broody pick up another one?"

"What's her name? I'm Miraval."

"How old are you? Did Broody take you off the back of a wagon?"

"Why's her hair filled with hay?"

The girls rattled off their questions one after another as Rana's attention bounced between each one. *Just what type of place is this?*

CHAPTER 3

The early morning sun shone throughout the Kingdom of Mari as a man in uniform ran through a makeshift military encampment outside of the city of Hellia. He stopped at a large tent with a bluebird holding a golden rose embroidered on the drapes. Entering it, he spotted a man with glasses scribbling onto a sheet of parchment.

"Good morning, general," said the man as he saluted.

"How can I help you, Lieutenant Galahan," said the man with glasses.

"Sir, I'm here to report on the morning's activities."

"I've told you before, lieutenant. There is no need to salute me. I'm just an accountant."

The lieutenant removed his hand from his head and placed them both behind his back. "But Sir, you are the sixth general, Sir, and due the respect of any other superior officer."

"A useless title, given to me because I saved the capitol a bunch of money. So that now the people in charge can go out whoring a little more than usual," said the general as he rolled up the parchment.

"But, Sir, you—"

The general raised his hand to stop him from speaking, "Look Lieutenant Galahan, sucking up to me won't get you any promotions. I'm from an unknown house, and I don't have any magical talent. I just happened to be good with numbers, and if not for that, I would be out there digging ditches with the rest of the men."

"Well, ya can't blame a guy for trying, everyone knows you've been summoned to the capital, and they're gonna need a replacement for you here. So, we thought maybe you'd put in a good word for one of us," said the lieutenant taking a seat opposite the general at his desk.

"Ha, if only that were the case. No, lieutenant, in truth, they'd probably demote anyone I tried to recommend. The more likely outcome I'd wager will be that they'll replace me with one of the sons from a noble house who's been playing with magic since he was three." Leaning forward to his desk, he grabbed the parchment and placed a silver ring around it. Standing up, he walked over to a corner and grabbed a leather bag that was hung on the wall along with a belt that had a bunch of pouches attached to it. He opened the flap of the bag and stuffed the rolled-up parchment inside, flinging it over his shoulder. "Come, see your superior officer off, won't you?"

"Well, it was fun while it lasted," said the lieutenant as he stood. He and the general then stepped outside the tent and into the cold morning air. The sun was beginning to peek over the horizon, as the two turned towards a carriage up a hill and began making their way towards it.

"Ya know, general, you never did tell us how you got this position," said the lieutenant.

"No, and I never had any intention to," said the general while chuckling.

"Ah, come on, you're the first non-mage to reach the rank of general in this kingdom's history. You can't just not tell us."

"Who knows, it might just be because I saved the kingdom from some overload or I blackmailed someone with too much power. Or, maybe, I saved some poor noble child who fell down a well."

"Okay, I get it, you're an ass who doesn't wanna talk."

"Now is that any way to talk to a superior officer?" asked the general with a smug expression on his face.

"No, but it is how we talk to a jackass superior officer who's going to quit before the day has ended."

"Too right, that it is," chuckled the general, "look, just tell the other cadets whatever you like, and I'm sure they'll believe it." The two men arrived at the carriage, and the general turned around, staring over the encampment as all the tent flags blew in the wind from the morning's breeze. The general closed his eyes, taking in a deep breath.

"You're not getting sentimental on us, now are you?"

"I'm retired now. You should allow this old man to embrace moments like these," said the general looking downhill at the soldiers below, making their way through the camp, starting their morning routines.

"A twenty-eight year-old retiree? That's a slap in the face of every soldier that will spend the next thirty years in service here."

"Who knows? Perhaps one of you will be unlucky enough to replace me since my time here is over. Strange things will always find a way to happen. You can never predict what fate the goddess has in store for us," said the general as he turned around, stepping inside the carriage. "Try not to get yourself killed, Lieutenant Gallahan, I won't be there to bail your ass out from now on."

The lieutenant clapped his hands together and gave a salute. "Fuck off and good day to you too, Sir."

The general saluted back, "Spoken like a true soldier," and the carriage pulled off.

Around an hour later, the general arrived at the military's main headquarters in the city. Stepping out of the carriage, he stared up at three blue flags mounted on top of the military base; each flag was embroidered with a golden rose. The general walked up the steps and saw ahead of him a man in uniform. He was holding a pipe in his mouth and standing beside one of the stone pillars of the building. The man stared down at him as if waiting for something to happen. The general paused for a minute, shook his head, and continued to walk up the steps.

"Ya know, I didn't expect you to do me the courtesy of actually meeting me out here. I figured you'd just fester in your office until I eventually made my way around."

"Hah, I've known you long enough to know you'd try to skip out without being seen as soon as you got the chance," said the man as he shook the general's arm.

"That was the plan, but it seems as if you've seen through my diabolical methods once again. Perhaps you're the one that should have been the general instead of me."

"Now that's a statement that I most certainly agree with," said the man joyously as he placed his hand on the general's back, leading him inside. "Now, come along; the first is waiting for you."

"And when did you start smoking again, those kids running you crazy already?"

"Hey, you try raising three children as they break everything in sight, and then you can judge my bad habits."

The military headquarters was a massive stone building with blue flags hanging on the walls of the corridors. The general and his associate walked down the halls toward their destination. Along the way, many people greeted the general and wished him luck after retirement.

"So, tell me, how was it being a big fancy pants general for these past eleven years? I heard about that nasty business you handled in the border wars a few years back. Did you really capture Urgana the War Bride?"

The general closed his eyes and nodded slowly. "Yeah, that wasn't exactly a high point in my career, but it was either that or have them wipe us out or starve us in. Plus, she ended up escaping anyway. So she was more of a temporary transport than a hostage."

"Hey, you won't see me questioning your actions. Survival at any cost is the rule of the battlefield. But still, you got to meet Urgana, that's impressive." The two stopped in front of a room with three golden roses painted on it. The man lowered his voice, "So ah, out of curiosity, did you hook up with any of the younger cadet girls?"

"What?"

The man leaned in close to the general as if making sure no one overheard his words. "My good man, you are the hero of the Border Wars. Defeated Urgana when she'd wiped the asses of four other generals before you. And through some mysterious circumstances that no one in the kingdom can understand, you were appointed to be the sixth general of the army. A position that, until you appeared, didn't even exist. You're a walking legend, mate. How you are not fucking every doughy eyed girl from here to the Sakari Wilds is beyond me."

"Says the man who's married with three kids. How is

Grettal anyway? She's still trying to get Henry to become a scholar?"

Before the man could respond, the door opened, and out came an older bearded man with a bald head. He saw the man's arms on the general's shoulder and made a coughing noise.

"Sergeant Coral, sorry to interrupt you and the sixth's loving embrace, but I need to speak with him."

Sergeant Coral noticed his arms still on the general's shoulder and pulled back saluting. "Good morning first, I was just—"

"Calm down, sergeant, I just need to speak to the sixth here, give us an hour or two, and you can have him back," said the first as he waved his hand in dismissal.

"Yes, Sir," said the sergeant, then he looked at the sixth general, "you can tell me about everything else later. Drinks on me tonight." and he walked off down the hall.

The first general nodded to the sixth and stepped to the side, holding the door open, "Come in sixth, we've been waiting for you."

The sixth general stepped into the office and noticed a desk with two empty chairs, each with golden embroidered trim designs laced across the edges of the furniture. But the room itself was empty, except for a bookshelf. Even the walls were just barren stone except for a few candles spread out across the room. The sixth general raised an eyebrow back at the first. "We? I don't see anyone else here."

"Oh, did I say we? It seems I misspoke. Perhaps old age is finally getting to me," said the first.

"I'm sure you and the rest are very eager for my retirement," said the sixth, walking inside, taking a seat at the desk.

"While I admit, I'm not fond of you personally. I harbor you no ill will sixth, I'm just curious as to why your position exists is all," said the first as he first closed the door behind the sixth. He walked over to a window, looking out at some stable boys that were cleaning horses. "Ya know, I started out as a stable hand myself."

The sixth raised his eyebrow, "Maybe old age has finally gotten to you if you can't remember your own history."

"Oh, I imagine they tell quite a different story in the military's history books," said the first chuckling. He stretched out his hand, extending out his palm, and slowly a small flame appeared above it. "My gift for magic came to me a lot later in life than most others. Whereas most developed the talent around the age of nine or ten, I didn't notice my talent until I was well over sixteen. My parents, who had already sent me off to the military, were as shocked as I was when it finally appeared."

The first stretched out his fingers a bit, and suddenly, the ember over his palm broke apart and shot towards different corners of the room, igniting the wicks of the six candles that were hung on the walls.

The sixth looked around the room at the recently lit candles and whistled in acknowledgment of the feat. "For a man whose talent started late, you certainly handle magic better than most. But I suppose that's why your battles are what the kingdom likes to put into the heads of tiny children." The sixth moved his hands in a flimsy motion. "The great battle mage Roman Heights, Hero of the Battle of Yulan, was made into the first general by the late Queen Nolana, and has been a pillar of power ever since."

"Pillar of power, that's a good one. The only difference between high noble mages and myself is that I wasn't taught any other magic to specialize in. By the time my magic came to me, I had grown too old to be trained in a traditional magic school, so I decided to just stay in the military," said the first general as he turned to a bookshelf beside him, grabbing a bottle of wine and two glasses.

Roman placed them on the desk, filling both cups, and slid one over to the sixth. "You know our military has some damn fine battle mages. Not a few of them were under your command until recently. So, tell me, did you ever take the time to actually watch them train, or did you just send them off to die on the battlefield with no regard to their actual skill?"

"On occasion, I would travel down to the mages quarters and ask them to explain how their spells worked. Not all of them, but the ones that would be used in battle most often. I'd like to think that I understand the basic principles of magic. Even though I myself am as mundane as your average farmer," said the sixth as he sipped from the cup.

"Good. Even if you can't perform magic, it's better to get an understanding of it. I, myself, was like that. Before my talent emerged, I was fascinated by it. But while other mages were being taught the different types of magic at their comfy little schools, I had war magic beaten into me almost from the moment I could summon a flame." Roman seemed to smile as he thought about past times as he sat down in his chair, "At one point, I found out that they had bets going to see who would break my shields the fastest, and that went on for years. But eventually, the day came when they could no longer break my shields. Instead, they began to wager on whose shields could last the longest against my attacks."

"An excellent story, Sir. A true testament as to why you are the first general," said the sixth as he took another sip of the wine. He then clapped with a deadpan face that showed he had no real interest in their current conversation.

Roman grunted at the false praise. "I told you that story to show you how I had earned their respect. How I overcame what they put me through. That, over time, they saw the man I had become. But you, I honestly have no idea who you are or what type of character you have." Roman rubbed at his beard. "Ten years ago, you appeared out of nowhere with no magical talent to speak of, no family to claim you, and her highness created a sixth general for you personally, wherefore the past four hundred years there had only been five." Roman leaned forward, looking at the sixth. "Which anyone would think is a giant honor. But every time over these ten years, when your Queen has summoned you to the castle, you somehow always found a way not to appear. Hell, I'm not even sure you're from this kingdom. And even still, our Queen Clarissa refuses to tolerate any question of your loyalty to her."

"I just happened to have been busy; the Queen knows this. You yourself should understand that being a general has certain levels of responsibility. No time for those social gatherings that you all masquerade as war meetings. But I guess even great generals have a need for gossip."

"Gossip, you say?" asked Roman as he stroked his beard. "Well, I guess there is a bit of truth to that. For many of us have often wondered about you." He stood from his seat, beginning to pace around the room. "As mysterious as you are, the only thing we generals have been able to find out about you is that you will go to extreme lengths to avoid meeting her highness." Roman pulled out a small pipe from his sleeve and ignited it with a snap from his fingers. "Which is why I went to such great lengths to keep the Queen's visit here today a secret." The sixth's face made a dramatic change from calm to more of a weary disgust as he clenched his fist on the chair. Roman gave a satisfied smug grin as he wagged his finger at the sixth. "Oh, that's an interesting expression on your face, sixth. I'd wager anyone would take it for a look of hatred and disgust if you weren't careful."

The sixth general slowly regained control of his emotions and took a small breath, relaxing his posture once again. "That was a good jest, first. But the Queen is hundreds of miles away in Jallenport on a diplomatic mission. Even with the use of airships, it would take at least a day or two to get here."

Roman took a few puffs from his pipe and gestured with it towards the sixth, while still having a grin on his face,

"Oh, that, well, that was a lie. A little misinformation and magic to have her image appear where needed. You see, sixth, I didn't misspeak earlier. I really meant that *We* had been waiting for you." Roman raised his hand as green energy began to swirl around it.

Suddenly, the bookcase behind him started to shake, "We are the royal military, sixth, and as you said yourself, being a general has responsibilities. One of which is attempting to please our Queen, who was very eager to meet you again. So, you of all people should understand and appreciate the need for secrets." Roman tightened his grip around the magical green glow, and slowly the bookcase that housed the wine given to him earlier began to slide left, opening a passage behind it.

From the dark passage into the mid-morning sun, a woman stepped out. She was dressed in a royal blue and purple dress with her neck and arms adorned with golden flowery bracelets as a golden crown sat atop her head. With hands folded over each other in front of her, she gracefully stepped into the light of the room and smiled at the two men, before focusing her attention on the sixth general.

"Hello, Victor, you look as wonderful as ever," said the woman as she entered the room smiling.

Roman bowed to the woman and turned back towards Victor, who had now adopted an unmistakable face of hatred as he grit his teeth and narrowed his eyes. Suddenly he began to feel a burning itch on his neck.

"Oh, my sixth. Earlier, I thought you disliked our fair Queen. But now I'm fairly certain that you hate her," said Roman as he took a few steps forward, placing himself between the Queen and Victor, lighting an ember in his hand. "But understand sixth, that you are in a room with two of the strongest mages in the kingdom, so perhaps you should think carefully before making any hasty decisions." Victor slowly relaxed the muscles of his face and tried to remain calm. He then placed his hands on the desk, lifting himself to his feet when he heard the Queen's voice.

"It's fine, dear Roman," said the Queen, placing her hand on Roman's shoulder. "Don't worry about Victor. In all of Ellendor, I am the one person that he could never hurt." The Queen stepped from behind Roman to the side of the table, waving her hand. And magically, the curtains of the room closed on the windows. "I'd like for the stable hands outside not to see me. As Victor himself said, I'm supposed to be on a diplomatic mission." She stared at Victor for a few seconds before noticing the grey veins on his neck, throbbing. Then, she raised her hand in Roman's direction, "Roman, please be a good man and give us some alone time. I have a private matter to discuss with Victor here."

Roman made a shocked expression before calming himself down. "My Queen, are you sure?"

"General, you said so yourself. We are two of the strongest mages in the kingdom, and I'm even stronger than you. With poor Victor here being born with no magical talent at all, I assure you, I will be just fine."

Roman stared at his Queen and then to Victor, who still had a look of disgust in his eyes, before bowing, "Yes, my Queen," and headed for the door.

The Queen followed behind Roman, locking the door behind him. She then walked back to the desk, waving her hand, and suddenly a shimmer covered the walls of the room, making it glow several different colors before fading away. "Now that's better, we wouldn't want anyone—" Before the Queen could say another word, she felt the warmth of hands around her neck. Not tightly, but just enough to feel the skin of his fingers.

The Queen sighed and turned around, still in the grasp of Victor's hands as they hovered over her neck. She gave Victor a look of pity as she gazed at him standing before her. His face had twisted into a mask of pain, disgust, and hate. The Queen reached up, pulling off the bracelet around her neck and tossing it on the table. She then grabbed Victor's wrists and pushed her throat into his hands, allowing him to feel the warmth of the blood flowing beneath her skin.

"My poor Victor, I see it still hurts to be around me." She rubbed at the grey veins on his throat as they began to stretch up to his jawline. "But don't worry, this is a pain you don't suffer alone. The feeling will soon pass." The Queen reached to her neck and moved Victor's hand aside, allowing him to see the same grey veins mirroring themselves on her skin. "See, you're not alone sweet Victor." She then reached her hands over and slowly began to caress his face. "We are the same. But look at you, you're trembling. Understand Victor, that no matter how much you fight this, you can never hurt me. We both know this."

Victor's face shook as he clenched his teeth and narrowed his eyes, trying his best to control his own body. But anything he tried to do to the Queen just ended up with his own body freezing the moment he tried to assault her. He soon lost the willpower to continue. Unclenching his teeth, his hands fell to his sides. His body began to tremble as he felt himself regain control. "What do you want?" he said in somber acceptance of his fate.

The Queen placed her finger under his chin, lifting his head so that their eyes met, "Now, don't be that way. I came all this way to see you. The least you could do is smile." Victor just turned his head away, not wanting to humor the Queen in her games. She sighed and began to pace the room. "Fine, if you must know, I need you to go to the Kingdom of Burlus and foster a certain agreement with King Nevander. He's annoying our borders with attacks as a way to get my attention. I need you to go and figure out a way to appeal to his good side. I can't afford to have him against me with what's coming ahead."

Victor placed his hand over his face lifting his glasses in frustration as he rubbed at the space between his eyes. "I gave you sixteen years; I even joined this damned military like you said. That was the agreement, sixteen years. I won't give you any more, you hear me?"

The Queen suddenly turned on her heels and marched back up to him, looking up at Victor defiantly. She was so close that Victor could see his reflection in her blue eyes. "You think I want this? I've searched for ways to fix... this. But during all this time, no spells, concoctions, seals... none of it works." The Queen realized her position and backed away from Victor. "No, as long I have to deal with it, then you will have to deal with me."

Victor went back to the chair at the desk, turned it towards the Queen, and sat down. He placed his hand on his head, moving it through his dark hair, taking a deep breath. "When am I leaving?"

The Queen lowered her head, closing her eyes while rubbing her hands across her sleeves, "There will be a carriage outside for you when you leave this building; you will travel to Aaron's Bay and take a ship to Krispick."

Victor dropped his head into his hands, "This will never end, will it?" Hearing no reply, he looked back up and saw the Queen staring back at him. "What? What else do you want?"

"You haven't seen me for years, and you haven't even once commented on my dress." She puffed out her cheeks as if pouting.

"What?" asked Victor, tilting his head.

The Queen raised her arms, spinning around, flaunting the gold ornaments draped throughout the dress. "I had it made especially for you, you know. The finest fabric I could find. It's actually quite extravagant, really. But the secret to it is that the whole thing is tied together by my magic. They said finding the fabric that would respond well to magic is actually quite rare, and it takes a full week's worth of training just to learn to wear the damn thing. But magic users can feel the vibrations of the fabric when they come near it. Roman was quite impressed when he felt it, the first time. But of course, you can't tell since you have no magical talent, so I guess it's wasted on you."

"I'm flattered," said Victor, rubbing at between his eyes again.

"You should be," she said, and she raised her hand, "but the trick for you is when I turn off the magic in the dress." The Queen snapped her fingers, and the lovely dress simply fell apart to the floor in a pile of silks, linens, and leaves, revealing a stark-naked Queen.

Victor began to stand, "What are—"

"Stop," said the Queen as Victor froze in mid-motion, with his words still on his lips. The Queen began to slowly walk over to him, allowing his eyes to view her entirely. "Two years, two long years," she took a step towards him, "and the only man I'm allowed to touch," she took one more step, "refuses to see me. And when I try to see him, he always vanishes." The Queen stopped in front of him, "Sit down, Victor." He sat back down in the chair. She removed her crown and placed it on the table and turned back to Victor placing her hands on his face. She leaned in and kissed him on his lips before slowly pulling away. "Ah, I've waited so long." Victor stared at her, noticing the grey veins on the Queen's neck as they slowly started to disappear.

"Speak, my wonderful Victor. That magic I cast earlier will ensure that no one will hear us."

Victor muttered out, "I... don't... want..."

The Queen smiled while looking down at the bulge in his crotch. "Oh, dear, are you sure? Because part of you seems to want me very much." The Queen twirled her fingers around his dark hair.

"It's... not."

The Queen placed a finger over his lips. "Victor, you say you hate me, but I know that I hate you. I can feel it deep inside me. But neither of us can stop what's about to happen." The Queen closed her eyes, embracing the moment," This... feeling, it never goes away. And it's much worse on me than it is on you. I swear men are so lucky. You see a pair of breasts, and your cock just jumps up.

CHAPTER 4

The next morning Rana awoke on a wooden bed next to another girl lying beside her. She felt the girl's arms wrapped around her belly as she opened her eyes into the morning sunlight that was shining in through a window above her. As her eyes focused through the golden streams of light, she squinted her eyes, looking around the room, and began to remember the night before. After meeting the woman and being taken inside, she was fed, bathed, and the woman even washed her shift.

The girl with her hands around Rana's waist snuggled up behind her in her sleep. Rana removed her arm from around her waist and lifted herself from the bed. She let her feet dangle off the side in the air and turned back, looking down at the girl in her slumber. She had called herself Pelly the night before. Looking around the room, Rana saw two other girls lying together on another bed in front of her. They had introduced themselves as Miraval and Renee.

I'm here now, but I need to get back home.

Suddenly, she heard the sounds of talking coming from outside the door. Leaning forward, she dropped to her feet and crept towards the door. The wooden floorboards beneath her creaking under her weight with each step. Cautiously, she opened the door partly and peered outside. But from her upstairs position, she couldn't really see anything, just the top of the tavern and the edge of the front door. But she was sure that she had heard voices. Rana took a breath and opened the door fully, stepping out into an air that smelled of ale and smoke. She moved out to a balcony and saw two men talking below her. One of them being the man she met last night. The girls called him Broderick. Beside him was an older man with a thick brown and grey beard with a sword at his side, puffing from a pipe in his mouth. She crept down to the edge of the balcony near the steps to get a better view, trying to be careful not to alert them of her presence.

"That's why I'm done with the mercenary life; I've set up a nice little shop here. And you at your age might need to be thinking about the same," said Broderick.

The older man placed his pipe down and sipped some ale from his mug, "Ha! And set up a little whore house like you did? The battlefield is where I'll die, not surrounded by a bunch of vipers waiting to fuck me and slit my throat."

Wait, whore house, is that where I am? Thought Rana as she gripped the edge of the wooden balcony listening in on their conversation.

Broderick laughed, "Well, at least I'll die with a hard cock in them, rather than a hard sword in me."

Under the balcony, Rana heard a familiar voice, "Well, either way, you both seem determined to die with someone getting fucked, just with different types of swords." And the two men exploded into laughter.

"Too right, too right," said the older man gesturing with his mug of ale. "Speaking of which, go check to make sure we've been paid, and everything accounted for. I don't want all of us getting fucked."

"Aye, father, try not to pass out drunk before I get back."

And the man's footsteps could be heard leaving out the back of the building. Rana tried to lean forward to see who the familiar voice belonged to. But suddenly, she felt a hand on her shoulder.

"It's not nice to be eavesdropping," said the voice.

Rana tried to jump up but slipped and fell on her butt with a loud thud. She glanced up to see the lady who took her inside the night before looking down at her.

"Oh my, you are lively, aren't you?"

"Well, what do we have here?" asked Broderick from down below. Rana peered down once again and saw the two men staring back up at her. "Come down here." Rana was hesitant, but the lady in front of her patted her on the shoulder.

"Now go on, he ain't gonna hurt ya none, he woulda done so by now if he wanted that." Rana sheepishly made her way down the stairs, heading over to the men. She kept her head down in front of them, but noticed some parchment on the table with the words, "Black Jewels" written on it.

"I picked this one up last night, says her name's Rana," said Broderick.

"I'm curious as to your process when it comes to selecting these girls. Are ya just into them young or are ya just starting a collection the way some people collect stones down by the river?" asked the old man eyeing Rana.

"Please, I have plenty of girls that are far plumper than her to suit me at night. I don't need a child for that. I'm planning to sell her off as a housemaid like the others after I get her trained up, which is a far better life than the one I found her in."

"Well, might I suggest that you hold off on the selling of that one, young Broderick?" asked the old man as he leaned back in his chair.

"Oh yeah, and why's that uncle? Have you fancied her yourself then? A new child for your war efforts. Although, I doubt a little girl as scrawny as this one would be much use on the battlefield."

The old man smirked, "You never were one for paying much attention, were you? I say that because ya little wench there can read, and from the way her eyes are darting back and forth across that piece of parchment there, she's a good reader too."

Rana's face jumped up from the parchment and noticed Broderick staring at her in amazement.

"You can read?" asked Broderick as he leaned on the table, taking another look at the little girl before him.

Rana's face darted to the old man who was smiling at her.

"No need trying to hide it now, girl."

"Yes, yes, Sir, I can," said Rana, dropping her head again.

Broderick reached forward, grabbing Rana's face, and squeezing her cheeks, forcing her eyes to meet his. "Well that's a rare thing in a street rat. So, tell me, who taught ya to read?"

"My father, he... he taught me."

"Oh yeah, and where is this father of yours? Can't imagine he'd left you to rot in my stables and ran off."

Rana shook herself free from Broderick's hand, pouting in front of him, "I don't know, he... there were bandits and he... disappeared."

"Oh, this ones got some fire," chuckled the old man.

Broderick frowned at his uncle while pointing a finger at him. "Are these the bandits you were paid to kill?"

"Who knows, they pay us to kill, and we kill, doesn't matter who they are."

"Fine, a reading maid will fetch a higher price anyway, doesn't matter who ya used to belong to. The thing is, you're mine now. You slept under my roof, and ya ate my food. So, unless that disappearing daddy of yours comes back to claim ya, that makes ya mine; ya got that?"

Rana scowled at Broderick, but before she could respond, she felt someone pulling her back. Quickly she was enveloped in the arms of the woman from the night before as she hugged Rana from behind.

"Now, now Broddy, the girl's been through enough. Give her some time to learn like the rest of 'em."

Broderick looked at Rana, then to the lady, and waved his hand in dismissal, "Fine, just take her and get her started."

The lady turned Rana around and playfully pushed her towards the back of the building. "Come on, baby, let's go."

Rana soon found herself in a much more beautiful room than the one she slept in. It had a soft bed with pillows. And she even saw that there was a big mirror over a dresser with a sitting stool. The woman walked to the end of the bed, opening a trunk, and pulled out a ragged brown and green tunic along with a pair of boots. She then walked back over and handed it to Rana.

"We can't have you running around all day in your nighties. It might give the wrong people some weird ideas. So put this on, and we'll get you to work."

"Thank you," said Rana taking the rags.

"Oh, so we do have some manners. Well, don't worry about it. We have a few others if those ain't to your liking."

Rana fiddled with the fabric for a bit while the lady went and sat down at the mirror to brush her hair. She put on the rags and boots, "What's your name?"

The lady turned around with her long hair brown still in her hand. "I was wondering when we'd get around to our names, although I'm a bit surprised the girls upstairs didn't tell you. My name's Tabby, a pleasure to meet you." she said, extending her hand.

Rana grabbed her hand and shook, "I... I'm Rana."

Tabby smiled. "Yeah, well, I knew that much, dearie. Now, I heard you tell ol'Broddy that your father was killed by bandits."

Rana's face saddened. "He's not dead... he's out looking for me, I... I know it."

"Oh, sorry baby, you might be right. Okay, then tell me what happened between your daddy and them bandits."

Rana thought for a second, "We were running, and then I fell, then he started fighting the bandits. Then, I fell again, and then I was here. I think."

"Ah, honey, I think you might have missed a few parts there, but maybe your father is still out searching for you. If he got away from them bandits. Goddess help him if he is." Tabby patted her lap, "You know we have similar stories of how we got here. My village was also attacked by some bandits."

"Really?"

"Oh, don't be surprised. Most of the girls here have some type of tragic story on how they ended up here. Sold into slavery or ran away from home. For some, it's as simple as their family couldn't afford to feed them or just didn't want them at all."

"But why... why would they do that?" asked Rana holding her arms.

Tabby stared up at the ceiling, "I'm sure those girls above us have wondered the same thing on many nights."

A young lady entered the room, "Miss Tabby, did you want..." She noticed Rana. "Oh, sorry, I didn't know you had company."

"Hey, Angela, it's okay. We were just having us some girl

talk, is all."

Rana turned to see the young lady who had entered the room. She couldn't hide the shock in her eyes after witnessing the young woman's face. She had two huge scars across the side of her face. One scar was over her right eye, down her cheek, and another was from her cheekbone to her chin. It left a large sunken in gash over her lips. Rana caught herself staring at the woman and turned her eyes away, trying not to be inconsiderate. But Angela just smiled.

"It's okay. Everybody has that reaction the first time they see my face; I'm pretty used to it now." Angela walked in and knelt before Rana, grabbing her hand, "It takes a while to get used to, but I find that this usually helps." Angela reached down and took Rana's hand, placing it over her face, and guided her fingers over the scars.

Rana felt the roughness of the disfigured skin as she ran her fingers across Angela's face. "Doesn't it hurt?"

"It did... for a long time it did. But not as much these days."

Tabby placed her hand on Rana's head, shaking her hair, "Angela here is our cook, she makes most of the meals for the customers here. We all listen to her when it comes to what's good to eat."

"Oh, that's right. Miss Tabby, we're almost out of pork and fish."

CHAPTER 5

A few days later, Victor arrived in the small port town of Aarons Bay. As the morning breeze flowed through his hair, he took a deep breath, smelling the saltwater in the air. Glancing down over the small town, he saw people moving throughout a horde of shanty houses that were spread out across the grass and sand. "Right, what a wholesome looking place," he said as he began to make his way down
48

and through the town. On the way, he stopped by one of the street vendors selling fish. "I'll take some of your cooked fish."

"Aye, that'd be five bronze," said the vendor, slapping a fish on an already warm stone oven. The man gave Victor a glance while the fish started to sizzle. "So, where ya from, mate? You're not from here, that's for sure."

Victor reached into his pocket and pulled out a few bronze coins, "I'm from the capital, just here to take a transport. Supposedly it's Gregory Klein's ship. You know where I would find it in port?"

"Old Greggy's ship, huh? He'd be down that way," said the vendor pointing to the left side of the city by the water. "You see them two twin ships with the squids on their flags. One of them be Greggy's. But he ain't meant to be leaving for another day or so, ya better off finding a place in town to bunker down until then."

Victor looked down the hill and tried taking stock of the city. "Have any suggestions; maybe a place where I won't be robbed so easily?"

The vendor laughed, "Aye, I see ya got your wits about ya. Try Miss Marshall's tavern. It might not be the fanciest place, but you're less likely to be finding a knife in your back before the morning."

"Thanks," said Victor, placing ten bronze on the table. He accepted the fish, munching on it as he made his way down the dirt road towards the left side of Aarons Bay. On his way, he noticed the state of the town was even worse than it appeared. Some of the homes had holes in the walls. Its people wore clothing that seemed to be little more than rags. And as one would expect in such an area, more than a few dubious people had been eyeing him as he made his way towards the port. There he would see the two ships that were mentioned. Both were holding anchor at the dock. Victor noticed a boy was sitting on the ground staring at him intently. He waved to the young boy, "Over here, lad."

"What can I do for ya, Sir?" asked the boy, walking over.

Victor watched as the boy's bare feet sunk into the dirt beneath him. "Which one of them is Gregory Klein's ship?"

The boy turned around, observing the ships before pointing to one. "That'd be Mr. Greggy's ship, Sir. The one with the blue squid on the flag."

Victor nodded and pulled out two silver, holding it out in front of the boy. "Now tell me lad, are you the only pickpocket here, or do I need to watch out for more?"

"Wha... I'm not."

"Lie to me, and you'll get no silver."

The boy looked Victor in the eyes for a second as if judging his seriousness, "Okay, you win, there's a few others, but they ain't here. Only I work the docks."

"So how bout you tell your other pickpocket friends to leave me alone while I'm in town?"

"Make it five silver, and we got a deal. I'm gonna have to share it with 'em and all."

Victor reached into his pocket and pulled out three more silver along with a dagger from his side. The boy eyed the blade nervously.

"Don't worry; I'm not gonna hurt you. You see those two men behind me. You know 'em?"

The boy glanced over Victor's shoulder, seeing the two men watching from up the road. He then nodded.

"When you leave, just tell them, you tried to pickpocket me, and I threatened you."

"Okay, I get it."

Victor placed the silver pieces into the boy's hand, "all right, be on your way then," and watched as the boy ran off. He placed his dagger back in its sheath where the men could watch him do it and started walking towards the ship with the blue squid on the flag. After a minute, he reached a large three-masted wooden ship. The vessel swayed in the water as the wood of the outer hull creaked under its own weight. Up ahead, there were a few men standing watch at the ship's entrance plank.

"Excuse me, gentlemen, is Mr. Klein's about?"

One of the men looked at him and spat off the peer, "Yeah, he's here," before turning and yelling, "Hey Greggy, some fancy pants' here to see ya." After a few seconds, Victor saw a hardy man with a full grey beard, who was easily twice his age appear. He made his way down the plank onto the peer. Walking and yawning as if he had just woken up, the man was dressed to fit the part with an open chest doublet and no underclothes. Spotting Victor, the man stopped and crossed his arms a few feet away.

"Aye, that'd be who we've been waiting for. You must be the man from the capitol. The ship leaves in the morn to catch the tide."

"I guess not that many military men come around here."

The captain cracked his neck and nodded at the city behind Victor. "Humph, outside of a trade once or twice a cycle, not much of anything comes around here."

Victor turned back, raising an eyebrow of concern at the disheveled state of the town, and nodded in agreement to the statement. "I guess this wouldn't exactly classify as someone's preferred vacation place."

"No, the vacation idiots are on my ship, tucked away until we sail, and I should be getting back to them," said the captain as he gestured to his ship. "You'll be staying inland tonight. I had a cabin for ya, but something came up. So I'll get something ready for ya come morn." The captain turned around and headed back onto his ship. "Try not to die before then. I don't wanna explain why I took a corpse across the waters deep."

A little while later, Victor arrived at the tavern that the vendor had mentioned. It seemed better than most of the buildings in town, but that wasn't much by comparison. He walked up the steps and into the building. Instantly, he felt the eyes of other patrons follow him on his way to the counter, where a young lady greeted him.

"Well, I ain't seen you before."

"Yes, I'm new here and would like a room for the night."

"Well, we sure got that, honey. I'll give you a room where you can see over the water." She pointed to a room upstairs that was the furthest to the left. "And are you expecting any company tonight?"

Victor laughed, "No. Sadly, I'm alone."

"Would you like some company then?" asked the woman as she dangled the key on her finger, licking her lips suggestively before cracking a smile.

Victor took the key and smiled, "No thanks, I'm not sure I could handle a woman like you," and walked up the stairs.

"Suit yourself, let me know if you change your mind."

After entering the room, Victor closed the door, locking it. He then reached into one of the pouches on his chest and pulled out a small plank of wood and a ball with a hole inside of it. Sliding the piece of wood between the top of the door and the frame to ensure it held firm, he then placed the ball on top of the wood carefully to ensure that it wouldn't fall.

Afterward he kicked off his boots and walked over to the window, watching the ships in the harbor, and noticing their flags. Both ships had identical flags, one had a blue squid flag, and the other had a red squid flag. "I guess they're part of the same company." He then glanced over and saw a man on a tower looking out to sea, while waving a blue and white flag down at the smaller ships in the water. Victor turned around and laid down on the bed. "I better get some sleep before nightfall, I guess," and closed his eyes.

CHAPTER 6

Days later, after arriving at the tavern, Rana was out in the streets of Lowtown with a basket, placing orders for items from the local street vendors. She stopped by an unattended vendor's shop, "Excuse me." No one answered, "Excuse me, hello!"

A man then stepped out of the shop, wiping his hands on his apron. "What can I do for you, little missy?"

"Mr. Brolly would like you to deliver the bread shipment

two days early," said Rana holding out a piece of parchment.

The man seemed confused, "Mr. Brolly? Wait, you mean Broderick? Ha, is that what you call him? Mr. Brolly, oh that's rich, I'll be sure to razz him about that later."

Rana made a pouting face looking down, and the man smiled at her, "Ah don't be like that," as he rubbed the top of her head, "You tell big ol` Mr. Brolly I'll bring it over in a day or so."

"Yes, Sir," said Rana, still sulking.

"Hey now, who's this," said a teenage boy walking up to the vendor, placing his hand on Rana's shoulder. Rana turned around to see two boys smiling at her. "We might have found ourselves something nice. What's your name?"

"Careful now boys, this one belongs to Broderick."

"Damn Broderick and his little house of whores," said the boy pulling his hand away from Rana and walking away.

"Don't worry about them sweety, just tell anyone who bothers you, that you're one of Broderick's girl's and you'll be fine."

But I don't wanna be one of Broderick's girls. "Ah, excuse me, Sir, but is Green Village near here?"

"Green Village? Ain't never heard of no place like that near here."

Dammit, how far away from home am I? "It's okay. Thank you, Sir."

She went on to make several more stops at different vendors. But at those stops, she was sure to call him Broderick instead of Mr. Brolly. Afterward, she took a break on the ground under a small tree in town. Reaching into her basket, she pulled out a piece of bread and started to chew on it while watching the people in town walk by. The town was a busy place in the day as people hustled back and forth. There were even other children moving about.

So many boys, I haven't seen any girl's my age out in town. I wonder why. Rana thought back to the girl she met in the alley the night of the fire. *I wonder what happened to her.*

One of the boys kicking the ball began to seem familiar to her. It was a small blonde-haired boy who was running about in a dust cloud in front of a nearby building with some other children playing a game with a little ball. They were kicking the ball amongst themselves and making the dust cloud grow even more significant with every heavy-footed kick that sent the ball bouncing off the side of a building's wall. But they didn't seem to care at all as they all gathered around the small boy enjoying their game.

"Well, lookie, it's the soaking wet girl Rana," said a girl's voice.

Rana turned to her left, the bread still hanging out of her mouth to see who had called her name. It was a brown-haired girl with a basket staring at her. Rana's memory came back to her as a night's experiences from days past flooded back into her mind. "Maggie... Maggie and Billy?"

Maggie smiled at her as Billy stopped playing his kickball game and started coming over to them. "I had wondered where'd you run off to; you even found yourself more clothes."

Rana glanced over Maggie and Billy and noticed that they also had different clothes on as well. "You look cleaner than the last time we meet too."

Maggie twirled around, showing off a clean blue and white tunic she was wearing. "I found me a sponsor. She puffed up her chest with pride, and he's a doctor and got plenty of money up in Hightown. Me and Billy down here running his errands for 'em." Maggie peered down at Rana's basket. "If you got pickings to be done, me and Billy can help," Billy took the basket from Maggie and thrust it at Rana.

"No, it's fine, I just finished."

"Then you should come with us. The Doc won't mind, and it's close by," said Maggie grabbing Rana's hand. Rana raised a brow at them unsurely, and Maggie playfully scowled back, "Oh, don't worry, he's a nice man. It'll be fine,

I promise."

Rana saw Maggie's cheerful face and gave in, "Fine, lead the way." And she and Maggie made their way through the streets until they reached the front gates of Hightown where guards halted them.

"Stop! What are you kids? Oh, it's you, Maggie. Tell the Doc I'll be over tomorrow, my shoulder's still nagging me." He noticed Rana. "Who's this one then?"

"She's helping carry the Doc's supplies."

The guard took a glance at Rana's basket and nodded his head. "Right, well, be on your way then, and if she's going to become a regular, have the Doc come by and vouch for her." They all then took off down the street towards the wall. Unlike lowtown where the streets were mostly made of wood, hightown's building were made of stone with wooden beams as the supports. Fountains were placed in the town squares for sitting and viewing pleasure as nobles casually went about their day. Rana gazed around at the people in fine clothing, compared them to her own state of cloth, and lamented her state of dress. After a small amount of walking, they reached Doc's house.

Maggie opened the door, and out came the voice of a man.

"Mr. Ericson, that leg of yours isn't going to get any better if you don't stay off it," said the man.

"I know, but my carrier was lame, so I was forced to take the message myself this time is all," said another man.

"Oh, you're back, just put the herbs on the desk there, we can start brewing them later," said the first man's voice as Maggie entered the house. Rana peeked her head in, and a handsome young man with dark hair noticed her and smiled, "And who do we have here, company?"

Maggie grabbed Rana and pulled her close. "This is Rana; she's a friend of mine."

"Well, hello there. I'm Astain. But mostly around here, everyone just calls me Doc."

"I'm Rana."

The doctor turned back to his client. "Okay, Mr. Ericson, you're good to go." And he ushered the man out. "And be sure to stay off that leg." He then turned back to Rana. "Well, miss Rana, will you be joining us for dinner. We're going to be having rabbit stew tonight, and you're welcome to join us."

"I won't be staying long; I just wanted to visit Maggie for a little while," said Rana shaking her head.

"Let's go, I can show you all the books and stuff the Doc has," said Maggie, pulling her away.

Rana noticed how Maggie kept a hold of her hand. *She's really friendly when she's not in an alley.*

As they scampered off to the back, the Doc yelled out after them, "Don't break anything in there."

"We won't," said Maggie.

In Doc's study, Maggie began showing all the odd things the Doc had. "He reads a lot and promised to teach me when he gets everything settled."

Rana looked around at the walls of the room, seeing each shelf filled with books, "So many, what are they about?"

Maggie pulled out a book from the shelf and showed it to her. "Doc said they got doctor stuff in 'em, like how to fix people that's been all cut up." Rana took the book and began reading a page. Maggie narrowed her eyes at Rana, tilting her head, "You can read?"

Rana closed the book handing it back to Maggie. "Yeah, sorry. My father taught me before... well, he taught me."

"Wow, ain't never meet a street girl that could read."

"Well, soon you're gonna be reading too since you said the doctor's gonna teach you," said Rana as she looked around the room. She was impressed by all the books and how nice everything seemed. The room had beautiful furniture with soft cushions, and there was a carpet throughout the home. But her wonderment ended as she began to remember what Maggie had said about sponsors a few nights ago. Rana leaned in close and whispered, "Maggie, he doesn't, uh... beat you, does he?"

Maggie's face turned bright red, "Wha... No."

Rana pulled back, keeping her voice low. "I just remember you saying that the ones with sponsors get hurt sometimes."

Maggie remembered her words and dropped her head, "Yeah, that's true. There was a couple girls who didn't come back, boys too even." Then Maggie lifted her head with pride. "But I was very careful when I picked ol` Doc."

"Wait, you picked him?"

"Sure did. I saw the people waiting outside his home a lot when I was sneaking around, and I wondered what they were doing here. Turns out Doc was out getting his medicines, and they didn't know when he'd be back." Maggie raised her finger in front of Rana. "So, I watched him for a few days after, making sure he was nice people and such. I had to make sure he wouldn't beat Billy and me, after all. And then, one day, I met him in the market and made him an offer that if he took care of Billy and me, then I'd do whatever he needed around the home."

Maggie placed her hands on her hips, shaking her head. "He didn't bite at first, but every day I kept pestering him till he gave in. It's a great deal since all I'm doing is woman's work anyway. Doc's even been teaching us how to cook."

Rana looked into Maggie's prideful face and laughed, "Okay, I'm sorry. Doc is a good man."

About an hour later, Maggie and Rana left Doc's home together as Maggie walked with her to the gates before stopping at the entrance. "Stop by from time to time or if ya ever in trouble. I'll get Doc to okay it with the guards." Rana walked out of the gate back into Lowtown and waved bye to her new friend. But as Maggie turned and started talking to one of the guards, Rana couldn't help but notice the cobblestones beneath Maggie's feet inside the gate, and the dirt beneath her own outside the gate. And with a saddened expression on her face to match the ping of jealousy in her heart, Rana made her way back through the streets of Lowtown towards the tavern.

A little while later, she arrived back at Broderick's tavern, which was at the time crowded with people. After entering, she headed back into the kitchen with the crowd laughing and joking when a man yelled out, "Hey Brodrick, let me get a discount on one of ya girls tonight since I'm such a loyal customer."

"No, can do, Manny. You will pay fifty silver for the night like everyone else."

"Huh, yours are double the price of the whores at Balisk's place."

Broderick poured a drink for another customer at the bar. "Well, take your pecker down to Balisk's then, I'll be surprised if ya manage to walk out with it still attached." The men of the tavern started laughing as Broderick gestured with his thumb and finger. "But from what I hear from the girls, you never had much to begin with." And the crowd burst into laughter again as the banter and insults began to fly through the tavern going back and forth.

Rana entered the kitchen to see Angela cooking in the back with some of the girls. Tabby walked in, tossing an apron over her head, and started cooking with the rest of them. "Now take that out to Lang's table, and Renee, get some carrots and onions from the cellar, we're gonna need to make a lot more stew." Tabby looked down and saw Rana. "Oh, Rana, perfect timing. Here put this on." Tabby grabbed another apron and tossed it over Rana's neck, handing her a bowl of stew. "Take that plate over to Andy." Rana gave a confused look back at Tabby as she mentioned the name. "Oh, that's right, you don't know our regulars yet. Take it to the table nearest the front door. The bearded man in a green hat ordered it, that's Andy, ya can't miss 'em. He's a big guy."

"Yes, Mam," said Rana as she grabbed the bowl and

59

headed back out into the tavern. As she began moving back into tavern air, she started noticing more things about the people in the room than she had before. Such as, many of them were carrying swords, while some even had small hammers and daggers at their waist. Rana walked down the middle of the aisle, trying to search for the man Tabby mentioned. Soon, she saw a huge man with a small green cap on his head near the door staring directly at her and waving.

She swallowed and slowly started to walk towards him when the patrons began to sing a rhyme about being in a war. Quickly, she found herself scooped up into a man's arms as he started to dance around while carrying her. She tried to balance the food, but it was no use. The speed at which the man spun her around sent the food flying to the floor, landing on another man's boots.

"Dammit, Manny, your little wench got me with the soup."

The man slowly put Rana down as she dropped to her knees, trying to pick up the bowl, "Ah, you complain too much, Daylon. You can still lick it up off the floor if you like. I've seen you eat worse."

But soon, the tavern began to quiet down as all the singing stopped.

"What's wrong with you all?" asked Manny, as he turned around and saw the giant man Andy standing before him. "Oh, hey, Andy, what's wrong big guy?"

"That was my food," said Andy.

Manny glanced down at the floor, seeing the spilled food as well as a very angry little girl glaring back up at him.

"Best leave the bowl for now," said a man's voice from behind Rana as she was once again swept off her feet as hands reached under her shoulders and snatched her up from behind. She found herself being pulled away fast back to the bar where Broderick was. She began to squirm but found herself quickly placed on the bar counter, looking at a brown-haired man with blue eyes. "You okay, muffin?"

Rana stared into the man's blue eyes for a few seconds. "I... I'm fine."

"That's a good muffin," said the man as he ruffled the hair on Rana's head and pointed to the ever-increasing panic that was beginning to emerge from near the front of the tavern. "Good to hear. Now watch carefully as you're about to see a very classic ass beating. A sight given to us by the ever ignorant and constantly stupid, Manny Rewland. This will be something you'll probably tell your children about."

Rana turned her face back to the confrontation and saw Manny waving his arms about, as the man's face seemed to go through a variety of emotions in just a small amount of time.

"Hey, Andy, I'm sorry. I'll get you another bowl, okay?" Manny turned around, "Hey, Broderick, bring my old pal Andy here another round of that stew on me."

"Can't," shouted Broderick with a smile on his face.

Manny snapped his head back towards Broderick at the bar. "What do you mean can't? Bring him another damned bowl."

"Oh, look, I think he's starting to sweat," said the blue-eyed man.

Broderick smirked at the blue-eyed man next to Rana and picked up a mug, staring at it as if it needed extra cleaning, "Well, the problem for you is that was rabbit stew, Manny. And Andy there caught it himself this morning, asking us to cook it for 'em. And my ladies here, being the sweethearts that they are, went out of their way to make Andy some special rabbit stew. And you know rabbits are rare this time of year, so we ain't got none in the back, hell we just ran outta pork." Broderick gave a cruel smile as the tavern guests began to step back after hearing his words. Manny quickly found himself alone with the giant of a man glowering down at him, gritting his teeth.

"You wanna take a bet how far he throws 'em Broderick?"

asked the blue-eyed man.

"Thirty silver, he hits the wall."

"I'll take that bet. My money says he goes over a few people but doesn't get enough height to hit the wall." The blue-eyed man bumped Rana on the arm, "You want in on this muffin? I'll even give ya three to one odds since Manny ruffled your apron and all."

Rana just stared at the man in confusion as Manny turned back to face Andy, "Don't worry, Andy. We can go somewhere else and I'll... argh," suddenly Manny was in the air sailing across the room, landing on a table and crashing into two other men near the wall.

"Hot damn thirty silver," said the blue-eyed man as he clapped his hands. "Call me lucky Jasper, the victorious."

"Dammit Andy, I remember you being stronger than that. I just lost thirty silver to Jasper because of that half-assed toss."

Jasper shook his head in mock disappointment, "Yeah, apparently our boy Andy here found himself a girl in town, and you know how they say a woman can weaken a man. Oh, and don't forget about me silver. A real man honors his bets."

"Yeah, yeah, fine. I'll have ya damned money."

"Dammit, Manny, get off me. Don't involve me in your mess," said one of the men Manny landed on. The two men quickly picked Manny up and tossed him back at the stomping-mad Andy headed in their direction.

CHAPTER 7

Victor laid in bed, listening to the sounds of footsteps outside his door as they paced back and forth.

"Come on, he's got money," said a man's voice from outside of his room.

"Yeah, well, I don't wanna get killed. He pulled a knife on little Eric, and he's only a babe," said another man's voice.

Victor thought back to the boy at the dock. *So, I guess his name was Eric, doesn't seem like my little scare tactic worked though.* Victor watched the ball on the plank that was wedged above the door and continued to listen to the men bicker with each other.

"Well, I ain't no babe, and I've got me a sword," said the first man.

"I'm telling ya, he looked like one of them military types. What if he's a mage?" asked the other man.

"Ain't no mage down here, they probably keep 'em locked up in the capital somewhere."

"Well, I ain't doing it. I ain't survived this long to get blown up by some mage. I'll stick to robbing farmers and such."

Suddenly, the door opened, and Victor stuck his head out to see two dimwitted looking men, "Excuse gentlemen, but if you plan on robbing me, then can you please get on with it. I would really like to get some rest before morning."

The two men seemed dumbfounded for a few seconds before the slightly balding one spoke, "Hey, how'd you know we'd be out here? Is that a fancy mage trick?"

"No, I simply heard you through the door. You both were quite loud."

The slightly balding man shoved the other man on the shoulder, "See, he ain't no mage."

Victor opened the door fully and stood before the men. "Gentlemen let me answer your questions. Yes, I am with the military, and no, I am not a mage, but if you try to attack me, know that I am very skilled and will kill you both."

The two men stood there in shock for a few seconds and looked at each other, before one spoke, "I'm done, Pue. I ain't messing with the military," and walked back down the balcony to the steps.

The other man followed behind, "You always been a scaredy-cat, we probably could'a taken him."

Victor shook his head, glancing down to see the lady who had given him his key at the counter, now by the door staring back up at him. She blew him a kiss and led the two men from before out the door. Victor walked back into the room, closing the door, and replacing the ball and plank before laying back down on the cot. "The world sure is a wonderful place."

The next morning, Victor set sail on Gregory's ship. He stared over the water at the shanty towns of Krispik, hoping never to return. But as the voyage started, he noticed fairly quickly that there were quite a few other passengers who were not part of the crew. The men and women aboard the deck were all dressed in nice clothes. The ladies all had on colorful dresses, while the men wore elegant doublets and fine trousers.

Well, this is certainly an interesting ship.

He started peeling an apple, deciding to wait until the captain had finished ordering the crew around before he would ask him about it. Eyeing the people on deck as they chatted with each other, he thought that they all seemed reasonable enough, if not a little bit out of place. That was until he glanced over by the railing of the ship and noticed a man with a cloak over his head. He was standing alone, gazing over the water. *Well, that one doesn't seem suspicious at all.* The captain finally finished giving his crew orders and began to make his way near him. Victor raised his hand, signaling that he would like to speak with him.

"What's it be, lad?" asked the captain with a tired expression on his face.

"Excuse me, but I was under the impression that the crown recruited this ship for my passage, I didn't expect so many other passengers."

"Yeah, you were wrong about that. Originally, I was headed to Stockton but was paid to change my plans and take you to the port city of Krispik in Burlus. And far be it from me to deny her majesty the use of my ship."

"Ha, and get yourself an easy payday in the process," said Victor as he munched the apple while waving an arm at the people scuttling around the ship. "So, tell me, who are these fine people that I'm going to be forced to travel with? I sure as hell didn't see them in port while I was there. And none were at the inn I stayed at. So, did you just conjure them up out of thin air?"

"Remember that other ship that was holding port yesterday? The one with the Red Squid flag. Well, that ship belongs to me brother. We have the business of transporting goods between ports. I make half the journey, and he does the other. Just so happened that this time the cargo be people as well as spices, rugs, and whatnot."

"And what of that one? The one in the cloak. He from your brother's ship?"

"Nah, that one's a mystery to me. He just showed up a day or two ago and asked if he could come aboard. I told him to plow off at first, but he offered up five gold pieces, and I ain't turning down the free coin."

"I'm guessing that one room you had for me, that something mysteriously happened to, would involve him."

"You'd be guessing right then."

Nope, not suspicious at all.

"Seems as if you have company," said the captain as he patted Victor on the back before walking off.

Victor turned around, confused by the remark only to see a man and a woman headed straight for him.

"Hello there, Sir. Are you with the Queen's military?" asked a man as he waved at Victor.

"Ah, yes, I'm here on business for the crown."

"Oh, excellent, I'm Francis, and this is my wife, Illyana. We are so happy to have protection on this trip. Just between us, this group of sailors appears to be more of the ruffian type, so I was worried for our safety until I saw your uniform."

"I'm happy my being here on your journey has eased your minds. I hope the rest of your trip is an easy one."

The couple gave hearty smiles as Victor struggled to keep his own.

"Well, now that we are acquainted, I simply must ask. What do you think of that terrible mess in the north?" said Francis.

"Which mess are you referring to, exactly?" said Victor, raising a brow.

"Surely you jest, the Starlight Queen's daughter has been kidnapped and spirited away. Stolen from her crib in the den of the night by a mysterious shadow. Or at least that's how the story goes." The man leaned in, whispering to Victor as if others were trying to listen in. "There's a rumor that she was stolen by our Queen Clarissa and will be held hostage to ensure diplomatic relations. They say the Starlight Queen hasn't slept a night since and has employed the aid of over one hundred tracers and bounty hunters in search of the child." Francis noticed Victor's face of shock. "You really didn't know? It happened like sometime a quarter moon ago."

Victor lifted his glasses, rubbing between his eyes and stretched the other hand forward to stop Francis from talking, "Forgive me, I have been on the road for the last half-moon, I haven't had the chance to hear any official reports."

"Oh it's been the talk of the ship since we started our little journey, trying to guess which kingdom took the baby," said Illyana clapping her hands while doing a little hop, "The Starlight Queen must be at her wit's end. It was her first child, you know. And they say the child was already showing magical talent. So she might grow up to be as powerful as the Starlight Queen herself. Oh, can you imagine a potential grand mage wandering around the five kingdoms with a group of bandits? It's preposterous."

Victor removed his glasses, pinching between his eyes again as his mind tried to understand what he just heard.

The man and woman looked at Victor in worry. "I'm sorry, Sir," said Francis. "I didn't mean to upset you; it's just all anyone has been able to talk about on this ship since we heard. And with you being a man of the military, we just assumed you'd known."

Victor slowly pulled his hands from his face, readjusting his glasses. "No, I'm sorry. I have been on assignment for a time, and it seems I have missed some things. Thank you for telling me this."

"Oh, no problem Mister...uh. I'm sorry, Sir. It seems we never got your name," said Francis.

"My name's Victor, Victor Krill," he said, offering his hand.

Francis shook his hand, and Illyana jumped again and clapped her hands together.

"Victor Krill, oh dear, are you the famous sixth general, the one from the battle of Ograham?" she asked.

Victor nodded, "Yes, that is I. Although I'm no longer a general, I have retired from that position, and am an ambassador now."

Francis made a face, "Retired, but you appear to be no more than thirty."

Victor laughed. "Early retirement for good service, I guess. But if you two will excuse me, I must head below deck as I have a few matters to attend to." Victor nodded to the two and walked off. *Dammit, Clarissa! Are you involved in this?* Victor shook his head. *Of course you are, when are you not scheming?* He headed down into the crew's quarters towards his room, but once he entered, he found the paste that he had placed on the door earlier had been broken. *Of course, as if I didn't have enough to worry about.*

Victor slowly opened the door with his hand on his dagger, glancing around the room. It was empty. He checked under the cot and out the window. Seeing no other place for anyone to hide, he sheathed his dagger and calmed down. He closed the door placing the same plank and ball above near the frame as before but added some of the broken paste to the ball to make sure it wouldn't fall because of the rocking of the ship. He walked over and sat on the cot.

"Right, so let's review my situation. One, the woman I hate most in the world, most likely stole the Starlight Queen's child. Two, I'm on a mission for that same evil bitch of a Queen to ensure that King Navender stays in cooperation with the kingdom. Three, someone just broke into my room searching for goddess knows what, also there's some mysterious cloaked guy on board who paid with five gold coins just to get on the ship."

Victor removed his glasses and laid down on the cot. "Oh, by the goddess, what's happened to my life." He closed his eyes to the world and awoke sometime later to the sound of knocking on his door. He wiped at his eyes, shaking his head, trying to get his senses as the banging on the door continued. "Hold on." He sluggishly opened his eyes and fumbled, trying to sit up and fell to the floor. "Wha... What do you want?" The knocking stopped.

"Sir, the captain, would like to see you," said the voice of a young man.

Victor tried shaking his head to clear his thoughts. However, everything he did just felt so sluggish, his body was slow to respond. "Tell him a minute; I'll be along in a minute."

"He says it's quite urgent, Sir; I can escort you if you—"

Victor yelled, "I said in a minute. It's morning, let me wake first."

"Sir, are you alright? It's mid-afternoon now, Sir."

Victor turned back to the window, "Mid-after, what?" and noticed that the sun wasn't shining where it should be, if it were, in fact, morning. "How long have I been out?" he asked himself. The man outside knocked again.

"Are you sure you're alright. Sir? There's a healer on board, I can call."

Victor snapped, "That won't be necessary!" As his voice echoed across his small cabin, he realized how he sounded and pulled his head back, lowering his voice, "tell... tell the captain... that I will be along shortly." He struggled to pronounce every word, as he heard the boy shuffling his feet outside the door.

"Ah. Yes, Sir, I'll ah... I'll go now."

Victor dropped his head down to the floor into his hands. "Great, now I'm... yelling at... children." He shook his head again and faced toward the door but noticed something on the floor. He crawled forward, picking up the item and waited for his eyes to focus properly on it. Blinking a few times until his vision cleared, he squinted to see that it was a type of plant before realization set in, "sleep root." He then looked up to the top of the door, and there was the little ball still on the plank.

He forced himself up to his feet and walked forward, leaning against the door. He reached upward, grabbing the ball and plank, placing them into his pocket along with the sleep root. *Forced to sleep, but... door wasn't... opened.* He opened the door and made his way towards the steps to the deck. "Why... is nothing... ever simple?"

On the ship's deck, Victor banged open the captain's door and leaned on the side of the door frame. The captain's room was a mess. Parchment, cups, and clothing were thrown about the floor; chairs were turned over and hidden under the large table in the center of the room. Red drapes covered the windows at the end of the cabin casting crimson lighting throughout the room as the sun shined in over the captain bed. Victor stared inside at the captain, who was sitting down at the table, looking at a map. "You... wanted to... see me?"

The captain glanced up at the disheveled appearance of Victor, who appeared as if he could barely stand inside the doorway. Victor's shirt was half undone, and his hair hung over his eyes as the captain raised an eyebrow at him. "Well, don't ya look like you're half dead? I didn't take ya for the type that would get seasick."

Victor forced himself back upright and walked toward the table. He reached down, steadying himself on the wood to ensure he wouldn't fall and lifted up one of the chairs from the floor and fell into it. "Someone... lit sleep root in my room, the after-effects... hard to shake off. Need... drink, preferably strong." He placed his hands over his eyes and realized he'd left his glasses in the cabin below.

"Fuck." The strain from trying to think in this condition was pissing him off. He focused his attention upwards and began watching as a golden chandelier swung back and forth with the ship's motion. Victor began to wonder if the ship was swaying or was he just losing control of his body. The captain stood up and walked over to a trunk near his bed, kicking it open. He reached in, pulled out a glass bottle, and snatched up a cup off the floor. Placing it before Victor on the table, he popped the cork on the bottle and poured Victor a drink.

"There, drink that," said the captain.

Victor eyeballed the cup as the liquid inside reflected the red light shining through the cabin and placed the drink to his nose. The fumes of the concoction stung his eyes as he threw his face into his sleeve as if to protect his now watery pupils from the dangers of suspect liquid.

The captain grinned, "Yeah, she stings like a jellyfish."

Victor mustered his courage, *Oh goddess protect me from the evil drink that I am sure will cause me great suffering,* and took the cup to his lips. He swallowed once, and he felt his throat begin to warm, then quickly swallowed again in anticipation of the storm that he knew was about to come. He didn't need to wait long, as the previous warm sensation in his throat had quickly turned into what felt like a raging fire in his lungs, as he coughed and gasped for air. Every breath felt as if flames were pouring down his neck. The cup flew from his hands spilling the rest of the concoction to the floor as Victor banged his fist on the table trying to distract himself from the strength of the drink.

"Aye, it's got a bit of a kick to it doesn't it? I've seen it bring the drunkest man out of his stupor."

Victor's face began to flush red as he muttered out between coughing fits, "What... is... that?"

The captain held up the liquor in the light and shook it around. "I'm not too sure, honestly. They say it's liquor mixed in with some type of magic and herbs or whatnot. I picked up a few bottles from a merchant who'd been in the Sakari desert a few moons back."

Victor gritted his teeth as he fought to hold back the coughing, with his eyes entirely red and filled with tears. "Appreciate... the... drink... but... why did... you summon me here?"

The captain looked down at Victor with confusion. "Huh, oh, that's right, someone got poisoned last night."

Victor began coughing and choking again, "What... how?"

The captain took a sip from the bottle and wiped his lips. "Seems, it happened while ya were off visiting the fairies. At first, I'd figured ya might'a have done it as some part of whatever mission you be on, but that seems unlikely now. Cause, if it were Queens business, then I'd not be butting in." The captain leaned forward and waved a finger at the still recovering Victor. "But now, seeing that it wasn't some type of mission, then I'd be asking ya to figure out who did it before any of my crew end up dead."

Victor stopped coughing and began testing out his scorched lungs taking in deep breaths. "Where's... the body?"

The captain leaned back into his chair. "The poor sods below deck, still in his cot. The wife found him dead this morning." Victor forced himself to stand, trying to regain his composure and a little bit of his dignity after the coughing fit.

"Aye Drew," shouted the captain as a man entered from outside. He waved his hand at Victor. "Take this man with ya to see that body down below."

Soon Victor was taken back below deck, where he entered

a small wooden cabin to find a woman in a cream-colored sundress with gloves on her hands squatting on her knees. She was hunched over the dead body of a well-dressed man in a waistcoat, while another crew member stood over them both. The other man noticed Victor and Drew and walked over to them.

"Hey Drew, who's that ya got with ya?" asked the man.

"Hey, Fenry, the captain sent 'em here, says he can find out who did the poisoning."

Victor responded in a gruff voice, still rebounding from the drink, "I… I can try." He then walked in and knelt beside the woman, placing a hand upon her shoulder, "Miss, can you tell me what happened?"

"I… I don't know, we went to bed together, and when I awoke, he just laid there," said the woman.

Victor reached out his hand, and after she wiped the tears from her eyes, she took it and raised to her feet. "Now, madam, I'm about to perform an investigation. Is there anything you can remember? Has your husband been acting weird for the last few days, or has someone been acting weird around you?"

The lady shook her head, "No, it was always the same. We would talk to people who we met on this trip. We were all here for an adventure, and Wilbert got along with everyone." The lady lifted her head to Victor, "Wait! He was talking to a cloaked man yesterday. He got on during our last stop. I didn't know him, but Wilbert was smiling when talking to him and didn't seem worried or anything."

Victor thought back to the cloaked man on deck. *Yeah, and there's the obvious conclusion.* He turned to the crewman, "Ah, Mr. Drew, was it? Where is the cloaked man that she speaks of now?"

Drew began to think, "I'd imagine he'd be in the mess of the ship with the rest, I spose, if ya want I can go round em up for ya?"

Victor raised his hand, stopping the man before he

could run off, "No, we're on a ship in the middle of the sea and won't make land for another week or so, it's not likely he has anywhere he can go."

"Ah, right, didn't think of that."

Victor placed his hand on the man's neck to ensure there was no pulse. "How many people know about this?"

"Ahh, only the lady, Me, and ol' Fenry here. The captain, he wanted to keep it all hush-hush like, so not to scare the other passengers."

"Right, let's keep it that way," said Victor as he stood up and met the lady's eyes. "Mam, I will find who did this, you have my word."

The lady stared up at him with red, watery eyes, "Thank You, Sir. I swear Wilbert was always nice to everyone. I don't know why someone would do this."

"Fenry, take the woman to my room and wait with her until I come for you."

"Yes, Sir," said Fenry as he ushered the lady off down the ship's corridor.

Drew began to follow them when Victor stopped him, "Mr. Drew, be sure to tell Mr. Fenry not to turn his back on the woman."

"What? You think she did the poisoning or something?"

"Not sure about that, but I am sure that she just lied to me about going to bed with her husband."

"How's that?"

Victor moved his attention to the dead man's hands, lifting one to check for any tearing of the skin or any signs of struggle. "She said she woke up and found him like this. Well, look at how he's dressed. You think he'd go to bed in a full waistcoat and doublet? So, either she dressed him herself, which judging by her size and his size, would have been quite the impressive task, or she was lying. Not to mention that she was still dressed herself. She even still had on her gloves. I can't think of many wives that would compose themselves so well, immediately after their

74

husbands passing, can you?"

Drew just stood in the door frame staring at Victor for a few seconds. "Wow, I'd not thought of all that. Are all of ya kingdom folks smart like that?"

"Don't worry; I can assure you I'm not as smart as you think I am. For, if that were the case, I would have found a way to properly retire." Victor noticed the confused look on Drew's face at his statement. "Don't worry about it, just head off and tell Mr. Fenry what I said."

Drew headed off down the corridor of the ship towards Fenry and the woman. Victor turned back to the body. "Right, well, let us see what secrets you have, Mr. Wilbert." Victor lifted open the man's coat, noticing some pockets inside his waistcoat that were meant to hold items, "Well this is extravagant, I wonder what you had in these." He then rummaged through the man's trouser pockets and felt his way down the seam of the leg, feeling for anything that seemed out of the ordinary.

Finding nothing there, he rolled the man onto his side, checking his backside for oddities. "Come on, I've never met a rich bastard that didn't hide a few secrets on them. If someone wanted you dead, then there must have been a reason." Victor felt something solid behind the man's back, trapped within the cloth of his waistcoat. "Ah-ha, got ya!" And pulled out his dagger, cutting a hole open in the fabric. He reached inside and pulled out another small knife with an ornate skull on end from a sewn-in scabbard. Victor held up the blade, staring at it in confusion. "What the hell kinda noble carries a blade like this."

Drew walked back in and noticed Victor holding the daggers. "What's those for?"

Victor just stared at it, "This one's mine," as he sheathed his dagger back at his side, "I'm not sure about this one, it was on him." He flipped the man's blade over examining the skull as Drew walked over, scratching his head.

"I guess even nobles carry daggers, nowadays," said

Drew.

Victor frowned, "It's not that he had it on him that's the problem. Questionable tastes aside, I think everyone should protect themselves. But the problem is where he had it. Plus, all those pockets inside in his clothing." Victor's eyes widened as he recognized the skull. He grabbed the dead man's wrist, placing the knife at his arm and cut through the fabric up to the shoulder, exposing the skin beneath.

Drew whistled, "Wow, that's one painted up noble." as both men stared at dozens of tattoos and scars along the man's arm.

"Where's the wife?" asked Victor.

Drew made a confused face, "Uh, in your room, like ya asked."

Victor jumped up and rushed down to his room only to see the door ajar. When he crossed the doors opening, he saw Fenry face down on the floor with blood leaking from a cut in his head.

CHAPTER 8

Mid-morning in the streets of Hightown, Rana, Miraval, and Pelly were out with Broderick on their way to pay a visit to the city magistrate's home. Soon they arrived at an arching gate to the large manor, and Broderick stopped and turned to the girls. "Okay, now you girls be good and only speak when I tell you to." The girls nodded, and Broderick looked at Rana, "And you, you just don't break anything, this'll be good for you to see how it's done." Broderick turned back to the gate and called out. "Hey in there, I got a meeting with the magistrate, open up."

A man walked into view, holding a sword, "Yeah, yeah, state your business." Broderick pulled the two girls in front of him, "I'm here to offer your lord the services of my girls here."

"Oh, it's you, Broderick. You coming here to peddle your whores again?" He glanced down at the girls, "And some more young`uns this time."

Broderick made a dramatic face while trying to imitate a noble's voice and posture, "My dear knight, you wound me. The whores from Lowtown are merely a part of my business ventures, but these girls here are pure virgin maids."

The guard burst out laughing, and Broderick switched to his normal accent, "Besides, I know the lord here likes 'em young."

"Aye, that he does," said the guard as he regained his composure while wiping his face, before turning to open the gate. The girls just stared at the large manor area until Broderick pushed them forward, "come on, no need to keep his lordship waiting."

"Are we gonna become whores like the other girls?" asked Pelly.

Broderick answered without looking down at the girl. "Yeah probably. But being the whore to a noble who can barely keep his cock up, is a far better life than being the whore of an entire city." As the group approached the steps to the manor, a man met them at the door.

No this isn't right. I'm not a whore. I have a home and a family. This... I have to find a way out. I don't belong here. Thought Rana, listening to Broderick as she made her way up the steps.

"Hey Broderick, you here to see the magistrate again? I figured he was waiting on someone today since he's been home all day."

"Hey Willow, been a while since ya been down to the tavern. What, ya found yourself a little lady friend to warm your bed at night."

"Nah, just been busy is all, I'll stop by again when I get the chance." Willow turned around, leading them inside. "Well, come along then. I figure he's been waiting for your arrival. No need to keep him waiting any longer."

Broderick gestured his thumb back over his shoulder. "I wish you would have told the guard that."

Willow turned and led them inside. They went through the main hall of the manor and into a large room. The room had two stories and was fully carpeted. Over to the right, she could see another smaller room with a table in the center with blue furniture inside. Directly ahead of Rana sat a man in fine clothing next to a bowl of apples looking over a few pieces of parchment. Broderick and the girls stood near the entrance of the room.

"Greetings magistrate," said Willow as he walked over, opening the curtains of one of the windows to let more light into the room. "I have brought some guests; I believe you were expecting."

The magistrate smiled, setting down the parchment, "Thank you, Willow."

"I have brought two girls to offer you as housemaids."

The magistrate stood up and walked over to the girls. He leaned forward, looking down and cupped Miraval's face in his hand, inspecting her.

"You certainly do bring me pretty ones, Broderick."

"Yes, I like to think I understand my lord's wishes very well," said Broderick rubbing his hands together.

The magistrate smirked, letting go of the girl's face. He approached Broderick, then noticed Rana beside him and pointed to her, "And what of that one beside you?"

"Oh, this one's new, only had her for a little while. Still getting her trained up."

The magistrate gave Rana an inspection with his eyes, "And how long before this one is, how did you say, 'trained up?"

"She still has to learn cooking, cleaning, knitting, and the such. So, maybe, half a cycle or so."

The magistrate frowned and stood back up to meet Broderick face to face. "Broderick let's be blunt here, you know about my pension for... young girls?" Broderick gave a skeptical eye but nodded his head. The magistrate turned around with his hands behind his back, stepping away, "Well, it seems my son also has this taste, and I plan to have him visit me soon, during his leave. My intention is to send him off with one or both of those girls that you have there. Where in time, they will wash his clothes, cook his meals, and warm his bed at night. But as you might understand, since this is my son, I would appreciate it if the girls were as well behaved as possible."

Broderick nodded, "Yes, Sir, I understand. Military life is a lot different than living in the comforts of your home. I used to be a mercenary man myself, so I'll properly explain to the girls what's expected of them."

The magistrate turned around and walked back to Broderick. "I appreciate your efforts, and you will be paid accordingly to our previous contracts. I figured this would still be acceptable, considering that mess you made two cycles ago."

Broderick's face turned serious. "It was a mess that needed to be made, Sir. Or did you not see what they did?"

"No, but I had heard what happened. Trust me, Broderick. I and the other nobles bear you no ill will. The continuation of the standard payment should indicate that," said the magistrate as he extended his hand to Broderick.

Broderick shook the magistrate's hand, "Yes, Sir, thank you for your continued business and understanding. I shall have the two of them prepared for your son's arrival, Sir."

"Your efforts are appreciated," said the magistrate. He then looked down at Miraval and Pelly, "I hope to see you ladies soon."

Miraval and Pelly both bowed to the magistrate, "Yes,

my lord."

The magistrate turned to Rana, "And after you're ready, maybe I will see you again too." He reached out and patted Rana on the head. But the moment he touched her hair, he gasped and snatched his hand away, looking shocked.

"Magistrate, are you okay, Sir?" asked Broderick in a panicked voice. The magistrate stood there stunned for a moment as Broderick called to him. "Are you okay, Sir?"

"Huh, oh... ah... sorry. It seems I contacted a bit of a shock when I touched her. Must be the carpet in here, it does that sometimes," said the magistrate as he regained his composure.

Rana made a face while rubbing at her hair. *I didn't feel a shock.*

"Uh-huh," said Broderick skeptically.

"Broderick, where did you say you found this one?"

Broderick raised a brow at Rana, then turned back to the magistrate, "Found her trying to sleep in my stables a little while back, why? You know something about her?"

The magistrate stared at Rana, "Huh, no, no, I just find her interesting is all." He turned back to Broderick. "Broderick, tell me again. How long did you say it would take you to have that little one, as you said, 'trained up?'"

"Half a cycle would do usually."

The magistrate stroked his chin, "If you can have her ready in time for my son to arrive. Then I'm willing to pay four times the amount."

Broderick's eyes bulged, "Fu... Four times," he pointed down at Rana. "For this little runt?"

"I think she might end up lucky for my son. And, on the battlefield, some luck would be a good thing for him to have."

"Ahh, yes, Sir, I will start her training immediately."

"And bring both those girls when you bring her for my son's arrival. I'll take them both as then they can stay together. I'd imagine they'd like that," said the magistrate as the girls nodded their heads. He walked back to the head of the table, "Now if you will excuse me, I have matters to attend to," Broderick bowed, and he ushered the girls out.

"Willow," said the magistrate.

"Yes, Sir."

"Get me more parchment. It seems I must send a letter to my son about his upcoming visit."

Broderick and the girls left the manor and headed out into Hightown. But, on the way back, Rana slowed her pace behind them. Broderick turned back to her, "What ya doing; keep up." After a few seconds, Broderick heard Rana mumble.

"Wanna whore."

Broderick raised a brow at Rana, "What's that?"

Rana lifted her head and shouted, "I don't wanna be a whore."

The nobles that were walking around them stopped, and all turned to look at Broderick and the girls. Broderick could hear them starting to whisper around him. He took a deep breath and sighed, "What's that? Oh, I've had this conversation before," and walked back to Rana while waving his arms around, drawing even more attention to himself. "Miraval, Pelly, listen here to what the little miss is saying and watch carefully. This'll be a good lesson for ya." He leaned forward, towering over Rana. "Alright then, if ya don't wanna be a whore, what do ya wanna be?" Rana stayed silent, and Broderick gestured his arms around at the people who, once again, started walking by. Although many purposely distanced themselves from the group, "What do you see girl?"

Rana looked around at the nobles, who were giving them narrowed glances as they kept their distance. "People."

"Yeah, people. And how many of these people helped you when I found you in my stables, huh?" Rana glanced around as people just stared at her and Broderick. Suddenly she felt herself falling as Broderick pushed her down onto the cobblestones. He knelt, grabbing the top of her hair, making her wince as he pulled her head back, "Call for help, go ahead, see if anyone of 'em comes to ya rescue."

I hate you; I hate you so much.

Rana opened her eyes and saw the disgust in people's faces as they continued to walk past them hurriedly. She watched as mothers pulled their children away, and as men turned a blind eye to her situation. A few of the men were even watching with smiles on their faces. Broderick let go of her hair, and she turned around to face him with hatred in her eyes, only to see the same loathing in Broderick's eyes as he stared off past her at all the nobles that were watching them. "Yeah, now tell me what you see, each and every one of them no better than the other. And they dare to judge us as if we're trash. If we died right here in this street, they'd still throw their little party tonight."

Broderick stood up and turned around. "Now come on. We're going back. You're gonna start your training today." Rana slowly stood up from the cobblestoned street and stared at Broderick as he stared down at her, "This isn't the first time someone's glared up at me with eyes like that, and it won't be the last. But if you expect to eat tonight, then you'd best remember who's feeding you." Broderick nodded ahead of her, "Remember you're my property, and all of them know it. I made sure of that. Or do you still think one of them will help you?" Rana glanced at the people around them and noticed the disgust in their eyes as they continued to whisper to each other. She bit her lip, wiped her clothes, and then reluctantly followed behind Broderick and the girls back towards Lowtown.

No one's gonna help me.

Later they arrived back at the tavern, and Rana saw Tabby at the bar handing mugs of ale to the customers. She noticed Rana and the girls come in and waved them over.

"Hey, glad you're back, go get yourself cleaned up, and help us out." Tabby noticed Rana acting odd, "You okay, honey? You looking a bit rattled."

"I'm fine."

And before Tabby could say anything else, Rana walked off into the back, grabbing an apron. Then, she returned to serve drinks. Rana never paid much attention before, but now she noticed that the girls would flirt with a lot of men in the tavern. She watched as a woman named Halva grabbed the arm of one of the men and began leading him upstairs, with his buddies down below making crude remarks about how he couldn't handle her, and how she had slept with one of them beforehand. Rana saw Halva just smile during the comments as she led the man upstairs, and suddenly the words of Broderick earlier on in the day came back to her mind. "Better to be the whore of some old geezer than the whore of an entire city," he had said.

Rana watched as the ladies of the tavern each spent time flirting with different men. Rubbing their faces and sitting on the laps of men whose names they probably wouldn't remember the next morning. But the women would go on and put on their smiles through this night and every other night. Rana felt as if she was there only to watch them as a silent witness to the harsh realities of the world. Her heart sank as she thought of her future here in the tavern or at the tent of some noble.

When the tavern was finally quiet, Rana cleared the tables along with Miraval.

"You can take the plates back; I'll finish wiping down the tables and cleaning up this mess," said Miraval.

"Okay," said Rana as she scooped up the wooden plates, taking them back into the kitchen, and dumping them into a bucket to be cleaned later. She took off her apron and wiped the sweat from her face.

"You wanna tell me what's been bothering you all night?" asked Tabby behind her.

Rana turned to see Tabby standing in the doorway with her arms folded as she hung up her apron.

"It's nothing; I'm just tired."

Tabby walked in, pulling out a stool and took a seat.

"Honey, I've been around here a long time and seen girls come and go. And that pained look you got there on your face there, be telling me that something's wrong."

Rana turned around, staring at Tabby with a serious expression on her face. "None of this is right. I'm supposed to be at home with papa riding on his horse. Instead, I'm here training to be some maid and... and..." Rana clenched her fists and lowered her head, trying not to tear up." Am I going to be a whore?"

"What? You mean like Halva and the girls," said Tabby, "Of course you not gon..." but after seeing Rana's face, so desperately trying not to show her emotions in front of her. Tabby gave up on trying to comfort the girl and sighed, placing her hand on her lap. "Yeah, I guess it would be best if I told you now. Hell, you would have found out anyway. Did you know that I was a whore? Hell, I probably still am depending on who you ask."

"Wha... but you and Broderick—"

Tabby just smiled. "Yeah, it's like that now, but in truth, I was just the whore he liked the most at the time. And lucky me, he decided to take me along with him after he'd had enough killing with his uncle. In truth, I done fucked men for money, for food, hell sometimes just for a place to sleep that wasn't on the ground or behind someone's shed. Then one day I met Broderick, and after we done fucked a few times and talked, he decided he liked me and kept me around."

Rana dropped her head, and Tabby just gave a pitying smile, "Oh, darling, I'm sorry. But I best tell you the truth. You might get lucky and become a maid. Broderick took you to one of his meetings right. So, you might end up working for some noble and doing good for yourself."

Rana looked up with disgust in her face. "The magistrate says he will pay a lot for me if I'm trained up for his son when he comes to town."

Tabby's eyes opened wide. "Wow," and she caught herself showing her excitement. "Well, that's a good thing. The magistrate is old, so he'll probably never," then she realized what Rana said, "wait, you said his son. Which one Cardon or Timothy?"

Rana shook her head, "He didn't say which one."

Tabby placed her hands on her knees, standing up. "Right, well, I've heard bad things about Timothy. But Cardon is liked by a lot of people here in town. He can be a hard ass, but I've not heard of him beating any girls before he left. But if it's Timothy," Tabby noticed Rana's face sink back into depression, "Oh, I'm sorry honey. I'll stop talking about it." Tabby stood and walked over to Rana, wiping her sweaty hair out of her face. "Look you're all dirty from the day's work, why don't you head on down to the washroom and get yourself cleaned up for the night."

"I don't wanna be a whore, Tabby," said Rana as her eyes began to water.

Tabby stared down at Rana, seeing the tears in her eyes. "I don't think anyone does honey; we just don't get much of a choice in this life, so we just make the best we can of it." She patted Rana on the shoulder and walked to the door before turning back to her, "Remember, I'm here if you ever wanna talk, Rana baby," and she walked off down the hall to her and Broderick's room trying to hold in her own tears.

Rana watched Tabby leave, before walking towards the back bathing room. She opened the door only to see Angela naked on her knees over a bucket of water with a towel in her hand.

"Oh! It's you, Rana, you startled me," said Angela.

"I'm sorry, I didn't think—"

The words froze in Rana's mouth as she gazed upon the scars along Angela's back. Angela saw her expression and began to self-consciously rub at her arms.

"Do they still look that bad?"

Rana walked in over the watery wooden floor, "No... they ah, I mean," she closed her eyes and focused her words. "How did... I mean, what happened?"

Angela just smiled, "It was my own fault."

Rana reached out her hand. "Can I?"

Angela dropped her towel, exposing her skin, "If you want, go ahead. I don't mind now. I did say it's the best way for you to get used to them."

Rana ran her hand down the scars on Angela's back. There were so many scars that she lost count. She continued moving her hand down across Angela's ribs, where the wounds wrapped around to her breasts. Rana stepped in front of Angela following the scars and saw atop one of her breasts amongst the scars was a large burn mark. Rana rubbed across it with her hand.

"Why?" Rana asked.

"Around two cycles ago, I tried to run away," said Angela, "and this is how I ended up."

"Did Broderick?" asked Rana, stopping her words as she saw the tears starting to show in the eyes of Angela's scared face.

Rana snatched her hand back, "I'm sorry; I didn't mean to hurt you."

Angela wiped the tears away and chuckled, "No, no, you're fine. I just thought that, after everything, you're probably the only one who'd want to touch me, even the other girls they just try to pretend they don't see the scars. But I guess—" Suddenly, Angela felt Rana's arms embrace her. Angela stiffened for a moment, not knowing what to do with the tenderness the girl was showing her, but she soon smiled and cradled the little girl in her arms. She could feel the little girl's breath on her neck as Rana began to tremble in her arms. Angela held Rana back, seeing the tears in her eyes.

"What's wrong?" asked Angela.

"It's not fair; you shouldn't... it's not right," Rana said

with wiping tears away.

It was then that Angela realized that this little girl was crying for her.

After a while, Rana stepped away from Angela with her tunic wet from the bathwater that was on her.

"I… I'll be back, I' mma go see Maggie. She… might be able to help," said Rana.

Angela gave a curious look. "Help? Who's Maggie?"

But before she could get a response, Rana was already gone. She had run out of the tavern door and down the street into the dark night of Lowtown. A little while later, she found herself getting closer to Hightown. But that night, a large amount of light was seen coming from inside the gates. She started following the lights and soon began to hear the sounds of music. Eventually, this would lead her back to the gates of Hightown as one of the guards noticed her wandering about.

"Hey, you alright over there?" asked a guard.

Rana stopped and glanced over at the guard, trying to catch her breath as she made her way over to him. "What… what's happening," she said as she stared up at the lights shining on the sides of buildings from over the wall.

The guard sighed, "No unauthorized people go into Hightown without permission."

"I… I am authorized, I work with the doctor."

The guard gave her a suspecting eye and then yelled out to another guard on the other side. "Hey Smith, is this the little girl that works with ol' Doc?"

Another guard walked over and saw Rana and started scratching his head as he looked down at her.

"I don't know, I remember there was another he came in and signed for, what's your name child?" asked the other guard.

"Rana, my name's Rana."

The guard noticed her dirty clothes and her unkempt face and reached his hand out to grab her. Rana jumped back shakily, and the guard pulled his hand back, seeing the mistrust in her eyes.

"Woah there, I'm just trying to get a look at that face of yours. You got that jungle in front of it."

Rana stopped her shaking and stepped back toward the guard, moving her sweaty hair out of her face and displaying it for them as one guard glanced at the other.

The second guard just shrugged, "You wanna tell the Doc why you didn't let his little hobby in the next time you go for a visit?"

The first guard thought about it and stepped aside, "Go on then, and don't cause any trouble."

Rana walked past the guards and headed toward the light, turning the corner toward the doctor's office, she then saw a party in the opening city square where the Doc's office resided. Lanterns were lit throughout the square, and the event was lively as people danced to the rhythm of the drummers, and ladies with fire sticks twirled them into the night sky. Rana was in awe of the spectacle. But then, she noticed something even more amazing across from a fire that was roaring in the center of the town square. Ahead of the dancing crowd was a woman in armour holding a sword. She had long brown hair that seemed to glow in the light of the fire.

The woman seemed to be discussing something with one of the male soldiers. Before she even knew it, Rana was moving towards the woman like the moths to the large flame in the center of the town square. She tried avoiding people and stuck to the shadowy walls of the buildings of the square, trying to get closer to the armoured woman. She made her way around, trying to keep the woman in sight as the crowd continued to block her vision. Eventually, she made her way close enough to hear some of her conversations with the man.

"How long ya in for?" asked the male guard playing with his dagger.

The woman stared into the fire, watching as the flames seemed to dance to the beat of the drummers. "Too long, but your commander thinks that Precillia Richards might still be in town. So, I'm to find out where she's hiding or track where she went and who's helping her."

The guard scratched his head. "You really think someone is helping her?"

The female guard made a pitying face toward the man. "Depends, you really think a girl of thirteen years from the high society of Bresham, would survive in this city on her own?"

The male guard raised his head in thought. "Well no, I guess not."

The female guard shook her head, "And here I wonder how she ever managed to escape this city's guards."

The male guard perked up, "I know, right? That's what the captain said, too."

The female guard stood up, shaking her head, "I need to go for a walk."

Rana watched from the shadows as the female guard started walking through the partygoers, weaving between them as if gliding on air. She was so fast that Rana began to lose her in the crowd. She tried to follow behind but wasn't sure if she could catch up. The woman vanished into the crowd again, and Rana dashed through the shadows of the buildings trying to catch a glimpse of her once more. Finally, she saw her as she disappeared behind a wall. Rana hurried her steps to try and follow behind the woman, and the moment she rounded the corner, she saw the woman sitting down on a bench just a few feet away from her. Rana froze. The woman turned her face to Rana.

"I thought you were looking at me," said the woman in armour. "But if you're gonna try to follow me, you need to be a bit sneakier."

Rana mumbled, "I...ah well—"

The female guard smirked. "Well, go on, spit it out,

you're here now."

Rana pointed at her, "You're a girl."

The female guard raised an eyebrow, "Aye, I am that, unless I sprouted a cock between now and my morning bath."

Rana calmed herself. "I mean, you're a soldier, and women aren't allowed to be soldiers."

The female soldier laughed and started to glance around at the buildings, "Yeah, I guess that would be the case out here." She leaned forward to see the other guards' horse playing and shoving one another. "Although one might be hard-pressed to call those... soldiers."

She turned back at Rana, who was staring back at her and leaned back on the bench, "It's true that it's uncommon for females to be soldiers." She then held out her left hand and began to wave her fingers like she was kneading the space between them. And slowly, an orange glow began to appear, turning into a small ember. "But it is common for females who possess magic."

Rana's eyes glimmered in the light of the tiny flame, and before she realized what she was doing, her fingers began to stretch out, trying to grasp it. And right before her fingers were about to touch it, the female guard closed her hand and smothered the tiny flame, bringing Rana back to her senses.

Rana stared at the female guard, "You're a mage."

The woman smiled, "You're really good at this; first you figure out I'm a woman and then a mage. I certainly can't keep any secrets from you, now can I?"

"Are there any more girl mages here?" asked Rana as she began to turn around, looking through the crowd of people dancing in the square.

The woman smiled, "Here no, but in the kingdom, yes. Most mages that are born are female. I think the score was seven out of ten mages are female. We just have a more natural reception to magic. The king and his son are an oddity in all the kingdoms." She narrowed her eyes and smirked. "One really has to wonder how that family keeps popping out boys in every generation."

"You keep score of boys and girls?" asked Rana as she turned back to the woman and tilted her head in confusion.

The woman laughed, "Well no, but when I was in school, we used to. We used to beat up on the boys a lot. During training, there would be like one hundred girls and maybe twenty boys, so we used to get into all kinds of messes during warrior training days."

Rana stepped closer, "How can I learn how to become a warrior too?"

The woman pulled a face, "You? A warrior?" She then looked in Rana's eyes and saw how serious she was. "Girl, there are only three ways a woman becomes a warrior. Either she becomes a Black Maiden, she's a mage, or she's born Sakari."

"What's a Sakari?"

The woman rubbed at her chin, "Well, there's a race of female warriors near the kingdom of Latrusa. All of their race has dark skin, and if their woman finds a man, not to their liking, I heard they kill them and pin them to stakes."

"Why?"

"You'd have to ask them; I've never met one before."

"I wanna be a warrior, what do I need to do?"

The female soldier pointed back to the male guards' ruff housing over by the fire. "You see those soldiers? They're all idiots."

Rana smiled at the bashing of the men being silly.

"But someone paid to have those idiots learn the sword. Whether it be the kingdom, or a rich family, or the king himself. Someone paid, they paid in gold. Do you have any gold?"

"I have two gold coins; a man gave me."

Rana dug into her pockets and pulled out the gold coins, and the female guard's face changed into one of surprise, "It seems I may have underestimated your resolve. I'm sorry, perhaps you are more determined than I first realized."

Rana smiled back at her.

"Tell me, child, have you noticed any new children around? Perhaps a girl with brown hair."

"What? Brown hair like mine?" asked Rana.

The female guard laughed. "No child you have blonde hair, that's more golden than brown."

A guard came around the corner and spotted the woman in armour. "Oh, there you are. The commander has come and would like to have a word with you."

The female soldier sighed, "I was wondering when he'd finally make an appearance." She stood up and placed her hand on Rana's shoulder. "Thanks for keeping me company, child. My name is Abigail. What's yours?"

"I'm Rana."

Abigail bowed. "Well Miss Rana, I look forward to seeing you again. But until then, find someone to teach you the sword, and that'll be a start."

As the female guard took off back into the group of the other soldiers, Rana stuffed the gold coins back into the pouch of her tunic. She then turned around and started to head back to the tavern when she saw the doctor's house in front of her and remembered why she had come running here in the first place. Making her way over towards the doctor's office, she knocked on the door, "Maggie, Billy, are you home?" No one answered. She knocked again but received only silence from within the house. With the sound of the party, she could barely hear her own knocking sounds herself. Rana then walked around to the side of the building, lifting herself on to a crate to see inside the window. Inside she saw the doctor asleep in his chair.

She looked around but didn't see Maggie. Saddened, she was about to lower herself back down to the ground, when the glimpse of the doctor moving his hand flashed across the side of her eye. Rana turned back and peered inside the window. This time she placed her hand above her eyes, near brows and drew her face closer to the glass.

She began squinting her eyes, trying to make out more of the shapes inside the house and saw something move between the doctor's legs. She focused hard on the object, and then she saw Maggie's face emerge from between the doctor's thighs and began moving up and down.

For Rana, time seemed to slow down as her and Maggie's eyes met. Maggie paused for a moment staring out the window at Rana before she continued. All the while staring at Rana's face in the window. To Rana, this moment seemed to last forever, as the two seemed to lock eyes with each other. Rana finally pulled herself away from the window in shock, turning around.

No, No, That's not Maggie. Maggie wouldn't... I mean... she...

To Rana, the world started to change. Everything just seemed wrong. Nothing made sense anymore. She tried to lower herself from the crate, but the moment her feet touched the ground, her legs gave out. She fell into a mud puddle, getting dirt all over her hands, clothes, and on the side of her face from the splash. Not even taking the time to clean herself; she just sat there, staring blindly into the crowd as they danced around like demons in her eyes. Demons that emerged from the large flame, that had come to get her.

The world seemed full of demons to her now. She stood up, trying to run but fell back down as her legs refused to listen to her. She looked ahead again, and demons near the fire started grabbing their heads and swaying in a strange motion. Rana once again forced herself up to her feet, willing her legs to hold her up. And slowly, one stumbled step after another, and she took off running back into the cobblestone streets. She barreled down the roads into the night and turned the corner towards the gate, only to crash into a man causing her to fall back down on the cobblestone.

"Wow, that was quite the attack," said a familiar voice as he placed a hand to his face. "Ow, what the hell is wrong with my head?"

Rana stared up with confusion in her eyes. She wanted to cry, or at least she thought she did. She wasn't sure anymore. She just wanted to run away.

The man noticed the strange look in her eyes, "Hey, are you okay?"

"I got... I mean... She was... But he seemed..." Rana just kept blurting out half phrases one after another.

The man shook his head at the sight of her muddy clothes and sighed, "Well, I supposed I can't just leave you out here like this. How bout we get you someplace safe for you to calm down?" He reached out to her.

Seeing the man's hand reaching for her, Rana quickly thought of the demons again. She began to yell uncontrollably. Her heart began pounding furiously inside her chest as everything started to become blurry as tears finally started pouring from her eyes.

"Woah, woah, what's wrong?"

Rana clutched her hands to her chest while balled up on the cobblestones as her heart refused to slow down. Her breaths were coming quickly in small gasps as she stared at the stones in front of her.

The man watched her as she clutched her chest on the ground. He knelt, placing his hand on her head. "It's okay, I got ya now," Rana began to hear a strange voice in her mind. It was quiet at first, but it quickly grew louder as it began to force all other thoughts away.

Calm yourself, you're safe now, child.

The voice repeated itself inside her head over and over, till the point where that phrase was the only thing in her mind.

Calm yourself, you're safe now, child.

The voice seemed peaceful and comforting to her. Slowly, her screams died out, her heart began to beat slower, and her breathing began to go back to normal. The man stayed over her till she completely calmed down.

You're safe. No one's going to hurt you; you can trust me. Now stand up.

Rana stood up,

Grab my hand.

She gripped the man's hand on her forehead.

Let's go for a walk.

And they turned and began walking out towards the gate and back into Lowtown. The whole, while Rana's mind was a jumbled mess. But she wasn't scared or mad anymore, just confused. It was as if she couldn't get a thought through her head before it became replaced by another thought. The one thing she knew for certain was that she was safe with this man and that she could trust him. They walked all the way back to Broderick's tavern and stopped in front of it. The man let go of Rana's hand, and the thoughts of the night started rushing back into her mind. She dropped to her knees, trying to catch her breath.

The man squatted down in front of her, rubbing her back. "Breathe, just breathe, it'll pass. Just give yourself some time."

Rana took a few deep breaths, then turned to see the man's face and her eyes opened wide. She quickly scurried away a few feet on hands and knees, before stopping and turning to face him. "You, I remember you."

The man stood back up, smiling and bowed his head, "Well, I'm flattered. The muddy princess remembers me."

Rana made a curious face at him and then looked herself over, realizing she was covered in mud again. Before scowling at him.

"I fell in the mud."

He raised an eyebrow, "Again?"

Rana stood back up, "Yes, so what?"

He pointed to her feet. "Well, at least you managed to keep your boots this time."

Rana puffed her cheeks, "Oh, forget you, what do you want from me?"

He rubbed his chin in a mock thinking posture, "A thank you would be nice, you seemed like you were in a really bad place back there. About to cry all the tears in the world, until this gallant knight came to your aid brought you to safety."

Rana pointed her finger at him, "You're not a knight; you used one of those tricks to make me follow you again."

The man gave an innocent smile, "Oh, for whatever do you mean, my muddy princess."

Rana stomped her feet, "Stop calling me that!"

An old man exited the doors of the tavern and noticed the two bickering in the street "Ahh, Jacob, I thought I heard your voice. Why ya back so soon? Figured I'd not see ya till I went back to camp."

The man with Rana smiled at the old man. "Just got sidetracked, father. I found a muddy princess and stole her away from the castle. Now I just gotta figure out what to do with her." Jacob pointed at Rana, and the old man's eyes followed his finger to look at her before he gave a cackling laugh.

"If that's true, then you're the sorriest knight I've ever seen, to steal a princess and then return her the same night."

Jacob made a confused face, before feeling a sharp pain in his leg as Rana kicked him in the shin. He lifted his leg, rubbing his shin only to see Rana run into the tavern past the old man who was clutching his sides in laughter as he followed behind Rana.

"Oh, the joy that children bring," said the old man.

Broderick saw Rana covered in mud with his uncle following shortly behind her. He tried to scold her, but she ran up the stairs before he could finish calling her name. His uncle grabbed a seat at the bar with a big grin on his face.

"What are you so happy about?" asked Broderick.

"Aren't children wonderful?" asked the old man.

CHAPTER 9

In the middle of the sea, the sun had finally set as the captain held a lantern over the dead body of an unknown passenger and the barely breathing body of the crewman Fenry, who was visibly in pain as he clenched his teeth with his eyes closed tight. Victor stared around the cabin noticing all the crates scattered about, "Why bring them to the cargo area?"

The captain frowned, "Cause I don't want a panic aboard my ship, and a dead body along with a missing murderous wife, are what people tend to panic about."

Another member of the crew was heard making his way down the stairs. He entered the room, followed by a man in a black cloak.

"I brought 'em, captain," said Drew making his way down the stairs.

Victor raised an eyebrow, intrigued by the unexpected guest, as he noticed the cloaked man leave Drew and walk up beside the captain.

The captain grinned at Victor, then nodded to the cloaked man. "It seems we had a special guest aboard the ship. Let me introduce you to Nahtalli of the Healing Circle; it seems he's a Grand Healer or something."

Victor scratched at his chin as his face turned to that of disbelief at the captain's words. "That would seem highly unlikely and quite lucky. Seeing as there's only like a handful in all the kingdoms."

The captain smiled. "Aye, that's what he said, but here we find ourselves with a fine opportunity to see if he is who he says. And I intend to use it." He gestured to the two men on the ship's floor, "If you'd be so kind sir, and show us some of that fancy healer magic?"

Nahtalli took a few steps forward and knelt by the dead man, "This one is dead, I can't bring him back."

"Aye, well, it was worth a shot." The captain then gestured to his crewman, "Well. what about Fenry there, can ya fix him then?"

Nahtalli placed his hand on Fenry's head and peeled away the wrap that had been set to try and stop the blood flow. "The wound isn't bad; seems as if he was struck from behind." He then moved his hands down to the injured crew member's chest, nodding his head.

The captain leaned over Nahtalli to see his crewman, "Aye, so my man is going to survive this, then?"

"Yes, he will survive this," said Nahtalli as he reached into his cloak, pulling out a small flask. Victor noticed a gold and green leaf jewel around Nahtalli's neck that was attached to a chain. Nahtalli reached down and lifted Fenry's shirt, exposing the man's skin. He then unsealed the flask he had pulled out and splashed a clear liquid onto the crewman's chest and belly. "That's to help with the poison." He then placed a hand on Fenry's abdomen, and everyone starred as Nahtalli's hand started to glow.

"This be my first time actually seeing this magic up close," said the captain.

Soon green and blue energy flowed from Nahtalli's fingertips down onto the liquid turning it green before vanishing seconds later. He then raised his hand as the magic began to race over the man's body before stopping above it. Green and blue streams of light hovered in the air over Fenry's skin, illuminating the dark cargo hold of the ship in swirling colors. Everyone gazed around the cargo bay as the magic shined in a revolving spectrum of blue and green light, before finally lowering onto Fenry's body and fading into his skin. They looked down towards the crewman as his labored breaths became more relaxed, and his face released the constant furrowing of his brows that it once had.

"He has a small amount of poison in his system, but it's not a strong type, I would imagine that the goal here was not meant to kill or they would have done it," said Nahtalli as he began rubbing his hands over his knuckles.

"So that light show is what all the kingdoms be fighting over, I take it," said the captain as he stared down at Fenry. "Well, it appears as if my man is doing better, so you have my thanks for that. I feel a lot better now about granting you passage aboard me ship."

Nahtalli placed his hands on Fenry's forehead checking his temperature, "Yes, I am grateful for you accommodating me on such short notice. But to ensure there is no lasting damage, I would prefer to stay here for another hour to continue his treatment. But I would expect him to be fully healed by tomorrow evening at the latest."

The captain nodded his head, "That's one problem done; the other is that I have an assassin on my ship."

"I'm more interested in why a Grand Healer was out here, to begin with, let alone in the right place to secure passage on this vessel," said Victor after waiting to ensure that the man was healed.

Nahtalli smiled, looking back up, "Oh my, does that also mean I am a suspect in this?"

"Just consider me interested in your current affairs. It's not as if Grand Healers are plenty in the five kingdoms, and finding one in these circumstances is quite odd."

"Yes, I can understand your interest in these events, but I'm afraid I must give you an unsatisfactory answer. I'm sure you are aware of the current state of poverty that the last port was in. I was in a nearby coastal town when I saw these large crew ships come by. So after I finished my business, I just assumed a bit of sea time would be my next adventure."

"So, you're a wonderer then."

"Indeed, I am. I go where the people need me."

"A fair enough answer, and given your group's history, I can't exactly question you."

"Your welcome to follow me along on my journeys until you are satisfied with the answer I have given you. I will not shun a bit of company on my travels."

"Unfortunately, that's likely won't happen. I also have my own goals to accomplish."

"A shame, but a path once cross will likely cross again."

Victor began to pace around the ship rubbing his hands on random cargo as he passed. "Technically, the man she killed was also an assassin. I think they were working together."

The captain hung the lantern on a hook as he began to rub the temple of his head, "Well, isn't that lovely, a war of treacherous assassins on my humble ship. To whom do I owe such a privilege?"

"Perhaps it's a sign from that sea goddess that sailors mention so much," said Victor as he ran his hand along the wall. He began to ponder about the situation he found himself in as he walked forward. *Why are assassins or whatever they are, playing hide and kill on this ship? And the fact that I'm here to see it can't be mere happenstance.* As he continued to pace back and forth thinking about the situation, he would occasionally feel something soft underneath his boot as he stepped around the side of the cabin in the dim lantern light.

He knelt and began rubbing the area below, feeling for what the object might be. Instead, he picked up a hand of some soft type of grain. Rubbing it between his fingers, he placed it to his nose and sniffed. Instantly he knew the smell. "Sawdust?" Victor turned to the others, "Captain, bring that lantern here, please." The captain raised an eyebrow, but grabbed the lantern back off the hook and made his way over to Victor, illuminating the area in the lantern's light. Victor picked up a handful of sawdust and showed it to the captain. "I don't suppose you had your men doing any woodwork down here?"

"What the blazes?" asked the captain.

They both began to scan over the wall beside them until the captain noticed a small black rag stuck in the wall. He reached over and snatched it out, revealing a hole in the wall as lantern light shined through from the other side. The captain closed one eye and peaked inside to the separate room. "Well I'll be damned. Some sods been drilling a hole in me ship, and guess where she leads." The captain leaned back and gestured for Victor to take a look inside of the hole.

Victor gave a smirk with a suspicious glance at the captain, but closed one of his eyes and peeked through the hole. And there before his one eye was his glasses lying on his cot. Victor's eye opened wide as he pulled back from the hole. "Oh, for the goddess herself, that's how they got that damned sleep root into my cabin."

"I don't get it. If they were after ya, why'd they kill that bastard there and nick one of my men? Which group of assassins is this anyway, ya figure that out at least?"

"Well, there are many groups of killers out there for you to pick from. The Pit of Vipers, the Black Maidens, the Mushroom group, a silly name, but non the less accomplished," said Victor as he placed his hands to his face and began to rub his eyes in frustration. "None of this makes any sense. Wait, actually..." Victor glanced around the dark cabin, "Captain, not just anyone can come back here, can they? I mean, usually, this place would be sealed off because of the cargo."

"Aye, it's guarded at all times by the crew."

Victor smirked at the captain and knocked on the wood near the small hole. "If that's the case, then who was able to get in here and make this hole."

The captain narrowed his eyes as he bit down on his lip, turning towards Drew, "Who's been on guard down here?"

Drew scratched his head, "Ah, I think Ark and Scubby have been doing it for the last few days, captain."

Victor took the lantern from the captain and walked forward, "Well captain, it seems as if we have a mystery and two subjects to question."

Around an hour later, Victor was back in the captain's chambers, with two confused looking crew members standing in front of them. The captain just stared at them for a second before popping the cork on a bottle and pouring a drink. "Now, boys, I was told you two were in charge of guarding the cargo during this trip."

A bald-headed man responded. "Yes, Sir, Cap'n, one of us been on guard at all times."

The captain smiled and poured a drink into another cup. "Ahh, good man Scubby, good man." He walked over to the two men and handed them both a cup. "But it seems like a night or so ago, someone managed to get in said room. Now none of ya would be knowing how that happened, now would ya?"

The two men stared at each other.

"Ah, no, Sir. I didn't let anyone pass. I guarded it all night like yah always be telling us," said Scubby.

The captain nodded his head as the door to the cabin opened. Nahtalli entered the room, closing the door behind him and walked past the two men. They stared at the man in the black hooded cloak as he sat down at the table.

"Well you two, go on and have a drink. Your captain's trying to offer out his generosity," said the Captain as the two men slowly drank from their cups. He turned around and glanced out the window of the cabin, "You see, boys, someone entered that cargo bay last night, and seeing how you two were the ones guarding it, I'd have to believe it was one of you, or that ya let someone else pass."

"But Cap'n, we guarded it like ya told us. We even took turns," said Ark.

"You boys have been such good lads," said the captain as he turned his back to the men. "It pains me to think that one of ya would betray me." The captain shook his head and whirled back around to face the men, "but nonetheless, betray me, is what one ya did."

"Excuse me, captain, "said Nahtalli, as the captain made a displeased look at being interrupted in his theatrical questioning. "But how many crew members do you have on this ship?"

"This ship has a crew of twenty. Why? What's it matter?"

"And of that crew, how many of them are magically talented," said Nahtalli as he twirled the golden leaf that Victor spotted earlier in his hands.

The captain laughed, "Is that a joke? I ain't got no mages on me crew. What mage wants to be a sailor?"

Nahtalli smiled at the captain. "Well then, it seems one of your crew is hiding a secret." He pointed towards Scubby.

"Because that one most certainly has magical talent and no small amount."

The captain made a confused face at Nahtalli. "What, Scubby? He's been on my ship for years. There's no way he's a mage."

Scubby glanced between Nahtalli and the captain with a confused face. "Cap'n, what's he on about, I ain't no mage."

"Yeah, that's what I want to know. You say he's a mage. Well, I can vouch for the last five years, he ain't been one."

Nahtalli turned to the captain. "I can only provide you with information, you are to do with that information, what you will."

Victor watched as Scubby pleaded that he wasn't a mage and thought of the cold confidence at which Nahtalli had spoken in his words. Then Ark and Scubby started arguing with each other, and soon, their conversation took a turn. It switched back and forth between innocent and guilty until the two men began blaming each other for all kinds of random things.

"Excuse me captain, if I may interrupt," said Victor.

The men at the table all turned to Victor.

"What, you figure you can make sense of all this foolishness?" asked the captain.

Victor waved his hand at the two men, "You say that Mr. Scubby here isn't a mage, and yet the grand healer says that he is a mage. So, if we were to go by the assumption that you're both right. Then the only answer where you both would be right would be if this man before us, is not Mr. Scubby."

"You think I don't recognize my own crew?"

Victor raised his hand, "No, I'm saying that magic can do some amazing things, including messing with our eyes. Captain, if you would be so kind as to ask Scubby here a question that anyone who's been on this ship for years would know."

The captain gave a skeptical look, but turned back to his

crewman, "Scubby, when we were at Archigo port a cycle ago, who did ya visit?"

Scubby scratched his head, "I went to visit Candy; girl's been sweet on me for years."

"Aye, that's what ya did."

"Please continue the questions, captain," said Victor as he stood up from the table and began walking towards Scubby.

"Alright, Scubby, humor the man. Name the last three ports we visited."

Scubby pursed his lips while thinking, "We were in Jalop, then Fowlhaven, and... oh yeah, Howlond, because Brone hurt his leg, messing around with them kids and their dog."

The captain smiled, "Everything seems right to me."

Victor walked over and stood next to Scubby and raised a finger at the captain, "One more question please."

The captain frowned, "Sea goddess help me. Scubby, tell me your mother's name."

Scubby frowned as Victor stood to the side of him and reached into one of the pouches that he had strapped around his chest.

"Cap'n, you know I never knew my moth... Ah!" Scubby yelled as he jumped back after Victor pulled out a vial filled with white powder from one of his pouches.

Victor and the captain were both surprised by Scubby's reaction as he jumped back. But then Victor smiled, "Well captain, this once is certainly a mage."

The captain looked between the panicked Scubby and the smiling Victor, "What happened, what's that be in your hand?"

Victor shook the bottle, "This is alagon powder. It prevents a mage from accessing their power until they wash it off. And Mr. Scubby here seems quite afraid of it. I expected him to start sweating from the sight of it. But he seems deafy afraid of it."

The captain turned back to Scubby, "What's going on here?"

Scubby glanced back and forth between the men and sighed, throwing his hands up in the air. "Okay, you win," he said in a much different dialect from before.

The captain twisted his face as he gritted his teeth. "Who are you, and what have you done with my crewman?" He drew his blade, pointing at the imposter Scubby.

The fake Scubby shook his head from side to side, "Who I am is not important. My mission is complete. So if you gentlemen would be so kind as to drop me off at the nearest port, I'd greatly appreciate it."

The captain stepped to the side of the table while still pointing his blade at the imposter. "Oh now we can't be doing that, not until ya tell us who ya are and what are ya doing on me ship."

The fake Scubby clapped his hands while laughing. "Oh, that would be fun. But sadly, some things are meant to be private."

Victor popped the cork on the vial and poured a small amount of the white powder into his hand. "Are you sure about that?" Victor threw some powder at the imposter's feet, making fake Scubby hop into the air, hurrying to place his back against the wall of the cabin. "We can always make you tell us, unless you believe that you can cast a spell before I litter this whole area in powder."

The fake Scubby began to panic as his eyes frantically looked around the room. "Keep that away from me."

Victor shook the powder in his hand while he took a step towards the imposter. "Your choice, either drop the illusion spell or—"

The fake Scubby snapped, "It's not some poultry illusion spell you fool, I'm better than that."

Victor raised an eyebrow in suspicion at the remark, "Well, either way, reveal yourself or be forced to."

The fake Scubby glanced around the room at the men

staring at him, "Fine." He closed his eyes and took a deep breath, and slowly his body began to change. His frame started to shrink as his skin began to turn a pale white. His pants fell to the floor, and the person who used to be Scubby turned into an ashen-skinned looking figure with Scubby's shirt hanging off one of its shoulders. Its appearance was human, but it had no hair, and its eyes shimmered like green and red gems. The captain made a disgusted face, "What in all the seas are you?"

The thing glared back at the captain angrily before turning back to Victor. "Happy now, Queen's dog?" Victor tilted his head at the name as the thing continued, "Oh yes, I know who you are, and your special relationship with the Queen." It pulled away from the wall, moving towards Victor appearing more confident. "Some have even tried to recreate that night you both shared back in Povish, but none have succeeded. Yet!"

Victor's frustrations overtook him, "And what of you oddity, did you learn all that in the shadows of your victims?"

It leaned forward while circling him carefully. "I have orders, just like you, or does your Queen's kill order count as more noble than mine?" Victor moved toward it with the bottle of white powder and thrust the powder-filled hand at the creature. It stammered back near the door of the cabin cowering with its hands over its head.

Victor narrowed his eyes staring at it, surprised by how fearful it seemed at the being doused in the powder, "Answer me this, why did you kill that man?"

It glowered up at him with hateful eyes, "Because I was told to. Do you ask questions when you're given orders?"

"Fine, who gave you the orders?"

"The House gives the orders you ungrateful bastard; I just follow them. We don't ask about the details."

"Then who do you work for? The Raven guild?"

The thing laughed, "Oh, piss on the Raven's Guild."

"Then who?" asked Victor right before the door opened

beside them.

"Cap'n, I brought you your supper from below," said a man in the door, before he happened to glance down and saw the pale white-faced thing's reddish-green eyes staring back up at him in the light.

"Oh, sweet mother of the seas," The man screamed before dropping the tray to the floor.

Victor's eyes opened wide as he and the thing both realized the door was unlocked the whole time. The creature leaped out the door, but Victor jumped after it hitting the deck hard but was able to grab its leg. He tried pulling it to him, but it frantically started kicking him wherever it could.

"Hold it there," said the captain as he rounded the table, coming to assist Victor.

"No. No. Let go. Just let me..." It nailed Victor in the face with its foot, "Go." And Victor's grip loosened just enough for it to break free. It scampered across the deck on hands and knees until finally breaking into a run.

The captain reached into his belt and threw a dagger at the running oddity. But the blade missed, hitting the mast off the ship instead. Victor took off, running behind it. The people on the deck were startled as the ashen-skinned thing ran through them before reaching the side of the ship. It jumped up, grabbing a rope, perching itself on the wooden rail above the water, trying to catch its breath.

Victor caught up to it, stopping a few feet away. "That was... a good run, but you have nowhere to go. We're in the middle of the sea and with days of travel left."

The ashen-skinned thing glanced between the water below and Victor. It noticed the crowd of nobles that it ran through earlier was gathering around them. They slowly moved in, staring, and pointing at it while whispering things to each other. The creature's facial expression changed from fear to resignation as it spoke so soft that Victor barely heard it. "I hate all of you." Then, leaning back, letting go of the rope, it fell from the ship down towards the water below. The crowd gasped as Victor jumped for it, clipping the side of the ship as he reached out his hand, trying to catch it. But it was too late as he watched it's body splash into the sea.

The captain leaned over the side, staring down into the water by Victor. "What madness, it willingly threw itself to the sea goddess."

Victor stared into the water, "I'm not so sure."

"What? You think it'll survive, out in the middle of the sea, days away from anywhere?"

"You shouldn't underestimate magic. I've seen it do impossible things," and he started walking back to the cabin, making his way through the crowd. "And I think that it was a she."

The captain followed behind, "Oh! And how ya reckon that?"

Victor rubbed at his face, where a few of the bruises were starting to show. "When she was busy kicking me in the face, I managed to get a clear view of something. Granted, I don't have my glasses. But I'm fairly sure I know what I saw."

The captain scratched at his beard, "Yeah, well, the sirens look plenty lovely till they start eating you alive. But goddess help us if any more show up."

Victor entered the door back into the captain's loft and saw Nahtalli still sitting down at the table and Ark asleep on the floor. "What happened to him?"

The captain walked by, "That was my doing, I figured I'd slip 'em some night essence into their wine to make sure they didn't try anything funny. Fat lot of good it did, that thing ran as if it had just woken up."

Victor turned to Nahtalli, "How did you know she was a mage?"

The captain picked up a wine bottle from the floor. "So, we're calling that thing a she now, are we?" asked the captain annoyed by Victor's casual tone towards the situation. He poured himself a drink, "Screw that, why did ya not help us apprehend her? You's a mage too, ain't ya?"

Victor sat back down at the table, "Healers are forbidden from taking part in any acts of aggression unless they are specifically targeted. And not many people are stupid enough to attack a healer nowadays anyway."

The captain leaned in with his hand on the table, staring at Nahtalli. "What, are ya some sort of rich fellow?"

Nahtalli threw up his hand dismissively. "Hah, hardly. Healers usually don't have many worldly possessions. Our travels don't really foster that type of lifestyle. Although there are a few that take up permanent residence in certain cities."

Victor stared at the necklace of Nahtalli, "Two hundred years ago, during the Manicil War, each side would hire healers. But oftentimes, the healers would be killed in battle while trying to heal others. Well, the Grand Cleric at the time seemed to have had enough of her students being killed in war, so she recalled all the healers from both sides of the battle. This action had a dramatic effect on the war, so much so that both sides stopped the war in order to negotiate with her."

The captain laughed, "Negotiate? With a healer? Why not just tie 'em up and make 'em heal?" Nahtalli frowned at the captain after his statement. And the captain shrugged back at him.

Victor shook his head and started rubbing the side of his face where he was kicked. "Captain, think of it this way. If there were a battle and each side had one hundred people. Who would win?"

The captain made a puzzled face, "Ahh, I'd gather either could win, I think."

Victor nodded, "Right, now imagine that one side had healers, and the other side didn't." The captain's face changed to realization, and Victor continued, "Right, so, whoever attacked the healers first, might as well surrender the war. And so, the Sunlight Accords were made with every kingdom now paying tribute or else they'd lose all healer support. Essentially the highest form of blackmail."

Nahtalli clapped his hands together while laughing, "Very well said. I imagine the High Mother was glorious that day. I shall relay your praise to her, the next time we meet."

The captain sat down at the table after pouring himself another cup before gulping it down, "I don't know what's crazier. That white she-thing that just jumped off my ship, or the fact that both of you are acting like everything that just happened was normal."

Victor chuckled at the captain, "You don't deal with magic very often do you captain?"

The captain lifted his cup in Victor's direction, "No, and thank the sea goddess for that."

CHAPTER 10

"Rana, wake up," said Miraval as she shook Rana, trying to awaken her from the night's slumber.

Rana rubbed her face into her pillow. And slowly, she lifted herself on her elbows from the wooden bunk, rubbing at her eyes. "What's wrong?"

"They're talking about you."

"Who, whaa?"

Miraval kept shaking her, "Come on, wake up, they're talking about you."

A minute later, Rana and Miraval were leaning down over the balcony, peering down at Broderick and the magistrate.

"I take it, you've been preparing the girl properly," said the magistrate.

"I don't think any of my girls have ever let you down before," said Broderick cracking his knuckles as he went behind the bar picking up a mug.

"While that is true for me, working in a mansion is a lot different than serving my son on a battlefield or in a barracks."

"I've trained her well this last month, I'll get someone to wake her, and you can ask her yourself," said Broderick waving his hand dismissively as he placed a few mugs on top of the bar, stacking them one on top of the other.

The wooden beams beneath Rana creaked, and the magistrate grinned as he glanced upwards.

"Oh, that won't be necessary, seeing as she's probably the one up above us right now."

Broderick glanced up but didn't see anything.

"Come on down, here little one," said the magistrate, and a few seconds later, Rana slowly made her way to the steps. The wooden boards beneath her creaked with each step, echoing in the silence of the empty tavern as she made her way down. On her way down, she noticed that Jacob and his father were over in a corner table having drinks. They spotted her coming down, and Jacob raised his hand, smiling at her before turning back to his father, resuming their conversation.

"What were you doing up there?" asked Broderick as he began tapping his fingers across the counter.

"Now, don't be mad at her, she has a right to know since it's her we're talking about after all. Plus, if you've ever tried to reason with children, you'd pretty much know you're just wasting your breath."

"Yeah well, boys just break stuff; it's the girls that turn

114

a man's hair grey. I swear I had less trouble with women when I was killing their men for a living," said Broderick as he shook his head at Rana coming down the steps.

The magistrate waved to Rana when she made it to the bottom step. "Come here, child." Rana walked over to the magistrate while looking nervously around the tavern. "Let me see your hand." Rana hesitated for a moment, but did as the magistrate asked of her, raising her right hand on top of his. "Now, tell me what have you learned in the month since I last saw you." As Rana began to speak, the magistrate closed his eyes and pressed his thumb into her palm. Rana looked to Broderick, who had raised an eyebrow in confusion at the magistrate before nodding at Rana to answer his question.

"I... I can clean, sew, and cook meals. Yesterday, Angela taught me to cook rabbit and turtle stew and..."

The magistrate opened his eyes and let go of her hand, "Good, good, it seems as if your progress is going well. But tell me, do you know why am I having you learn all these things? For what purpose?"

"Ah... I was told that I'm to serve your son."

"Correction, you're to serve my son on the battlefield. This will not be easy, child. On the battlefield, people die all the time, now granted you will be at the main camp, but—"

Rana's eyes open wide, "Can I learn to be a warrior there?"

"Warrior, you want to be a warrior?"

Broderick just waved her words off, "Don't listen to her, Sir. I caught her waving a stick around a few days ago outback; she was playing at being a knight."

The magistrate rubbed his gray-haired chin, "Well, in between your chores, perhaps you could have some of the men teach you basic defense. You will, after all, be in a military encampment. I can't imagine a better place to learn, can you? Who knows, you might have some secret talent for war."

"So I won't be a whore then?"

Broderick slammed his hand down on the table, causing the stacked mugs to come crashing back down. Rana flinched at the sound of the noise as it echoed through the tavern.

"Enough child, go fetch the morning sheets in or something."

Rana stuck her tongue out at Broderick. He reached out to grab her, but she jumped back and ran into the kitchen and out the back door. Broderick turned back toward the magistrate, "Sorry about that, Sir. She will be properly trained by the time you receive her."

The magistrate waved a hand, "I have two children and three grandchildren, I'm very much aware of how they are. It's good that she's spirited, perhaps it will help her adapt to camp life in some aspect. My son will be visiting next month from the front; I will bring him to meet the girl then."

Broderick nodded his head, "Yes, Sir," as the magistrate stood and made his way out. Jacob and his father watched him as he walked past them and out of the tavern doors, being followed by Broderick.

Jacob's father nodded to his son. He then stood and walked to the door by Broderick while Jacob walked out the back of the tavern towards Rana.

"So, what was this about, the magistrate of the whole city visiting you in the crack hours of the morning," said Jacob's father as he watched the magistrate disappear around the corner of a building.

"That dear uncle is a right fine purse, in exchange for that little runt back there," said Broderick, turning back towards the bar.

"Aye, I remember you mentioning that. Exactly how much are we talking?" asked Jacob's father as he sat at the bar, grabbing the mug the magistrate left, shaking it to see if any ale was left.

Broderick looked around and leaned in, "a hundred

gold pieces."

Jacob's father tilted his head, placing the mug back down on the counter, "A hundred gold for that little scamp, and you never bothered to ask or wonder why?"

"What? Of course not, I just figured he liked her. Plus, she can read, so that hiked up the price a bit, I'd bet."

Jacob's father just shook his head, "Boy, I swear, you have no eye for these things. You have a girl from goddess knows where in the five kingdoms, who speaks proper, can read better than most nobles. And now suddenly not just a noble, but the fucking town magistrate is willing to pay a noble's ransom for her. And you don't think to ask yourself why."

"Yeah, you're right, you think I shoulda asked for more?" asked Broderick as he rubbed at his chin, shaking his head in agreement.

Jacob's father just stared at his nephew, "You really are your mother's child."

Outside the tavern in the early morning sun, Rana was swinging a stick around in a mock fighting stance. She swung hard, making the small stick create a woosh sound as it cut through the air. Jacob exited the tavern, sitting down on the steps watching her as she began to make, "Ya!" noises with each swing. She was kicking up a surprising amount of dust with her movements.

"Ya, know, you've got terrible form."

Rana ignored him and kept swinging her stick around, and Jacob watched as the small amount of dust began to swirl around her as she continued to spin around, looking very random.

"Well at least you're able to kick up a lot of dust from your troubles. But your arms are too high to attack anything properly. You need to space your feet for the impact if you plan to block."

Rana stopped swinging her stick, and the dust at her feet settled. Turning to Jacob, she reared her arm back, launching the stick in his direction. The stick went hurtling over his head and bounced off the side of the tavern wall.

"Woah, watch out," said Jacob as he ducked his head from the high flying branch and watched as it landed on the ground near his feet.

"If you're just going to make fun of me, then leave," said Rana as she wiped beads of sweat from across her forehead with the sleeve of her tunic.

Jacob reached down, picked up the stick, and flipped the small piece of wood in his hand. "Hey, now, I was giving you solid advice." He performed a few practice swings with the twig testing its weight before walking over and holding out the stick for Rana to take. "You're swinging that thing around with no trace of form or skill. Why do you want to fight anyway, aren't girls supposed to be prissy and dream of being in a castle with knights saving them from the bad people?"

Rana snatched the stick back, "Girls can be fighters as well, I saw a lady knight before. She had magic and armour. I'm going to be like her. She told me to find someone to teach me the sword, but everyone I ask just laughs and sends me away."

"And you didn't ask me to teach you? My lady, I am in the highest offense." Jacob shook his head in a disapproving manner.

"You're not a knight or a warrior; you just know some freaky magic is all. And you don't... well, I've never seen you with a sword."

Jacob slowly stopped smiling and, in a formal tone, announced, "A thousand pardons, please forgive me, my muddy princess, for not introducing myself. I am Jacob Highland, second in command of the Black Jewel Militia. An army of over four hundred men. I myself have partici-pated in no less than ten skirmishes, the last two of which were, The Battle at Serihan and the latter being The Battle at Brigards Tower."

"If you're a knight, then, where's your sword?" asked Rana frowning suspiciously at Jacob.

"Well, knights carry their swords in war or when guarding something, and I at the moment, am doing neither. So here I am, swordless."

"Then show me, if you're such a great warrior."

"I will do just that," said Jacob, smiling. He then raised his finger and tapped Rana on the nose, "But only after you learn to ask me like a proper lady." He whirled around on his heels, walking back into the tavern while wagging his finger. All the while, he heard some very unladylike words coming from the small girl with the stick.

Inside the tavern, Jacob saw his father sitting down at the bar with a drink in his hand. He walked up, taking a seat beside him, and was passed a mug of ale.

Jacob's father wiped the ale from his beard, "You and that little one seem pretty close."

"She didn't try to kick me again. So that's a plus, I guess. Seems she has this dream of being a warrior maiden, like in the fairy tales."

"Everyone wants to be something until they realize what it costs to get it," said Jacob's father as he whirled the ale around in his mug.

"And how's that?"

"If you took a hundred men and put them in a room and asked which of them wanted to be surrounded by wealth and whores. How many you think would raise their hands?"

"Seeing how that's most men's dreams, I'd say all."

"Then say you gave all those men swords and said that whoever was left alive by morning would get everything he desired. How many would still stay in that room." Jacob gave his father a suspicious look. "Exactly, most men are cowards when they have to risk anything of importance. But of those men, a few of them would hold up their swords and start hacking away at their fellow man."

"Perhaps those people just liked killing?"

"Did you like to kill when I found you? I gave you a choice, either stay where you were or become my son. So, tell me how many men have you killed for money, over the years?"

"That's different; we were at war."

"Murder for some lord we don't even care about, so we could get his coin. My, aren't we noble." Jacob's father took a sip from his mug. "No, I gave you a choice, and you chose to kill to survive."

"You know, you really know how to take the joy out of life."

"I've been told worse," said Jacob's father chuckling. "My point is that this world has a habit of creating monsters. People who were willing to make hard decisions in order to get what they wanted. Sometimes you'll call those monsters Queens and kings, and other times you'll call them father."

Jacob stared at his father before considering his words. Then he nodded to the back door. "Fine then, my monstrous father, why take an interest in the girl then? Is she going to be another piece in this monster puzzle of yours?"

"Probably not, but try sticking to her for a while, there's something off going on with her. Get her to open up to you, and we'll see where it leads."

"What thoughts you got going in that head of yours old man. Every time you take an interest in something, it usually ends up with me, almost getting killed," said Jacob rubbing his face in frustration as his blonde hair fell over his eyes.

"My, aren't you sounding unappreciative of the life I gave ya. I took an interest in ya, and now ya lead an army."

"And that just proves my point."

Jacob's father chuckled, "Fair enough, let's just call it a hunch, and we'll see how the game plays itself out."

Suddenly Rana came stomping her way into the tavern

towards the men. She stopped in front of them. Rana looked up at Jacob and put on a smile while batting her eyelashes at him. "Sir, Jacob Highland, would you please teach this poor young lady how to become a proper fighter with a sword?"

Jacob and his father just stared at the girl for a few seconds.

"And thus, my monstrous game has begun," said Jacob's father before taking another sip of ale.

A few days later, Rana was braiding Pelly's hair when Jacob popped his head into the room.

"Hey, come downstairs. I've got something for you," said Jacob.

The other girls smiled at Rana, giving her knowing looks.

"Oh, haven't you been spending a lot of time around Jacob lately," said Miraval.

"Jacob is really handsome too, so perhaps Rana is growing up faster than we thought," said Renee while making kissy sounds.

"Oh, stop it, all of you," said Rana smiling, as she held out Pelly's braided hair. "Here Renee, you finish up; I'm gonna go see what he wants."

"Oh, I bet you are," said Renee.

Rana left the room to the sounds of giggling behind her. She followed Jacob, who was carrying a large brown rag in his hand down the stairs. She skipped a few steps to catch up to him.

"Did you get it? Is that it?"

"Aye, I have it here," said Jacob opening the back door to the cavern with Rana following behind him.

Outside of the tavern, Jacob placed the rag on the ground, unfolding it to reveal two different wooden blades and one long metal sword. Rana stared at the blades. The two wooden blades were about a foot and a half long with little jewel symbols carved into their hilts. The metal sword was over two feet long and shone in the morning sun. There was a white cloth wrapped around the hilt of the blade and the name Vindel was etched into the metal. Rana pointed to the wooden blade. "What are these two?"

"There practice blades to teach sword fighting."

Rana picked up one of the wooden blades, swinging it around. It felt lite in her hands, and it was easy to move.

"When will I get a real one?"

"Well aren't we impatient? But I'm guessing you never tried to hold a real sword before?"

"No, father never let me touch his."

Jacob stood up and walked behind Rana, "Well, go on then, try and lift mine."

Rana knelt and placed her hands over the hilt of the large metal blade, gripped it tightly and lifted the sword. She struggled at first but managed to lift it into the air. "It's kinda heavy."

"Okay, now set it back down. It's heavy because you're weak at the moment, so that's why we're gonna have you train with the wooden swords and have you get stronger. Because you're small, a blade for you would probably be a little longer than a foot. How old are you anyway, ten, eleven?"

"I'm thirteen," said Rana, stomping her feet.

Jacob smiled after teasing Rana. He then picked up the other wooden sword handing it to Rana. "I'm not sure you understand how swords work yet."

"Sure I do, you cut people with them. And then they run away."

Jacob shook his head at the little girl before him as she began to practice swinging her wooden sword, "I wonder if this is how father felt with me."

The two practiced together for little over an hour with Jacob whacking Rana on the bottom and back whenever she made a mistake. She would swing, miss, and get whacked.

122

She would try to block but get pushed down from the weight and get whacked again. Almost every attack from Jacob ended up with her in pain from either taking an attack or failing to answer back with her own. At the end of it all, she'd lay on the ground a crumpled mess of sweat, loose hair, and ruffled clothes, as the mid-morning sun cast shadows upon them from the tree behind her.

"No fair! You're stronger... I can't block," said Rana trying to catch her breath. "And you move too fast for me to catch."

"Then don't," said Jacob.

"What? But then, you'd hit me?" asked Rana, rubbing sweat from her eyes.

"Only if you stand still." He noticed the confused look on Rana's face. "Okay, I'm bigger than you, so if it's hard for you to block my attack, then your next option is not to be where I attack. In war, you can't always fight the same way; sometimes, you will fight people who use bows, poisons, daggers, maces, magic, and all kinds of other tricks to win. And that little sword won't protect you from all that."

"Then, what am I supposed to do? I need to learn to fight."

Jacob knelt, placing a finger on Rana's forehead. "The most powerful weapon you will ever have is here. It's a little cliché, but it's true." Jacob pointed to his own head. "This weapon has saved my life a hundred more times than my sword has." He reached under Rana's arms and lifted her to her feet. "So, let's start again, we only have a few weeks before you're off to the battlefield." Rana nodded, wiped her face on her dirty sleeves, smearing some dirt on her cheek, and gripped her little wooden sword. Jacob smirked at the sight of her. *The muddy princess, indeed.* He then nodded for her to attack as their training continued until sun set as Rana collapsed on the tavern's back steps. Jacob walked over, smiling, "You know, you're really terrible at this."

Rana struggled to lift her face to Jacob in an attempt to

curse him but ended up just giving up on the effort as she just closed her eyes, embracing the pain. "My everything hurts."

"Why do you want to learn to fight so much, aren't girls supposed to want to be all prim and proper?" He said sitting down beside her on the steps.

Rana opened her eyes, staring up at the stars as they began appearing in the night sky. "My father said he used to be a fighter. He didn't want me to learn, but I used to watch him train with a sword when I was little. I remember watching him from the window as he swung his blade around in our yard."

"You didn't play with the other kids in the town or fight with them?"

"It was just Papa and me. We lived alone near the woods. He sometimes took me to town, but no one ever really came out to where we lived. It took two days just to get to the next town. Oh, and Ms. Buggle, who would come and give me snacks, but she was old, so I didn't see her that much."

Jacob just stared at Rana.

"What? Why are you looking at me like that?"

"You really are small, are sure you're thirteen? You speak well for a child, although it sounds like you lived a sheltered life."

Rana frowned up at Jacob "I'm not a child. And yes, I'm thirteen... I think. And Papa taught me how to read, and about the goddess and other stuff. Home was much better than here. I even had a horse. Her name was Samilly. Why, how old are you?"

"I'm twenty-four. What about your mother? I doubt any mother wanted her daughter to wind up here, in the back of a tavern training in ways to murder people."

Rana rolled to her side away from Jacob. "It's not murder, it's protection." Papa said he used to protect people. And mother wasn't around much anyway; it was mostly Papa and me. Every now and then, she would come home with toys and stay for a few days, but then after a while, she'd be gone again when I woke up. Papa would just smile and say, 'she'll be back soon."

Jacob replayed Rana's words in his mind, *it's not murder, it's protection,* and started shaking his head. *Wow, this really is what father must feel like around me.*

Rana turned back around and looked at Jacob. "What about you? That old guy is your father, right? Did you grow up like a noble to become a knight, you don't act like the people papa warned me about?"

"Me? A noble? As if... Nahh, I'm just a child of war," said Jacob laughing while Rana made a confused face at the statement. Jacob placed his hand on her head, rubbing her hair. "It means my mom was probably a whore in a military camp somewhere on some battlefield, had me and either died or left me in the camp."

Rana shook her head and sighed, "Why are only women whores? The men come here every night. Why can't you men be the whores."

Jacob burst into laughter and Rana narrowed her eyes at him as he patted his knee trying to regain control of himself. "I'm sorry... I just... You really are sheltered. Most men are whores, but I supposed if you wish to see men who have taken up to profession. Then you'd have to visit the Kingdom of Ursjun. The Queen and noble ladies all have male concubines there."

"What's a concubine?"

Jacob placed his face in his hands, trying to hold in the laughter, "How... how have you lived here and not gotten this information? Surely you must hear the men and the woman at night. What do you think they're doing here, playing four Queens?"

Rana leaned out her arm and started hitting Jacob on the lower back, "I know what sex is, I just don't know all the words is all."

Jacob pulled his hands out of his face wiping tears

from his eyes. "Oh goddess, you... you really are a muddy princess." He then raised his hand up in front of Rana, trying not to laugh. "Well either way; I was told I would have probably died if I hadn't had a talent for magic." A small amount of blue magic appeared around his fingers and arm and began slowly moving around. The blue streams of light glimmered in the night across Rana's eyes as she stared up at it. "Found out later that, since I didn't receive any proper training, my magic core just naturally settled on blue magic."

"Why's it called blue magic?"

"Hmm, how to explain that? Well, in the magic school, they probably call it something different. But for us unedu-cated people. Magic is separated into colors by what it does. Green magic involves trees and the earth. Red magic involves things like fire. I think people call healing magic, white magic. And my magic is blue because it's mind magic. I found out later than my type of magic is rare, or at least that's what I'm told." Jacob dropped his head, "Father found ways of using that to his advantage, but I'm pretty sure there's more to it. I just never got any real training, so I don't know that much myself." Jacob dropped his hand, letting the magic fade. "Well, by the time the old man found me, he figured he could get some use out of me, and I've been with him ever since."

"But you just called him father, is he like a religious man or something?"

Jacob scratched the back of his neck, "Yeah, well, there's a reason for that, he—"

Suddenly, the tavern door opened, and Pelly came out with freshly braided hair. She glanced around before finally spotting Rana on the steps beneath her.

"Rana, Tabby was wanting for us to come back down; people are starting to come in; we have to tend to the tables or Broody will get mad," said Pelly.

This time Jacob made a confused face, "Broody?"

Rana struggled to get up, moaning at her aching muscles, but managed a smile at Jacob, "It's what we call Broderick when he starts yelling at us," and she and Pelly ran back inside of the tavern.

During the next two weeks, between maid training with the girls, cleaning, and running errands around town, Rana practiced with her wooden sword. She swung at the air, trying to remember how to block and parry with Jacob showing up every other day or so to correct her on what she was doing wrong. Until one day, Jacob showed up with a dark-haired lady in what appeared to be horse riding trousers and a blouse. Rana stopped as the two approached, and Jacob gave a wave with his usual smile. "Hello there, muddy princess, I see you've been having a good time."

Rana pointed her wooden blade at him, "Where have you been, you were supposed to—"

Jacob raised his hands, "Whoa, whoa, before you bite my head off, I brought someone for you to meet," and then gestured to the lady.

"Hello, there," said the woman.

"Hello, I... ah, I'm Rana."

"She's even cuter than I thought. My name's Dessi. When I heard that Jacob had been spending all his time around a little girl, I just had to come and see."

Rana stared at Jacob as his face shifted to one of tiredness and then back to the lady again, "Are you a warrior too?"

"Well I am a member of the Black Jewels, but I'm a different type of warrior."

Jacob coughed, "Rana, why is it mostly men become warriors instead of women?"

"I don't know... because you're bigger?"

"Well, that's the main part of it, I guess," said Jacob. "Remember when you tried to pick up my metal sword, remember how it was hard for you to balance and hold correctly?"

Rana nodded. "Yes."

"Well every sword is either that heavy or heavier. And you're already small for your age, so even when fully grown, I doubt you will be able to swing an average-sized blade right."

Rana looked at her hands and began to compare them to the size of Jacob and Dessi's. "What should I do then?"

Jacob placed his hand on Rana's head and ruffled her hair, "Rana, you told me before that you just wanted to protect yourself, well there are a lot of ways to do it. So, I'm just going to change your training a little," Jacob turned to Dessi, "You're up."

Dessi shrugged and patted her sides, pulling out two small sharp blades from some hidden place instantly.

Rana's eyes widened at the trick as sunlight glimmered off the edges of the blades. "Wow, what are those?"

Dessi grinned and held out one of the small blades before Rana. "Go on, take it, and try not to cut yourself." Rana reached forward, taking the blade from Dessi's hand. It was barely the size of the lady's finger, and even in Rana's hand, it barely outstretched her palm.

"They're so tiny," said Rana as she rubbed the side of the blade against her finger.

"Any blades, even ones that small, can kill a man. You just gotta know where to cut." Dessi took the blade back from Rana and maneuvered it between her fingers before flicking her wrist and sending it flying into the side of the tavern wall, embedding it into the wood. "And if you want, I could teach you how to use a lot of blades, each one, a different size." The look in Rana's eyes as she stared at the blade in the wall was all the indication that Dessi needed. That afternoon, Rana spent her time throwing, slashing, and bumping the little blades off the side of the tavern wall.

The next morning inside the Tavern, Jacob's father and Broderick were sitting at a table.

"So where have you been, you got another contract?" asked Broderick.

"Not yet, but things are starting to get bad over in Grent, heard that the people in villages near there are up and disappearing. The king is too high up to care about some raiders at the edge of his territory, so some noble Duke will probably send for us."

A few thuds were heard against the back walls of the tavern. Broderick sighed and continued talking. "And you don't think they'll handle it themselves or hire someone else?"

"Nahh, there's no other militia for a hundred miles, and the king's soldiers are either here doing fuck all or at the border waiting for a war that means fuck all. So, I figure after enough people get looted, raped, or killed, someone will show up for us."

Jacob walked in through the back of the tavern and sat down at the table. "Alright, Dessi's outback playing momma with the girl."

A few thuds were heard again. Jacob's father nodded to the back wall, "We heard."

Broderick shook his head, then pointed to the back of the tavern. "You really take value in that runt? Why? You've seen dozens of girls come in and out of here. At least with the noble, he has the excuse of his son, which will be here any day. But you, what's your game?"

"She's a young woman who wants to learn how to fight, and I'm a military commander. I'd say that's enough reason for me to be interested," said Jacob's father while taking a sip of ale.

Broderick narrowed his eyes, "Whatever, just make sure that if you're gonna do something, do it after I get my money. It's not like—"

A few more thuds were heard against the wall, along

with mumbled instructions from Dessi. Broderick stood up from the table. "Oh, great mother's behind, I'm not gonna have a wall if this keeps up." He walked to the back of the tavern and yelled, "Stop that blasted banging. Go to the market and get them to deliver more wine and meat."

"Hey, Rana, watch this," came Dessi's voice into the tavern.

"What are you... Dessi, no, no, don't you dare. Ah! You bitch, you could've hit me."

Broderick walked back into the tavern, mumbling to himself and sat back down, taking a swallow of ale. "If you're gonna raise that runt to be another Dessi, that probably isn't a good idea. They're too emotional..." He noticed that both men were staring at him, "What?" They both nodded at his shoulder, and Broderick's eyes followed to see a small blade sticking out of his vest's leather. "Ah fuck, that bitch." Broderick ripped the blade free from the leather throwing it to the floor as both Jacob and his father gave a hearty laugh.

A little while later, Dessi and Rana were finishing up the market orders when Dessi stopped, "Oh! Let's stop by Holland's shop; I need to order something."

"Who's Holland?" asked Rana curiously.

Dessi took a left turn down a street with Rana following behind her, "Holland's an armour and weapons maker. He's usually the one who we buy weapons from when we're in town. He made my knives and Jacob's blade." The two walked together past the gates into Hightown until they came to a place with burly men banging metal with hammers.

"Hey Holland, are you in there?" yelled Dessi.

Two men came around the corner with buckets of water in each hand.

"Yeah, who is it," said an older gray-haired man in a leather apron. He spotted the two girls. "Oh, it's you Dessi.

Did Oscar send you to get some work done?"

The younger man with the buckets dropped them and started stretching. "Hey, Dessi. What you doing here?"

Dessi smiled at Holland, "Nope, I'm here for some personal work. And why's Jasper here? Figured you'd be out doing the dumbest things you could find."

Jasper put up his fists. "Careful now, them be fightin words. And as you know, I've already proven I can handle two women at once." Jasper started bouncing around, throwing punches in the air.

Dessi shook her head, "I really don't see what Prinja and Keltre see in you."

"How bout I drop my trousers and give ya a look, it's quite impressive if I do say so myself."

"Hello again, Mr. Jasper," said Rana as she recognized the man from the night of the tavern bar fight.

"Oh, hey, if it isn't the little muffin. What you doing here." He pointed his hand at Dessi. "This evil she harpy dragging you along on her errands today."

"That's not nice," said Rana frowning, "Dessi has been treating me well and teaching me things. I'm going to become a warrior."

"A warrior, you say," said Jasper rubbing at his chin while looking at Dessi with a smug look on his face. "Yeah, she can certainly do that. But be careful you don't want to end up a heartless shrew like her or—"

"Oh, shut up, you twit. No one cares about your silly jests."

Holland walked past Jasper, "Don't mind this dumbass," waving for Dessi to follow. "Alright then come inside, won't be able to discuss business with all this noise."

Jasper gave a displeased look at Holland, "Well, I'm off anyway. Gotta pick up some herbs and such. I'll be back ya old coot, try not to burn the place down before then." He then strolled off down the street, whistling a weird toon.

Inside they sat down at a table while Holland grabbed

three mugs, setting two in front of Dessi and Rana. He grabbed some bread off the shelf and handed Rana some to munch on. "Your kid, Dessi? If I had known, I'd have sent you a gift."

"Not mine, but I do feel quite motherly with her around. Jacob asked me to take care of her for a while."

A moment of sadness passed through Rana's mind as she glanced down at the table. *I have a mother.*

Holland filled two mugs with ale and Rana's with water from the bucket he had just brought in. "You still high on Jacob then, figured you'd have ended up married to some nobleman by now."

Dessi placed her hand over her heart while playfully fluttering her eyelashes at Holland, "You just don't understand the ways of a maiden's heart, Holland."

"Aye, ya have me there. My father always said he'd have an easier time becoming an Archmage than understanding my mother, and I guess I followed suit." Holland pulled out a chair and sat down, rubbing at his neck. "Alright, so what ya got for me? You didn't come here just to make me feel old, now did ya?"

"I brought you a gift that only your keen eyes would appreciate," said Dessi as she reached to her side and pulled out two more blades from hidden places and laid them on the table.

Holland picked one up and started twirling it around, examining it. "Humm, seems too light for throwing, you'd want the base and the tip to be heavier. The weight's all wrong."

"Those things almost got me killed. Half the time, they barely hit where I was aiming."

"Yeah, they'd do that when made like this. So, what ya doing down in Heftan? That's a long way away."

"I didn't say I was in Heftan," said Dessi with a raised eyebrow.

Holland placed the edge of the blade on the table and

scratched it across the wooden surface, leaving a mark. "This is Heftan metal. It's harder than what we got here. So, they can't temper it as much without it breaking. And there's flaws in the blade. So even if the metal was perfect, whoever did it probably wasn't skilled enough to do a proper job of it." Holland flicked the small blade back on the table. "What happened to the ones I made ya before? It was a couple dozen, I think. That should have been enough to last for a while."

"Well, there were problems with my last job. And the next thing I knew, I was in a carriage barreling down a hill and throwing blades faster than the sky drops water," said Dessi picking back up the blade.

"I heard about something happening over in Heftan. Some clans were trying to merge or something."

"Yeah, seems the bride of one of the chieftain's sons killed an elder of a rival clan. It was a whole mess."

"And let me guess, you're gonna say you had nothing to do with it?"

"Oh, I had everything to do with it; after all, it's what I was paid to do. The local lord down there was afraid that the clans would merge and start raiding the villages even more than they did before. And now they'll be fighting each other for the next hundred years."

Holland sighed, "I often wonder just how many pots Oscar has his hand in." He drummed his fingers on the table, thinking. "Alright, I'm guessing you're going to be needing more blades, real ones, not that junk you just handed me."

Dessi leaned back into the chair, "Yep, four dozen this time."

Holland stood and walked to the window, watching as the men worked the metal, "Alright, come back in four to five days."

"You treat me so well Holland, one of these days a woman's gonna snatch you up, and you'll be too busy to take these orders."

"Keep your well wishes, I'd like to think I have enough women bossing me around." He then nodded at Rana, who was finishing her bread. "What about that one, you said you're teaching her. You want her getting a small dagger or something?"

"Actually can you make another dozen small practice blades? Nothing fancy, but just for her to get the hang of what I'm trying to teach. As long as they fly straight, they'll do."

Holland watched as Dessi patted Rana on the cheek while talking to her. "Aye, but you really think it's wise to be teaching her that. I can't imagine the life you've lived is one you'd like for others to have."

Dessi's eyes stared past Rana as if in a daze, "Who knows? But she'll decide what she wants. It's not a decision I can make for her."

"I'm not a child. I want to learn."

Dessi smiled and hugged Rana pulling her face into her bosom, "That's right. We girls gotta protect ourselves from the evil, lecherous old men like Jasper and old Holland there."

Holland made a displeased face while pointing to the door, "Oh, be off with ya; I have work to do. Go play mother somewhere else."

Dessi stood up and began leading Rana outside.

Holland spoke in a low tone when she reached the door, "You're favoring your right side, what got ya."

"You always were good at noticing things. Arrow grazed me. Got a few extra stitches to add to the collection," said Dessi placing her hand over her right side.

"One day, that reckless streak of yours is gonna get ya killed; no one's luck lasts forever."

Dessi turned to Holland, her happy face replaced with one that seemed tired and sad. "Maybe, but it'll be a choice that I made, not one that someone made for me," she said before walking out the door once again, wearing a smiling face. "Let's go, Rana; we can grab something to eat on the way back."

The two walked down the streets of the city, passing the gates into Lowtown.

"Don't forget to practice with your new toys now when they arrive, I'mma need you to be as good as I am in a few years."

"I'm gonna practice whenever I can," said Rana. She glanced around the city at the people and noticed a man and a woman kissing by a well. "Ms. Dessi, can I ask you a question?"

"Sure, what is it?"

"Are you in love with Jacob? The old man said you were chasing him."

Dessi raised an eyebrow at Rana before following her gaze to the couple that were enjoying each other over by the well. "So, you've become interested in boys, have you?"

"What? No, I mean... there's nobody I like. But you and Jacob seem to get along, and Holland seemed to act as if you liked him."

"Hmm," Dessi stared into Rana's eyes and, as if making up her mind, "Honestly, I don't know. I've known him since he joined the old man. And we've taken care of each other for as long as I can remember." Dessi snapped her fingers, "It's probably better to just say I picked him."

Rana frowned, puzzled by the explanation. But before she could ask another question, she heard someone calling her name. Turning around, she saw Maggie holding a large sack in her arms, followed by Billy.

"Hey, Rana, what ya been up to? I haven't seen you in like forever," said Maggie as she walked up, dropping the large sack on the ground at her feet.

Rana turned her head away for a second as she instantly remembered the night of the festival. The vision of Maggie's face in the window, flooded her mind. But she quickly forced the thoughts away, turning back and smiling, "Oh, hey, Maggie, I've been busy working a lot, so I didn't have time to visit. They're teaching me a lot there." Rana glanced around, "Where's the doctor?"

"He's been gone a few days; said he had a sick patient outside town. Me and Billy just been restocking while he's been out." Maggie looked up at the lady standing beside Rana and nodded in her direction, "Who's this, she with you?"

"Oh! I'm sorry. This is Dessi. She's... um... she's one of my teachers."

"Hey Dessi, I'm Maggie. You teaching Rana how to become one of them fancy lady folk for some nobleman, I bet. Ever since we met, she been talking kinda fancy," said Maggie, wiping her face with the sleeve of her tunic.

Dessi smiled, "That's right. Before I'm done with her. Rana's going to be dancing at balls with lots of little noble boys vying for her attention." She placed her hand on Rana's shoulders, rocking her back and forth a bit, "But what about you, little Maggie, do you have dreams of being a noble lady, surrounded by admirers?"

"What? Me? I got no dreams like that. Sides, I already got us a sponsor myself. The doctor takes good care of Billy and me here." Billy just nodded his head. "Don't mind, Billy, he can't speak, but he does well enough."

"Well, it's a good thing he has you to take care of him then," said Dessi smiling down at the little blonde boy rubbing his head. "You know, you remind me of a little blonde boy I knew a long time ago."

"We do right by each other," said Maggie as she hugged Billy from behind.

"You can play with your friends, and I'll finish up the errands," said Dessi as she stepped behind Rana, giving her a little push on the back.

"But you don't have to—"

"Nonsense, I needed to handle a few things anyway. And your toys won't be ready for a few days still. So, I'll drop by the tavern again when everything's ready," said Dessi as she made her way off into crowds in Lowtown.

"Oh, Rana, you've got to come with me, I want to show you something," said Maggie with a giddy look on her face.

Rana watched Dessi disappear into a mass of people, before turning around to follow behind Maggie and Billy as they headed down the street and back to the doctor's office. She stepped inside their home as Maggie went into the back while Billy took a seat on the floor, opening up the sack they had with them.

Rana turned around again and noticed some parchment and a few herbs scattered across the doctor's desk. She walked over, picking up an herb, twirling it in her fingers. The parchment on the desk seemed to have some weird writing on it. She couldn't make out all of the words but assumed it was for ingredients to some type of medicine. Maggie strolled back in clutching a book to her chest and laid it down on the floor in front of Rana.

"Look," said Maggie.

Rana knelt on the floor and inspected the book, but didn't notice anything particularly special about the cover.

Maggie waved her finger over the cover of the book. "It's a book about the human body; it tells ya all kinds of stuff." Maggie opened the book a few pages, "See, it says here. That... the...spine of the... sub... sub... subject... is co... co... conecked to the... skull and—"

Rana was confused as she watched Maggie continue to struggle to make out the words of the book. She wondered why this was so important. Then Rana's eyes opened wide as she shouted out, "Maggie you're reading."

Maggie gave Rana a big smile, "Yep, and Billy can too, or at least I think he can. It's kinda hard to know, what with him not being able to speak and all." Billy gave Maggie a discouraging glance, narrowing his eyes at her before he went back to sorting out herbs from his pack. Maggie chuckled, "I'm just kidding Billy, I know you can read." She turned back to Rana, "The Doc's been teaching us all kinds of things."

Rana pointed back at the desk with the letters and herbs. "So that mess over there belongs to you and Billy, then?"

Maggie blushed a bit, "Ah, well, I'm not so good with my letters yet, but I'll get better. And, one day, I'll be a doctor myself." Maggie playfully poked Rana in the chest, "You're not the only one who's trying to get out of here, just you wait. Me and Billy are going to become the best doctors you ever seen." Maggie walked over and picked up the paper from the desk, "The doctor said that... What, what's the matter?"

Rana gave a puzzled face, "What do you mean?"

Maggie put the papers back on the desk and placed one hand on her hip with the other pointing to Rana. "Don't *what do you mean* me. I learned to read people a long time ago. Every time I bring up the Doc; you make this kinda sad face. What? You don't like 'em?"

"No, it's not that; it's just..."

"It's just what? The Doc's been treating me and Billy real good. He ain't beat us or nuthin, right Billy," said Maggie walking back over to Rana.

Billy nodded his head.

"No , no, it's nothing like that," said Rana as she glanced back at Billy, then grabbed Maggie's hand, "Come here for a second," and led Maggie into the back room.

"What's your problem, Rana?"

Rana peeped out the door and made sure Billy didn't follow them and then turned back to Maggie. "It's just, remember the night when all the people were dancing in the street with the fire?"

"Yeah, what about it?"

Rana dropped her head, "That night, I had come by to see you. I swear I knocked on the door but, I guess the noise was too loud. So, I went around to the window and ah... well... I saw you, you... um... were."

Maggie sighed, "And you saw me with the Doc's pecker

in my mouth. I thought I saw a face in the window that night. Didn't realize it was you though."

Rana looked up at Maggie in shock at her statement. "Ah... well, yes... I didn't think he'd make you do things like that. He seemed—"

"Make me? You know how long it took before he'd let me do that?"

Rana's eyes opened wide in shock, "Let you, you mean you wanted to do that?"

Maggie shook her head, "No Rana, I...want... to survive, and doing that makes sure that I will. Not just me, but Billy too." Maggie noticed the questions written across Rana's face. "Look Rana. The Doc is a man. A... single... man, who has money and respect. Do you know how many women come round here, batting their eyes at him? And those women want husbands. But do you know what those women don't want? Humm? Two little brats hanging around. So, either I take care of Doc and live in his nice house, with him buying me the nice clothes, and teaching me the books and the letters. Or me and Billy go back to begging on the street, begging to people who wanna do a lot worse than what the Doc gets."

Rana lowered her voice, "I... I... sorry. I just thought."

"And you thought the Doc made me do it," said Maggie as she shook her head. Noticing Rana's sad face, she stepped forward, wrapping her arms around Rana, "Thank you for caring about me, Rana."

Rana hugged her back.

"But I'm okay here, really. And the Doc's not so bad as far as men go. You should see him. He gets all flustered and nervous when I grab his pecker."

"Maggie!" said Rana in scandalous shock.

Maggie laughed, "Well, it's true. But really, Rana. You have no experience with boys? Even I kissed Billy before."

"What? But do you like Billy?"

"What? No, but I wanted to know what it felt like to kiss

a boy. And Billy's a boy like any other." Maggie pounded her palm with her fist, "You should kiss Billy, it's not like he'd ever tell anybody." Maggie turned to get Billy, but Rana stopped her.

"No, stop that," said Rana as she started playfully hitting Maggie.

Maggie laughed while raising her arms to fend off the light impacts, "Fine, fine, but you're gonna end up kissing somebody eventually. Better Billy than some old toad for your first kiss. I'm fourteen, and I known girls that had babies a year past me."

Rana pouted, sitting down on the floor, "I'm fine; I don't need that stuff. I can't be like you. It's amazing how you got with the doctor so fast. It seems like I meet you on the street, then next thing I know, you live here. Really, Maggie, you get along with everybody." Rana stared at her hands, "But I just want to run away. From the tavern. From this city. From everything. But I don't have anywhere else to go."

Maggie calmed down and sat on the floor beside Rana. "It looks that way, but I get scared too, Rana. I think about what if the Doc beat Billy or me. Or if he'd rape me and kick Billy out. I know it sounds silly now cause Doc's all nice to us and everything. But the guards and other men's been looking at me funny lately. And I know what happens to the girls when they get my age, if they on they own out here. And Billy's my responsibility. He's been following me ever since we met. If something happened to him, it'd be my fault."

"You really do care about Billy, don't you?"

"Of course I do, he been following me around since forever, and it's not like I just take care of him. When I was hungry on the street, Billy would bring me food. No idea where he got it from, but whenever things got bad, and we had nothing to eat. He would disappear, and soon he'd come back with food for us to eat. We survive because of each other. It'd be wrong for me to live in Doc's house and not have Billy with me. I told Doc the same, and he just smiled and nodded his head, saying, we're both a package deal, so if he was gonna get one of us, then he was gonna get the other too."

Rana nodded and started twiddling her thumbs, "I understand, but... when did you... ah... well."

"Start putting Doc's pecker in my mouth?"

Rana blushed. "Ah, Maggie, how can you just blurt that out?"

Maggie giggled, "I'm sorry, your face is just too funny. The truth is I was delivering some grendel juice to a whore house, and I just decided to ask them girls there for their advice. I mean, they know a lot about men, right? After I told them bout Doc, they seemed happy enough to help. So they gave me a plan, and one night when the doctor was at his desk, I came in crying to him about how I felt bad he was taking care of us and all that. I made sure to throw myself into him, rubbing my face in pants, and sure enough after a little time. I felt it start to rise, so I just grabbed that pecker and started rubbing."

"Stop saying it like that," said Rana placing her hands to her face.

Maggie struggled to hold her laughter, "After that, he takes care of Billy and me, and I take care of him. The lady Tabby said that no good man can refuse a crying maiden, and it worked."

"Wait, Tabby? Did you say Tabby?"

"Yeah. What, you know her?"

"That's... that's where I live; Tabby lives there too."

This time Maggie's face turned to shock, "You live in a whore house?"

Rana's face turned red again as she tilted her head at the floor, "Well... yeah... but they call it the tavern... and I don't... well, I don't really see anything... sometimes I hear them at night, though."

Maggie burst out into laughter rolling around on the

floor, "And here I am talking about rubbing peckers when you go and live in a whore house."

CHAPTER 11

The captain's ship arrived at the port of Krispiick, and Victor watched as the crewman lowered a plank. The port city had seen the benefits of the commerce that its pristine trade route had granted it. The walls of the buildings were made of white stone that shone beautifully in the morning sun. And most of its people were dressed in beautiful summer clothes. Men in elbow-length doublets and women with breathable silks wrapped around their bodies in all kinds of colors.

Victor watched as passengers left the ship, making their way into town. "This certainly seems like a wonderful place to live. Everyone's walking around without a care in the world. Makes you wonder what kind of fun secrets they hide behind this wonderful visage." he said while gazing over the city as the captain approached.

"Aye, it's perfect for the people that think war is something out of a fairy tale, but at least it seems free of murderous white she-beasts."

"What's that captain, you don't appreciate the joys of the city."

"Oh, I appreciate its coin well enough, but everything here seems to clean. And I don't trust anything that hasn't been through the dirt a few times."

"Well it seems there are still a few things we can agree on."

He and the captain exited the ship and walked down onto the docks.

"Still though, it's a nice change from Aarons Bay. The people here aren't giving off a vibe that screams that they want to kill me and loot my body for the joy of it." He watched as the people in port went on about their day. He could see the fresh produce stalls littered through a nearby market area as children ran about playing near the water.

"So, captain, you headed off again?"

"Aye, Stocktons only a weeks voyage away as long as the winds are right. I'll give the men and guests a day to enjoy the town's pleasures, as the ship gets new supplies for the journey ahead. But I'd expect to be off soon enough." The captain turned to Victor, "I want to say, it was a good voyage with you. But you seem to be the type of man that trouble tends to follow. So, in truth, I'm glad to have ya off my ship."

"What? And here I thought that sailors were the type for adventure and treasure on the high seas. Perhaps the tales I hear of your type gallivanting across the dangerous open waters are all but a lie."

"Aye in my younger days, this would be a tale to tell. But I'm old and wise now. And having murderous magical shapeshifters around every corner ain't good for business."

Victor sighed, "I'm sorry about your man. You seemed to have been with him a while."

The captain took a deep breath of sea air as he gazed over the water at the seagulls flying off into the distance. "We rarely get to decide how we go back to the mistress. I asked the healer to give a prayer for the lad."

"Where is Mr. Cloak anyway? I haven't seen him since we docked."

"Ya missed him then; the boys said he left as soon as we meet land. Just walked off and wandered into town."

Victor shook his head, "Nope, not suspicious at all." He noticed a man in a dark uniform standing on the docks who seemed to be staring at him and the captain, "Is that someone you know?"

"No, I don't dock here often enough for someone to be waiting on myself." A woman in uniform soon ran up and joined the man. He pointed at Victor, and the two began walking toward him and the captain.

"Hello Sir, Are you, Mr. Victor?"

"Yes, that is me. How may I help you, Mr?" asked Victor, narrowing his eyes at the man.

"Ah, yes, sorry, I'm Dekol, and this here is Frenka. We're to escort you to the capitol," said the man as he presented Victor with a piece of parchment.

Victor gazed over the two. They both had dark hair. Dekol's hair was short while Frenka's was long and down to her back. He took the piece of parchment, scanning it over, "Forgive me, but I wasn't aware of any escort. I was told this would be a solo journey."

"Yes, Sir, that was the plan. But I was given orders to hasten your travels under our escort; the king would like to speak with you as soon as possible."

"And I'm guessing; I don't really have a choice in the

matter."

Dekol shrugged, "Orders are what they are, Sir."

Victor lifted his glasses and rubbed his face in frustration and turned to the captain, "Well, it seems I must be on my way, captain. I wish you good sails."

The captain smirked, "Already getting into more trouble, be off with ya then." He turned around walking back onto his ship.

Victor left the docks and journeyed into the city with Frenka and Dekol at his sides. After a while of walking with his escorts, he spotted two other similarly dressed people waving at them up ahead.

"These two are Thaddius and Mova; they are with us. We have an airship right outside the city that will take that to the castle."

Victor nodded at the two as they joined the group, and they all began walking towards the exit of the city. Thaddius was a large man with a beard and had the sides of his head shaved down. His uniform seemed too small for his muscular frame, and Mova was a short-haired woman whose uniform was cut short at the bottom, revealing her legs. Victor glanced between Frenka and Mova and noticed the contrast between the two women. Frenka with her long flowing black hair and Mova with her short blonde cut. It seemed to him as if the two women personally went out of their way to be opposite of each other.

Wonder what the history is there.

The group stepped outside of the gate, and there was an airship hovering above the ground. The bottom seemed similar to that of any regular sea ship, it had a mast, but no sails were attached. The body of the ship was made out of stretched lumber and held together by metal beams. But alongside each of the metal beams along the vessel was a liquid encased in glass throughout the ship. The liquid inside glowed red as the craft hovered over the ground.

Victor looked over the vessel nodding his head in

approval, "Well, if you're going to rush me, it's nice that you have such a nice toy to offer me a ride in."

A woman on board the ship peered over the side and waved to the group below. Victor saw Dekol wave back at the woman as she turned back, throwing a rope ladder down to them. It unwound itself on the way down, hitting the ground as the wooden steps clanked against one another.

Frenka tugged on the rope before placing a foot on a step, then spoke in an odd accent. "Well, there no need to wait. We climb now." And they all climbed up to the top of the ship. On the deck of the ship, they were greeted by another female soldier.

"This is Crispa; she's the one who controls the ship," said Dekol.

"I appreciate you giving me the ride," said Victor, extending his hand to her.

Crispa shook Victor's hand, "Welcome aboard; I hope you all are ready to go. I wish to get back home to my daughter; she's teething, and my man wouldn't know his way around a wet nap without me being there."

"We are at your whim now Crispa, whenever you're ready," said Dekol with a grin on his face.

Crispa walked over the ship and stood in front of a wooden platform that held a large red crystal. She placed her hand on it, and the liquid inside the glass of the ship started to glow a bright red. The ship slowly lifted into the air and propelled itself forward.

Soon they were high in the sky as Victor leaned over the railing staring down at the ground below. In the air, they were able to cover land very quickly; an area that would have taken days to travel was now being covered in a matter of hours. The terrain of Burlus wasn't treacherous by any means. The land was green and flat, and many of the villages they passed on the way seemed to have many people just going about their day. The land was green and fertile with the soon coming harvest as Victor looked down, seeing the common people handling the land with plows and bisons in the fields.

Nothing about this trip is making sense. Okay, fine, Clarissa wants me to play politics here. But why are they rushing me? What difference would a few days make? What does the king want from me? Victor shook his head, annoyed at his situation. *And once again, I'm stuck in another shit hole situation. I should have known I'd never be free.*

"Have you not been on an airship in your kingdom?" asked Thaddius as he walked over beside Victor.

"Oh, on occasion," said Victor coming back from his own thoughts. "I have taken them when needed. But it's still a rare thing to book passage on one." He looked over at Crispa as she navigated the ship. "I was told it takes a decade of training just to fly these things, and not many mages are willing to dedicate their talent for that long, just to learn to fly a ship. Especially in a war where these things might as well be a big bullseye in the sky. At one point, I heard a pilot refer to it as 'training for ten years, just to learn how to get shot down in ten seconds."

"Aye, not many in our kingdom take up the trade as well. Crispa, there is only one of twenty that we have on call."

Victor raised an eyebrow at Thaddius while smirking, "Oh, are you sharing top-secret military information with another kingdom, Mr. Thaddius."

Thaddius bellowed a laugh, "Please, as you said, these ships do not last long in a battle. Wars are won with troops on the ground, not these shiny fragile trinkets in the sky. One good blast, and this whole vessel would be nothing more than kindling."

"So, are you a mage Thaddius?" asked Victor as he stretched out his arms and embraced the wind as it flew against his face and through his hair. He was surprised the wind was so soft considering the speed at which they were traveling.

"Aye, all of us here are since we're assigned to protect

the prince. Well, except Dekol over there, he's mundane. But honestly, I'm not sure the kingdom could afford it if that man were to be given any type of magical ability."

Victor watched as Dekol lifted a rope into his arms, carrying it over to the other side of the ship. "It's said that seven out of every ten mages are female. So how did your magic appear?"

Thaddius glanced over at the three female mages on deck, "Nothing as grand as other's stories, I'm sure. My father and mother were both mages. One day my father had frozen a bucket of water trying to show off. And me wanting to be like my father tried to mimic him. I didn't freeze the bucket, but I managed a few ice chunks in the water. After that, they sent me off to train."

"Well, I admit that with all you magical prodigies surrounding me, I do take some comfort in knowing that your man Dekol over there is a mundane like myself. Just the two of us non-magical men trapped in a sea of magic and politics, at the whim of royalty."

Thaddius laughed again, "You'll soon realize how wrong your words are if you spend any time around the man."

Victor gazed from Dekol, back over to Crispa, who was starting to sweat a bit. "It appears as if our driver is becoming weary."

"We're almost to the kingdom now; usually we have them go for only an hour or two before swapping them out, but Crispa wanted to do the whole thing in one trip," said Thaddius as he shook his head at the pilot.

"Well, if you'll excuse me, then," said Victor as he lifted himself back from the rail of the ship and left Thaddius, walking over towards Crispa. "You seem to be having yourself a fun time," he said to the woman navigating the vessel.

"Just a little longer, and as soon as we clear those mountains, you'll be able to see the capitol," said Crispa as she smiled at Victor with small beads of sweat running down her face.

Victor reached inside his pocket and pulled out a handkerchief, showing it to Crispa and gestured it towards her. She nodded her approval, and Victor began to wipe the sweat off of her face. "You seem quite dedicated to getting home Miss Crispa."

"Well, I got a decent amount of rest before they found you, so I figured I could make it in one trip. Plus, my little one is waiting for me to get back. This is the first time I've been away from her for more than a day since she's been born."

"I take it; this is your first one?"

"Aye, that she is. The darling of my eye and all that mushy stuff. It's funny; you never think of yourself as the doting mother until you're holding the little rascal in your arms. What about you? You have any kids of your own?"

"Not to my knowledge, no. Although that was the plan before I was sent on this mission," he watched as she maneuvered her hands around the crystal. "Tell me something, why does it take so long to learn to fly these things?"

Crispa looked around at the other mages on deck. "It's not that getting the ship into the air is hard, per se. It's the amount of precision needed to focus your magic on so many things at once that often has mages running out and quitting during the training. Most mages focus on one thing at a time, move this item or blow this thing up. But ship piloting is different. We have to learn to push our magical energy outward into these crystals and ensure that our magical current is equally stabilized throughout the whole ship, or we go flying out of control. While at the same time extending our magical barriers the length of the entire ship. Whereas a mages barrier usually only protects themselves. That way, we can prevent the effects of the strong winds up here. If I were to drop my shields now, just the wind force alone would send us all flying overboard."

"That honestly sounds like a giant pain in the ass, if I

were to be completely honest."

Crispa laughed, "That's what most of the men say. Out of all the flyers that we have, only one man was able to properly learn to become a pilot. I'm guessing your type is just meant for blowing things up."

"I can't argue with you on that," said Victor as he peered over the horizon and saw the city of Burlas come into view.

The ship flew over the kingdom as Victor watched the people below go about their business in the mid-day sun. The city was massive in scale, with a wall surrounding it that was taller than the buildings inside. Stone and marble structures littered the inside of the city, with more wooden structures nearing the gates. While forestry and farmlands may have precluded their journey to the city of Burlus, the surrounding area was more of the same flat green land with roads that spread out from the city in all directions.

And in the center of it all was the Castle of King Nevander. Crispa glided the ship down inside of the gates of the city, over and above a large wooden platform next to a tower. She slowly moved the ship next to the tower, and two men lowered a plank from the tower onto the vessel. Crispa dropped her arms from the crystal and took a deep breath as the ship hovered in place over the wooden platform.

"Woah, finally home," said Crispa.

A woman ran across the plank and over to the crystal, "Welcome back, Crispa, I hope you had fun."

Crispa patted the women on the shoulders, "She's all your Bella; I'm off to see my baby." She waved at Victor and his crew before heading down the tower.

As the crew left the ship, Victor turned around to see the woman who had just come aboard, placing her hands on the red crystal. Once the two men pulled the plank back, she took the ship back off into the sky.

Victor watched as the flying ship quickly vanished over the kingdom before walking down the tower and joining the crew over to some nearby stables.

"We can take the horses up to the castle," said Dekol as he grabbed the reins of a steed.

Victor grabbed a horse and mounted it, "I was told this would be a diplomatic mission, I assumed I would be sitting in front of a table talking politics. But this hurry makes me think your king has other plans in mind. Tell me, what exactly does he want from me?"

"Honestly, I have no idea. I was just told to gather you from the city and expedite your travels here and bring you to his majesty," said Dekol as the rest of the crew mounted up as they rode off into the city.

"Well, let us not keep your king waiting then."

They all rode off through the city until they reached the castle. Dismounting their horses, they entered into the large stone halls of the building. The structure itself was massive on the inside. It had stairs on each side of the lower levers, each leading to a different tower of the castle. Dekol led Victor through the main hall and up two flights of steps until they reached the throne room at the center of the castle.

"Wait here. I shall inform the king of your arrival," said Dekol as he headed off into a back room, leaving the other three guards behind.

Victor gazed up at the throne and noticed behind it was a portrait of the king holding a sword with a large red jewel embedded in its golden border. But what Victor found odd was that the crown from the portrait was also there just hanging off the edge of the throne. "Does the king normally just leave his crown unprotected like that?"

"Usually, yes, he very rarely ever wears it except during ceremonies," said Thaddius.

Victor noticed that on each side of the room were portraits of previous kings, all wearing that same crown. He walked over and examined one of the portraits. Each one was embroidered in a golden border and had a large black stone at the base. Victor stopped at a picture of a blonde-haired man holding an apple. "This is Arenhal, the father of the king."

Frenka nodded, walking over beside Victor, "Yes, I'm told he was wise king and very beloved by people during his reign."

Victor noticed that Frenka accent again, but he couldn't place where she might be from. "He was the king who helped establish the magical division system that all schools use today,"

Frenka smiled and clapped her hands together in excitement by Victor's words. "Well, don't you know a lot. The Green System was made by him, although some claim it was not."

Victor rubbed the ornate golden border of the painting, inspecting the portrait. "He found that children are predisposed to gravitate to one element or another; his magic shielding technique is the standard used by every military mage in every kingdom." Victor turned around, thinking, and saw Frenka narrowing her eyes at him. "What, is there something wrong?"

"No, it is just not common to have non-mage be so well versed in kingdom's magical history, especially one from different kingdom. I am not from kingdom myself, but I was trained here, and you seem to know more than me."

Victor continued to look around the room, focusing mainly on the other pictures of previous kings. "Magic is like anything else in life; it has rules that it must follow. If you understand the rules, then you can manipulate it."

"Yes, you sure you not mage, you certainly think like—"

Suddenly the doors to the throne room opened as a man walked in with two girls at his side giggling.

"That's right, ladies, if you were to be so lucky, one of you could be at my side as I..." the man said before noticing the people in the throne room. The guards saluted the man as he smiled, "Oh, stop that, especially you Thaddius. You know I hate when you guys start all that formalness. Except for you Frenka, please do keep saluting me. In fact, join me in my bedchamber tonight; you might teach these lovely ladies some magic tricks."

Frenka made a tired face, "No, Sir, but we have guest."

"Why are you acting all... oh a guest, did you say?" Victor walked into view of the man. "Ah, so we do have a guest, ladies if you a would be so kind as to give me some time alone with my guards and Mr."

"Victor Krill, I am an ambassador from the Kingdom of Mari."

The ladies giggled as the man escorted them back out of the door and returned to shake Victor's hand.

"Greetings, Mr. Krill, no doubt you've come to see my father about the treaty. I am Prince Saffron Montavia, heir to the throne of Burlus."

Victor shook the prince's hand, "Yes, that is correct. Thank you for welcoming me to your kingdom."

"It's not his kingdom yet," said a man's voice. The two turned toward the door and saw Dekol enter with a man beside him who was wearing a royal uniform. "He still has a lot to learn before he's worthy of being called king."

The prince performed a bow, "Hello father, will you be teaching me these lessons today, or will you have someone else do it per usual?"

The king huffed, "He gets that smart tongue from his mother. Begone boy. The emissary and I have business to discuss."

"Well, come along then, perhaps the girls haven't left the palace yet," said the prince as he waved for the guards to follow as he turned away.

Dekol glanced at Victor and back to the king, "Sir, perhaps I should stay for security, in case—"

"Boy I am, the strongest mage in existence. Do you believe I am incapable of protecting myself?"

Dekol dropped his head, "Ah no, Sir, I just."

"Go on to Saffron, that boy is the one who needs your

concerns, not I," said the king waving his hand towards his son's back.

Dekol noded and hurried after Saffron.

"His father fought against me in the Trecholm war, gave me this scar on my neck. Now he's dead and his son watches over mine like a wet nurse. Fate surely laughs at us when we try to plan out our lives," said the king shaking his head as Dekol disappeared out the throne room doors.

"You are very kind and trusting, then," said Victor.

"Ha! Trust has nothing to do with it, figured it'd get that son of mine to understand what it means to be king. To always have someone nearby who wants to kill you. But if anything, he now seems even more aloof." The king sighed as he walked toward the throne, "What about you emissary, what's your story? That bitch of a Queen Clarissa sent you here to make me happy?"

"She wishes for you to stop attacking the Frilling Mountains near the border," said Victor following behind the king, noticing how easily he turned his back on a soldier from a different kingdom.

"I'm sure she does. She can't afford a war with me with that other crazy bitch Millandra losing her mind after her brat was stolen. It's only a matter of time before she comes knocking." The king sat down on the steps to his throne, rubbing his knee, "I swear, the worlds going to shit. We got four dumbass Queens and my son who's so flamboyant that he might as well be one himself."

Victor chuckled at the king's words and gestured up to the crown, sitting on the throne. "Tell me, your highness, do you usually leave your jewelry unattended like that?"

The king turned around, noticing the crown, "Oh, that thing? A useless golden bobble passed down throughout history. They might as well melt it down and sell it scraps for all the good it does."

"I take it you're not big on ceremony then."

"Now that's putting it lightly. I can't stand the stuff. But while power can get you a kingdom, policy is what keeps a kingdom. And I can promise you it's not my power that feeds my people. It indeed keeps them in line well enough, but it's not what keeps their bellies full at night."

"But it's your power that gives you the privilege to make policy. Only a fool negotiates with the weak."

"That's what my father used to say," said the king as he stood up, grunting. "Alright then, tell me, emissary. Who are you then? The powerful or the weak."

"In front of a grand mage, I'm sure most would consider me the weak one," said Victor laughing.

The king placed his hand on Victor's shoulder, "It's too late to have me think of you as a simpleton now emissary. We both know power and strength are two very different things." The king stepped back and undid the collar of his shirt, revealing a long scar across his neck that went deep into his chest. "Have a look. This is strength. And this was done by a man with no magical talent at all. Conviction! That's what did this to me. The resolve to do what needed to be done."

Victor stared at the scar in amazement, "How did you even survive that? It seems as if it should have been fatal."

"With the same conviction to live through it, that he had to end it, that's how," said the king as he released his shirt collar. "Alright emissary, I've shown you the power, now let's talk about that policy. Here's what I want from you. I need you to find someone for me. A girl, thirteen or so named Fairline Hasher."

Victor pondered for a second, "Surely there are people more qualified than I that could—"

"Oh aye, there are, and all of them have failed me in this task. Tracers, trackers, all come back to me with nothing, and of the last group I sent, not a single one managed to come back at all. But you are the Queen's little miracle boy, Hero of the Battle of Prelone Valley, so if my own men can't find her, then the answer is simple. Use someone who's not my man to do my dirty work. Especially if that someone managed to best Urgana in battle. That story has traveled far and wide, Demon of Flowers."

Victor closed his eyes and took a deep breath, "And this is how we make policy?"

"Aye, it is."

Victor lifted his glasses, rubbing between his eyes again. "Agreed, I accept. Though it's not like I had much of a choice, is there? This isn't a negotiation, but something more akin to blackmail."

"And blackmail is the best type of negotiation; it means I'll get what I want."

"I will need information on the girl in order to find her."

The king nodded and pulled off a ring, "Aye that you will." He tossed the ring to Victor. "Go to my record keeper, give him that, and he will have all the information you need to start you off properly."

Victor twirled the ring around noticing the image of a large black ox head in the center with four smaller golden stars scattered across the top, "I will depart after I get the information I need," Victor turned and began walking out of the throne room.

"You're not fond of mages are you, emissary?"

"And how's that?"

"Ever since you've entered this room, you haven't bowed or tried to kiss my ass. No, your grace' or your majesty'. And not once did I sense any hostility or fear in you. So, do you hate nobles or just all mages in general?"

Victor turned around to the king and bowed, putting on a silly aristocratic voice, "Your Majesty."

The king bellowed out a laugh that sounded throughout the throne room. "Oh, you most certainly hate both, to even stand there and mock a king. But, be careful emissary, a lesser man would find fault in your actions."

Victor stared back into the king's eyes, "And a lesser king would find enemies in shadows that don't exist."

"Guards!" shouted the king, and soon two men entered the room, "Please show our guest here to Sir. Eunwalt's chambers. Ensure that he doesn't get lost on the way." The king turned his back to Victor. "I look forward to our next opportunity to talk... policy, emissary." The guards then ushered Victor out of the throne room.

Victor was taken through corridors and downstairs until he finally reached a wooden door. Pushing it open, he saw an assortment of books on each wall and parchment scrolls atop a table. An older gentleman holding more scrolls in his hands appeared from behind a corner.

"Oh, I thought I heard the door open. How may I help you?"

"The king asked us to bring him to you," said the guard.

"Oh, well come in," said the older man, "I'm Eunwalt, what can I do for you?"

Victor walked into the room, pulling out the ring and placing it on the table, "I was told to get information about a girl from you."

Eunwalt picked up the ring, examining it, "The girl, oh yes, you must be another one hoping to find her then. Well, perhaps you will fare better than the last bunch." The old man glanced over at the bucket of black gemstones. "Sadly, it seems they weren't up to the task." He dropped the two scrolls on his desk, "Here, have a seat," as he walked over to the shelf, grabbing a small stick with engravings on it. Victor sat down, and the old man walked back to him, handing him the stick. Victor stared between Eunwalt and the stick, raising an eyebrow in suspicion.

"Smell it," said Eunwalt.

Victor hesitated for a moment unsure what to think of the old man before him, but he took the stick from him and placed it under his nose and slowly sniffed the wood. The stick began to glow blue as a small amount of magic went into Victor's nose. Quickly the image of a brown-haired girl in a red dress filled his mind. Victor shook his head, dropping the stick and began rubbing his eyes, "What was that?"

The old man knelt, picking up the stick, holding it in front of Victor's face, "It's a memory stick, its mind magic, you see. Certain memories can be implanted into it."

Victor removed his glasses, shaking his head, trying to disperse the memory from his mind. As he opened his eyes, he noticed a bucket filled with large black gems in a corner. "So that was the girl, I take it."

"Yes, but from three years ago, she's older now," said the old man walking back around and placing the stick on his desk.

Victor blinked his eyes, still trying to drop the memory from his mind, "And how am I to find this girl?"

"She was last seen in the city of Passala, but she was lost during a fire."

"And what if she perished in the fire?"

"No. If she'd have died, we would have known."

"Okay, so I have a brown-haired girl's face stuck in my head, and she was lost during a fire. Is there anything else to go on?"

"Perhaps now you see why it has been so difficult to find her. One of our tracker groups almost found her once, but their untimely deaths in a fire complicated the matter."

"Well, that certainly sounds dangerous. Was there anything else odd about the fire? You know, other than the death of your men and all."

Eunwalt smirked and thought for a moment before answering, "In truth, the fire was the result of a pyromancer who was accused of treason. Somehow, they'd gotten ahold of the girl. Needless to say, they did not take to the idea of being captured, fondly. And in all the confusion, the child escaped."

"Is the child magically talented?"

"There is no record of her showing any signs of the talent, but one wonders how she escaped a burning building surrounded by guards, without the aid of magic."

"Any places in the city where she could have gone for refuge?"

"The house of a man named the Goose. His wife and the pyromancer seemed very close. The guards investigated there the night she escaped, but perhaps there's more to be found."

"I guess that will have to do," said Victor as he stood up from the table.

"Wait, wait, I still need an impression." Eunwalt walked over to a cabinet and pulled out a small device with a small needle along with a black gem and placed them on the table. Victor noticed a significant burn mark across the man's left arm as he placed the items.

Victor raised an eyebrow at the device, "And this is?"

"An impression device," said Eunwalt, "it's very simple. We take a drop of blood and place it onto the gem. Then the gem will glow red as long as you are alive. This allows us to know if something has happened to you or not. You were in the throne room, correct? You should have seen the gems next to pictures of the royal family. It is the same thing. We'd need to inform your Queen if anything were to happen to you."

Victor looked at Eunwalt, searching his face for lies. "And it just requires blood?" Eunwalt nodded. Victor reached to his side and drew his dagger, "Then, I'll do the honors myself." He nicked his thumb with the blade and placed it on top of the black gem, and in just a few seconds, the gem started to glow red.

Victor exited the castle and saw Dekol and Frenka waiting for him, "So I'm guessing you two will be my babysitters for this journey."

"We are to provide you with any assistance you need," said Dekol.

"Well, you can assist me in finding some new attire. You two may fit in. But I'm guessing a soldier of Mari's outfit won't do me any good here."

The two escorted Victor to a clothing shop in the city where he picked out dark blue trousers, doublet, boots, and a cloak.

"It's always good to have new clothes. It really makes you feel like a new man," said Victor patting down his new outfit.

"They do suit you, but what that thing you keep strapped across your chest, with them pouches?" asked Frenka.

Victor adjusted the belt strap of his pouch bags. "I keep an assortment of tools in here. Unlike you mages, us regular folk need to be prepared with medicine and goods to help us on our long travels."

Frenka walked up, tapping her hand on the little pouches on Victor's chest, "And those little satchels have everything you need?"

Victor mounted his horse. "Not everything I need, but it gets the job done, usually. Don't worry, If I find a problem I can't handle, I'll be sure to let you both handle it."

And they all rode out of the city towards Passala.

That night they made camp alongside the road as they sat around the fire.

"Okay, ask your questions," said Victor as he poked the fire with a stick.

"What do you—" said Dekol before Victor cut him off.

"The way you two keep glancing back and forth to each other is a sign of anxiety, so either you two are waiting for me to go to sleep so that you both can have a tumble, or you're both trying to decide who's going to go first."

Dekol coughed, "Oh, well, there are rumors about you. Not just you, mind, but all the generals of Mari. But you're the only non-mage to be appointed to such a station."

Victor turned to Frenka. "Is that the same for you too?"

Frenka folded her arms in front of her, "I just wanna know if you been fucking the Queen."

"Frenka," said Dekol in a scandalous tone.

"Oh, don't Frenka me. You been thinking it too. A lowborn non-mage becoming general. He might not be fucking Queen, but he certainly fuckin someone with lots of power."

Victor gave a hearty laugh as the two stared at him. "I do appreciate your honesty Frenka, but I'm going to have to disappoint you both. The Queen wishes to be rid of me more than anyone." Victor warmed his hands on the fire, listening as the embers crackled in the flames. "As you both said, I'm not a mage, and most mages seek out other mages to mate with. Is that not true even with you Frenka?"

"Aye, that be true, I would prefer I marry mage if possible. But it is not true that men lining up for chance to wed Frenka." She placed her hands under her chest and lifted her breasts, "Frenka blessed with large front side for sure, attracts men well enough, but they soon find I not refined enough for themselves, so courtship does not last."

Victor smirked at how Frenka treated herself, "That prince of yours seemed quite interested."

"Ha," chuckled Frenka. "That fool only interested in adding to collection of whores. I sooner bed ol' Dekol before I ever let stupid prince have his way with me."

Dekol blushed and gave Frenka a disapproving stare.

"That accent of yours, where are you from, Frenka? Certainly not here."

"Oh, gods no. I from one of mountain clans north of city. When hunting, father, attacked by bear. I blacked out, but father said that I let out such scream that it sent bear flying through air. After that, he brought me to capitol, and king's guard picked me up after I found to have affinity for war magic. Got stuck guarding stupid prince ever since."

"The first time they met, Saffron tried to squeeze her

breasts as his royal right, and she decked him face-first into the mud," said Dekol as he laughed. "The king announced she was to be his personal guard the instant he found out. I never seen him laugh that hard before. I think he was smiling for days afterwards. And Saffron just kept on being himself, just with a black eye."

"Yes, well, fat lot of good it do; he still tries to grab Frenka during training, no matter how much I whack him around."

"And, what of you, Dekol? How did you end up finding your way into the king's service?"

Dekol just shrugged, "Honestly, I'm not sure myself. My father was a rebel who started an uprising against the king. Both he and I never inherited the gift of magic, although my mother had the talent. I'm told that my father and the king somehow found themselves against each other in a vicious battle where it was my father who placed the scar on the king's neck. After quelling the rebellion, he stripped my mother of her title but allowed her to stay in comfort and just drafted me into his service. And that was the end of it."

"The king showed me that scar. He seems to hold your father in high regard."

"He told me that fighting my father was the first time he felt afraid on the battlefield. And hoped I'd instill the same fear in Saffron."

Victor narrowed his eyes as he heard a noise outside of the camp. He poked the fire once again, "Your stories are sounding a lot more interesting than mine. And here we are now, all together on the hunt for a little girl whom I'm not entirely sure even exists." Victor said as he continued to hear rustling noises in the grass around them.

Dekol placed his hands on his neck, popping it for relief. "Well, we should probably get some rest now. I'll take watch; we'll be wanting an early start to tomorrow's journey."

Victor laid himself down on a blanket and made himself comfortable, closing his eyes. And every now and then he would hear the sound of shuffling around their camp, "fine with me; I could use a little rest."

A little while later, Victor felt a tug at his boot. "I know, I've been hearing them for a while now. How many do you think there are," said Victor in a low tone as he laid there with his eyes closed.

"Oh, well, I think there's dozen, maybe more," whispered Frenka.

Victor looked over and saw a sword and an empty blanket where Dekol was. His eyes opened wide. *What the? I heard whatever that was in the grass, but I didn't hear the man right beside me. How in the world did he—.* Then abruptly, out of the darkness came the sound of men screaming in pain and confusion. Suddenly a beastly image appeared and started moving in the shadows.

"Wha... what's happening?" asked a man's panicked voice from the shadows. But confusion and the sounds of more men screaming were his only reply. "Ah, screw it, just kill 'em already," said the man. Suddenly eight men rose from shadows into the dwindling light of the campfire. In a swift motion, Victor was to his feet with Dekol's sword in his hand, blocking an incoming overhead slash. He took the blow by kneeling, allowing the force to push him to his knees. Victor grabbed dirt in his hands as the man's momentum carried him forward and over Victor's shoulder.

Victor lifted himself with the man on his shoulder, sending him flying through the air. He then focused on the next charging man and quickly stepped left, dodging another incoming blade, elbowing the man in the face, and throwing the dirt into his eyes. He parried another man's attack allowing him to pass and piercing the dust faced man's chest with Dekol's blade.

Victor then kicked the man free from the blade, spinning around to face another attacker, only to be confronted by a flaming body rushing towards him. Victor jumped out of the way as the burning man screamed past him in pain, falling to the ground dead.

"Sorry, was that one yours?" asked Frenka as she hit a man in the face with the butt of her sword before twisting her elbow and slashing the man across the neck, leaving him falling to his knees, gurgling blood on the ground.

Three more men tried to rush Frenka, but black tendrils enveloped one man's face as he was pulled down to the ground and devoured in the shadow of the creature from before. Frenka blocked one man's blade and stepped forward placing her hand on his chest, "Alagalam," said Frenka, and the man's body stiffened. Frenka then placed the man between herself and the other attacker.

"Dammit, Egon, move," said the man who was frantically poking at Frenka as she dodged behind the paralyzed man. The man screamed in frustration and stabbed his companion through the gut trying to hit Frenka, only to glance down and see Frenka on her knees, gritting her teeth up at him with her sword stabbed into his chest.

The man fell over, and Frenka stood back to her feet, surveying the area, before finally lowering her sword. "Well that was fun," said Frenka as the shadowy creature appeared again.

"I'm guessing that thing is you're doing," said Victor as he gestured his hand at the mysterious thing coming towards them.

Frenka smiled at the creature, "Aye that it is." She waved her hand in front of it, and the shadows began to peel away, revealing Dekol, who was holding a small dagger.

"It's still hard to see when you do that Frenka," said Dekol rubbing his shoulders and rotating his arm.

"What was that anyway?" asked Victor.

"Just bit of illusion magic," said Frenka. "It only works at night, I reflect the shadows onto Dekol, and he turns into vicious beasty. I thought of it because of late-night stories father would tell sisters and me about the Lapinya to make us behave. It works plenty well at scaring people, though."

Victor wiped the blood off Dekol's sword, "Yes, the visage was quite unnerving. Are there any left alive?"

Frenka pointed to a pair of knees sticking up out of the shadows. "I think that one you sent flying earlier still alive, doubt fall itself killed him."

"The one that I pulled down is still breathing somewhat," said Dekol.

"Okay, let's drag them over to the fire. Frenka can you recast that shadow spell back on Dekol?" asked Victor. "Sure, but he can't stand too close to fire or illusion won't work."

"That's fine, Dekol, keep your distance, and just appear intimidating."

A little while later, one man woke to the feeling of water being poured on his face. "Wha... what the bloody hells," said the man while coughing. He shook the water from his eyes and saw his companion bound and gagged next to him, making mumbling sounds, and realized he was also bound. The man stared up to see Victor and Frenka looking back down at him. "Fuckin hell." The man spat on the ground and clenched his teeth. "You won, so what do you want from me?"

Victor placed his hand on the man's shoulder and leaned in, "Good, you understand the situation. That shortens things a bit. You are going to tell us who sent you and how you knew where we were."

The man laughed, "Now, why would I do that? You'd just kill me afterwards."

Victor leaned back upright, "Well, that may be true, or we could just feed you to that." Victor pointed out to the darkness. The two men turned their heads to the left and low to the ground they could see it. A shadowy creature with eyes white as pearls slowly prowling around the campsite.

"What the hell is that!" shouted the man.

"We're not too sure actually, but we do know that it won't come near the fire. So as long as you're here, you're safe. But

166

if you won't talk, then I might as well just feed you to it, in hopes it'll leave the rest of us alone."

"That, that thing's not real, she's a mage. I saw her cast the flames. It's probably fake."

Victor shook his head. "Frenka, if you would be so kind as to help me escort the gentlemen up." Frenka walked behind the man, grabbing his tied wrists, lifting him up.

"Hey, what are you—" said the man as he struggled to balance himself.

"Hinatsu," said Frenka as a gust of power pushed the man forward, forcing him to roll over the ground as he lost balance, ending up on the ground several yards away.

"You pieces of shit, I swear, I'm gonna—" The man stopped as he saw the shadowy creature slowly creeping forward. "Back, stay back, damn you," the man rolled over, planting his face into the ground, lifting himself to his knees. After getting himself upright, he stood and dashed back toward the camp. "No, no, no, stay," but before he could reach the camp, the shadowy creature collided with him, dragging him off back into the night. All that was heard were his screams and the sound of something tearing before everything went back to quiet.

Victor took a step back and grabbed a piece of wood, tossing it on the fire. "Well, now that didn't seem pleasant at all." Victor then turned to the other man who was bound and gagged, who was by then visibly crying. He walked over and removed the gag.

"Please don't send me out there, I don't... I don't—"

"Shh, shh, it's okay. It's okay, as long as you tell us who hired—"

"I don't know; I swear I don't know. Addy just said it was some old guy promised 'em easy coin just by off'ing some guards when they left town. Never said nothing about you being no mage."

Victor turned towards the shadowy creature that had once again started to prowl around the campsite, "And you didn't see this old guy?"

"No, I swear. We was just doing what we was told, is all."

Victor knelt in front of the man, "It's okay, I believe you, we're not gonna toss you out there."

The man tried to steady his breath while turning back to look at the creature, "Swear, that's all I—" said the man before he felt a sharp pain. He turned back to see a dagger in his chest and Victor staring into his eyes.

"But you..." were the man's final words as his head slumped down onto his neck.

Victor slowly pulled the blade out, placing his hand over the man's face, closing his eyes, and laying him down on the ground.

"You can always tell lots about man by how he kills," said Frenka.

"Really? And what does it say about me?" asked Victor solemnly.

"You made it quick and did it when he was not looking. Murder be still murder, but at least that one had compassion."

"I can't let them go back and give information on us."

"Oh, I know. If you not have done it, I would have, or Dekol perhaps."

"I killed the other one," said Dekol as he walked up with the shadows peeling off of him the closer he came to the fire. "He didn't get off as easily as this one. I needed to make him scream for the effect we needed."

"Right, well, I hope you two got enough rest, there's no need to stay here with the corpses around," said Victor.

"Hand me back my blade, and I'll go fetch the horses," said Dekol as he strapped the sheath to his side.

Victor handed him the blade, "Thanks for that."

Dekol took the blade, placing it back in the sheath and walked toward the horses.

Victor and Frenka began to roll up their belongings.

"Perhaps next time, we will get a full night's rest without

someone trying to kill us," said Victor as he turned to Frenka. "Those words you said before you cast that magic. I take it; those are your links?"

"Aye, I can say in head, but saying loud feels easier to control," said Frenka as she tied a rope around her blanket. "You sure you not mage, you know a lot of magic stuff for normal fella."

"I had mages which I commanded in war, so I took the time to learn how magic worked in order to use them properly. They told me how using magic, to them, felt like how you move an arm or foot, so they commit a word to memory as if they would move a muscle. And the moment they say the word, their bodies unconsciously cast the magic."

Frenka lifted her blanket, tossing it over her shoulder. "That pretty much it, yeah. Except, if use too much magic, then pass out from headache we get. You never woken from magic hangover before. It not fun time." She turned to see Dekol walking back without the horses with his hand hovering over his blade. "Dekol, what wrong? Where are horses."

Victor stood up to see Dekol staring off into the wooded darkness, as he made his way back to the fire. Victor walked up beside him, "How many more?"

Dekol closed his eyes, listening, "Can't tell, not a noisy bunch, but they're out there."

Victor placed his hands to his face, rubbing between his glasses as frustration started to set in once again. "Right, well then, no use prolonging what's about to happen." Victor stepped forward, placing his hands over his mouth, and yelled, "We know you're out there. Are you going to try and kill us, or are you going to hide in the shadows till the sun comes up?"

A few moments of silence passed before a voice echoed from the woods, "Well, seeing as you're so inviting. How can I refuse such an invitation?"

Soon the sounds of rustling through leaves were heard.

Victor stared into the darkness of the woods as the sounds began to grow louder and closer. Creeping slowly out of the darkness of the forest, appearing into the dim light of the fire, stepped a dozen men in dark uniforms. They appeared out of the woods holding swords at the ready.

Victor shook his head, "Well, they certainly appear tougher than the last group." Dekol gave him a displeased glance. Victor smiled back at him, shrugging his shoulders before he raised his hands to show he was unarmed. "Thank you for that. Now am I to assume that you gentlemen wish to kill us? Because if so, you're much better dressed than the last group, although I can't promise you'll fare much better than they did."

"Why thank you, my men do pride themselves on their dress," said a man stepping out of the shadows wearing the same dark uniform as the others.

"And may I ask you who you are, Sir?" asked Victor.

"I am captain Cardon Burgess of the king's military second battalion, and these are my men. And who am I speaking with?"

"I am Victor Krill on a mission for his majesty King Nevander; these two with me are royal guards, Frenka, and Dekol." Victor dropped his hands, "As happy as I would like to be to think we are on the same side, I do somehow find it questionable why a captain of the Imperial military is almost a half-moon away from the frontlines. Especially since we've already had one group try to kill us tonight, I'd rather not be at the mercy of a second attempt."

"I can see your point there," said Cardon as he rubbed his chin. "Fine, allow me and two of my men to come forward, and we can discuss this. It seems only fair as you have two of your own."

Victor glanced at Frenka and Dekol as they nodded their heads in acceptance. "Agreed," said Victor as he gestured for them to come over. Cardon walked forward into the light with two soldiers, both of whom now had their swords sheathed.

Cardon leaned to the side of Victor, peering over by the fire, seeing the dead bandit's body, "I assume he was one of the bandits."

"Aye, he and a few others are scattered around here. Is there any particular reason your men were just out in the dark spying on us?" asked Victor.

"We camped nearby, then we heard the sounds of fighting, so we came to investigate. Its standard military practice to not draw attention at night by lighting a fire, as it seems that you yourself can now attest to. But since you seem to have taken care of all of the night's attention. Would you mind if we shared your fire?"

Victor laughed, "What, you want to rest beside the dead bodies?"

"Oh, my men will move them far enough away so that nature can take its course without worrying us."

"Dekol, Frenka, do you know this man?" asked Victor, turning his head between the two.

"No, but I have heard of him. He fights under General Bradley, and it would make sense since he is from this area," said Dekol.

"I don't know much about other parts of military," said Frenka.

"Well, Dekol's word works for me," said Victor to the captain. "Have your men move the bodies and join us around the fire. I doubt much more sleep will be gotten before sunrise anyway."

All the men sheathed their swords and began moving the bodies from the area, while Victor and Cardon continued talking.

"You said earlier it was suspicious that a captain would be out here," said Cardon. "But If I'm not mistaken, Victor Krill is the sixth general of Mari. And if you're him, I'd think that would be even more suspicious than myself being here." Cardon raised an eyebrow in Victor's direction as the fire crackled.

"You have me there. I am indeed Victor Krill of Mari. My Queen and you king are trying to play nice, and I'm stuck in the middle of their stupidity."

Cardon laughed despite himself, "Oh my, that sounds like you've been given quite the heavy burden then. I do recognize the uniforms of those two with you, I've seen it from time to time on my visits to the palace. So, I do believe your words. Plus, I highly doubt a spy would willing admit to being the general of a different army."

"While there have been many days that I wish I weren't myself, I've learned just to play the hand that life has given me and make the best of it. What about you, captain? Dekol said you were from this region, what brings you back home?"

"Ah, yes, well. It just so happens that the magistrate of Passala is my father. A little while back, he asked that I visit him. Just so happens that I found time to do so. And you, Sir, may I ask why the king's royal guard is off killing bandits in the countryside? I'm sure the common people appreciate the gesture, but that is hardly the station of the royal guard."

"Nothing too mysterious, there was a fire at Duke Richard's manor. I was sent to investigate. So, it seems we both are headed to the city of Passala."

"Ahh, yes, I've heard about that, but what is there to investigate? The man was a traitor to the crown, and justice was served; I'd heard."

"Yes, well, we're out here to try and find the cause that would compel a man to betray his king as it were. All trees have roots, after all."

CHAPTER 12

Pelly and Miraval sat on the tavern steps, watching as Rana tried and mostly failed to throw small knives into an old piece of wood sticking out of the ground.

"Why do you want to fight so bad, you wanna get yourself killed?" asked Pelly.

Rana's blade missed the wood landing in the dirt, "Dammit." She turned to Pelly while walking towards the piece of lumber. "I used to watch my Pa train with his sword, said it was the only thing he really ever knew how to do." She reached down and started digging knives out of the ground, "Since he's not here, I figured I'd teach myself."

"But that's not a sword; you're just throwing knives around."

"It'll be a sword one day. I just gotta get stronger and bigger."

Miraval gave Rana a look over, "You're the smallest one here; I don't think you'll be getting much bigger."

"I know I'm small; you don't have to remind me," said Rana, frowning.

"Was your father a soldier or something?"

"I'm not sure, I mean, he never had any armour. I just remember the sword. Sometimes I remember him polishing it," Rana lowered her head, trying not to start crying, "Wha... what about you two? You never said where you were from."

"I'm from Scottsville, Pa used to raise horses," said Pelly as she began to stare off, "Then one day the raiders came, they took Ma and me. Don't know what happened to Ma. One day they took her, and she never came back. Guess they sold her. A few days later, they dropped Renee off in my cage, along with a girl named Harper. Broderick bought Renee and me and brought us here. He didn't have enough coins for Harper, though, don't know what happened to her."

Miraval placed her arm around Pelly as she tried not to start crying.

"At least your parents wanted you," said Miraval in a disgusted tone as she frowned. "Broderick bought me from my father. Not like it mattered much. It was just another day that drunk beat me; just this time, it was where people could see. Broderick just walked up and offered to buy me. At least now I know how much I'm worth. A whole four gold pieces, after haggling down from eight." Miraval shook her head and bit her lip in disgust as if trying not to think about it anymore.

"Wait, so Broderick just goes around buying girls, then?" asked Rana.

"Yeah, I forget that you've only been around for a month or so, so you wouldn't know. Broody's been doing that for years, according to the ladies here. He will buy young girls and turn them into maids and such for the nobles in Hightown. But he only sells to the noble that promise to take care of us."

Rana made a confused face, "So you won't be whores?"

"Not all the girls become whores, Rana. Broderick actually works really hard with the nobles to get us good homes."

"But what about the girls upstairs, isn't he making them... well... have sex for money?"

"All them ladies upstairs came to Broody because they wanted to work here. He treats them much nicer than the other places. And haven't you noticed that Tabby mostly handles the girls anyway? It just seems like Broody does because of the girl's safety. No one's gonna beat the girls if Broody would then beat them, if not him, then one of his uncle's men. He's gotta keep up appearances."

Rana dropped her head and began thinking. "Oh! I thought he was making the girls upstairs be whores."

Miraval shook her head, "Rana you really are a little dummy. I learned that part in my first week here. If Broody was such a bad guy, you think he'd let you be out here playing with knives? He says he's training us to be maids, but he mostly just leaves us be most of the time."

Suddenly Rana's mind began to think of the times when she was with Broderick. The time when he pushed her down in public when the crowd of people were watching a little girl spout off to him in the street. How he never made her stop training with Jacob or Dessi.

Rana stood up from plucking a knife out of the ground and walked past the girls into the tavern seeing Halva.

"Where's Broderick?" asked Rana.

"He ain't come out yet, so I'm guessing still back there," said Halva as she pointed to Broderick's room in the back.

Rana headed into the back of the tavern and pushed open Broderick's door only to see Tabby naked on top of him. Broderick sat up, pausing when he saw it was Rana, but stayed stiff as he noticed the blades in her hand.

Tabby stopped her grinding on Broderick and turned around. "Ahh, Rana, baby, what's wrong?"

"What's wrong? The girl just barges in holding blades, and you ask what's wrong," said Broderick in an annoyed tone.

Rana took a deep breath and stormed up the bed.

"Now you hold on one—" said Broderick.

"I'm sorry!" Rana shouted.

Broderick narrowed his eyes as his mouth hung open, "What?"

"You been taking care of me, and I thought you were being a stupid bully and taking girls and having sex with them and—"

Broderick fell back down to his pillow, "Oh, for the mother's sake."

Tabby started laughing.

Broderick adjusted himself beneath and raised an eyebrow at Tabby, "Really? You enjoying this foolishness?"

Tabby began to wipe tears from her eyes while trying not to laugh, "I'm sorry... but you must admit... it's pretty funny." she said before dropping the sheet over her breasts and extending her arms to Rana, "Oh, come here, baby."

"Tabby!" said Broderick as she turned her attention back to him. "I hardly think now is the best time to nurture that motherly instinct of yours."

Tabby glanced down at her own nakedness and her situation, "Oh... well, I ah... suppose you're right." Tabby patted Rana's face. "Be a good girl and give us a moment, dearie."

Rana then realized what they were doing, and shyly

nodded her head before taking a step back before heading to the door.

The two watched as Rana left the room.

Tabby placed her hand on the sheets, squeezing Broderick's hand beneath it, "Thank you for waiting."

Broderick slid his hand from under the blanket, revealing a short blade that he had hidden under the sheets, "Yeah well, I know how you feel about them, you always calling them your babies and all."

Tabby laid down on Broderick's chest, "They're the only children I'm allowed to have."

Broderick placed his hand on Tabby's head and held her close.

Rana stepped outside of the tavern to clear her head and bumped into Jacob's father.

"Whoa there little one, don't knock this old man down," said Jacob's father.

Rana bumped off him and stumbled back, "Oh, sorry."

Jacob's father started glancing around, "No worries, child, where you running off to in such a hurry?"

"Ah, nowhere, Sir."

"Well, seeing as we're both here, and I won't see that nephew of mine till later. Would you mind entertaining this old man for a little while, I was told to pick something up today. And a little bit of company would be nice."

Rana thought about it, then agreed to accompany Jacob's father. They began to walk up the street together through the town.

"So, tell me little one, how goes your training?"

"Ah well, I can properly wash clothes and make over twenty meals now. And I can—"

"Ho-ho, I'm sure you can, but I'm asking about your other training. The one that Dessi's been teaching you."

"Ah, well... Wait. How do you know about that?" asked Rana as she stared up at the old man.

"Well since I'm the one who told her to do it, I'd imagine

I'd know quite a bit about it. But, I'd prefer if you told me."

Suddenly, Rana remembered where she'd seen the old man, "Your Jacob's Pa," she said, and the old man laughed.

"So, it seems I am, but you can just call me Oscar."

"Is Jacob here? I haven't seen him since Dessi started teaching me the knives." Rana started searching around the area for signs of Jacob.

"Nah, he went to handle an errand for me. He should be back in a day or so. Dessi went to meet him. What about you, are you able to stick those blades into anything yet?"

"Yesterday I made 'em stick a lot," said Rana as she made a few throwing gestures.

Oscar gave a warm smile, "You'll have to show me when we get back."

The two turned the corner and ended up in front of a shop with a sign that had the image of a black fish holding a needle in its mouth. A bell above the door made a ringing sound as they entered the shop.

"Greetings and salutations," said an old lady with an odd accent.

"I see you're still speaking like a loon Addison," said Oscar.

"And I see you're still as much of an asshole, as I remember," said the lady in a different accent. "So, what are you doing here, can't imagine you showing up to get your hems tucked in." She noticed as Rana stepped out from behind Oscar and started looking around at the clothing in the shop. "What's this, you picked up a new kid since the last war, aren't you a little old to be fostering children at your age?" asked Addison as she reached into a cabinet, pulling out a bottle of wine and two mugs.

Rana gazed around at a large amount of clothing and fabrics that were littered throughout the shop. Colorful sheets of all colors hung from spindles, and mannequins stood in stiff poses as their wooden bodies displayed a particular fashion for any onlookers that would happen to view them.

Oscar took a seat at a table by the window as the door closed, "Something like that. Where's Jasper, he was supposed to meet me here."

"I'm back here, old man," came a voice out of the back of the store.

"Well, hurry up, you're the one who wanted to meet me here."

Jasper came out of the back of the store, wearing a silly red hat with a bunch of green feathers sticking out of it. "And here I was trying to be all mysterious. Oh, hey, you brought the little muffin with you. How ya been, honey?"

"Hello again."

Jasper walked up, patting Rana on the head, "Heard you been trying to become like Dessi, out there throwing knives like a warrior princess."

"I'm getting good too. I'm making them stick a lot more," said Rana as she flicked her wrist while smiling.

"Oh I'd bet, Dessi's a good teacher. Don't tell her I said that, though. I gotta keep treating her like shit, or she won't appreciate me anymore," said Jasper as he winked down at Rana.

Rana was confused by Jasper's statement, but smiled back at him.

"Enough with your foolishness, what news do ya have," said Oscar shaking his head as he watched a few kids outside of the shop's window kicking a ball around to each other.

Jasper turned back to Oscar and shrugged his shoulders. "Why must everyone spoil my fun?" He reached into his doublet and pulled out a small book, opening it and flipping through the pages. "Fine, it seems the capital of Dresha has an issue. Some masked man is running around, killing nobles. They've started to call him Queen's Bane."

Oscar laughed, "Of course they've given him a stupid name. I'm sure he's the talk of all the cocktail parties. What's he doing all this for?"

Jasper tapped the pages of his book. "That's the weird thing, so far he's killed nobles across three different kingdoms. Apparently, he leaves messages claiming that he's the true king of all the five kingdoms."

"Alright then, so he's probably skilled, but alone. And his little war has nothing to do with us. Let the Starlight Queen deal with his rampage then. Anything else?" asked Oscar as he rubbed his beard.

Jasper closed his book and taped it against his head while lowering his voice and leaning in close to Oscar, "They a say a servant girl caught him in the Queen's Clarrisa's bed-chamber completely naked wearing nothing but a mask."

Oscar shook his head, "Your ability to lie with such a straight face is as amazing as it is frustrating."

Jasper threw up his hands before pointing the book at the old man, "Oscar I'm hurt; this is solid intel, I promise." He then glanced down at Rana beside him and squeezed her cheek. "But you believe me, don't you muffin."

Rana slapped his hand away and narrowed her eyes at him as she puffed her cheeks.

Oscar shook his head in annoyance, "Fine, that's enough. I need you to stick around for a while. Something may have come up."

Addison took a seat at the table with the men. She poured a drink for them both, "So outside of dealing with this dumbass, are you going to tell me what you want, or are we going to just reminisce about the old days?"

"We got another job," said Oscar, taking a sip from the mug.

Addison folded her fingers together, leaning forward, "Oh, anything fun?"

"Your type of fun? Ah...no, but it's a job, and it pays. Some nobles down south are having a problem with raiders, I think. So, we've been asked for some muscle to help smooth things out. I'mma need ya to send out for a few guys."

"Oh, they're talking about boring stuff again; come on muffin, let's go try on some fancy clothes that make us look like we have sticks up our asses," said Jasper grabbing Rana's hand dragging her along.

Addison shook her head at Jasper, before turning back to Oscar, "Well, let's see, Angus and Malon have set up shop nearby. But if you can wait a little longer, then we can get Gregga and Larpris from Florence. David is setting up a group in Belvon but, it's not really up to snuff yet."

Oscar drummed his fingers across the table, thinking, "Nah, leave Belvon to attend his own. Get Gregga and send for Malon, he's got a few mages with him, might come in handy."

"You expecting some trouble?"

"Nah, just being careful."

"That means you've heard something. I'm not one of your kids Oscar, I know you. You never do anything unless it leads to something else."

"Apparently some people are disappearing in the outer villages near Nollage and Nyril. The locals are claiming its ghosts or a curse or something."

"And you think differently."

"Not sure, could be just a few rogue mage nobles or could be the second coming of the shadow king. No harm in being a little cautious. I'd think we both understand that better than most," said Oscar as he watched Jasper help Rana into a pair of oversized trousers, tucking her tunic inside as he tied the waist.

Addison made a mockingly noble gesture with her hands, "As always through the time, an idiot with a blade."

"Is just as deadly as a noble with a blade," said Holland standing in the door with the sound of the bell ringing.

"I was wondering when you'd show up," said Oscar.

Holland walked over, taking a seat at the table, "Between you and them kids of yours, it's a wonder I ever get the chance to ever leave the furnace."

Oscar laughed, "Well, you won't be leaving anytime soon, either. I need polished armour and blades for fifty men in a week's time."

Holland dropped a satchel on the table, "Well, fuck, you're gonna put me in the grave before I ever retire." He reached inside the bag and pulled out a cloth and slid it over to Oscar. "Figured I'd drop it off on the way since you insisted, I come here."

Oscar raised a brow skeptically at the cloth and then back to Holland, "What's this?" He asked as he unrolled the fabric and saw twelve small knives, with four of them having holes on the end. "I appreciate the gesture Holland, but I'm more of a swordsman myself."

Holland gestured to Rana over in the corner as Jasper slapped a large hat on her head, "I believe it was for the youngling over there with the clown. Dessi placed the order."

"And I'm guessing that I paid for these trinkets," said Oscar as he picked up a blade and inspected it.

Holland reached over the table, grabbed Oscar's cup, and took a sip, "Obviously, my lord is very generous after all."

"Humph," Oscar nodded over to Rana, "Well, little one, come over here." Rana dropped the large hat on her head and waddled over in her oversized pants to the table, seeing the blades. She turned to Oscar and Holland, waiting for permission.

"Go ahead, they're yours after all," said Oscar.

Rana grabbed a blade and began inspecting it, rubbing it against her fingers, "It feels different than the other ones."

"Of course, it does, that's what quality feels like. Not like those kitchen knives you had before. The weight balance is perfect for throwing; they'll cut the air like a sparrow in the breeze."

"Why is it you only get poetic when talking about blades and hammers? I've never heard you talk about a woman that way," said Addison.

Rana picked up one of the curved blades with the hole in the end, "What's this one?"

"Well if your meaning is to do any damage, then it won't be with a sword as it's too heavy for ya since you're small. You're gonna need leverage. So, place your finger into the hole child, now grip the ridges on the blade. Yes, like that. Start practicing with it. You'll understand how to hold it properly in time. Especially if Dessi is teaching you."

Addison stared at Rana as she tried to find a holding angle for the blade, "And so, it begins again with another one it seems."

Oscar grabbed the bottle of wine, refilling his cup, "Do you object, Addison?"

"No, the world isn't so lovely that it would give me the right to object. And this one seems to want it."

"Rana, it seems I will be here longer than I'd thought. You can run along. Jacob and Dessi should arrive sometime later today. If you see them, tell them where I am."

"Yes, Sir," Rana walked back to the table, placing the blade back amongst the others." Can I... can I take them with me? I want to practice more."

Oscar pursed his lips in thought before nodding his head, "Alright, run along then, just try not to kill yourself on the way," he said, wrapping the blades back in their cloth and placing them into the satchel.

Rana slid off the oversized trousers and rubbed her tunic back flat, "Thank you," she said before she ran out the door.

Addison reached down, picking up the discarded trousers and began folding them in her arms, "You sure you wanna start her off with blades already? I'd figure poisons would work better for her age. Better for her not to have to look into the eyes of the people she's killing until she's a bit older. You gotta wean her into it, like taking a bath in hot water."

"And how old were you when The House taught you needlework?" asked Oscar.

"Why that's exactly my point Oscar, I mean, just look at how much of bitch I turned out to be."

Holland coughed out his wine.

Outside of the shop with a satchel in tow, Rana rounded a corner, seeing a crowd of people gathered near the gate to Hightown. Over the crowd, she saw men on horseback wearing dark uniforms. A little away from her, she saw a boy standing on crates trying to get a better view.

"What's happening over there?" asked Rana when she made her way over to him.

"The magistrate's boy has returned from the front," said the boy as he hopped up and down on the crate excitedly. "Ya wanna see, there's room up here for another," said the boy as he reached his hand down to pull Rana up.

"No, thanks, I'm okay down here," and pulled away from the boy as she watched the men on horseback.

"Suit yourself then."

When the men had made their way through the crowd, Rana turned around and ran back down into the streets of Lowtown. Later she found herself back at the tavern walking in with her head down.

"Rana dear, have you heard? The Gen—" said Tabby.

Rana ran upstairs to her room, trying to avoid anyone.

"Right, well, I guess that means you have." Tabby took off her apron, laying it on the counter, "Girls mind the bar for a minute will you," as she followed behind Rana. She slowly entered the room to find Rana sitting on the floor beside her cot with a bag in her arms.

"Mind if I sit?" asked Tabby.

Rana looked up at Tabby but didn't reply. Tabby sighed and walked over, sitting down on the floor by Rana.

"I'm guessing you found out the magistrate's boy has come to town."

"He's not supposed to be here yet," said Rana gripping

the top of the bag tightly in her hands.

"I thought you were excited to be going off to the front."

"The girls say he just likes young girls; he uses them and gives them to the men."

"Yeah, I heard that too. But some of them have become wives I've heard."

"So, I'm just to be a whore then? What if I wanna decide what I wanna be?"

Tabby took a deep breath staring up at the ceiling. "That's how it was for most of us, either we'd whore ourselves out, or we'd starve. In war, we'd be raped to death or raped and left to die." Tabby slid some hair out of Rana's face, "You know my daddy was a fisherman. He used to take my sister and me out into the waters from time to time and show us how to throw a net. He'd always say, 'Just because a woman isn't expected to do a man's work, doesn't mean she shouldn't know how to do it."

"My papa used to make me ride horses, said girls need to learn how to ride them."

Tabby smiled, "Sounds like our pa's had something in common. Mine would borrow his friend's horse from the barn to teach us how to ride them. He always wanted his girls to know how to take care of themselves. Then suddenly one day, raiders came, killed every man they saw and locked the girls in cages. They kept us in that cage for days as they traveled. Only letting us out at night so they could put their cocks in us. Then one night after they were done with us, we snuck out, stole their horses, and ran away. I'm not even sure they searched for us. But we hid in the woods for days until we were sure they were gone. We found a lake a couple miles away, and we caught fish to eat. Eventually, we made our way to a nearby town. Two half-naked girls in rags come riding in on horses. Some of the people there even knew my father, but they wouldn't help us."

Rana looked up at Tabby with watery eyes, "Nobody helped? Why?"

"Had their own families to take care of, I guess. At the time, I hated 'em for not helping sissy and me. Eventually, we found a man who would house us in exchange for what every man wants." Tabby closed her eyes and took a breath. "And of course we did, we didn't care anymore. All we had to trade were our bodies, and he had food and warm beds. And after a week on the road barely eating, cold and wet. You'd be surprised what you don't care about anymore."

Tabby started rubbing the back of her hand again, "I swear if I could give you a better life, I would. But this... this really is truly the best I can do, baby."

Rana closed her eyes, taking a deep breath before laying her head down into Tabby's lap, "I know."

CHAPTER 13

Victor and crew passed through the gates of the magistrate's manor, being escorted by captain Cardon.

"You seemed to be much the town hero here," said Victor.

Cardon pulled the horse up near the stables of the manor. "Ha! If only. It's a quiet town, so the lowborn simply wish to have something to speak about. Today it's me and my valiant return; tomorrow it may be a large fish that was caught at the lake."

"Welcome home, young master," a man said as he grabbed the reins of The Captain's horse.

"Ahh, Willow, my friend. Has father been told of my arrival?"

"Yes, my lord. He awaits you inside."

The captain escorted Victor into the manor and into the main hall, where an older man sat at a table reading over a piece of parchment. "Greetings father, I hope everything is well with you."

The magistrate smiled at the appearance of his son. He stood up from the table and walked over to greet him, "My boy, welcome home. You've finally arrived, and it seems you've brought company."

"Yes, father, these are some of the men who work under me and allow me to introduce Victor, Frenka, and Dekol. They are investigators sent by his majesty, King Nevander."

"Investigators? Is there something that I need to be aware of?" asked the magistrate as he shook his son's hand in greeting.

"No sir, it's a simple investigation into the estates of Duke Richards," said Victor.

"Ahh yes, terrible thing, that. What would possess a man to betray his king like that? But where are my manners? You must be tired from your long trip. Take a seat." The magistrate waved over at a man, "Henry, prepare some wine and food for our guests."

"Thank you, magistrate," Victor said as he took a seat, "That's what we are here to find out. Why the duke turned his back on his king."

"Well, I shall arrange for you to have the freedom to search the manor's grounds or what's left of it for that matter. The city guards still have the area closed off," said the magistrate re-taking his seat at the table.

"Thank you, Sir. Can you tell me anything about Duke

Richards?"

"Well this was just the duke's vacation home. He would often bring his family here during certain times of the season. It was very odd for him to be here during this time of the year. But here he was."

"Any idea as to why he was here?" asked Victor.

"Sadly, no, for his time here, he never attended any gatherings. Kept his family locked inside that manor of his mostly, I heard."

"Tell me, did you assist in the attempt to arrest Duke Richards?"

"Me? Goodness no, I merely lent the services of the city's guard to the arrest. I fear I would have just gotten in the way had I attended."

"Forgive me, you grace; I was under the impression that you were a mage."

"Ha, to my shame, I was gifted with healing magic, and father refused to send me to the High Mother for training in my talent. Said it wasn't magic meant for a man. Nowadays, even at my best, I'd struggle to heal minor wounds."

"My apologies for bringing up such a subject then. Were there any survivors of the manor?"

"To my knowledge, only the duke and his wife were killed and their two girls were captured. The servants are all serving new houses now or have left the city entirely."

"I see, well, thank you for the wine, good sir."

"Will you not be staying for breakfast, surely you must be tired after your journey."

"Perhaps later, I do intend to return, but I'd like to see the manor as soon as I can. Thank you for your hospitality," said Victor as he stood up from the table.

"Willow, please escort our friends here to Duke Richards and inform the guards that he is to be given access to the grounds."

"Yes magistrate" said Willow as he nodded and escorted Victor and crew out of the room.

"So, father, what was so important that you asked me to return, your letter never said what exactly."

"My boy, I do believe I have procured something precious for our family. A girl of remarkable potential."

"A girl? I doubt I needed to travel all the way back for one of those; plenty hang around the camps at the wall."

"Not like this one, I felt it when I touched her. She's gifted, but the power is odd compared to either talent that we have."

"You seem rather confident in this. Okay then, and where is this girl now, if she's so gifted?"

"Broderick is keeping her until your arrival."

"Broderick? The whore monger? I'm starting to think that maybe your age has finally caught up to you father," said Cardon laughing.

The magistrate smiled, "Yes, for as unlikely as it sounds. I had trouble believing it at first myself. But there's no mistaking it. The power was there. He doesn't know she has the gift; I doubt even she knows it. If you were to acquire her and mold her to your liking, then perhaps her power alone might raise our family's standing. Something strange is happening in the world, and fate has dropped this jewel into our hands."

"Fine, let's say I believe you. But if this girl were so important, why didn't you just take her, rather than leave her with the whore monger?" asked Cardon, folding his arms across his chest.

The magistrate walked over to the window. "You weren't here for that mess two cycles ago between Broderick and the nobles. I'd like not to find myself in a similar situation. And since he's given this house girls before, if possible, I would prefer to have us pursue the natural course of things. Then no one would have a reason to ask questions."

The magistrate turned back, facing his son. "Don't you

think it's odd that a moon ago, Duke Richards was killed? Then suddenly out of the blue, this girl appears. And now we have a royal investigator on our doorstep. No, no, no, He's here trying to find her I can assure you. Probably the bastard daughter of some highborn noble or something. Richards more than likely stumbled along to some type of secret, and that's why he's dead. We need to be careful, or else we'll suffer the same fate as his family."

The captain walked over by the window with his father and watched as Victor and crew rode out of the manor gates. "Alright, let's say she is valuable. What do we do now? If I just up and leave with some strange girl in the middle of the night, it'll only be a matter of time before he finds out. And then both of us will end up like Richards. If they'd do that to a duke, you'd be certain they'd do even worse to us."

"Perhaps if we hid her in another city for a day or so, I doubt he'd notice if you went amiss for a short amount of time." The magistrate glanced over at his son and smiled, "You've been on the road for a half-moon captain, surely no one would think it odd, if this evening, you took the troops out to experience the pleasures of the city."

A little while later, Victor arrived at the burned down manor of Duke Richards.

Victor whistled, "Even some of the stone seems to have melted."

"Sir, why did you not inform the magistrate about the girl you're looking for?" asked Dekol.

Victor began rubbing the charred lumber, "Dekol I'd prefer if you just called me Victor. And the reason I didn't tell the magistrate is because nobles are always looking for ways to screw each other over. And this girl, if they found her, would just become another pawn in their endless game of stupidity. So, if possible, I'd like to keep them ignorant of that piece of knowledge."

"The way you speak, you don't seem fond of them nobles," said Frenka.

"It's not a matter of fondness. I've seen how they manipulate anyone and everything for power. So, I've learned that it's in my best interest to be wary of them," said Victor as he pushed a piece of wood. "Frenka, I don't suppose your magical talent includes being a tracer?"

"Sorry, different magic. Besides, you need personal thing of theirs anyway?"

Dekol turned to peer over the city, "How are we going to find a single child in this city, where do we even start?"

"Oh, I have a few ideas. Sadly, they are tedious and time-consuming," said Victor as he stood up and called out, "Mr. Willow."

Willow stopped talking to another guard and walked over to Victor. "Yes, Sir."

"Willow, the night of the fire, did any of the men witness anything strange?"

"One man said that he saw a small shadow near a wall, but when he yelled out to it, it disappeared."

Victor rubbed his chin, "Did he say what the shadow looked like, its shape?"

"No, Sir, he said that he saw it for only a second after he yelled out to it, it was just gone."

"Well, that sounds vague, and I'm sure me questioning him myself will be just as fruitless. Okay then, Mr. Willow, anything else?"

"Ah, No, Sir, no one else has come forward saying anything else."

"Of course not, that would make things too easy. Tell me, Willow, what do you think would make a man betray his king?"

"Ah... gold, maybe?"

"Perhaps," said Victor tossing a piece of burnt rubble away. "Mr. Willow, please provide my friends here a list of the servants that were on duty at Richards manor the night of the fire. And if they are still in the city, their current place of employment. Surely not all of them left the city that night. The magistrate mentioned that a few of the other houses had probably taken some in."

"Yes, Sir, I think I can do that," said Willow as he ran off.

"A simple man, but eager to help," said Victor. "When he returns, I want you two to start questioning the servants that remain in the city. And don't specifically bring up the girl."

"And what you be up to while you send us off on fool's quest?" asked Frenka.

"I suddenly feel the need to start investing in today's youth."

Dekol and Frenka both made a curious face at Victor.

A little while later, Victor found himself at the gates to Hightown. He turned to a guard standing on watch. "Excuse me, Sir, if I were to go on the hunt for a pickpocket in this city, where would I start?"

"Ah, so one of the little bastards got ya, did they? Well, I doubt anything will come of it at this point, but you could try your luck down by the lumberyard. Old Nelly's always finding things for them to do. Or the Goose's warehouse, I heard he puts a few boys to work down there."

Victor thanked the guard and walked off into the direction he was pointed towards. He soon arrived at the lumber yard and walked up to an older man skinning a log with a drawknife, "Excuse me, good Sir, who's in charge here?"

The old man slammed the drawknife into the log and turned to Victor as he wiped the sweat from his face, "That'd be me for now. The name's Nel, what can I do for ya?"

"I heard you sometimes employ the children of the city here."

"Aye, that I do, keeps the little bastards busy for the most part. Why, did one of 'em take something of yours?"

"No, nothing like that, I'm merely here to ask questions involving an investigation."

Nel looked Victor up and down before calling out, "Pike, get out here." Soon two boys emerged from around the corner covered in dirt and sawdust. "Alright, boys, this man has a few questions for you, answer 'em so he can be on his way."

Victor sat down on a log, "Have any of you lads noticed any new children in town within the last moon or so? A girl, perhaps."

The two boys glanced back and forth to each other, "Sorry, Sir, we haven't noticed anyone like that," said Pike.

Nel raised an eyebrow, "You sure, boy?"

"Yes, Sir."

"What about you, young lad?" Victor said to the other boy.

"No need to question that one, boy's a mute. Hasn't spoken a word since he got here," said Nel gesturing to the other side of the mill, "There's a few other boys on the other side around, if ya want to talk to 'em."

"Yes, thank you," said Victor as he stood up and walked forward around the lumber mill.

When Victor had turned the corner to the mill, Nel looked down at the boys, "Pike, what you boys do is your own business, but try not to bring trouble to my doorstep."

"But we didn't bring him here."

"Maybe not, but you did lie to me, didn't you?" Pike dropped his head, ashamed. "I've known you long enough to know when you're not being honest with me. I won't ask what you know or what he means to do. Just be careful. Nothing good has ever come from people like him showing up here asking questions." Nel nodded them away, "Alright, now get back to work," and the two boys ran off.

Victor asked the boys on the other side of the mill about the girl that might have appeared recently, but they all denied knowledge of such a girl. He could tell some were lying, which was to be expected. He understood that, no kid wants to rat out a friend. But it was the way that Pike turned to the mute boy. It was as if he was asking for permission. It was that look that interested him. Surely the boy must know something. Victor decided to wait until the boy left work and follow him.

Hours later, the boys all began leaving the lumber yard. The mute boy left for the streets of Lowtown with Victor trying to blend in behind him. The boy took a few back alleys, but Victor managed to keep him in sight, and watched as he made a few stops. First, a bakery, then another place with a few other kids, and then down the street into another small alley. Victor waited until the boy took a right before he followed behind him. He walked into the alley, making his way to where the boy turned right and peered around the corner, trying to catch a glimpse of the boy. And instead of a glimpse, he saw the boy right in front of him, staring into his eyes.

"Fuck, I was never any good at following people," said Victor, "I bet Dekol would be laughing at me right now. Outsmarted by a child."

The boy just stared at Victor, not saying a word.

"Okay, I get it, I'm caught." Victor tossed up his hands, walking over to the side of a building, and sat on a wooden crate. "Alright, there's no use lying now, so let me explain. That alright with you?"

The boy shrugged his shoulders.

"Okay, I'm on a mission from the king to find a girl who was with Duke Richards the night his manor burned down, but she apparently escaped during the fire. I assume you know her."

The boy smiled.

"Well at least I was right on that I guess," said Victor to himself and glanced back to the boy, "Tell her my name is Victor Kr... goddess help me, I'm telling a mute boy to tell someone my name." he reached into his coat. "And, of course, I have no parchment." he dropped his head, "The best-laid plan falls apart because the witness can't speak."

The boy picked up a stick and began drawing in the dirt, and to Victor's surprise, he saw that the boy had spelled his name. Granted, it was with a *K* instead of a *C*, but it was his name none the less.

"You can read?" asked Victor in amazement, "Oh... ah, I just want to talk to her, please tell her I mean her no harm."

"Well, that's good to hear, Mr. We'll be sure to pass the message along," said a child's voice from above him.

Victor glanced up to see a boy on the ledge above him, bouncing a large stone in his hand. He noticed that it was one of the boys he saw the mute boy with previously. "Am I really that bad at tailing someone?"

The boy smiled, "Yep, you're bad. I've seen old ladies who do it better."

The sound of giggles echoed in the narrow alley, and suddenly, children started emerging from all different places.

"Can you get off now?" asked a voice from below Victor. He stood up, and a small girl popped out from under the crate he was sitting on.

"I suppose you all look out for each other here?" asked Victor chuckling with a smile on his face.

"Aye, we do. If you'd tried to hurt Billy, we'd have pelt ya with rocks," said the boy above Victor as he continued bouncing the large stone in his hand.

"I was gonna poke your bum with this," said the little girl from the crate as she revealed a sharp piece of metal.

More giggling came from the children as Victor nodded and bowed to the little girl. "Well, my humble bum truly appreciates that my lady."

Victor turned back around and saw that the mute boy had vanished. With a quick glance, he could find no trace of him, "Goddess, he's like a mini Dekol. I've really gotta get better at this." Victor then scratched the top of his head, inspecting all the children who were still smiling at him. "Well, technically, I think I've accomplished my mission." Victor turned to the boy above him with the large stone. "What's your name, lad?"

"Drebbel, is what everyone calls me here," said the boy as he lowered himself down onto some crates, before jumping to the ground.

"Well Drebbel, since I've done what I came here to do, you guys want to get something to eat?"

Drebbel raised an eyebrow at the statement, and Victor led the children out of the alley and into a tavern. Soon Victor was surrounded by children at a table filled with food.

Victor looked down at Drebbel, sitting next to him at a table, watching the boy stuff his face with food. "I'm grateful and all, but what made you trust me, instead of pelting me with those rocks earlier?"

Drebbel scarfed down a piece of meat, "Becooose, usoooally," he swallowed "if they want one of us, they just take us away. No one ever tries to talk to us. It's always, *'Come `ere boy or come `ere girl.'*"

"Do they do that often down here?"

"Not really. Sometimes for the girls, if they older, not so much for us boys though," said Drebbel as he swallowed some water.

Victor smirked as he watched all the children around the table, laugh and giggle with their mouths full, "I only see two girls, where are the rest?"

"Broderick gets most of the girls before the other adults can, there at his place, probably?"

"Broderick huh, who's he?"

"He owns the whore house by the gate. But he's not a bad man or anything; he just makes the girls work. Cleaning floors and cooking and what not. He's like you; he talks to us. He even paid to fix Groggy's leg when he fell."

"Sounds like quite a man," said Victor as he waved over

a waitress, "How much is all this?"

"One gold, twelve silver, Sir."

Victor reached to his side and pulled out a jingling bag, he then pulled out two gold pieces and placed them in the waitress's hand, "Bring a round of fish for them as well if you would."

The waitress took the gold and smiled, "Yes, Sir."

Victor placed the pouch back at his side and noticed Drebbel eyeing it, "Eyes off the gold, I doubt you want to be stealing from the crown." Victor playfully shook Drebbel's head and grabbed a piece of meat for himself.

After eating, Victor walked out of the tavern as the children all ran off in different directions with full bellies. He then turned to Drebbel, who was smiling and patting his stomach, "Know any good place to shack up for the night, where people won't try to rob and or kill me?"

Drebbel was silent as he thought, "The Goldfish is where all the rich people stay when they come to town."

"The Goldfish it is then. Okay, if the girl decides to see me, tell the boy that he can contact me there," he wished Drebbel well, as the boy ran off with the other kids. Victor then turned and began making his way back towards the magistrate's home. After entering Hightown, he encountered Frenka and Dekol outside of a house as they were talking to a servant.

"You two have any luck?" asked Victor.

"None yet," said Frenka, "people say Richards had no company. And wife stay locked inside room for days. Then guards attacked, and fire happened."

"But the story is weird. Why did the wife lock herself in the bedroom? Some claimed to have heard weird noises as they passed by a room a night. What about you, did you find anything?" asked Dekol.

"I'm not sure yet, I found some kids who might know where she is. But nothing certain yet. Apparently, there's a guy named Broderick who seems to collect the little girls of this town."

"That sounds sick," said Frenka as she grimaced.

"That's what I thought also, but the kids who know him all claim he's a good guy."

"And so, hunt continues then?"

"I don't think the hunt will ever end. Between warring kingdoms and hunting for little girls, I'm starting to wonder what's the point of it all."

The three began walking off up a hill when Frenka noticed Victor slowing down and staring off into the distance.

"What wrong, Victor? You look bothered?" asked Frenka.

Victor stopped and turned around peering over the city "There's another place I should probably check before it gets dark, you two can head back to the magistrates if you like. I shouldn't be long." Dekol and Frenka glanced at each other and then walked back to Victor.

"We are here to help on this," said Frenka. "So, no fair leaving us out. You should rely on us more."

Victor smirked, "Sorry, I'm not used to this whole three-man team thing."

Frenka raised a brow, "You mean two-man and woman thing. Do not group me with Victor and Dekol's silly sex."

Victor chuckled, "Fair enough. When I was at the capitol, I was told that the wine merchant here was friends with Duke Richards, so it's probably a good idea to go check out his storage warehouse. Plus, I was told that he hired a few kids from town."

"Then let's go," said Dekol as he stared into the sky, "We still have some time before sunset."

They walked off again as Victor continued to think of all the information he had on the girl, but was unconsciously walking at a slower pace than usual. Frenka noticed him rubbing his chin, mumbling to himself, and walked back to him, wrapping her arm around his.

The physical contact woke Victor up from his thoughts

as he looked over to see Frenka, who was wagging her finger at him.

"Victor think too much, should learn to embrace life and act in moment."

"Even if half of those moments are people trying to kill us," said Victor, allowing himself to be dragged along by the dark-haired woman.

"Exactly, me and Dekol have learned that even if we must protect stupid prince. He can't be stupid prince all time. Only half time, so I decided to live a full life in that other half. It has worked very well over years."

"I'm starting to wonder which one of us has the most depressing outlook on life," said Victor as he just stared at Frenka shaking his head.

"Why choose? You have stupid Queen, and I have stupid prince, and they both be pain in asses until we die, or they hopefully get us killed."

Victor couldn't help but laugh as the three continued to make their way through Hightown, occasionally stopping to ask for directions to the Goose's warehouse.

A little while later they arrived at the warehouse in Hightown as men were loading wine barrels onto a wagon, while a portly man watched over them. The warehouse was the largest out of all the nearby buildings and was made entirely of stone with wooden support beams throughout the building.

The portly man watched another barrel being loaded when he noticed Victor and crew walking towards him.

"Hello there, do you have any business here?" asked the portly man.

"Yes, we're trying to find who's in charge here," said Victor.

The man noticed Frenka and Dekol's uniforms and took a step back, "I'm in charge here; why would you be searching for me."

"Ah, so you would be the Goose then, I was told that

you hire children to work down here sometimes, we'd like to speak with them about a girl that has gone missing. Victor turned, glancing inside the warehouse, seeing two small boys rolling a barrel on the ground from one place to another."

"Ah... ah... yes, I'm Freddo Ball, but people call me the Goose. But we don't hire girls here, only strapping young lads who can handle the work."

"Tell me something, Mr. Goose; I was told that you were friends with the late Duke Richards, is that true?"

"I... I... well... yes, that is true... but I mean... we didn't... we had nothing to do with that mess."

Victor began walking inside the warehouse with the Goose, Frenka, and Dekol trailing behind. The air was damp and chilly inside, much cooler than the streets. And he could see traces of spilled wine scattered throughout the floor of the warehouse. Victor was impressed by the sheer amount of volume the man had managed to accumulate. There were three levels of wine barrels stretched throughout the warehouse. And from the moment he entered, he could smell the scent of several different types of wines in the air. All of them, mixing their scents together to form a wonderful aroma. So much so that his mouth began to water with every breath he took.

"You must do fairly well, Mr. Goose, this is quite a large collection of goods you have managed to get a hold of," said Victor as he continued around the warehouse.

"Ah... yes, my family has been in the wine business for the past two hundred years. We have a collection of vineyards throughout the local area that supply us."

Victor watched as several boys shuffled back and forth throughout the building, moving from one area to the next with different items. They all wore ragged clothing, and many wore hats. Some were carrying small wooden planks that were meant for wine barrels; others were carrying tools to some of the larger men. But the one that caught

Victor's attention was one of the two boys over in a corner painting the Goose's logo on some freshly made barrels over in a corner. They wore rags like all the rest and had on hats, but the boy's hat on the left seemed newer and bigger than the rest of the boys that he noticed running around and through the building.

"How many boys do you have working today," said Victor as he made his way forward, still looking around.

"I... uh... think a little more than ten, they're good for small jobs and don't cost that much," said the Goose as he pulled out a small handkerchief and began dabbing at the sweat that was starting to appear on his face.

"And if I heard you correctly, you said you don't hire girls." Victor stopped behind the small boy in the big hat. He tilted his head down and noticed that the boy was trying to hide his right hand. But Victor could see it poking out of his sleeve. The skin was disfigured, and more than likely covered more than just his hand.

"Well... I... mean, I usually don't..."

Victor lifted the hat off the child as their long flowing brown hair fell out and dangled down to her back. Victor looked down into the face of a petite girl, "Well hello there, honey, what's your name."

The child was indeed a girl as she stared back up at Victor and over to the Goose with her eyes starting to water. The Goose sighed and extended his hand to the child, who quickly ran over to him and took it.

"She's... she's mine, the bastard daughter of one of my lovers. I'm quite the ladies' man around town, you see," said the Goose as sweat dripped down his face.

"And how did she get that burn mark across her hand?" asked Victor.

The Goose scratched his neck nervously, "Why...why... she was cooking with her mother, that's how it happened. Children are always prone to getting into messes, you see, and this one is no different."

Victor shook his head at the portly man, noticing his round features in very sharp contrast to the thin little girl beside him, "You're a terrible liar, Mr. Goose, anyone with eyes would know that's not your daughter, just by the sight of you two together."

The Goose sighed, "My wife said the same." He then turned to Victor with stern eyes, "Are you going to turn us in?"

Frenka frowned at the overweight man and the girl, "Orders are orders, Victor. We have to take girl if she one we need. But she seem different from image I remember."

Victor looked at the portly man and the little girl clinging to his side and scratched the top of his head, pitying the two, "No, we're not turning you in, but if my assumption is correct, I will have to take the girl." Victor reached into one of his pouches strapped across his chest and pulled out the alagon dust and poured some into his palm, walking over to them. "I'm trying to find a brown-haired girl, but she doesn't appear to be who I'm searching for. Did you cast any magic on her to change her appearance?"

"What? No, I'm no mage."

Victor sprinkled some of the dust on the girl's shoulders and head as she stiffened, holding on to the Goose's hand, shutting her eyes.

Victor stood back and watched the girl's face, waiting for her appearance to change. But he noticed that after a few seconds that nothing happened. Victor smiled, "Okay then, seems she's not the girl I'm here to find."

The Goose sighed and squeezed the girls hand, "So... you're really not going to turn us in after all?"

Victor shrugged, "For what? All I see is a father trying to take care of his daughter. And quite frankly, that's none of my business. But I would suggest that you get the girl out of the city. If someone is searching for her, eventually they will make their way here, and I doubt those rags and that hat are going to keep fooling people forever."

The Goose looked down at the girl smiling and then back to Victor, "Yes, Sir, we've already found a safe place for her, we're just waiting for her to be accepted."

Victor nodded, "Well, I'll be on my way then, I still have work to do. I wish you both well on the path you've chosen."

Victor turned to leave but felt someone grab his fingers. Glancing back, he was surprised to see the little girl holding onto him with her scarred hand.

"Thank you," she said as she stared up at him.

Victor smiled back at her. "Be safe out there," he said while patting her on the head, knocking off some of the alagon dust.

And then Victor left the warehouse with Dekol and Frenka beside him.

"Do you know who she is?" asked Frenka as they walked back down the streets of Hightown.

"She's his daughter, didn't he say so?" asked Victor with a knowing grin across his face.

Frenka narrowed her eyes at Victor, "No fair, hiding things from us."

"Hey, you're the one who said I think too much. So why not both of us just try and live in the moment."

CHAPTER 14

Moonlight shone through the window upstairs into the room the girls slept in. Rana laid in the bed, watching the cracks in the wood of the ceiling, thinking about what she was going to do about the magistrate's son.

I have to leave. I have to go somewhere. But maybe if I go with him, he might know where Green Village is. No, they just want me as a whore. I can't just—

The door opened, and Miraval walked into the room,

she tried to be quiet, but the wood creaked under her feet with every step. Rana rolled over in the bed, smushing her face into the pillow.

"Rana, are you okay?"

"I'm fine," said Rana's muffled voice from beneath the pillow.

"Do people who are fine just stay in their room all day with their heads buried in pillows and not talk to anyone?"

Rana lifted her face, "Fine, I'm not fine. It's just... it's not fair."

"What's not fair?"

Rana threw her hands in the air gesturing at the room, "This, all of it, I'm to be a maid or a whore, or probably both, the way that manor lord looks at me. He keeps grabbing my hand and rubbing it when Broderick takes me to see him."

"So, you mean being a girl with no money or family isn't fair? Oh, is that why you been playing with knives, do you mean to kill him?" asked Miraval excitedly with her eyes filled with the joys of a potential scandal.

"What? No, I just want to be able to protect myself, like papa. And If I can do that, then no one would be able to make me do anything I don't wanna do."

"That sounds like a nice dream."

"But it doesn't have to be, we can—"

"Rana stop," said Miraval as she raised her hand, "Not everyone wants some crazy life like you. And the ones that do..." She paused and caught her words before her eyes seemed to accept what she was about to say, "The ones that do end up like Angela." Miraval pointed to her face. "The scar on Angela's face that no one talks about. Well, now I will talk about it. Angela was supposed to be a maid for some noble a few years ago. But she tried to run away for a better life, just like you want to do. Broderick found her some days after. Said men had took her, beat her, cut her, and raped her again and again. She said they held her down and took turns. And when the nobleman came for her and

206

saw her face, he didn't want her anymore. He took another girl, and now Angela is stuck here in the kitchen, or getting grabbed on every time she delivers some food."

Rana sat up on the bed. "I... I didn't know."

Miraval pointed her finger at Rana, "Of course not, you never asked us. We all try really hard when Broody shows us off to them nobles. But you always say, I don't wanna be a whore. You think we don't know what happens to some of the girls Broody turns into maids? Some become normal maids or mistresses. But that's still better than my daddy beating on me every day for dropping the water or not cleaning fast enough, or being locked up in some cage while people come by squeezing us and checking to see if we got all our teeth like it was for Pelly. I understand you want to be strong and a warrior, but not all of us want that. Most of us just want to be safe and not some crazy warrior maiden from the fairy tales."

"Hey girls, get down here, the kitchen needs help." came Tabby's voice from downstairs.

The girls looked at each other, and Mirava headed for the door with Rana slowly trailing behind. Miraval stopped in the doorframe and turned back to Rana. "Rana, I'm sorry for saying that, but you need to think about how we feel. Tabby said Broody found you trying to sleep in the stables. Can't you think about what would have happened to you or to any of us if Broody wouldn't have taken us in? My daddy would still be beating me, or Pelly still locked in that cage, or we'd be dead. We all know it's not the best life, but it's the best we probably gonna get. So at least try to think of the trouble you cause us when Broody is trying to find us nice homes."

"I... I didn't mean to make it sound that way," said Rana with her head hung low.

"I know you didn't, but not everyone wants to run away from here. For most of us, this is the only place we have that's safe to run to. We ain't got nowhere else." Miraval walked back to Rana, grabbing her hand, "Come on, let's see what Tabby wants," and they headed out the door together.

Walking out onto the balcony of the tavern, they stared down at the lower floor. It was now filled with people. Looking ahead, they saw the usual crowd of black jewels members, but along with them were some of the soldiers in dark uniforms that Rana saw earlier that day. Many of the girls had already started flirting with the uniformed men, expecting to make a profit from the night's services. Rana started walking down in shock at the sight of the uniformed men.

No ones gonna help. I'm stuck here.

Miraval tried to call out to her.

Why... why is this happening. What can I do. I don't have anything.

Miraval tugged on her arm, "Rana, what's wrong?"

"Huh?"

"What's wrong? Come on. Let's go see what Tabby wants."

"Oh... ah... yeah," said Rana as she allowed Miraval to guide her downstairs into the kitchen. The scent of fresh stew was in the air as they entered, and Rana saw Pelly and the rest of the girls already at work.

Tabby was stirring a pot when she saw the girls enter, "Okay, girls, put on your aprons, we got a large crowd tonight. And Rana, do try to handle yourself well, okay. I'm sure that captain's out there tonight."

Rana nodded as Miraval tossed an apron over her head, turning her around, tying it behind her back.

"Rana, take that fish stew out to table six," said Tabby as she began to drop more vegetables into a large cooking pot.

Rana grabbed the plate and made her way back out into the tavern, through the crowd placing the wooden saucer on the table.

"Three cheers for the captain, he sure knows how to treat his men right," said a soldier swinging his mug of ale through the air, while squeezing the breast of a woman in his lap.

"Right, although this one's still a little small to do a man right," the soldier said as he gave Rana a hard slap on her bottom, that sent her skipping forward trying to catch her balance. Rana didn't get mad; she just looked at the man sadly and walked back into the kitchen.

"What's wrong Ronnie, trying to find a woman to match that cock you got? I think even that one might be too big for ya," said another soldier with Halva sitting on his lap.

The men of the room started laughing.

"Well, what about that one with the scarred mug, do I get a discount if I plow her?" Ronnie said as he grabbed Angela and forced her on his lap. "Come `ere darling, how about a little kiss." The man tried to rummage his fingers up her skirt as Angela struggled to free herself.

Rana found herself moving back towards Angela about to try and help, but just stopped and watched as Angela struggled as she thought about what Tabby and Miraval had said. Seconds later, Broderick snatched Angela out of the man's lap.

"Sorry, Sir, this one happens to be my family. So sadly, she's not on the menu for you," said Broderick as he sent Angela running back into the kitchen past Rana.

"Ah, come on, I was just having fun," said the man, whining.

"There's plenty of other fun to be had, I can assure you, Sir," said Broderick as two other girls came to the man and started rubbing on him.

Broderick made his way back to the bar, where another man was sitting having an ale.

"You seem used to handling these types of men," said the man in average clothing as he took a sip of ale and tilted the empty mug for Broderick to see.

"Bah, they're just men trying to work off some steam, they'll be good and sensible after a night's romp. What about you? You hoping for a girl for the night?" asked Broderick as he refilled the man's cup.

The man turned back, smiling at the uniformed men, "For the night? No, but a particular servant girl, that's why I'm here."

Broderick thought for a second and gave a smirk, "You must be the magistrate's boy, I was wondering when you'd get here. Why ya not in uniform like the rest of 'em?"

"I'm home for the first time in years; surely, you wouldn't blame a man who would prefer to wear normal clothes during his homecoming."

"Right, well, I imagine you're here to inspect the brat, follow me then," said Broderick as he walked out from behind the bar and looked over to Rana, who was about to grab a mug off the counter. "Rana, you come with me," he said, as he headed into a back room with Cardon. The two men sat down at a table, and Rana followed in behind them shortly afterward.

"Close the door," said Broderick, and Rana did as he said. "Now come here. I want you to meet someone."

Rana slowly walked forward as the man turned to greet her, "You're the magistrate's son?"

"That is correct, how did you know," said Cardon.

"I saw you ride in with those men today."

"I guess we did attract some attention. Do you know why I'm here?"

"I'm to become your maid, at the military base," said Rana with her head down rubbing at her fingers. Broderick tilted his head over at her noticing that she was being unusually timid this time.

"That's right, so is there anything you want to know beforehand?" asked Cardon.

Rana stayed silent for a second before raising her head to ask a question. But stopped herself and dropped her head again, "No, Sir, I understand I'm to wash your clothes and cook for you."

210

Broderick leaned his elbow on the table with an eyebrow raised at Rana, "What's wrong with you? I thought you were excited to ask him to become a fighter or something. Like you did with the magistrate."

Cardon blinked in shock at Broderick's words, "A fighter?" He then turned to Rana, "Sorry dear, we don't teach girls to fight in camp unless they have some type of magic, and even then."

Rana's heart broke as she stood there, hearing the man's words. She tried holding back her tears as she clenched the front of her apron in her hands. She began moving her head back and forth and took a deep breath before looking back up to face the men.

"Can I... can I go back to the kitchen now, Mr. Broderick, Sir?"

Broderick bit his lip as he saw the pained expression on her face and her eyes that seemed to have tears just barely holding on at the bottom of her eyelids.

"Go on then, take a break for a while. Come back when you're done."

"Th... thank you, Sir," said Rana as her lips began to quiver. She turned away from the men as the tears slowly began to fall from her face and opened the door, exiting the room. After pulling the door closed, her emotions finally took over her as she took off running through the kitchen, past Tabby, who was hitting Jasper with a spoon. She ran out the back door and into the darkness at the back of the tavern.

A few seconds later, Jasper walked out of the back of the tavern with some bread in his hand, "Hey muffin, where'd ya go," he said softly into the night. Jasper closed his eyes and listened to the sounds that came from the darkness. In between the sounds of a dog howling at the moon and the insects singing their songs into blackness, he heard the whimpers of a crying girl coming from the stables. Walking over, he found Rana crying into the hay and began to make a joke. But after seeing her, he instead just walked into the stables and sat down beside her. Jasper slowly wrapped his arms around Rana, pulled her into his arms, laid her head on his chest, and allowed the little girl to cry as long as she needed.

Eventually, Rana lifted herself from Jasper's chest, looking up at him, "I... I'm sorry."

Jasper smiled down at her while rubbing her hair. "For what? I make women cry all the time; it's kind of a matter of course at this point." He wiped the remaining tears from Rana's eyes, "Now come on muffin, tell good ol' uncle Jasper what's wrong."

Rana gazed up into Jasper's smiling face trying to think.

Jasper patted her on the back, looking around the stables, "Don't worry. Good old uncle Jasper knows how to keep a secret. I promise that no matter what you tell me, it'll stay between you and me." They both heard a dog howling at the moon again. "And that dog, but dogs are loyal, so you ain't gotta worry about them so much."

Suddenly, all the weight of the past month hit Rana's heart as she laid her head back down on Jasper's chest. "Everything's all wrong; I miss papa and everyone from home. I don't wanna be here anymore. I don't understand why I'm here; I don't understand why the bandits came. I don't understand anything; I just wanna go home. Why can't I go home?"

Jasper held the little girl to his chest, patting her head again, "It's gonna be okay now. Let it all out. Tell uncle Jasper where home is."

Rana sniffed and rubbed her tears into Jasper's shirt, "We had a little house in Green Village back in Drinland and..." Rana felt Jasper's hand slide off the back of her head. She looked up to see Jasper squinting his eyes down at her. "What's wrong? Did I..."

"Did you say, Drinland?"

Rana nodded, "Yes, why? Is it... is it far from here?"

"Honey... that's leagues away; we'd have to cross the seas even to get close to it. And even then, we're talking months."

Rana started shaking her head, "No, I was there before I came here. I fell into the water, and I woke up here."

Jasper started rubbing his head, "Well, either way, it's going to be damn near impossible to get you home from here. Do you think your papa's still out there trying to find you?"

"I don't know. I mean... I hope he is, but I don't know how to find him. I'm stuck here, and soon I'll be off at someplace with the magistrate's son."

"Oh, that parts easy to deal with," said Jasper with a chuckle.

"What, really? How?" asked Rana as she pushed herself up, staring back at Jasper.

Jasper poked her nose with his finger, "The answer is simple. Me, and you should run away together."

Rana rubbed at her eyes again and stared at Jasper as if he went crazy, "What?"

Jasper threw his hands out, "We should run away, let's hop on a horse and ride away from everyone. We'll live off the land, eat with fairies, and do little dances to celebrate our new found freedom." He bobbed his head while waving his hands in an imitation of a dance.

Rana giggled at his silly expressions despite herself.

"There we go, nothing better than a smiling muffin. Now, are you feeling better and ready to run away?"

Rana lifted herself from Jasper, stumbling in the hay. "You're a silly person, Mr. Jasper."

Jasper waved his finger, "Nope, nope, if you want me to become your knight in shining armour, you must refer to me as uncle Jasper; otherwise, us running away together starts sounding a bit weird. People might think that I'm as depraved as that magistrate who has that stupid statue of himself in town. So, you must ask uncle Jasper for help when you need it, then I shall swoop in like a real hero."

Rana laughed, "Okay, okay, I'll call you uncle Jasper."

"Now there's some sweet words to my ears," said Jasper as he lifted himself up. A book fell out of his shirt and landed on the hay. "Oh, my book. Can't let that run away from me." He reached down and picked it up, slapping at the loose hay that had attached itself to it.

"What's that?" asked Rana.

Jasper finished shaking hay from between the pages of his little book, "Oh, this is my book of secrets. I write down everything that's interesting or that I plan to do inside of here. It's filled with the mysteries of all the kingdoms. When it's finished, I plan to sell it and make a tidy profit." He looked down at Rana, "speaking of which." Jasper reached into his pocket and pulled out a piece of charcoal and started writing in the book.

Rana tilted her head, squinting her eyes suspiciously at him. "What are you writing?"

Jasper finished writing and placed the book back into his shirt. "My next mission, of course. Now come along, let's get you back inside before we both get in trouble. Tabby can be evil when she don't get her way." Jasper reached his hand out for Rana to grab, and she took it squeezing his fingers. "That's a good muffin, now remember, you gotta be a brave girl for a few days till I can take care of a few things, but soon I'll come get you, and we'll run away together to live with the fairies."

Rana and Jasper walked back into the tavern holding hands. She really did feel better. Even though she knew he was lying to her, it didn't matter. He sat there and listened to her cry and complain and because of that, it felt like a lot of weight she had been holding inside of her had been lifted.

As the two entered the kitchen, suddenly, a crash was heard inside. Both of them peaked their heads out of the kitchen and saw that a brawl had broken out between some of the black jewels and the captain's men. Fists were flying as men from both sides cheered each other on.

"What the hell is going on here?" asked the captain as he exited the room with Broderick behind him.

"Hey Captain, Baylon challenged some rat to a scrub, we're taking bets on who'll be the winner."

Broderick noticed that the men that were fighting had broken a table and two chairs in their struggle against each other. "I'll be adding the damages to the bill for the girl," said Broderick to Cardon.

Cardon chuckled and nodded to the two brawling men, "You know the man my boy's fighting with?"

"Yeah that's Prat; he's a tough bastard. Gets into fights down at the mill a lot."

"Care to make a wager on this?"

"What ya have in mind?"

"My man wins, then the food and the girls are free, that Prat of yours wins, I pay double for the girl."

Broderick considered, but shook his head, "The girls make their own money. I won't gamble that. Smaller wager, your boy wins, and you don't have to pay for the furniture, Prat there wins and ya cough up six gold pieces."

"Accepted," said Cardon as he yelled out, "Baylon, you shit for brains. I swear if you lose this fight, you'll be clearing shit ditches for a month."

Broderick frowned at Cardon, and Cardon grinned back at him, "What? It's a captain's job to give his men proper motivation."

The two men squared off again. Prat kicked at Baylon, but Baylon dodged, only to catch a left fist to the right side of his face instead. He stumbled back, stabilizing himself off his right leg and focused again on Prat just to see the big man charging at him. Baylon jumped up, kneeing Prat in the face and making him stumble backwards. Prat gritted his teeth and squinted his eyes. Baylon clapped both hands together and brought them up under Prat's jaw, sending the man stumbling back once again and falling over onto a table and passing out. The men in uniform cheered as Baylon grabbed his sides in pain, breathing heavily as blood leaked out of his nose.

"Goddess that fucker was tough; it was like hitting bricks with me hands," said Baylon as his buddies started patting him on the back, congratulating him.

Cardon walked over, "Alright, let's go, Baylon, time to go get you patched up. You did a good job tonight."

"But Captain, what about the girls?" Baylon whined as he looked at the other men celebrating with women around their arms.

"Seems to me like you've already gotten fucked over once tonight, no need to go in for a second round," said Cardon as he patted Baylon on the back. "Come on, up ya go" and threw the soldier's arm over his shoulder, walking with him to the tavern doors.

"I'll fuck twice as hard in your honor Baylon," shouted one man as Cardon and Baylon left the tavern with the sounds of laughter following behind them.

Broderick walked over, shaking his head at Prat, who was passed out on his broken table. He grabbed some ale off a nearby table and splashed it in Prat's face. But the man stayed knocked out. "Alright well, drag his ass over to a corner somewhere, can't just leave 'em in the middle of the floor like this. When he wakes up, tell 'em to fix my damn table." Broderick turned back around and saw Rana staring. "And you, get back to work. Until you're paid for, you still gotta earn your keep round here."

Rana went back into the kitchen and reached for another plate but noticed Tabby leaning out the door, talking to someone. She leaned back and called to Rana. "Rana baby, that girl named Maggie is outback with a boy, waiting for you," said Tabby. "Go see what they want and come back, we still gotta feed them boys out there when they done cleaning up after Prat."

Rana walked towards the back of the kitchen and peeked out the door, seeing Maggie and Billy standing outside.

"What are you two doing down here?" asked Rana as she stepped back out the door.

"We're waiting on you, what else? Billy here said that..." Maggie stepped forward and placed her hand on Rana's face, "You've been crying, your cheeks are flushed, and you got them eyes all red."

Rana began rubbing at her eyes, "It's okay; it's nothing."

Maggie narrowed her eyes at Rana.

"Really, it's nothing, I promise. What did you say about Billy?"

Maggie stepped back, "Okay, if you say so, Billy told me that a man's been looking for you, and he wants to meet you."

"Meet me? What, man?"

"Don't know, just said he wanted to talk with you."

"And you brought him here," said Rana glancing around into the shadows.

"Of course not, Billy lost 'em. But Billy thinks he's a good man and wasn't lying. And he's better than me at knowing if someone is good or not. Oh, and get this, he said he was from the kingdom," Maggie said with a suspicious face. "Rana you some important lady and not telling us?"

"I don't wanna meet anyone from the kingdom," said Rana quickly in response.

Maggie seemed disappointed, "Alright, it's your decision, but Billy said he was a good man, and Billy's never wrong about these things." Maggie pushed Billy. "Come on, Billy; we gotta get back before the Doc starts to worry."

Rana started to think as they began to leave, "Wait."

Maggie and Billy stopped, "Rana you okay, I figured you'd be glad to meet someone wanting to get you from out of here."

"I am... it's just... I mean, are you sure he's a good person? Papa always told me not to trust noble people."

Maggie smiled, "That's what Billy thinks, and I've never known him to be wrong on anything when he's made up his mind. Plus, we can just run away if we need to."

Rana heard the sounds of the uniformed men inside as they started to sing. She dropped her head sighing before staring up at the stars in the sky, "Well, I guess it can't hurt anything now. If you guys think it's okay, then I'll meet him."

Maggie patted Billy on the back joyously, "I knew you'd want to meet him. Don't worry; I know just the spot. Just leave everything to me. Let's go, Billy," 'said Maggie as Billy waved at Rana, and they disappeared around the corner.

Rana went back inside the tavern.

"You done talking to your little friends?" asked Tabby.

Rana nodded.

"Well then, back to work, I swear these boys hungrier than pigs."

CHAPTER 15

Maggie and Billy passed by the gates of Hightown, just in time to see the doctor with his key in the door and his medical bag in hand. He waved at them as they approached through the torch-lit streets.

"Oh, there you two are; I was starting to get worried. I know you're both from the streets here, and don't worry about bad things happening to you, but that doesn't mean that I won't worry about you," said the doctor.

"I'm sorry, we were just visiting Rana, is all. We probably

should have told you where we were going. I still haven't gotten used to having somebody looking after me. Usually, it's me that does the looking after," said Maggie dropping her head.

The doctor placed his hand on her shoulder, "Well that's fine as long as you understand. I mean, it's not like I'm used to having someone around that I start worrying about. Usually, I just treat the patients and send them home. So how bout we both just take our time and figure things out as we go. I imagine we both still have a lot to get used to."

"Okay, that's a deal. What'cha got that for? Another patient out of town?" asked Maggie, pointing to the Doc's medical bag.

"Oh, that's right, I was summoned to the magistrate's home to treat a patient. Would you two like to come along?"

"Of course, let's go," she said smiling, as she walked forward, grabbing the doctor's hand. All three of them walked up the dark street of Hightown.

A little while later, they arrived at the gate to the magistrate's manor.

"Hello, doctor," said Willow.

"Hey, Willow, where's the patient."

"He's inside; dumb fella got into a brawl with Prat from the mil. He's messed up something bad."

Willow ushered them inside to see a bare-chested man with half his face starting to swell lying down on a table. Willow walked over and opened the drapes allowing the moonlight to shine into the room over the unconscious man's body.

As Maggie walked into the room, she couldn't help but breathe in deep. The room smelled fresh and clean, unlike the streets of Hightown, or even the doctor's home. Everything smelled so fresh; the room was decorated in lush dark blue furniture with carved wooden seats. She even saw two bookshelves on either side of the window that Willow opened. A large carpet spread out throughout the room and was much more beautiful than what even the doctor had.

"I gave him some night essence to ease the pain, but that will only do so much," said Willow.

"You did fine. I will give him a look over," said the doctor as he began to feel his way across the man's rib cage, "Okay, he's got two cracked ribs. Swelling from repeated blunt trauma," then he turned to Willow. "You said he was in a fight with Prat, well this is his work alright, I've treated a few of his victims. He's left-handed, so he tends to use it a lot when fighting, and the right side of this man's face has surely seen some better days. Billy hand me my bag, please." Billy walked over and lifted the bag in his arms for the doctor to take. The doctor lifted the bag and placed it beside him, taking out five vials and laid them across on the table. "Okay, Maggie, which one is used to stop swelling?"

Maggie looked at the vials, picking each one up and trying to pronounce the words scribbled on them. "Su. Su. Sujune, Ara...Aramont, Lil...ly, ah! I know it's Lilly Oil."

"That's correct." He pulled a chair over and lifted Maggie into it, having her stand on the cushion. "Okay, now put a small amount of the oil on your fingers and rub them over the swollen area."

"Should you not be doing this yourself, doctor?" asked Willow with a concerned look on his face.

"Don't worry; he simply has some mild trauma, all fairly simple to treat. He's actually the perfect subject to train on since there's no real threat to his life." The doctor turned back to Maggie. "Oh! No need to apply too much, just a small amount will have the desired effect." He grabbed Maggie's hand, pulling out a cloth from his jacket. He wiped the oil from her fingers. "Okay, now, place your hand here," The Doctor guided Maggie's hand along the man's mid-torso. "This is the rib cage, now listen to the man's breathing habits."

Maggie allowed the doctor to guide her hands along the man's rib cage. Every time they applied pressure to a particular spot, she could feel the vibrations as his body began to tremble from his labored breathing.

"See, right there, that's an indication of either a cracked or bruised rib," The doctor grabbed his bag and set it down on the floor in front of Billy, "Now it's your turn, Billy. Show me which medicine we use to promote bone healing." Billy opened the doctor's bag, rummaging around for a few seconds, before coming out with a vial that had green powder inside of it.

"That's right, I swear, I have the smartest students," said the doctor taking the green vial from Billy and turning back to Willow, "I didn't have time to turn it into an oil. Excuse me, Mr. Willow, can I trouble you for some water and a bowl, and perhaps a spice grinder if your kitchen has one."

"Huh... oh, ah, yeah, I can get some from the kitchen."

"I'll help get it, you can't carry all of it," said Maggie, hopping down from the chair. "Where's the kitchen here?"

"Ah, right, well follow me," said Willow, making his way to the kitchen with Maggie. As they left, she heard the doctor start lecturing Billy about the medical stuff.

"Your father teaching you two to become doctors too?" asked Willow as he led Maggie down a shadowy corridor that was alight with candles on the walls. "I didn't realize the Doc had kids."

Maggie smiled and decided to play along as she walked beside Willow, "Yep, papa promised to start teaching us this year." The rest of the house smelled of old furniture and the candle wax that had fallen from the wall mounts and coated areas of the floor beneath. They usually didn't burn all the candles it seemed, as she noticed a decent amount of the candles were more than half-melted, while some others looked to have been freshly lit.

"Thats nice, my father was a hunter. He taught me how to use bows when I was a kid."

"Do you still hunt now?"

"Yeah, when I can get out of town. I got pretty good with a bow too. I like to think paw'd be proud."

"I've just started learning from papa, but he said I'll catch on quick. Gonna be as good as him one day," said Maggie as she took a turn down another hall. "Wow this place is big," she said as she looked ahead into the shadows of another corridor. Maggie stopped behind Willow only a few doors into the hallway, turned, and stepped into the kitchen. He walked toward some shelves and reached up to grab a bowl. Grabbing one, he placed it on a tray with a flagon of water. "Now where'd she put that mixing bowl?"

"I'll go ahead and take this back," said Maggie, grabbing the tray.

"Oh, ah, sure, I'll bring the mixer when I find it, try not to get lost on your way back."

"Okay," said Maggie as she shuffled back down the corridors with the tray in her hands. She remembered where to go and could easily find her way again. Compared to navigating the streets at night, one or two dark corridors weren't enough to make her start worrying. She turned the corner and knew that the doctor would be up ahead after the main hall.

"Did you know they're training that girl with knives? She honestly thinks she will become some female warrior or something," said a voice from behind a door as Maggie began to pass.

Maggie heard them and stopped. Seeing that the door was ajar a bit, she peeped in and saw a man in a chair talking to the magistrate.

"I think she did mention something like that when I was there. It doesn't matter anyway. We just need to get her out of the city before that investigator finds her," said the magistrate.

"Where is he anyway?"

"Willow said he was at the Goldfish."

"The girl's not a problem; we can use her afterward. But if the crown finds out. I'm not sure all this is worth it. Why not just give her up and be done with it?"

"You say that because you can't feel it, I can feel this power, and I've never felt anything like it. Even in the high nobility. If we can add that girl's power to our own, then perhaps we might..."

"You got lost, didn't you?" asked Willow from behind Maggie.

Maggie's body jolted from the surprise of Willow appearing being her. She almost lost control of the tray in her hands, as the flagon clanked on the saucer.

"Who's out there? Is that you Willow?" asked the magistrate's voice from inside the room.

Maggie stepped back from the door as Willow opened it, "Yes, Sir, the doctor needed a few things from the kitchen, so I went to fetch them."

"Oh, so he's arrived already. Have him visit me when Cardon's man is tended to."

"Yes, Sir," said Willow as he closed the door and looked down, smiling at Maggie. "Come on, I'll show you the way back, it's just past the main hall."

When they arrived, the doctor set Billy to stirring the medicine together in the bowl and showed Maggie how to set the oil and wrap the wound properly. Soon after that, they were finished treating the man.

The doctor wiped the sweat from his face and looked down at Maggie, "That should do it, you're still too small to bandage a man properly, it seems. Well the torso mainly, but I imagine that will change as you get older and bigger. Billy, on the other hand, is plenty strong for his age; I guess that lumber yard work is paying off. Pretty soon, you'll be stronger than me."

Billy smiled while trying to make a manly pose.

"Oh, doctor, the magistrate wished to see you after you had finished," said Willow while smiling at Billy.

"Oh, okay, well, we can go immediately if you'd like. He should be fine on his own now that he's been treated. And probably fit to travel in a few days," said the doctor to Willow as he turned to Maggie and Billy, who were putting the vials back into his bag and cleaning up. "You two wanna meet the magistrate?"

Maggie pretended to think about meeting the magistrate, but shook her head, "Nah, Willow's gonna show us how to shoot a bow."

"I am?"

"Yep, you said you were good, and I think Billy would like that."

Billy thought to himself for a moment before nodding in agreement.

"I mean, it's kinda dark, but we can shoot in the stable if ya like. There's plenty of light in there."

"Okay, let's go then," said Maggie as she dragged Willow by the arm out the room.

"Don't hurt yourselves," she heard the doctor say as they left.

Rana and Billy followed Willow outside to the stables with his bow.

"I'm surprised you want to learn; usually girls don't like bows."

"Well I don't really, but Billy seems to," said Maggie as she pointed over to Billy, who was already attempting to string the bow.

"Hey! Be careful; the Doc'll kill me if you hurt yourself. Here, you need to hold it like this," said Willow in a panic as he rushed over to Billy.

Maggie walked over and sat on a bundle of hay, laughing as Willow tried his best to teach Billy the proper way to nock an arrow.

I wonder who they were talking about. They said something about a girl. A girl with the power of them nobles. Does she just order people around?

A little while later, the doctor walked out of the manor to the stables and saw Willow trying and failing to teach Billy how to properly use a bow. He turned to Maggie, who was sitting and kicking her legs in the air.

"Is training going well?" asked the doctor.

"Well, he's got more arrows in the ground than he's got in that hay, but not bad for a first day, I think."

"Let's go, Billy," said the doctor. Billy handed the bow back to Willow, strolling back over to them. The doctor rubbed Billy's head, "Enjoyed yourself?"

Billy nodded in satisfaction.

"Well, if you want to learn, you can always come back when you're not working. That is if Mr. Willow doesn't mind."

"Oh no, I'd like that. The boy's strong and can pull the bow well enough for his age; I think he'll be a good hunter in time, just needs some training."

"You hear that Billy, you wanna try being a bowman?"

Billy smiled, nodding his head, and striking an archery pose.

"Then it's settled then. I entrust you to take care of your student Mr. Willow."

"Aye, that I will."

The doctor patted Billy on the back as the little boy waved back at Willow.

"And you little girl, listen to your father, and you'll be a good doctor in no time," said Willow as they neared the gate.

"Did he say something about a father?" asked the doctor.

Maggie laughed, dragging the doctor out the gate by the arm. "Who knows? Maybe he wants us to pray for him at the goddess's statue."

CHAPTER 16

Victor awoke to the sound of knocking at his door, "All right, hold on, I'm coming," he said as he stumbled out of the soft bed. *I finally get to sleep in a nice bed again, and of course, someone wakes me up early in the morning.* Walking to the door, he removed the ball and plank trap that he had placed earlier and opened the door. But once opened, there was no one there. He poked his head out into the Goldfish hotel hallway, searching for signs of anyone, but sure enough, it was empty, only a vase filled with flowers.

Victor rubbed his chin in confusion as he turned around to see Billy sitting on his bed, rubbing the soft pillow that Victor just had his face buried in. Victor turned back to the door and then again at Billy, confused at how the boy got past him into the room., "How'd you do that?"

Billy just sat on the edge of the bed, smiling as he started kicking his feet in the air.

"Eventually, I'm gonna find out how you do that," said Victor, closing the door. Billy clapped his hands together and grinned as Victor shook his head yawning. He walked over to a dresser, picking an apple from a bowl of fruit. He then turned, tossing it to Billy, who was inspecting all the fancy stuff in the room. "I'm guessing that since you're here, that means that the girl has decided to meet with me." Billy nodded, and Victor reached down, grabbing his boots, "Okay then, guess that means I should get dressed."

A few minutes later, they both left the Goldfish Hotel while munching on apples. The morning was heavy with a dew that soaked the grass and the streets as Billy led Victor back down towards Lowtown.

"I would ask you to tell me where we're going, but I don't imagine that'll do me much good."

Billy stopped and pointed to a building off in the distance.

Victor followed the boy's finger, but only saw only the tops of houses in the distance. "Right, well, off in that direction, it is then," he said as the two continued till they reached a boarded-up disheveled building. "Well, this looks peaceful," said Victor as he gazed up at the very in shambles looking building. He tried to open the door, but it was locked. He applied a bit of force with his shoulder but found that the door was solidly in place. "Okay, you sure this..." said Victor as he turned back to Billy only to notice he was gone again. "Right, I should have expected that." He glanced around for another entrance that he might be able to use.

228

Seconds later, Victor heard some shuffling from the inside and the sound of wood hitting the floor. The door slowly opened, and Billy was standing there before him. Victor walked inside. "You really gotta show me how you do that," he said to Billy as he walked past him. The house appeared as if it hadn't been used in years. There was no furniture, just an old chair off in a corner by the window and a lot of dust. Some of the walls seemed to have been either torn down or half completed, and there was a small hole in the roof where sunlight was shining through.

Victor walked around the room for a moment but didn't notice the girl around anywhere. "You sure we got the right place? I mean..." He turned around to see Billy sitting down against a wall, eating some bread. "I guess that means we wait. You mind sharing a piece of that bread? I'd say it's only fair since I gave you an apple."

Billy looked at the bread for a few seconds before finally breaking a piece off and holding it out. Victor walked over, taking the food, and sat down beside Billy. "You know, you really are the best conversationalist anyone could ask for. A person could tell you all their secrets and never have to worry about them getting out. I mean you'd have to keep it a secret that you can read, kinda. But what noble person would even begin to think that you could anyway. Those bastards would just assume you couldn't and never question it." Victor clenched his fist, "Fuckin nobles."

Billy poked Victor in the side.

"Huh, what?"

Billy spelled out the word "Noble" in the dust on the floor and pointed at Victor.

"I'm not a noble; I grew up with wooden horses and goats. Not magic and a stick up my ass. My father was a farmer all his life, and I never..."

Victor stopped talking as he heard someone enter the room behind him.

"Billy, are you here yet?" asked a young girl's voice.

Billy clapped his hand three times.

"Did you bring the man with you?" asked the girl.

Billy poked Victor again and pointed to the wall.

Victor nodded, "Ah… hello, My name's Victor. Are you Fairline Hasher, who was at the Manor of Duke Richards when it burned down?

"Fairline? You didn't…" said the girl, and then there was a moment of silence that hung in the air, but it finally broke with, "Ah, yes, that was me, why are you looking for me?"

Victor raised an eyebrow at how the conversation was going and glanced back down at Billy, who just shrugged back at him. He narrowed at the boy suspiciously, but decided to follow along.

"I was asked by the King of Burlus to find you."

"But what if I don't want to be found?"

"Then I will leave, I have no love for the king or any nobility. I am just doing what I was asked."

"And if he asked you to drag me back with you?"

"Well, in that case, the king can rightfully go fuck off."

The sound of girls giggling was heard. Suddenly the sound of wood hitting the floor was heard, and a door opened. A blonde-haired girl walked out, followed by another brown-haired girl.

"Rana, what are you doing?" asked the girl who was following behind the blonde one.

Victor noticed that the brown-haired girl following the blonde girl was the voice of the one that he was talking to.

"It's okay, Maggie," said Rana to the other girl before turning back to Victor. "Am I the one you want?"

"No, the girl I need has brown…" Suddenly the image of the girl he was sent to find flashed vividly into his mind in an image so strong that it left his vision blurry and his ears ringing. He glanced back at Rana, whose hair and face were changing to that of the image. *What the hell was that?* He raised his hand to his face, lifting his glasses and covering his eyes.

230

"Are you okay?" asked Rana.

Victor shook his head, "Yes... yes, it's just a headache." He turned back at Rana, who now had brown hair and green eyes.. "You're the one I was sent to find; I remember brown hair and green eyes."

Maggie scratched her head while lifting a piece of Rana's hair. "Are you sure he's okay, Billy?"

Billy gave a thumbs up.

"You're the one who said Billy is never wrong. And I think it might be a little too late to start questioning that now. So, we might as well hear him out since we're here now."

Maggie smiled back while grabbing Rana's hand, "I did say that, didn't I?" And the two turned back to face Victor together.

"While I appreciate both you girls' determination, I really do. Tell me, little one, what do you plan to do? Are you planning to live the rest of your life in this town?"

Rana thought about Victor's words, "Can... can you give me a day or two to decide? I still don't know what, I mean... I've never met the king before. And papa always used to tell me to stay away from the nobility. That they don't mean me any good."

"Your father was probably right. I've spent half of my life around them, and I don't trust 'em," said Victor as he stood and shook the dust off of his clothes.

"Where are you going?" asked Maggie.

"Me? I'm going to grab some breakfast; I'm starving. What about you, little man? You going to the lumber yard? Wanna grab something to eat on the way?"

Billy stood up, nodding to Victor.

"Billy," said Maggie.

Billy just shrugged his shoulders and walked over beside Victor.

"You're just gonna get up and leave? Don't you have any more questions?" asked Maggie.

"I've delivered my message. It's Fairline's decision to make now. It's her life, after all. I'll be in town a few more days if you change your mind. Billy knows where to find me," said Victor as he and Billy headed out the door.

"Well he and Billy sure seem to have gotten close," said Maggie shaking her head before playfully pushing Rana. "Fairline Hasher, your name's Fairline?"

Rana sheepishly dropped her head, "Well yes, that's the name my papa gave me."

"And the king wants you? Are you like a noble, or like a runaway princess, like the ones in stories?"

"What? No, I mean I don't think so."

"I knew you were lying about your name when we met, but I'd never guess. Oh! Does that mean I can start calling you Fairline now, or your highness?" asked Maggie pointing her finger at Rana.

"What? No, don't do that."

"Yes, my Queen, I shalth do'ith whatever'ith yous'ith command'ith," said Maggie in an odd tone as she knelt.

"Stop that," said Rana as she started shaking Maggie playfully.

"Okay, okay, Rana, it is," said Maggie as her tone changed to that of a serious nature, "But you know Rana, I don't think he was lying about what nobles are like."

"Yeah, you might be right. Papa said never to trust them. But if I go to a military camp. People fight there. Maybe they'll end up teaching me."

"Listen, I was at that magistrate's house last night with Doc treating a patient, and I heard him talking to a man about some girl who wanted training. And he didn't sound like he was keen on the idea at all."

Rana placed her hands on her face, "But maybe... Oh, I don't know, Maggie. I just don't know what to do anymore. None of this makes sense. It's all so stupid. I'm supposed to be back home with papa, and instead, I'm here. And I was told that Green Village was really far away, so how am I supposed to get back home if I can't even find it. And even if I did, I don't even know if papa is waiting for me or if he's out searching for me." Tears started to form in Rana's eyes as she continued to spew words from her mouth. "I just... I just wanna go home. And nothing ever works... I don't wanna be a whore...but I can't run..."

Maggie grabbed Rana's shoulder, holding her tight, "Rana, look at me." Rana stared up at Maggie as her world started to crash around her. "If you don't know, then I'll tell you what to do. You should go with that glasses man, he didn't seem bad, but that magistrate, I don't—"

"But he's with the nobles, and papa said..." shouted Rana.

"Rana, I know, but you heard him. He don't like them nobles none either. And since that man and the magistrate's boy is in town to get you, you probably ain't got much time left." Rana tried to push Maggie back, but she held onto her firmly, "I know it's hard, but you gotta decide before they come get you."

Rana pushed Maggie back with all her might. "What you mean like you did with that doctor's cock in your mouth? I don't wanna be..." Rana's words froze in her mouth as the regret of what she had just said began to sink in. "Wait, that's not. Maggie, I'm... I'm sorry, I... I didn't..."

Maggie turned her head from Rana and frowned. Rana could see the impact of her words on Maggie as her lips began to quiver.

"Yes... that's what I decided to do," said Maggie as she slowly turned back to Rana. But now it was as if she wasn't looking at Rana. It seemed as if she saw through her as her face began to lose all signs of emotion. Her brows unfurrowed and her voice began to lose its compassionate tone.

"Maggie, I... shouldn't—"

"Why... it's... it's true, it's not like you lied or... or

233

anything," said Maggie as rubbed at her shoulders. With tears beginning to escape from her eyes, Maggie faced Rana. "I did... what you said. I let the doctor use me. As... as much as he likes."

"Maggie please, I"

Maggie closed her eyes, taking a deep breath, trying to stop the tears, and trembling of her voice. "No... no... I get it. You... you don't wanna end up a whore like me." Maggie dropped her arms, "I'm a whore, right, Rana."

Rana grabbed Maggie's hand and pressed it to her face, staring her in her eyes, "Slap me."

"What! I'm not gonna do—"

"You have to!"

Rana tried to get closer to Maggie, but she stepped back away from her. Rana then grabbed Maggie's shoulders and forced her back against the wall of the house. Maggie tried to free herself.

"Stop... I don't have—"

Rana clasped Maggie's hands in hers again, placing them on her cheeks while looking up to her with watery eyes, "Papa always said, real friends would fight one day and be okay the next. You can hit me, kick me, but I want us to be okay, please..." she mumbled as tears started to roll down her cheek. "Let us... let us be okay. Please let us be okay."

Maggie felt the cold tears on Rana's cheeks as they rolled down onto her fingers. The sight of the tearful girl in front of her made Maggie's frustrations and tension drain from her body. "You really are a handful; you know that." Maggie sighed, "Fine, we're okay; you can let me go now. This is... this feels funny."

Rana let go of her and took a step back, wiping at her tears. "Do... Do you forgive me?"

Maggie smiled, "Not yet. First, give me your right hand," she said as Rana reached out her hand. Maggie grabbed it, then squeezed Rana's hand till she winced from the pain.

"Owe, that hurts," said Rana as she tensed her shoulders and squinted her eyes, trying to bear the pain from Maggie's squeeze. Rana felt the bones of her finger grind against each other as she grit her teeth before feeling the hot fiery impact of a hand across the side of her face. Maggie had drawn back and slapped Rana with her other hand so hard that Rana almost fell down. But Maggie held her hand tight, pulling her back up to her now wobbly legs and steadied Rana on her feet, before letting go of her hand.

Rana quickly placed her hand on her cheek, trying to hold back more tears from the pain of being slapped. Maggie then grabbed Rana's face, trapping her hands on her cheek, leaned in, and kissed her. Rana's eyes opened wide as her and Maggie's lips pressed against each other. Maggie held their faces together for a few seconds before finally letting Rana go.

"Wha... I mean... but why. I don't?" asked Rana, fumbling her words while still clutching her sore cheek from the slap.

"After a fight, you should always kiss and make up, didn't your papa ever teach you that?" asked Maggie, wagging her finger at Rana.

"Yeah, but I don't think he meant to actually do it," said Rana, pouting and rubbing the side of her face.

"Oh, hush you, big baby. Didn't you want us to be friends again?"

Rana dropped her head, "Yeah."

"Then, we friends again. Now let me see that cheek of yours," said Maggie reaching out her hand towards Rana's face.

"Why?" asked Rana as she stepped back, concerned another slap might come.

"Now, Fairline Hasher, friends let other friends see their cheeks," said Maggie, placing her hand on her hips.

Rana cautiously stepped forward, allowing Maggie to remove her hand from her face.

"Oh, it turned color real fast. I got ya pretty good."

"You don't have to brag about it."

"Sorry. Hey, why did that guy say you had brown hair anyway?" asked Maggie as she reached forward, grabbing a lock of Rana's hair.

"Huh, what do you mean? I do have brown hair."

"No, you have black hair. I have brown hair," said Maggie as she grabbed a lock of her own hair and held it besides Rana's own hair in front of her. "See."

"I mean, mine might be a little darker, I guess. But they look the same to me."

The two girls stood in the light shining down through the roof, holding each other's hair, trying to decide which one of them had the darker shade.

Eventually, Maggie dropped Rana's hair. "Both him and you are just weird," said Maggie as she walked toward the door. "But I like weird. Anyway, we been here too long, I need to go back to the Doc's office, he asked me to sort the herbs today, and I need to get started." Maggie walked out the door before sticking her head back in," Remember Rana, whether ya like it or not, you will have to make a decision soon. I pray ya make the one that makes ya happy." Maggie left the building and took off up the street.

Rana then left the building, walking back down the street to the tavern. When she arrived, Tabby immediately noticed the bruise on her cheek.

"Oh, did you get into a fight with the boys this time?"

"No, I just bumped into something."

"Well it must have been pretty hard for you to be trying to hide your face like that."

Tabby leaned down, removing Rana's hand, "You bumped into something that looks like a little hand?"

Rana sighed, "It's fine; we made up."

"I'd like to hope so; they got you pretty good too, not sure you could stand more of those,"

"That's what she said."

"So, it was a girl. Alright then, let's put something cold

on it to make sure it doesn't swell much."

Tabby took Rana into the back of the kitchen, where they spotted Angela coming out of the cellar with a bundle of meat. "Oh, Angela, good timing, hand me one of those pork wraps." Tabby sat Rana down and placed the cold meat on her cheek. Rana winced at the cold feeling against her sore skin.

"Tabby, do you think the general's son will let me keep learning my knives after I go with him?"

"What! Of course, he will! I mean Broderick said..." Tabby looked into Rana's face and sighed, "Honestly, baby, I don't know. I mean, I hope he will. But men like that will only do what makes them happy. And that man, in particular, I asked the girls in town about him, and they say he was very controlling of them when he was younger. But that was years ago. I'm not telling you this to scare you; I want you to be brave, but—"

"Maybe I can run away like you did, Tabby."

Tabby bit her lip, "I suppose I won't be able to stop you if you do. But just be safe, baby, and try not to get into too much trouble, okay." The room was silent for a few seconds as they both struggled for words to say.

"Can I go lay down for a while?"

"Huh, oh, sure. That cheek might swell, though. So, try to keep the meat on there till it goes warm; I'll send Angela up to get it later."

"Okay," said Rana as she left the kitchen and headed up to her room. She laid down on her bed and couldn't help but think about the things Maggie said. *Maybe I should go with the man with glasses. Maggie and Billy trust him. Or maybe he knows where Green Village is. He said he didn't like nobles. If I ask him, maybe he'll take me home.* And with thoughts of home in her mind, she fell asleep.

Later on, that night, Rana was awoken to the sounds of someone knocking on the door. She found that the meat she had on her face had been taken away, and the side of her face had swollen, but only a little. She walked over, opening the door and saw Broderick standing in front of her.

"It's time; you should get your things."

Rana peered out behind Broderick and saw some of the dark uniformed men near the door.

"But I haven't said bye to anyone. I mean... I thought... he's not supposed to come get me yet."

"Yeah, seems like something has come up, and the captain has to return immediately, so go on and get your things."

"Ahh... ahh," said Rana as she turned around, looking around the room confused. She wiped her eyes and headed back into the room, trying to think of anything she could take with her before realizing that she had nothing. She walked back over to Broderick with her head down. "It's okay, I... I... don't have anything."

"What about those little knives and wooden sword you been playing with?"

Rana's head lurched up, "Oh my knives," Rana rushed back to the bed and lifted the sheet to see a satchel and a small wooden sword." She then stuffed the wooden sword into the satchel with the knives and made her way back to the door. I... I'm ready, I guess." But Broderick just stood there looking at her.

"Aye, that you are," said Broderick as he knelt and patted Rana's head, shaking some dust free from her hair, "Listen girly, it's going to get hard from here on, I've done the best I could for ya. But the rest is up to you."

Rana clenched her hands on her bag, "Yes, Sir. I promise I'll be good."

Broderick hugged Rana cradling her head in his hand. Rana was shocked by the gesture but couldn't help herself, but to hug him back. He let her go and stood up. "Well, let's not keep the captain waiting."

Rana and Broderick walked down the stairs to the waiting Cardon.

"Sorry for the short notice Rana, dear, but I was summoned back to the front faster than I had anticipated."

"I understand, Sir."

"You're too small to ride a horse that far, so I had father prepare a carriage so that..." Cardon knelt and placed his hand under Rana's chin, inspecting her face. "Your face is a little swollen, did someone hit you?" Cardon narrowed his eyes back up at Broderick.

Rana shook her head, "It's okay. I just got into a fight with one of my friends, is all. It's nothing really."

"Okay then, well, that's fine, I guess, children are known for ruff housing, just the same as anyone else. But as I said, there is a carriage waiting for us outside to take us most of the way."

Rana stood beside Cardon, and he reached into his coat, pulling out a bag of coins that jingled, handing it to Broderick.

"In due of services rendered, here is your payment, with extra because of the inconvenience."

"I appreciate your consideration, Sir, and I do hope we can do business again," said Broderick accepting the bag.

Cardon placed his hand on Rana's back and led her out of the tavern and towards a waiting carriage. Rana clutched the satchel with its wooden sword in her arms once again as she exited the tavern for the last time.

The air outside was cold and chilled her skin. She could see the moon high in the sky above her as she stepped down onto the dirt. *I guess Maggie was right; I should have probably gone with the glasses man...* Rana placed her foot on the carriage steps. She looked around one last time, only to see the faces of Maggie and Billy staring back at her from around a corner before she was ushered inside of the carriage doors.

CHAPTER 17

Maggie and Billy were walking down the streets of Lowtown towards the tavern.

"I just wanna give her this before her face gets extra puffy," said Maggie holding up a vial of lilly tears, "then we can head back."

Billy made a sleepy face while stretching.

"You didn't have to come, you know, I woulda..."

Suddenly they heard the sounds of men and the neighing of the horses from up ahead. The two stopped and rushed to stand in the shadows near the tavern where Rana worked. They peeked their heads out around a corner and watched some dark-uniformed men outside the tavern standing beside a carriage.

"What are they doing here this late?" asked Maggie.

Billy gave Maggie a knowing smile.

"Okay, yeah, they came for that. But why the wagon?"

Seconds later Rana exited the tavern with a small bag in her hand, followed by three uniformed men. She saw Rana glance around into the night before their eyes met. But it was only for only a second as she was escorted inside the carriage. The man behind her climbed up top with the driver, and the other two men hopped on horses. And with the sound of a crackling whip, the carriage lurched and crept off into the night.

"Billy, do you still remember where that glasses man you met lives?"

Billy nodded his head.

"Let's go then; we gotta tell him Rana's been taken. He'll do something."

Victor awoke to the feeling of someone shaking him out of his slumber. He opened his eyes to see the little boy Billy rocking his shoulder. Victor shook his head, "I'm awake, okay, okay. What's going on?" He sat up, rubbing his eyes as Billy pointed to the door. Suddenly there was a knock outside as Billy strolled over, opening the door.

"Wait, don't open..." Victor closed his eyes as the door swung open. After a few seconds of nothing, he opened them to see Maggie standing in the doorway leaning on the frame with sweat running down her face.

"What? How did you?" asked Victor.

Billy walked up and handed Victor the ball and plank

from his hand.

Victor looked to the door and down to the items in the boy's hand. "How in the goddesses name?"

Maggie came through the door sweaty and out of breath, "Oh... Oh good, he's... here. "She bent over breathing heavily while resting her hands on her knees. Gasping for air, she tried to catch her breath as sweat ran down her face, dropping to the rug beneath her feet.

Victor squinted his eyes at the girl as the night's dreariness slowly faded away. "Are you okay? Wait, you're that girl from the house, what's going on?"

"You have to... go get Rana."

"What, who? Who the hell's Rana?"

"That... Fairline girl or whatever you called her... the dark men took her."

Victor stood up, reaching for his doublet, "Wait, what? Start from the beginning. What happened to Fairline?"

"The magistrate's... men took her and left the city."

"Shit, in the middle of the night?" Victor turned to grab his things, but then when he turned back to Maggie, "Wait, was this her decision or—"

"No, she hadn't decided yet, we were talking about it and... well... I don't think she wanted to go with them. And I saw her when they took her, and she didn't look none too happy about it."

"Fuck," said Victor as he began to get dressed, "Okay, when?"

"Just now, me and Billy ran here as soon as we saw them take her."

"Shit, alright, come in."

Victor turned to the sidewall and started banging on it. "Dekol, Frenka, wake up, we got work to do." He sat down on his bed and slid on his glasses, boots, and undershirt. Soon Dekol and Frenka walked into the doorway.

"What's going on?" asked Dekol as he spotted the two children.

"I fucked up; The girl's been taken, grab your things, I'll explain on the way."

Dekol and Frenka took off back down the hall.

Victor turned back to Maggie, "How'd they take her?"

"Ah... They had horses, but they put Rana in a wagon."

"Good, that'll slow them down," said Victor as he threw his pouch belt across his shoulder.

A minute later, Victor left the Goldfish and saw Dekol and Frenka already dressed on their horses. "They left through the front gate on horseback, but they had the girl in a carriage, should slow 'em down enough for us to catch up."

"And here I thought we'd have us an easy night," said a man with a sword walking up from the shadows.

"I told ya we should've snatched up the girl when we saw her running in," said another man following behind him.

Victor groaned at the appearance of men, "We don't have time for this," He glanced over and saw Maggie and Billy still at the entrance to the Goldfish staring out at them. "Frenka, Dekol, kill them all. They'll report back to the magistrate, and those kids will be in danger."

Dekol and Frenka dismounted and grabbed their blades, slapping the horses on the sides and sending them running off as more thugs started appearing from around the corners of nearby buildings.

"Yeah well, let's see how that goes for yo..." a man said before a blade pierced his throat as Dekol dashed past Victor, slicing two other men before they even had time to draw their blades.

Frenka crossed swords with one of the thugs, and two other men rushed at Victor with their blades drawn. One man swung at Victor, but Victor grabbed his arm mid-swing and hit him in the throat with the palm of his hand. The man shook, dropping to his knees, while the other man swung at Victor's head. Victor ducked and threw his elbow into the man's ribs, then punched him in the face. Through his fist, he could feel the man's teeth crack under the force as the man stumbled back with his hands over his mouth.

"Yoooo bastoood, I'll—"

Victor's dagger pierced the man's throat as he drove the blade deep into his neck and twisted it out. The man's body fell limp to the ground as Victor was tackled from the side and pinned to the ground. The man sat on top of Victor, punching him in the face.

"I got you know now fucker," said the man on top of Victor as he then clasped both his hands together, raising them above his head and brought them down hard towards Victor's face. But Victor shifted his weight just enough to have the man's clubbed hands crash into the cobblestone road beneath him. The man reeled back in pain as he crushed his fingers on the stone and felt a sharp pain as Victor embedded his dagger into the man's stomach. The man gulped and then looked down to see the blade in him and fell over to the ground beside Victor, twitching as blood began to seep from his mouth. Victor struggled to his feet and stabilized himself before pulling his blade from the man's body and holding it in front of him. He could taste blood in his mouth as he placed a hand to his lip.

"Fuck, busted lip."

He stared at the blood on his fingertips as the world around him started to shake a bit. He realized his vision was kinda blurry from the man knocking his glasses from his face, or maybe it was from the two punches to the face the man had got him with. He wasn't really sure, but he didn't have time to wonder about it as he noticed that two more men were quickly heading in his direction. One had a sword, and the other was wielding a club. Victor reached into his pocket, pulling out the small rock that Billy had handed him back.

"Perfect chance to use it, I guess."

He flicked the small rock towards the men, and it started making a whistling sound as it flew through the air. Victor covered his eyes, then suddenly it exploded in a blinding light, which caused the two men to grab their eyes in pain, screaming. Even the man with the sword dropped his weapon to cradle his eyes. Victor, not immune from the quick flash of light, squinted his eyes in recoil and charged the two men. He slashed the disarmed man across the throat, sending more blood gushing out onto the cobblestone. The man with the cub was swinging wildly and blindly but managed to club Victor on the back, sending him to his knees in pain and dropping his dagger to the ground. Victor gritted his teeth, trying to get up, but another man jumped on his back.

"Gotcha now, sweetheart," said the man.

The thug with the club cleared his eyes and saw his partner on Victor. "Hold 'em down; all I need is one crack at his head."

The man held the club above his head and with a cruel smile and brought the club down. Victor closed his eyes for the impact, but the impact never came. Instead, all he heard was a clunking sound.

Victor opened his eyes to see the club bouncing off the cobblestone a few feet away. He looked up to the man who had the club and saw that he now had a blade sticking out of his chest, with Frenka twisting it inside him. She kicked the man free from her blade, and the man holding Victor released his grip, trying to back away.

"Wait, wait, I surrender, there's no need to..."

Frenka walked up to the man and, with a single swing, lopped his head off as it rolled across the cobblestones with its mouth open as if still trying to finish his pleas. Frenka turned around, grabbing Victor by the shoulder, and lifting him to his feet, patting him on his shoulder with a smile on her face.

"You did good, I think you got three or four of 'em," said Frenka.

Victor grunted from the effort to stand and smiled back,

"Not my personal best, but I think I did okay. Why aren't you using magic?"

"I am trying not to burn down these buildings," she pointed to two men coming towards them warily, "Oh, but they will do for test fire, you want to join in, or should I?"

Victor waved her on while clutching his sore shoulder, "You go on. Have your fun. I'll just... I'll just sit this one out."

Frenka dashed towards the two men, deflecting one man's blade as sparks flew from the metal colliding. She tripped the other man, sending him tumbling to the ground. The man who she had just deflected came back with a slash at her head. Frenka leaned back dodging the blade, and landed with her back on the ground beneath the man. She pointed her hands up, "Holana," and her hand shot flames up the man's body and into the night air.

The man screamed and started patting himself before falling to the ground rolling around in pain. The other man that she tripped was back to his feet and soon noticed that he was the only one left. He started looking around in a panic before turning around to run and stepping straight into Dekol's blade as it pierced his throat. Frenka walked over to Dekol. "I got six, what about you, boys?"

"Four, I think, maybe," said Victor as he started rotating his arm, inspecting the damage. "I'm not sure anymore."

The man on Dekol's blade dropped to his knees and slid off to the ground. "I didn't count," said Dekol.

Victor shook his head, sarcastically, "You should count Dekol, or else I have to assume I beat you."

"That is no fun. You were over there, right?" asked Frenka as she lit a fire in her hand, walking forward. "Let us just... Wow," said Frenka as she leaned forward and peered out in front of her. "You really outdid yourself this time."

Victor turned around, walking up behind the two and stood there in a loss of words. The road before him was littered in a mass of dead bodies. There were slashes, cuts, dismembered arms and legs throughout the street. Victor tilted his head at Dekol in shock.

"You said, kill them all," said Dekol.

"I... I... that I did but," said Victor, still in disbelief. He shook his head, trying to regain his senses, "Okay let's round up the horses. I'll marvel about this later." Victor turned back around and saw the two children still standing in the hotel's doorway, watching them. Both of their mouths open as if in shock.

"Get away from here, before someone comes, there's gonna be a lot of questions in the morning, and you don't wanna be near it." Maggie and Billy ran off, with Victor watching them disappear into the night. "I'm sure there is gonna be some type of punishment for subjecting children to visual brutality that I'm gonna suffer for this."

Dekol and Frenka came back with the horses. They all mounted up took off down the street through the city and through the front gate. Frenka leaped down from her horse, inspecting the track, "The carriage went left, around two hours ago, maybe."

"Right, let's go then, we have to play catch up," said Victor.

"I cast shadows so they not see us coming."

CHAPTER 18

Rana had been staring out the window of the carriage for hours, watching as the sun crept over the horizon. *I wonder what Maggie was doing there. I wonder if I will ever see her again, or Pelly, or Miraval. I wonder if Papa is searching for me. How will he find me if I'm off with the captain? Maybe Mama will come for me; I haven't seen Mama in so long. Maybe she will come one again, see the house is gone and come looking for me.*

These thoughts flashed through Rana's mind back and forth throughout the night as the men rode on, but something was weird. Rana didn't feel sleepy at all. In fact, her mind was more alert than ever as she continued to think about random things. It started sometime last night in the carriage. Her senses were over alert. She could feel every vibration of the carriage and hear the birds singing to the morning sun, even though some of them were far off. Everything to her just seemed to be so alive this morning.

"Keep up the pace. I'm going in," said Cardon's voice from outside.

The carriage door opened and Cardon swung himself inside, setting himself down to get comfortable, before noticing Rana looking at him.

"Oh you're awake," said Cardon, "Sorry about the abrupt leaving. But things never go as planned in the military. But everything will be okay. We're just going to drop you off in the next city over for a few days. After that, I'll come for you after things in the city have calmed down."

Rana furrowed her brows at him while rubbing at her shoulder, "So you're not taking me to the military camp?"

"No, not yet; we just needed to get you out of the city first is all. But no worries, soon I will come back for you, and we'll take an airship from then on out. Have you ever ridden an airship before?"

"No, Sir."

"Ah, then you're in for a treat, they are much faster than horses. Being hundreds of feet in the air is a feeling every-one must experience at least once."

"Ah, Mr. Captain, will I be able to be a knight after we get there? I even brought my sword and knives to train with."

"A knight? Ah yes, I remember Broderick saying you wanted to be a warrior. Well, the front doesn't have any female knights on the line. But if you behave, I'm sure we can find something to keep you occupied."

Rana's heart sank as she realized that Cardon wasn't

taking her seriously about her desire to learn.

"Why do you wish to fight? Your talent hasn't even manifested yet. You could wind up like the old man for all we know."

"My talent?"

"Yes, your talent. Wait, so you didn't know after all? Well, considering the sad state father found you in. No, I guess you wouldn't." Cardon snapped his fingers, "No worries, though, we'll soon get you sorted, and you tested; you might even end up being of some use to our family after all. Maybe then, you can..."

The carriage slowed, creaking to a halt.

"Hey, what's going on out there?" asked Cardon as he banged on the top of the carriage.

"Something's on fire," said Rana as she began to smell smoke in the air.

Cardon frowned at Rana before he started smelling the burning of wood, "Stay put, something's not right," before stepping out of the Carriage. Rana got up from the seat and peered out the bars on the door.

"There's a cart on fire in the road, Sir," said a guard.

"A what?" Cardon walked up to see a man and a woman in vividly colorful tunics with flower crowns on their heads, dancing around a flaming cart in the middle of the road, "What in the name of the goddess? I demand to know what is going on here."

The man and the woman kept dancing around the flames, chanting their song. But now the smoke was beginning to sting the soldier's eyes. The man turned to the soldiers and started thrusting his crotch in the guards' direction while making obscene hand gestures. One of the guards began to snicker.

Cardon turned to his guards, "Go and remove these people and whatever that is, from the road. And I would appreciate it if you used force," he said with a scowl.

Two men moved forward on horseback, but after a few

steps, the horses collapsed on the ground.

"What in the, it's a trap. Kill those two," shouted a guard.

Suddenly out of the brush and trees came six figures dressed in black. Pulling the guards off their horses and slamming them on the ground before they could get the chance to draw their blades.

Rana jumped up from her seat, grabbing the bars of the carriage window, and watched as the shadowy figures took down the guards. One masked figure appeared in front of the bars to peer inside and stared directly into her face, surprising Rana, and causing her to stumble back to the floor before the figure dashed off. *No, no, no, the masked people who attacked Papa are here.* Rana began shaking nervously as she reached for her bag, grabbing her wooden sword, and placing her back against the other side of the carriage. As shadowy figures dashed past the openings outside the bars of the carriage, she heard the screams and groans of men in pain as horses neighed and metal clashed. *I'm sorry Papa, I don't know what to do anymore.*

Soon the sounds outside the carriage calmed down, and silence settled into the atmosphere, but Rana dared not move from her spot in fear that they would snatch her away. Through the bars of the carriage, all that she could see was the light shining inside, through some nearby trees.

Outside the carriage, Cardon watched as each and every one of his men was subdued. He turned back around, grabbing the hilt of his sword, but the moment he turned to draw the blade, a hand grabbed the hilt and prevented it from leaving its sheath. Cardon's eyes flared as the masked man who was dancing and thrusting a moment ago was directly in front of him.

"Hello there my happy Captain; I hope things find you well this morning," said the masked figure in a deep growly voice.

"Who are you, people?"

"Who, us? We are a traveling circus. I do so hope you're

enjoying this morning's entertainment."

"I am most certainly not," said Cardon as the air around the two men started to swirl. The wind hit the ground creating a small dust cloud as Cardon overpowered the man forcing his blade from the sheath and slashing at the cloaked figure. But the blade missed as the cloaked man jumped back to avoid the blow.

"Woah, that almost got me," the cloaked man said while trying to shake the forceful feeling from his hand.

"I assure you, the next one won't miss," said Cardon as he assumed a fighting stance.

The cloaked figure threw both hands in the air while moving his fingers, "I wouldn't suppose you'd wanna give up, seeing as I have your men and all."

"I'll cut you down first, and free my men second."

The masked man sighed, "Fighting mages, is too much of a pain. I'll let you girls handle him."

"It's too late to beg—" said Cardon before he was suddenly lifted from his feet and slammed against the side of the carriage, making it side across the dirt and forcing Rana to try and stay upright inside.

The masked man whistled at the sight, "Eww... that looked painful."

Cardon struggled while pinned to the side of the carriage because of some type of magical force. He gritted his teeth as the lady who was dancing earlier, and a cloaked female figure had cast a spell that was pinning him there.

The masked man walked up to Cardon, "See, isn't it better when mages fight each other? Kinda evens out the playing field, doesn't it?"

Cardon began to struggle, trying to free himself, "You... won't... get."

The masked man cracked his knuckles, drew back, and punched Cardon in the face so hard that it knocked him unconscious with a single blow. "And that'll be the end of that." The two mages released their spell, and Cardon slumped to the ground as the masked man started rubbing his fist, "Woah, that fellow there has a solid jaw. My poor fingers." He then playfully jumped over Cardon's body and slowly opened the carriage door while bowing. "Come on out, I'm here to take you away." A few seconds passed, and no one came out of the carriage. The masked man looked to the female mages, and they nodded back to the carriage. He peered inside to see Rana huddled against the wall of the carriage holding her wooden sword.

"Ahem, my lady. I was sent to pick you up and take you away."

"I don't know you, what do you want," said Rana glowering at the masked man.

"My apologies, I am Friggy the Iggy, second son of Sliggy and Miggy," said the masked man as he wiggled his fingers at Rana in a weird manner. "And you are to come with me to be my future bride and live in my castle made of cotton."

A small amount of laughter was heard in the air from some of the other cloaked figures. "Give the girl a break you fool, we wanna off before someone shows up," said one of the men trying to hold in his laughter.

The masked man shook his head, "You guys are just sticks in the mud. Go on and admit it, this was more fun than following Molan's big ol' hairy ass throughout the mountains each and every day." The masked man turned back to Rana and removed his mask. And Rana's eyes opened wide as she was greeted to the sight of Jasper's blue eyes and face, "I think I remember promising to take a little muffin away, but maybe she's—" Suddenly Jasper was falling back landing on the ground as Rana had thrown herself into his arms landing on top of him.

Jasper began laughing and rubbing the little girl's head, "I take it, this means you coming with me then."

The two female mages stood over Jasper and Rana, smiling down at them.

"And I distinctly remember him saying he wasn't good

with children, I think he might have been lying to us Prinja," said the female mage in the colorful tunic.

Jasper glared up at the two women and shook his head while narrowing his eyes, "Now don't you two start getting any ideas."

Jasper stood up and set Rana on her feet before wiping her eyes. "Now remember what I said, if you want my help you gotta ask."

Rana nodded, wiping a tear from her eye, "Will you help me, uncle Jasper?"

Jasper threw out his arms, "Of course, muffin. Don't ever be afraid to ask for help." He said as he rubbed her head. He then turned to Cardon's body, which was still passed out on the ground and gave a wicked smile.

And within minutes, Rana was in Jasper's lap riding through the forests with a mysterious group of people. "Where are we going?"

"We have a camp a little over a day's ride from here," said Jasper as he steered the horse down a trail, "You can get some sleep if you want, I'll make sure ya don't fall."

"I'm not tired."

Jasper laughed, "Not yet, you aren't. But that's june dust in your hair. Sooner or later, you're gonna be sleeping like a baby. Had to make sure, the sleeproot didn't affect ya, if anything went wrong."

"What's june dust?"

"A dust that keeps you awake. I'm guessing you haven't been to sleep since I told Broderick to cover ya with the stuff if ol' captain showed up. We're on it too. But we just used it. You've been on it all night."

"But I feel fine," said Rana, and less than an hour later, she was passed out in Jasper's arms as they continued through the forests.

CHAPTER 19

An hour or so later, Victor and crew arrived at a carriage stranded in the middle of the street. It didn't take long to find that Cardon and his men had been tied to a tree on the side of the road. Walking up to the tied men, Victor noticed they were asleep.

"My, they look so peaceful sleeping away like that," said

Frenka.

Victor noticed the ashes from what seemed to be a half-burned cart up ahead. "Dekol, go check that out, would you?" He and Frenka walked over to Cardon and his men asleep under the tree. "What do you make of this?"

"Well, I do not see girl among them. So I guess someone took her."

Victor yawned while popping his neck, "I guess the only ones who have the answers are this lot. So how ya wanna wake them?"

"I could just start kicking them until they woke; that'd be fun," said Frenka as she glared down at the sleeping soldiers. She reached out her hand, placing it on a soldier's head, shaking it. "And they pretty knocked out too. I wonder what happened to them. Maybe sleep spell, but on so many would be hard. So yes, they will be hard to wake, so I would suggest kicking them."

Victor raised an eyebrow at Frenka, "Subtle, but probably not the best way." He walked over to his horse, grabbed a water pouch from its side, and returned to Cardon, turning it upside down on the captain's head. "This seems familiar for some reason."

Cardon woke from his slumber and started coughing and gasping for air. "What... what's going on..." asked Cardon in between fits of coughing out the water.

"That's something that I would most certainly like to know myself," said Victor as he corked the water pouch.

Cardon blinked his eyes in confusion, trying to shake away the water and the now bright morning sun from his eyes, "Victor? What... what are you doing here, where's the girl." He said as he glanced around the area.

"Once again, another question that I would like the answer to."

Cardon struggled to try and stand up but soon realized that he'd been tied up with his men. "What is the meaning of this? Release me at once."

Victor frowned, "What do you think, Frenka?"

"I do not know, those men besides you look pretty comfy, it would be shame to wake them during nap."

"I wholeheartedly agree," came a voice through the air, "We can't let them go. Not until I get some answers."

Frenka jolted back up and started searching around, "I know that voice. Prince Saffron, where are you?"

Suddenly behind them, the world began to warp as Prince Saffron emerged with a dozen men and women at his side. It was like the world turned into a water painting that started leaking onto the ground, and through the mixture of wet dripping colors, stepped Prince Saffron into vision.

Dekol walked up with a half-charred plant in his hand, "Hey, Saffron," He then turned to Victor, "It seems the cart was filled with sleep root."

"Well, that explains why the guards are sleeping. That stuff had me out for a whole day," said Victor.

"You not seem surprised that Prince Saffron is here Dekol," said Frenka, glaring at him suspiciously.

"Why would he be; he found me the first night I started following you. He even brought us food from that little city you all were in," said Saffron laughing.

"Why you following us in the first place, don't you have better things to do?" asked Frenka.

Saffron mockingly made an offended face while placing his hand over his chest, "How could you say that? Two of my best friends leave the city without me, on some magical quest. And you expect me not to follow. I'd have figured that you'd know me better than that by now, Frenka. And I missed your breasts, have they grown again?"

Frenka swung at the Prince as he ran and hid behind Dekol.

"So violent, you mountain people are all the same."

Cardon stared on in amazement at the group's antics, "Are... are you really Prince Saffron?"

Saffron turned his attention to Cardon, "That I am, and

if it is to my understanding. You tried to steal something that belongs to us." The Prince turned to Dekol, "Is that the way of it, do I have it right?"

"That's pretty much correct, yes," said Dekol.

Saffron turned back to Cardon squatting on the ground before him, "Oh, well now, that does certainly sound like treason to me. So, one has to wonder, just what am I going to do with you?"

CHAPTER 20

The side of Rana's face felt warm as she listened to the sounds of a heartbeat. The smooth and steady bumping of the rhythm of it was calming. It reminded her of her father when she used to sit on his lap and read to her. She'd snuggled her face close, feeling the warmth of his chest against her cheek. She felt safe again as if everything was merely a dream. That Broderick, the glasses man, Jacob, they were all dreams. She was back home again, and she felt her father's arms around her as he held her close.

"Papa, did I fall asleep again?"

She rubbed at her eyes, yawning up into her father's face. But as the sleepiness faded from her vision, she realized it wasn't her father. Instead, she was greeted by the image of Jasper's sleeping face. She had fallen asleep on top of Jasper. She stared up at him, confused, and noticed they were on a large bed together and he had his arms wrapped around her. Glancing around, she saw that they were in some type of large tent. She could see the sun shining through the fabric. Rana began to think back, but could only remember being on Jasper's horse as they went through the forest.

"Well, I was wondering which one of you two was going to be the first to wake," said a familiar voice.

Rana looked over to see Oscar with a blade in his hand, cutting into a piece of wood. She peered around the tent once more before sitting up on the bed. "Where am I?"

Oscar kept chipping away at the wood, "You're in my tent. That boy Jasper walked in here with you in his arms and plopped down on my damned bed. He said he brought me a present and passed out. You two been out for a full day since ya got back." Oscar chipped away at the wood a few more times, before examining it to make sure it was to his liking. Then placing the wood and blade on a table beside him, he leaned over in his chair at Rana and grinned.

"It looks like it's about time for you to make a decision, little girl."

"What? What do you mean?"

Oscar pointed to Jasper. "The boy Jasper there has been with me for about eight years, I'd say. And throughout those eight years, he's never once asked me for a damn thing. He just did his job and made his little jokes. That was, until a few days ago. When Jasper comes marching up to me and outright begs me to take ya in. Now with me being the generous man that I am, how could I refuse the request of someone who's given me such good service. But it makes me wonder why Jasper would take such an interest in ya so quickly and why in the hell was the magistrate after ya. So, my little oddity, you're gonna answer all the questions I have for ya."

Rana started nervously looking around the room and then down to Jasper, who was still passed out. She noticed that he had large claw marks across his chest and shoulders.

Oscar smirked, "Oh no, there's no one to save ya this time. You're gonna make a decision here and now. Either you answer my questions and stay here with Jasper and my boy Jacob, or ya try lying to me. In which case, I'll sell ya off to some bandits and you'll be locked up in a cage for the pleasure of whoever buys ya next. It's your choice."

Rana looked back down at Jasper and closed her eyes before looking back at Oscar, making up her mind, "I'll answer your questions, Sir."

"Smart choice. Now first, tell me, what's your name?"

Rana clenched her fist, "Fairline, my name's Fairline Hasher."

"Well, little miss Hasher. What did the magistrate want ya for?"

Rana shook her head, "I don't know, all he did was start touching me every time he came to visit."

"Yeah, I'm aware of his habits, but you were meant for his son. So there has to be another reason for him to try and sneak ya away in the middle of the night," said Oscar as he started rubbing at his beard thinking. "Fine, where are ya from?"

"Green Village in Drinland, that's where me and papa lived," said Rana as she squeezed Jasper's hand, "But... but uncle Jasper said that was far away, is that true?"

Oscar leaned back into his chair and sighed, "Aye, he was right on that; it's at least half a cycle away from here just to get to Drinland." He drummed his fingers across his knee, "Ya seem like ya telling the truth, then how did ya get here?"

"Papa and me were being chased by bandits. They kept chasing us and calling him Reginald. But they caught up to us, and I fell, that's when Mr. Richards found me and took me to his home."

Oscar rubbed his head in frustration, "Wait, so you were in Drinland when you fell, but Richards found you here?"

Rana closed her eyes as memories flashed through her mind and slowly started nodding her head, "Yes, I... I think so."

Oscar sighed and stood up from his chair. Walking over to a table, he poured wine into a cup. "What about your father then? You said his name was Reginald."

"No, that's what the bandits called him. I don't know why they did that. Papa's name is Eulan Hasher, and my mother is Evalene Hasher." Rana found that now that she was telling her story, it was as if the words were just suddenly coming out of her mouth without her even thinking about it. She didn't realize that hiding who she was for so long had caused her to keep so much pent up inside.

Oscar took a large gulp from the cup, "Fine, but one things for sure. Duke Richards died because of you. So that makes me question why was the Duke hiding ya in the first place?"

"I... I don't know, I was only with Mr. Richards a few days before the men came and then the fire started. That's when Broody found me."

Oscar just stared at Rana while swirling the mug of wine in his hand.

The flaps to the tent opened as Jacob walked inside. "Is she awa... Why good morning muddy princess," said Jacob as Rana smiled at his appearance. Jacob turned to his father, "How goes the interrogation of the damsel, surely you didn't make her suffer your questioning for too long?"

"I'm starting to think I'm the one who's gonna be suffering if I continue to question her. The things she's telling me ain't adding up. She thinks she's telling the truth, but—"

"I am telling the truth," said Rana as she slammed her hand down on top of Jasper's chest, making him cough in his sleep. "Oh no, I'm sorry I didn't mean to..."

Oscar raised an eyebrow at the little girl huddled over Jasper, before turning back to Jacob. "Be that as it may. You can take her. She wanted to learn to fight, right? Take her round the camp and get her paired up with Dessi." Oscar poured himself another cup of wine, "I'm gonna need to be properly not sober before I question her again," and he began to chug down his drink.

Rana narrowed her eyes at Oscar, giving him a disapproving look as Jacob laughed.

"Okay muddy princess, get down from there, and I'll show you around."

Rana crawled across Jasper and lowered herself to the rug and walked over to Jacob. She stopped, turning back to glance at Jasper.

Oscar raised his cup in Jasper's direction, "Don't worry about the idiot, he'll wake soon enough, and I'll send him your way when he does."

Rana turned back around and allowed Jacob to usher her out of the tent. Outside, Rana could see a bunch of other tents and fires set up as she followed behind Jacob. The camp had a lot of people that were going about their day. Men who were banging wooden stakes into the ground and Rana even noticed some women who were holding swords as she followed Jacob through the grounds. They strolled through the camp as Jacob pointed and waved at different people.

"Is this a real army?"

"Well, there's not that many of us here at the moment, but were more or less capable of fighting anything that needs to be fought. We're pretty famous in the five kingdoms, as Jasper so elegantly likes to say, 'The Black Jewel Mercenaries are a name to be feared by both ally and enemy alike. For our foes, we attack their homes while they sleep, and to our friends, we attack their purses so that they can sleep."

Rana peered downhill towards a stream where a group of naked men were washing themselves in the waters. Their pale bodies seemed to glisten in the early morning sun. The men were all very muscular. She could tell from their frames as they dumped buckets of water over themselves. One of the men turned and saw her up the hill and waved at her and Jacob with his cock dangling freely in the early morning sun. Rana stared as if in a daze at the men.

Jacob shook his head and dragged Rana away, "That's probably not the best thing for you to see so early in the morning." Jacob continued to usher Rana through the camp as the people around them began smothering the fires of the night before. They walked forward until they came upon another group of half-dressed, bare-chested men.

Rana looked over to see two men fighting against each other with swords and shields. One man was larger than the other one and had a bigger blade. He pounded away at the smaller man's shield forcing him to his knees while holding the shield above his head. The large man swung down at the smaller man again, but this time he rolled over and tried to slash his sword at the larger man's leg. The larger man planted his sword in the ground blocking the smaller man's blow.

"Good try, but mistake," said the large man.

The smaller man's blade clanged off the embedded blade and he tried to pull his arm back after hitting it, but it was too late as the larger man had leaped forward and grabbed the smaller man's sword hand, bending his wrist until the blade dropped from his hand and gripped the neck of the smaller man with his other hand. The smaller man struggled in, the larger man's grip until his face started to turn color. The crowd around them roared with cheers as the smaller man started tapping, the larger man's arm, and he was let go, falling back to the ground.

"Dammit, Molan, I thought I was gonna die that time," said the smaller man rubbing at his throat.

The larger man smiled as he reached out his hand to the smaller man, "You did good that time; it was good idea to go for legs." he said in a thick accent.

The smaller man grabbed his arm, lifting himself up while continuing to rub at his bruised throat, "It sure didn't feel like I did good."

Molan smiled at the smaller man, then turned and saw Jacob with Rana. He walked over to them, "Yo, Pretty Boy, you come to get ya`self refreshed on the glory of me kicking your ass?"

Jacob placed his hand under his chin, "I think you might be misremembering how our last fight ended, Molan."

Rana noticed Molan calling Jacob "pretty boy" and glanced up at him; she had never paid much attention before. But now in the light of the sun and them both not covered in sweat, she could see that Jacob had a beautiful face. He had a sharp jawline, green eyes, and golden hair, whereas Molan was big and burly with a thick beard.

Molan cracked his hands in a fist, "Perhaps you'd like to show me once again."

"Sadly, I'm busy showing our new recruit around, so perhaps another time," said Jacob as he placed his hand on Rana's shoulder.

"You mean this little thing, I figured she was a new toy of yours," said Molan as he gestured down at Rana.

Jacob laughed, "Not mine, one of father's."

"Old man, huh," said Molan as he took a better look at Rana, "Well, she probably grow into something if she lives long enough. Who you using to break her in?"

"Handing her off to Dessi first, see how she does."

"Well, makes sense; she does not look big enough to hold sword yet. Not even small one."

Rana narrowed her eyes at the man. *I know I'm small, why does everyone have to keep pointing it out.*

The small man walked up behind Molan and noticed Rana, "Hey, it's the muffin Jasper rescued. That was a fun little mission."

Molan pointed down at Rana, "This is what funny man borrowed men for? He comes up out of blue, asks to borrow men and takes off into the night, and comes back with this?" Molan rubbed his chin, inspecting Rana again. "Okay, now I interested; if funny man and old man want her, then that makes her special."

"Happy to see you awake little lady, you were sleeping pretty hard on Jasper during the ride to camp," said the smaller man as he patted Molan on the back, "Come on Molan, you still gotta beat Trilan's ass, he said he's up next."

Molan smiled and tossed up his hands and started walking off, "Oh well, send girly my way if you want her broken in another way," he said while laughing his way over to the other men.

"Break me in? What does that mean? Will he be training me also?" asked Rana with an innocent expression in her eyes.

Jacob frowned down at her in astonishment, "How is it possible you lived at Broderick' s', and don't know what that means." He placed his hand on her shoulder, "Whatever, just stay away from that one. I don't think you want his type of training." Jacob placed his hand on Rana's back and began pushing her off towards another part of the camp.

"Why? Is he dangerous?"

Jacob bit his lip, thinking, "He's not really dangerous, it's just he's from the mountain clans. They have different ideas on how they pick women for themselves. And I'd rather not have father have to deal with that. So, it's best to say he's dangerous to you if he takes an extended interest in you."

They soon found Dessi sitting beside three other ladies. She saw them coming and waved them over.

"Well, looky here, if it isn't my two favorite people together. Did you come to visit me? I feel flattered," said

Dessi.

"Hey Dessi," said Rana as she felt a wave of relief come of her at the sight of the dark haired woman. "I'm glad to see you again. I got better with my knives. Do you want to see?"

"Knives," said a lady behind Dessi, "You're taking a protege already? And with Jacob? I knew you two were hot for each other, but to have a baby already. Dessi, I'm shocked."

The girls around them started giggling as Dessi swirled around frowning at them, before turning back to Rana.

"Rana, let me introduce you to the giggling harpies over here," said Dessi as she started to point out the ladies around her. The girls' names were Keltre, a blonde lady with green eyes. Prinja, a brown-haired lady with black eyes who kept flipping a spoon in her hand and Julianna, another blonde girl with blue eyes who was playing with dirt in her hand, making it whirl around her fingers.

"Hello," said Rana to the girls.

"They're all mages," said Dessi as she waved her hand at the girls, "Juli, as you can see, does mostly ground stuff, while Prinja and Keltre are both wind mages. Keltre can even fly. They were the ones who rescued you with Jasper."

Rana recognized one of the women from the raid on the wagon, "Thank you for coming to get me."

"Oh, well, doesn't she have manners," said Prinja as she leaned forward inspecting Rana, "Tell me something, what is it about you that's got our man all worked up. I always figure that only me and Keltre could get that bastard to do anything."

Rana rubbed at her shoulder shyly, "I don't know? Uncle Jasper said he'd come to get me, and we'd go and live with the fairies."

Prinja burst into laughter, "Uncle Jasper... goodness, he's got another one. The other girls call him that too. Well, he's off with the fairies now, after getting hopped up on that june dust. Thankfully since we're mages, we can fend off the worst of it."

"Can you really fly?" asked Rana.

Keltre smiled, "Hardly, I can barely lift myself off the ground, but I can definitely send someone else flying. You must not have seen what me and Prinja did to that captain a few days ago."

"I was inside; I only felt it shake. But... but I heard him." Rana turned to Jacob. "Was I really asleep all day?"

"Yeah, to you it probably felt like last night, but that was almost two days ago," said Jacob, "The effects of the dust can really strain the body, so you wind up crashing at the end of it. Jasper just strolled into father's tent, said a few words, and passed out with you in his arms."

"Yeah, me and Keltre had to use magic to wake him up after we watered the horses," said Prinja. "He really pushed himself, making it back to camp."

"But she looked so cute when she was asleep," said Dessi.

"Well I'm happy you feel that way," said Jacob. "Since father elected you to be her teacher."

"Good, I was afraid he'd hand her off to Molan or Jasper, and she'd end up as some type of freak. At least with me, she'll end up a competent killer."

Keltre pointed her finger at Dessi, "Hey, you can talk bad about our man when you find a way to get your own."

"Ah, don't worry about Dessi, baby," said Prinja as she leaned over and kissed Keltre. "She's just mad and sexually repressed. I don't think our boy Jacob's done put his cock in her all year. She's gonna be coming to us looking for some girl fun sooner or later, with all that frustration she's got pent up inside her."

Dessi's face started to blush, and she bit her lip, pointing at the two women. "How dare you say—"

Jacob quickly wrapped his hands around Dessi's mouth, holding her down. "Speaking of sleeping beauty. I heard that was a fun little mission. Did he really make a fire and start humping the air?" asked Jacob as Dessi mumbled some interesting words between his fingers.

"Oh that he did," said Prinja as she suggestively wiggled her fingers at Dessi, "it was the hardest thing ever just to keep a straight face during the whole mess, although Keltre was the one dancing with him."

"Hey, it was much better than just hiding behind the trees like a squirrel, although blocking the sleep root made it hard to concentrate," said Keltre.

"I still don't see how you two deal with him," said Dessi as she calmed down, removing Jacob's hand. "All he does is tell stupid stories."

Keltre smiled, looking over at Prinja, "Well, it's more like we love each other, and we just like having him around, but he ain't so bad after a while. And he's always fun."

"He's an acquired taste," said Prinja.

"Yes, I imagine many things are," said Jacob, "But who am I to decide the way into a woman's heart?"

"Maybe not her heart, but I'm sure Dessi's been waiting for you to find your way into that cunt of hers for a while," said Prinja as she once again wiggled her fingers in Dessi's direction.

Dessi kicked at the ladies as they started smiling, "Oh, shut it, both of you."

"And with that, it seems I have to go back and be anywhere other than here," said Jacob as he patted Rana on her head, "I shall leave you in the hands of these capable although somewhat questionable ladies." and he quickly walked off.

"Oh, he's running away," said Prinja.

Dessi stood up, "Well, as much as I enjoy the company of you girls and your annoying schemes. It's time for us non-magical people to get some training in." Dessi led Rana away from the girls down towards more tents, "Did you have time to grab your blades before the captain got you?"

"Yes, I have... well, I think I have them. I fell asleep on the way."

"They're probably with Oscar then. Okay, for now, you can practice with mine." Dessi slapped her legs and pulled out two blades, handing them to Rana as they arrived at the edge of camp where Dessi pointed to a log on the ground, "Okay, try slamming that log with the blades."

Rana took aim and threw the first blade, and it stuck in the log.

"Not bad, you really have been practicing."

Rana threw the second, but it missed and landed on the ground.

"That's okay, you've gotten the basic understanding of it, now it's just a matter of practice. So, let's try again."

For the rest of the day, Rana spent her time throwing blades until her arms felt like they were about to fall off. She practiced with a few types of Dessi's blades, all of them different sizes and shapes. She spent most of the time missing, but she found that if she focused really hard then oftentimes, she'd get them to stick. Hours and hundreds of throws later, Rana laid sprawled out on her back on the ground.

"I don't think I can throw anymore."

Dessi noticed the sun beginning to set, "Well that's enough for today, I don't think we'll move camp for a few days, so we'll start again tomorrow. Let's get you cleaned up." Dessi and Rana headed off to another tent that had a few other women inside alongside some buckets of water. Dessi stripped Rana down and began to wash her back as she sat on a stool.

"Are you not gonna wash, Dessi?"

"I have a bucket and washcloth in my tent, besides you're the one who worked up a sweat today. I swear I haven't seen so many misses in a long time."

Rana dropped her head, "I'm gonna get better, I just gotta practice more." She turned to Dessi as she rolled up her sleeves and dunked the cloth into a bucket of water. "How long did it take you to become good with your knives?"

"Oh, years, a lady named Addison was one of the people who taught me for a while, but that was a long time ago."

Rana noticed that Dessi's hands had a lot of scars across her knuckles and up her arms. "How did you get so many scars?"

"Oh, I still need to have these taken care of, I had forgotten with everything being so busy. I got a lot of these on my last mission in Heftan; I was going to be the Queen of a warrior clan."

"Oh, I thought you wanted to marry Jacob."

Dessi frowned down at Rana before grabbing her shoulders and shaking her. "Why does everyone keep bringing up Jacob? I swear you're no better than Prinja and Keltre."

"I'm sorry, I'm sorry," said Rana laughing.

"Now sit still and let me finish washing you, let's just put your hair up first." Dessi reached to her waist and pulled out two metal rods with sharp ends and a hairpin from off a nearby table. She started rolling Rana's hair into a ball, pinning it in place with the clip and sticking the rods in on either side. "There, now you look all cute."

After getting cleaned, Rana walked back over to her clothes to put them on.

Dessi stopped and narrowed her eyes at Rana, "Hmm."

"What?" asked Rana.

"We really can't have you wandering around in rags anymore. You're gonna need something proper. But Addison is a few days back, so I guess we'll have to make do with what we got." Dessi walked over and started rubbing Rana's clothes between her fingers. "I guess we can put some pockets inside of this. I'll ask around tonight in camp. Think you can find your way back to Oscar's tent?"

Rana nodded, "I can."

Soon, she and Dessi left the bathing tent and split up, with Rana heading off back towards Oscar's tent. On the way, she began to notice even more people around their makeshift fires as the sun started to set. She made her way through the camp but forgot which direction Oscar's tent was. *I think it was this way.*

Turning around, she found herself face to face with two girls staring back at her. Rana jumped in surprise as the girls stared at her. The girls were different; they both had skin that was much darker than hers, and their hair coiled in on itself and stood up instead of hanging down. Their clothes matched as they both wore skirts and tops that exposed their stomachs. And on each of their heads, their hair was pulled back into two small balls covered in a white cloth and tied.

"She jumped," said one girl to the other.

"We don't see other girls here, you new?" asked the other girl.

"You want to play Krump?" asked the first girl, as she held out a small leather ball.

Rana just stared at the two girls.

"You here, not many girls here, so yes, you must be new," said the second girl.

"Ah... who are you?" asked Rana.

"Oh, she speaks," the first girl said in mock surprise as she threw the ball into the air.

"She not likely seen Sakari before," said the second girl, shaking her finger in the first girl's face. "So we must introduce..."

"Sakari!" shouted Rana in recognition, so loud that it startled the two girls as their ball landed on the ground. "I've heard about Sakari; you are warriors."

The first girl looked to the second, "Are we warriors?"

"You kill five men; I only kill one. So maybe you the warrior?" asked the second.

"Five men?" asked Rana in surprise.

"What your name, I'm Momo and this sister Jomo," said the first girl

"I... I'm Rana."

Momo smiled and grabbed Rana's hand, "Well Rana,

now we friends, so you come to play Krump now?" Jomo then grabbed Rana's other hand, and together, they took her through the camp.

Rana was lost in the pace of the two girls, with how fast everything was moving. "But I don't know how to play Krump."

"No worries, we teach you, it's simple. I throw ball, and you catch."

They continued to drag Rana through a small part of the camp, where she noticed other Sakari men and women scattered throughout the crowd. They arrived outside a tent, and Jomo tossed the leather ball to Rana. She tried to catch it but dropped it as it was heavier than she assumed it would be. She knelt and picked up the ball.

"This is kinda heavy."

Suddenly the tent flaps opened, and Jasper walked out, holding his little book in his hands.

"Uncle Jasper, what are you doing here?" asked Rana as she dropped the heavy ball on the ground with a thud. She noticed that he had a much more serious expression on his face than usual.

"Oh, muffin, I was wondering where'd you'd wandered off to," said Jasper as his face resumed its usual smile.

"Uncle funny man, uncle funny man," shouted Jomo and Momo, as they danced around him, with Momo climbing up on his back and wrapping her hands around his neck.

"Oh, wow, all the muffins are here. What are you three doing today? You're not getting into any mischief, are you."

Jomo smiled, "No, we play Krump with this one."

Jasper glared down at Jomo, "Oh no, you don't, you promised that you'd use proper kingdom speak with me. And I expected you to keep your word."

"But proper kingdom speak hard, too many words," said Jomo pouting.

"A promise is a promise, and I expect you to keep it," said Jasper folding his arms with a stern look on his face.

Jomo dropped her head, "Yes uncle funny man." She then took a deep breath. "How are you today, Sir. We have been playing with our new friend. Her name is Rana."

Jasper patted Jomo on the head and turned to Momo, who was still on his back with her arms wrapped around on his neck. "And what do you have to say to me?"

"I am not like my sister Jacinta, I have properly learned the kingdom tongue like you told us," said Momo.

Rana scratched her head at the name. "Who is Jacinta?"

Jasper smiled down at Rana, "I see they got you too. They call each other Jomo and Momo because it's just easier for them to say. Jomo's real name is Jacinta, and Momo's real name is Makeba." Jasper reached around, grabbing Momo and setting her down on the ground. "They just speak broken kingdom tongue because apparently Jomo," Jasper raised an eyebrow at the Sakari girl, "doesn't like to take her lessons."

"But kingdom tongue stupid, Sakari tongue better," said Jomo before seeing Jasper looking back down at her unsatisfied. "I mean, I promise that I will continue to study uncle funny man."

"Uncle funny man?" asked Rana.

"Yeah, they got that last part from Molan. He calls me that. Ever since they heard him say it, they haven't spoken my name once. Well, either way, I'm happy I got to see my three favorite muffins before I had to leave again."

"What? You're going to leave?" asked Rana

"Yeah, I'm headed over to Nyril. Apparently, some people went missing over there, so Oscar asked me to check it out. They say it might be ghosts."

"Oh, okay," said Rana as she slumped her shoulders.

"Hey now, don't act like that. I'll be back soon enough, and then I'll tell you some stories. Besides, it seems like you're already making new friends," he said as he rubbed the hair of Jomo and Momo.

"Yes she new... I mean, we have become good friends,

uncle funny man," said Jomo.

"Alright, I expect you to take care of your new friend. She's my family now, just like you two are. So, you all best behave and get along."

"Yes uncle funny man," the two Sakari girls said in unison.

Jasper shook his head, "Of all the things for you to learn from that Ala-go ha ma neway Molan."

"Ala-go ha.... what's that mean?" asked Rana.

"It's Sakari, essentially it means. A dumb pile of shit," said Jasper as he turned back to Rana. "And you, be good till I get back. Then I'll tell you the stories of the fairies."

"Yes, Sir, uncle fun—"

"Don't you dare."

Rana giggled as Jasper patted her on the head and walked off through the camp.

"Okay now uncle funny man gone, it's time for us to play krump," said Momo.

"I go see if uncle funny man, not break him," said Jomo as she walked inside the tent.

Momo walked a few feet away from Rana, who had picked back up the krump ball in her hand. Momo raised her hand. "Throw."

Rana weighed the ball in her hand, "It's too heavy, I can't throw that far."

"Oh, you no have talent; I fix to make Krump easier," said Momo as she walked back over to Rana and tapped the ball in her hand. Brown light emitted from the ball and disappeared. A layer of dirt puffed into the air around the ball before falling down over Rana's hands and arms. Instantly, the ball felt a lot lighter.

"There, all better, now it feels better to play Krump," said Momo as she walked back, "Toss," and she spread her arms out.

"You can do magic too?" asked Rana as she stared at the ball, watching the dirt disperse from it.

"Yes, me and Jomo have talent, but can you play Krump?"

Rana tossed the ball to Momo, but her arms were still sore from her knife lessons with Dessi, so the ball didn't fully reach Momo and fell on the ground before her.

Momo giggled at Rana, "You really weak; you will need practice for Krump. You need power."

"No fair, I'm just tired from training."

"Oh, what training?"

Rana pulled out one of the metal rods from her hair and looked around till she saw a nearby piece of wood. "Okay watch," she showed Momo the spike before narrowing her eyes in concentration and launching it at the wood. Her arms were still tired, but she focused hard and launched the rod. It pierced perfectly and embedded itself inside.

Momo's eyes opened wide as she smiled, "Oh, you good. What is that?" she pointed to the other rod in Rana's hair.

Rana pulled the other rod out to show her, "They are spikes, I will use them to fight."

Momo lifted the metal rod from Rana's hand and smiled, "Yep, yep, spike Krump. We throw ball; you throw spike."

Rana laughed while going to pick out the other spike from the piece of wood and placed it back in her hair, "Well, I don't think I'll be having you catch these spikes."

"Yes, I could not catch spikes, but we have spike catcher inside."

Jomo peeked her head out of the tent, "Why you out here, come come; we play Krump."

Momo grabbed Rana by the hand and led her into the tent where Rana saw a man bound and gagged. He was held up against a large piece of wood. The man's face was bruised and had dried blood from where a few gnashes had been opened up.

Momo handed the spike back to Rana, "See," and pointed to the bound man, "spike catcher."

The man noticed Rana staring up at him and made a few muffled noises trying to speak to her. But Rana just stared at him in shock with the spike in her hand.

Jomo walked over and pointed at the spike in Rana's hand, "What that?"

Momo smiled, "She can play spike krump with that."

Jomo clapped her hands, "Later you show, but no spike Krump now, just Krump. We wait for mother and old man." Momo tossed the leather ball to Jomo.

Jomo felt the weight of the ball and looked at her sister, "You made soft?"

Momo pointed to Rana, who was still in a staring contest with the man, "I teach, she weak, not catch."

Jomo nodded in understanding and turned around, throwing the ball at the bound man's head. It bounced off, and Momo caught it before it hit the ground. The man made a growling noise before getting smacked again in the face with the ball. The two sisters continued to throw the ball at the man's head and chest, trying to catch it before it hit the ground. But if one of them didn't catch the ball, the other would walk over and slap the other sister. Sometimes on the hand, other times on the arm or chest, but they never hit each other in the face.

Rana just watched as the two girls went back and forth with the ball, between themselves and the bound man, and realized how horrible things would have been if Momo hadn't taken off the magic from the ball earlier. The man was getting hit, but the soft ball was barely doing anything other than annoying him.

After a few more throws, a Sakari woman entered the tent, followed by Oscar. Her coiled hair was pulled back in a long-braided ponytail with a golden cloth following throughout the entire braid. It fell down, looping around her neck. She wore kingdom clothing with pants and doublet with a blade on her side, along with beaded bracelets on her wrists. Rana noticed she had a large scar over one of her eyes as she glanced around seeing Rana and the two girls.

"It would seem as if someone else has beaten us here," said the Sakari woman.

Oscar glanced at the bound man and smiled, then turned and noticed Rana staring back at him.

"And what do we have here?" asked the Sakari woman after noticing Rana, "A little intruder perhaps?"

Jomo and Momo stepped beside Rana, "She friend, we played Krump."

The Sakari woman laughed, "Friend, you and this little kingdom girl? Where did she come from? I never seen her before."

"That one's mine, Gregga," said Oscar stepping forward, "How she managed to get here, I'm curious about, but she's mine nonetheless."

The Sakari woman smiled at Oscar, "Oh, you claim her, then?" She leaned down at Rana. "Then that means you must be special." The woman turned back to Oscar, "You always pick up fun toys, what so special about this one?"

"Perhaps, I'll tell you one day. But I think we have more important matters at the moment," said Oscar.

"Fine, another time then," said Gregga as she walked over to the bound man rubbing her fingers on his face. "I have a new toy to play with as well," she reached down into the man's pants, grabbing his cock and began squeezing it as she bit his ear, "and I think mine would be a lot more fun."

Oscar walked over and grabbed a chair, "And here I thought you preferred your own kind, have you started taking a liking to us after all these years?"

Gregga smiled while rolling her hands over the man's penis, "Well, I doubt he will be as much fun as Jasper was, but it's always fun to try new... things."

Oscar raised a brow, "I doubt Jasper would refer to those years as your slave as...fun."

"Oh, you be surprised what a man likes after a little foreplay," she said as she removed her hands from his cock and patted his crotch before walking away. "But maybe you and your little toy kingdom girl there would like to watch?"

What? No, I don't want to watch. Are they going to make me watch? Thought Rana.

Oscar twisted his lips at the thought, "I somehow think you'd enjoy that more than I would, ungag him, and let's get this over with."

"Oscar you really should learn how to show a girl a good time, but fine," she said as she ungagged the man who started coughing and breathing heavily.

"You people are sick, you and these little dark cunts," the man spat at the two girls. Jomo and Momo hopped back laughing before Jomo whacked him in the face again with the ball.

"Ah, damn you," said the bound man.

The two girls started giggling again as they went after the ball.

"Well it's nice to see your tongue still works, cause I'mma need you to answer some questions for me," said Oscar.

"I don't know anything; I was just out hunting when I was grabbed by these people. They beat me up and brought me here."

"I swear, I have done more interrogations than I can count, but the reason I keep doing them is because the more I do, the better I get at them." The sakari woman walked over and placed a small table in front of Oscar and spread out a few items on the table. "And through these interrogations, people more often than not claim that they did nothing wrong. But here we have some of the items that you were caught with. An expensive-looking dagger," Oscar waved around the dagger admiring the craftsmanship, "it probably costs more than your average farmer makes in a month. Then we have three gold coins, and a hand-drawn map of this area, and it even has details I didn't know about. That'll come in handy." Oscar put down the blade. "So, please, tell me the lie that's on the tip of your tongue just waiting to come out, that you think is gonna get you out of this situation."

The man scowled at Oscar, "I'm a hunter and I—"

"Okay, we're sticking to the hunter story, I figured you'd have changed it after I showed the dagger, but..." Oscar nodded over at Gregga, "That's a fairly common one but, maybe he'll spice it up. I do so love a good story." He then turned his attention back to the bound man. "Oh, sorry, I interrupted you, please continue."

"Wha... wha... this isn't a joke, I'm from Krelin Village. I was just out hunting when I was grabbed and brought in here. I really don't know who you people are, and truthfully I don't wanna know."

Oscar scratched at his shoulder, "Is that it? I figured there'd be more this time." The man stayed silent. "Oh well, I guess not everyone is an expert when it comes to lying. They all can't be Jaspers after all." Oscar pointed to the man's boots, "Your boots are too new and expensive-looking to be from any type of respectable hunter. Any hunter worth his bow would have broken them in ages before he ever took them hunting." Oscar tapped the side of his mouth, "Your tone of voice is all wrong for Krelin Village, they speak more lowborn. Your speech is more city man than country hunter. Hell, if you would've spent any time in Krelin, you should've been able to figure that out. But at the very least, that tells me that some nobles are involved. So that's a start."

The man's face grew dark, "Who are you, people?"

"Oh, my apologies, I am Oscar Highland, leader of the Black Jewel mercenaries. On a mission to find out what's happening to the people out here. I don't suppose you'd know anything about that, now would you?"

"Mercenaries," said the man in a disgusted tone, "I've heard of you before. Aren't there more important battles for you to fight, rather than be out here? What? You're going to tell me you're out here trying to protect peasants?"

"Aye, that I am. Granted, I'm not exactly fond of the

people out here, but I am a fan of their coin."

"What does coin matter, we're out here doing important research. The kind that will benefit the whole world."

"So, you mean, you're using lowborn people as test subjects for your experiments." Oscar stood up, "I've been through this before, you can kill 'em now."

"You don't want to ask him where his friends are hiding?" asked Gregga.

"Oh, I guess that could be a thing to ask." Oscar turned back to man, "Do you wanna perchance tell me where your stupid friends are before I have you killed?"

The man seemed confused, "What?"

"Sorry, I guess this is going a little fast for you. Let me explain properly. Very soon... you are going to die in this room. Do... you... want to tell me... where your... stupid friends are? You would be making things much easier for me."

"Do you? Do you think this is some type of joke?"

"I find it quite funny, yes. A group of silly nobles playing savior of the world, by killing low borns. I'm sure you tell yourselves all kinds of wonderful pleasantries at night. That the ends justify the means or some shit like that."

"You dare," said the man as the air of the tent began to move. "I thought to play the common hunter to learn who you were." The man broke the bindings on his hands with ease, sending splinters flying across the room. "But you lowborn scum are not worth the dirt you stand on." He then reached up and snatched out the restraint around his neck.

The air began whirling around the room as his voice echoed. "I am Fredrick of house Normat, you all are nothing before me." Fredrick whipped his hand forward and sent a wave of force so strong that it sent that table with its items flying across the room, tearing a hole in the tent. Gregga jumped back to avoid the table and landed on her butt.

The man hovered in the air, glowering down at them. He pointed his hand at Oscar. "I will rip this whole place from the ground, starting with you. "Exormite!" he said as a wave of blue force leaped out of his hand towards Oscar so strong that it rattled the tent. And just as quickly as it came, the force vanished before him." The man seemed confused until he saw Jomo and Momo channeling magical power. "You're both mages," he said in surprise.

"Okay, girls bring him down," said Gregga.

He looked around to see a large amount of dirt and rocks hovering above his head. Suddenly, it all came crashing down on top of him, pinning him belly first to the ground and covering him in pounds of dirt. Jomo and Momo then hopped on top of him, patting the soil, making dust clouds.

"Well that was certainly fun to watch," said Oscar patting dust off his clothes.

Gregga stood up, coughing and waving dust away, "Did you know he was a mage?"

"Of course not, I just assume everyone's a mage, especially nobles. That's why I wanted him held around your little munchkins."

Two dark-skinned men ran into the tent with blades in their hands but stopped when they saw Gregga hold up her hand at them.

"That was fun; he was flying," said Momo as she packed the dirt down on top of the man with her sister.

The man slowly began to open his eyes, coughing out dust.

"Well that didn't take long, hello again," said Oscar.

He saw Oscar and tried to lash out at him, but noticed he couldn't move a single finger. "What... what's happening? What have you done?"

"Oh, well, you threw a little temper tantrum, so I had these two hold you down," said Oscar as he pointed to Momo and Jomo, who were sitting on the pile of dirt on top of the man with their legs crossed.

He twisted his neck to see Jomo and Momo smiling back at him.

"He packed down good, he stuck," said Momo.

"What, get off me this instant, I demand you release me."

"Actually, while you were out, I had a great idea on how you could be of use to me," said Oscar as he glanced around the tent to see Rana huddled over in a corner under a table. "Ah there you are. Rana, can you find this man's blade I had a moment ago. I'm sure it's around this tent somewhere. Will you get it for me? I need to finish my conversation with him before we continue." Rana slowly began to ease from under the table, "There ya go, I promise Mr. ahh, what was your name again?"

"I swear, I'm gonna—"

Oscar threw dirt at the man's mouth, "Higgins, let's call him Higgins. I promise Mr. Higgins won't be doing any more magic tricks." Rana started to search around the room for the blade, as the man began to cough up dirt.

Oscar pulled out a flask of alcohol from inside his cloak. "Sounds like you have a bad cough Mr. Higgins, wanna drink?"

"Wh... wha..." said the man between coughing fits.

Oscar shoved the flask into the man's mouth. He coughed up a lot of the liquid as his eyes began to water.

"Feeling better now?" asked Oscar with a grin on his face.

"Okay... I... I surrender."

Oscar looked over at Gregga, "Oh, I think he's finally understanding the situation he's in." Then he turned back to the man and playfully started slapping the side of his face. "Shame it's too late, but them's the rules of war."

"Wait... wait... my family has money; they will pay you handsomely for my return. More than those peasants have given, I assure you."

"Oh, we've reached the bargaining stage, figured he'd curse me a few more times, to be honest. Okay, then boy, make me your offer. I am a businessman, after all."

"Five hundred gold, my family owns a shipping business. I'm sure they'd pay at least five hundred gold for my safe return."

"Woah, that's a lot of gold Oscar, think you'd want to take him up on that," said Gregga.

"Yeah, but some things are worth more than money," said Oscar as he smiled down at the man. "You see, Mr. Higgins. I'm going to use you to help me protect my investment."

"Wha... what do you mean?"

Rana walked up, shaking, and clutching the knife against her chest.

"Oh, I see you've found it. Good. Rana dear, have you ever seen someone die?"

"No... no, sir," said Rana, with her knees shaking.

"Ah, good, hand me the knife," said Oscar as he reached out his hand over the man's head.

"Wait... wait... what..." said the man as his head bobbled on the ground.

Rana held the blade out in both hands. Oscar smiled, "It's not so bad." Oscar reached out for the blade, and quickly made a fist around Rana's hand on the hilt, then gripped her other hand, slapped it closed on the other, and then drove the blade into the man's neck with Rana's hands around it. The man gasped from the shock of the blade entering his throat as the sound of gurgling blood was heard from his mouth.

Rana winced from the pain of Oscar, slapping her hands to the blade. She felt something on her finger as she looked down to see the man's blood coming out of his neck and onto her and Oscar's hands. Then slowly, she started to glance between the bloody blade still in the man's neck and Oscar, who stared back into Rana's eyes.

"Congratulations on your first kill."

Rana's eyes opened wide in terror as she tried to pull away. But Oscar kept a tight grip on her hands over the blade. Keeping her locked over the now dead man's body.

Her eyes began to water. "Let go, let go," said Rana as she desperately tried to free herself, but Oscar's grip was tight, and he was strong. No matter how hard she tried, she couldn't free herself. "Please, let me go. Please..." Oscar did not say a word. He just held her hands in place as she sobbed uncontrollably in front of him as the moonlight shone down on them from a hole in the top of the tent.

After a minute or two, Oscar finally removed his hands from Rana's. She didn't respond; she just stayed over the man's body with her hands on the blade. Oscar stood up and walked towards the exit of the tent before turning back to Gregga. "She's not to leave the tent tonight."

Gregga nodded and walked out with Oscar while leaving the two men to stand outside on watch. "See that the kingdom girl stays here," she said to the men as they nodded in acceptance. Gregga then ran up in front of Oscar and stood before him.

"Did you plan that?"

"No, I saw an opportunity, and I took it."

"You were not given permission."

"Would you have given it, had I asked?"

"No."

"Then I was right not to ask."

"There will be a price."

"There always is."

Gregga kneed Oscar in the stomach, making him bend over in pain, and before he could regain his balance, she struck him in the face with her fist, sending him crashing to the ground. The dark skin men of the camp just started laughing at the sight. But the kingdom men stood up and started coming closer to Oscar and the woman. Gregga knelt beside Oscar as he spat blood onto the ground and lifted himself onto his elbows.

"Your kingdom men are coming to Oscar, are we finally going to have some fun together?"

"Halt!" yelled Oscar out to his men. "I have this under

control," he said as he shook his head, trying to shake off the blurriness from his eyes. "Well, go on, then, you're not done yet, are you. That's two, but I took three?"

Gregga smiled, "A man of pride you are, Oscar." She pulled out a small blade and stabbed Oscar in the back. He clenched his teeth as one of his arms went numb as he felt the blade sink in. Gregga leaned in close to Oscar's ear. "The price has been paid; your son is now safe from me. Congratulations, Oscar, you are now forgiven." The woman stood up, ripping her blade free of Oscar's body. "Get a healer; the commander has proven he is a man of honor tonight." A few men came over and picked Oscar up off the ground.

"Take me back to my tent and get Frillin to come patch me up," said Oscar as he turned his head to Gregga. "A pleasure doing business with you, Gregga."

Gegga nodded and smirked, "Go on and lick your wounds. We'll take care of your little kingdom girl tonight."

The men escorted Oscar away.

Inside the tent, Jomo and Momo sat atop the dirt above the man's body, staring at Rana in silence. After some time, Rana lifted her head and removed her hands from the blade. She tried wiping the tears from her eyes but ended up just smearing blood on her face. Rana pulled her knees up to her chin and wrapped her arms around her legs, beginning to rock back and forth while staring at the dead man's body. She then looked over to see Jomo and Momo still on top of the body, sitting with their legs crossed, staring back at her.

"What do I do now?" asked Rana to the two girls.

Momo looked at Jomo, "Sister."

Jomo looked at Momo, "Sister."

The two girls crawled over the man's body towards the blade that was still in his neck. Momo pressed down hard on the blade, causing more blood to ooze out of the man's neck. Then both girls began rubbing their hands in the man's blood and patting his neck with heavy force, splashing blood on their clothes and arms.

Rana just stared at the girls as if she were watching them through a window; nothing seemed real to her anymore. The girls then began to rub the blood on each other's faces before turning to Rana. Rana just kept her hands cradled around her knees as Jomo and Momo approached her. Both girls began to rub the man's blood on Rana's face before wrapping their arms around her and holding her in each other's embrace.

Momo rubbed her bloody face against Rana's face, "Sister."

Jomo rubbed her bloody face against Rana's face, "Sister."

And once again, Rana began to cry as her tears mixed in with the now dead man's blood before falling from her face.

CHAPTER 21

Victor rode back into the city of Passala behind Prince Saffron, and a very weary faced captain Cardon riding next to him. Much like Cardon's first return, a crowd of people gathered in the streets like before, but now they were offering well wishes to the prince and the royal family.

Prince Saffron waved at the people who had gathered and threw on his best smile for them as he passed, "I do so love the common people, the way that they cheer for me. The way they claim that they would do anything for me. Why, it makes a man want to hold them in his arms. Don't you agree with my unloyal captain?"

Cardon just dropped his head as they strolled through the city streets and made their way towards the home of the magistrate.

"Oh don't be that way captain, I could have had you and your men bound and gagged as we marched throughout the city; instead, I sent your men back to the front, and you're atop a horse and still seem ever so much the hero of the kingdom. I'd say I'm being rather generous considering the situation of things," said Saffron as they entered the gates of the magistrate's manor.

Willow ran out of the stables holding a bow over his shoulder, making his way up to the captain and the prince.

"Greetings, your highness, and welcome back, my lord. We were all surprised to hear you had left so early. But we would have prepared better if we had known you were off to meet Prince Saffron."

Saffron smiled at Willow, "Now, now, don't be too hard on your lord, you must understand that some things need to be kept quiet, especially for members of the royal family." The prince turned to Cardon with a grin on his face, "You never know where you might find a traitor in our mist these days."

"Oh, yes, Sir, I understand," said Willow.

Saffron looked over the manor and then noticed the bow over Willow's shoulder, "Oh, are you a hunter?"

"Oh... ah... Yes, Sir, I was training that boy over there before you arrived, he's my ah... trainee."

Saffron caught a glimpse of a boy trying to string a bow over by the stables. "Wonderful, perhaps while I'm here, we could go hunting. I fancy myself quite good at it."

Willow's eyes lit up, "Oh, that'd be wonderful. To get to hunt with the prince, it would really be an honor."

"Tell me good Sir, is the owner of this manor still here?"

"Huh? Oh, yes, Sir, he was informed of your arrival a little while ago and awaits you in the main hall."

Saffron dismounted the horse, and the rest followed suit. He walked up to Willow, patting him on the back, "Well then, lead the way, my good man."

Willow led the group into the main hall, where the magistrate was waiting. His attention was focused out the window as the group entered the room.

"Hello there magistrate, I hope you don't mind me stopping by unannounced. After having a talk with your son, I just had to come and make an introduction."

The magistrate turned and bowed toward the prince. "Of course not, your highness, please, you and your men take a seat. You are welcome in my home." The magistrate noticed Willow behind the prince. "Ahh, Willow, please give me some time alone with our guests. We have sensitive matters to discuss."

"Huh... oh... yes, your grace," said Willow as he turned to leave.

"Don't forget, Mr. Willow, I expect you to keep your word about the hunt."

Willow smiled back at the prince, "Oh, yes, I will go now to see if I can gather more bows," said Willow as he happily left the room, with the prince's guards closing the door behind him.

The prince walked over to the large table at the center of the room. He began sliding his hand across it, feeling the engraved designs along the tabletop. "How are things magistrate, everything going well for your family?"

The magistrate turned back to Saffron with narrowed eyes. "I'd heard that you were the flashy type, an animal that likes to play with his food before he kills it. I assume you've gotten all the details out of my son."

Saffron frowned at the magistrate's words, "And here I was hoping that you'd try to deny it. You know, I've seen many fathers forsake their sons for their own sake. But I guess not all sheep are of the same stock." Saffron plucked an apple from a bowl on the table. "But you are mostly correct; still, I wish to hear the story from you personally. Who is this girl that everyone seems to be so fascinated with?" asked Saffron as he took a bite out of the apple.

"And if I tell you all I know, what assurances do I have that you won't strike us down after I've given you what you want?" asked the magistrate.

Saffron raised his hand for a moment as he finished chewing the apple. "Oh, that's good." He looked around the room before turning back to the magistrate. "Why, absolutely none, both of you might be dead by the end of this day. But at the very least, you telling me now ensures that you and your son will get to live a little bit longer." The prince walked over to Dekol and handed him the apple, rubbing Dekol's shoulders. "You took a brave gamble trying to steal from the crown. And I respect that, I really do. But I would surely not expect such a brazen man as yourself to be so squeamish when it comes to gambling on the consequences of those same actions now."

The magistrate stared at the prince for a few seconds, "Fine; the girl had an odd power about her. Something unique, I'd never felt it before."

"Yes, I was told that," Saffron turned to Victor, "And I assume father sent you to find this girl."

"I was under the impression that she might have been a child of yours. Well, either yours or the kings," said Victor.

"Ha! Perhaps if it were a boy, but a female heir to the throne hasn't been born in the last five hundred years. Father would have smothered her the moment she was born if that were even possible." Saffron turned to the magistrate, "You said her power felt different, how could you tell?"

"I have the talent for healing, and as all healers are capable, if I touch a person of magical talent, then I can get an understanding of their power through how it reacts to mine."

"Well then, that makes this easy." Saffron strolled over to the magistrate and offered his arm. "Take a peek inside and tell me what you see."

The magistrate stared at the prince's forearm.

"Well, go on then, I won't bite," said Saffron.

The magistrate grabbed the prince's arm and closed his eyes for a few seconds, "No, it's different, it's strong, but it's smooth." The magistrate removed his hand from the prince's arm, "No, her's was more rigid, and the prince's power is stronger, they're too different to be the same. Your talent is smooth; the girls' was more violent. Like it was fighting against itself inside of her."

"Well that doesn't sound pleasant at all," said Saffron as he turned to his men, "Dekol, you said you couldn't follow the trail of horses that you found?"

Dekol finished chewing on the apple that the prince had given him, "No, after a while, the trail veered off into too many directions, there was no telling which was the true path," said Dekol.

Saffron shook his head on his way back to the table, "That's a shame; it appears as if you still have your work cut out for you, Victor."

Victor was watching a piece of white fabric hanging down from the second floor, but he turned to the prince after hearing his name. "What? You expect me to find her again? With no information to go on." He nodded over to Cardon. "After they let her slip away to goddess knows where."

Saffron grabbed another apple from the table while strolling around the room, "Of course, you're our secret weapon. Obviously, you may keep Dekol and Frenka with you." The prince pointed the apple towards the captain and the magistrate. "Oh, but I do suppose your right, these two did ruin a royal investigation. That crime, at the very least, does carry consequences." The prince placed his hand under his chin in mock contemplation, "but killing a mage is so wasteful. Oh! I know. Men would you please chop off one of the magistrate's arms."

"What!" said the magistrate.

"You can't do..," said Cardon as he tried to stand, but one of the prince's guards held him in his seat, and another man placed a knife at his throat as three other guards walked forward grabbing the magistrate, dragging him towards the table slamming him down on top of it.

Saffron smiled at Cardon, "Oh, I imagine I can. What do you think, Victor? Am I being unfair to one of my subjects?"

"The man already tried to kill us once already, by sending goons to the tavern I was staying at. He won't get sympathy from me," said Victor as he noticed that the white cloth he saw before on the second floor was now gone.

The prince clutched at his chest in mock surprise, "Goddess no. Perhaps we should hold a public execution and just be done with it. I surely don't feel safe in the home with this murderer." The prince then turned to Cardon, "And if the father was involved in the attempted murder of an imperial investigator, then surely the son was too," said Saffron as the guards held out the magistrate's left arm while keeping him pinned to the table. One guard pulled out a blade from his sheath. "No, I'll do it. Father always said a man should do his own dirty work. Gotta inspire moral in the men and all that." The prince pulled out his own sword from the sheath at his side and walked around the table.

"Your highness, please, I'll do whatever you ask," said Cardon as the guard held the knife to his throat.

"Don't worry; I'm a fair man. No father should have to watch their son die. So, I promise, I'll kill you after your father has passed out from the blood loss. But first, let's see about that arm, shall we." The prince turned to his guards while waving his blade around. "Now hold his arm out straight, I would like to make the cut as clean as possible," said Saffron as he raised the blade above his head.

"Your highness, I beg you to reconsider," said the magistrate.

"Sorry, but you should understand, responsibilities, and all that. Can't have such an untrustworthy man in my mist." The prince's face changed as if an idea struck him. "Actually, will you be attending my wedding in the coming month?"

"Huh!" said the magistrate in a state of confusion and panic as he was held firmly against the table.

The prince lowered his blade to his side and leaned his face in beside the magistrates on the table. "I'm asking if you will be attending my wedding magistrate."

"I... I... ah was not aware of your majesties ceremony, but if you would allow me, then I will most certainly be there," said the magistrate.

Saffron pulled back to his height, "Good, good; then I guess I will let you keep that arm of yours after all. Can't have any one-armed men walking around on my wedding day, it would upset my darling bride," said the prince as he sheathed his sword. "But tell me magistrate, seeing as you've tried to steal from the crown and tried to assassinate one of its own representatives. How am I to assume you won't try something again?"

"I'll do anything my lord desires; I admit my mistakes; I was weak."

"Oh you certainly do sound repentant, tell me, magistrate, have you ever heard of the Sakari bonding process?"

Victor raised a brow at the statement.

"Your Highness?" asked the magistrate in a state of confusion.

"It's an absolutely marvelous technique, It's some type of magical bonding ritual. It makes you absolutely subject to the whims of the contract holder. I also heard it leaves a nasty mark on your back, but such is the price of loyalty, I suppose. I've heard it only works on those with talent, which luckily you two are blessed with."

"I... I... I mean... surely that won't be—"

294

"Guards, I've changed my mind, slit the captain's throat, would you make sure the magistrate sees it."

"No, wait I... I accept your offer."

"Good, and what of you, my dear captain?"

The captain spoke without hesitation, "I'd already accepted a lifetime of service to the crown before father got me involved in this mess. So, I imagine now it'll be no different than it was before."

Saffron wagged his finger at the captain, "Oh, I like your resolve, okay then men and ladies, please lock these two down in the cellar where they may have a proper father-son bonding time until proper arrangements can be made."

The guards released the magistrate as he fell to the floor rubbing the back of his neck. Saffron nodded to his guards, and they removed the blade from Cardon's neck.

Victor watched as the two men were ushered away and noticed that the white cloth was back hanging down from the second floor. It seemed like part of a dress to him. "You are a very forgiving man, prince," said Victor.

"Well, I do not wish to have my lady wife think of me as a savage if this one-armed gentleman were to show up at our nuptials. I would simply die of embarrassment."

"I was not aware of such an event upon my arrival, I would figure it would be the talk of the kingdom," said Victor.

"Oh! That's because we haven't announced it yet, but it will be proclaimed soon enough, that I am to marry Laura of House Dunblane. Honestly, though, she is quite the docile woman and quite boring. I much prefer the fiery type. Speaking of which, Frenka, how about you and I—"

"Piss off."

The prince threw up his hands, "...and thus the boring Laura of house Dunblane it is," as he walked towards the door. "Come men; I do believe I mentioned something about a hunt earlier. Dekol are you any good with a bow nowadays?"

"I think I can still manage at a decent range," said Dekol as he stood up and followed behind the prince.

"Splendid! And Mr. Victor, I invite you to join us as well. I still have matters I wish to discuss with you." The Prince and Dekol strolled out of the room with his guards following behind him.

Frenka buried her face in her hands, "Goddess that man's annoying."

Victor turned to Frenka, "Is he always like that?"

"Always... every second... of every day."

"He seems... exhausting."

Frenka pulled her hands free of her face and sighed. "You would not believe number of messes he got us into." Frenka gestured over to the door, "Only one who never seems bothered by it is Dekol out there."

"Actually, does the prince often ask to marry you, that seems like quite an opportunity to turn down. Is that how he shows he cares?"

"Yeah, I think I will not want his type of caring."

Victor laughed, "I imagine a life chained to him would be quite complicated."

"I already have life chained to him; I just not give him satisfaction of bedding me," said Frenka, shaking her head. "Did you know that idiot has bed chambers lined with alagon stones?"

Victor's face twisted into confusion. "Wait, so the prince of the kingdom, one of the most powerful mages in the land, sleeps in a room that he can't cast magic in?"

Frenka nodded her head while throwing up her hands, "You see, even you find it stupid. That is type of man I am forced to deal with."

"You really do have your hands full," said Victor to Frenka as she rubbed at her temples. Victor shook his head at her frustration and glanced up to the second floor of the main hall. "You up there, you're gonna show yourself, or should I have the frustrated mage here send fireballs at

296

you."

There was a ruffling on the second floor before a girl popped her head up.

"Do you often spy on your lord's proceedings?" asked Victor.

"I ahh... well," said the girl.

Another girl appeared from the doorway upstairs, "Please forgive her, my lord, she's always been the curious type."

"And who might you ladies be?" asked Victor, staring up at the two girls.

"We're the housemaids, Sir, I'm Miraval and that one's Pelly." Miraval stepped out of the door to the railing, staring down at Victor. "Ah, may I ask a question of you, Sir?"

Victor waved to the girl above him, "Go ahead. How may I be of assistance?"

"Were they talking about Rana earlier, is she the girl that disappeared?"

"Rana? No, that's not," then Victor remembered that the little girl Maggie had once called Fairline the name Rana before. "Yes, did you know her?"

"Oh, I knew it. Was she really taken?" asked Miraval.

"Sadly, yes. Come down here, you two; you're not in any trouble. I'd just like to ask you some questions."

The two girls looked at each other before slowly making their way down the stairs and standing before Victor.

"How do you two know Rana?" asked Victor.

"We both worked the kitchens at Broderick's, my lord," said Miraval while trying to straighten out her skirts.

Victor raised a brow at Broderick's name, being brought up again, "I'm not a lord, just talk to me as you would each other. Now, tell me more about this... Broderick?"

"Oh! Well, he owns the tavern near the gate in town. Well, it's a whore house really, but he treated us nice enough."

"So... Rana worked in the kitchen of a whore house?" asked Victor.

"Yes, Sir, we lived there together before coming here."

"You don't look so well Victor," said Frenka, noticing that Victor's face seemed to constrict after each question he asked.

Victor pulled his hands to his face while leaning back into the chair, "One of you girls fetch me some wine, please, I imagine I'm going to need it."

Two mugs of wine later, Victor was rubbing the stubble of his beard, "Okay, so... Broderick found Rana sleeping in his stables and took care of her in the whore house. But not just her, he apparently takes in a lot of young city girls and trains them to be maids for the nobles of the city. But he just so happened to bring Rana along with you to the magistrate's home, where the magistrate took a liking to her. Is that about right?"

"Don't forget she likes throwing knives," said Pelly as she nodded her head. "She had gotten pretty good at it too, even was getting a couple of them to stick."

"Yeah, Jacob was teaching her all kinds of stuff," said Miraval.

"Wait? Who's this Jacob then?"

"Oh, he was a guy who came to the tavern a lot to see Rana, to train her."

"So he was one of the captain's men?"

"Nah, he was one of Broderick's friends, I think. Broderick used to be a fighter; his friends always stop by to see him. I think it's called the Black Jewels."

"That's a mercenary group, seen 'em in capitol before. King even used them against small rebellions before," said Frenka.

"Excuse me," said Pelly as she ruffled her apron while staring down at her feet, "But is Rana gonna be okay?"

Victor stood up from the table, "I'm going to try my best to see that she is. When I find her, I'll bring her back to visit." Victor said as he started walking to the back of the building towards where the men had taken the magistrate and Cardon.

"Where are you going now?" asked Frenka.

"Going to have a talk with our dear magistrate," said Victor as he made his way down into the cellar area of the manor. Upon entering he noticed that Cardon and the magistrate had been bound to chairs with their hands tied behind their back. Cardon had been bound in metal bracelets to ensure his power wouldn't allow him to escape. Victor walked in, taking a seat in an empty chair.

"I'm surprised they left you with no guards; the Prince is awfully trusting," said Victor to the two men.

"Foolish sentiment," the magistrate scoffed. "And where would we go, even if we could escape, no one would harbor us as enemies of the crown."

Victor shook his head, "Magistrate, I must ask. Why risk your position and apparently your life over a girl, whether she be powerful or not? Surely after witnessing what happened to Duke Richards, one would think that would give you pause."

"I have no reason to answer your questions now."

Victor shook his head while looking up at the ceiling, then took a deep breath, trying to let out his tension and frustration that had built up over the past days. "Magistrate, I'm tired. I haven't had a good night's sleep since this whole mess started. And now my suffering persists only due to you and your son's bungling. I've had two groups of people try to kill me. One attack your son can attest to, and as for the other group, I'm fairly certain they were sent by you yourself. So either you answer my questions this very second, or I will visit such monstrous acts upon you and your son, that you'd have wished the prince would have killed you himself."

The magistrate froze for a moment at the cold assuredness at which Victor had spoken his last words. The room was silent for a short while as the magistrate turned his head to his son. Then he slowly began to speak. "None of you understand, only one with the gift of healing would.

299

That girl is different. I have been around the mightiest mages in the kingdom. And even in my experience, that girl is singular."

"What? You're gonna tell me she's stronger than the king," said Frenka entering the cellar.

"No, it's not power; in truth, my son in terms of talent is stronger than her." The magistrate shifted in his chair, uncomfortably. "Magic follows rules, every mage in every kingdom, their talent flows according to these rules. But hers doesn't, from the moment I touched her head, it was like her talent was trying to attack me."

"If she's that dangerous, why try to nab her? Sounds like a lot of pain if you ask me," said Frenka.

"You're not a true born noble Frenka," said Victor as his eyes narrowed on the magistrate. "Among the noble families, magic power is more valuable than coin. If he had managed to get a hold of a new type of magical power. Given a few years and if that girl's children possessed the same power as her. Who's to say that they couldn't topple a kingdom or, at the very least, get themselves a monopoly on whatever discoveries her magic would bring."

"Exactly, just the sheer fact that these possibilities now exist is worth more lives than I can imagine."

"How did you find this girl after the fire? I can't imagine she just strolled in here one day," said Victor knowingly.

"By chance, that is exactly what happened; a flesh peddler in town named Broderick brought her to me."

"A flesh peddler," said Frenka, "how old was girl again?"

"The king said she was thirteen or so, but she appeared to be ten, maybe eleven," said Victor.

The magistrate coughed, "Be that as it may, his name is Broderick, he supplies most of the nobles in this city with maid services, you may question him yourself if you like. But he seemed to have no knowledge of the girl at all."

Frenka just tossed up her hands. "I still don't think all this trouble will be worth it."

"Perhaps not, it could all be a waste of time; her power could turn out to be turning water purple. But at the very least, it's worth checking into," Victor stood up from his seat, "I thank you gentlemen for your time, and I hope never to see you again." He then left the room with Frenka, following behind.

"You can be quite the vicious man, Victor, I heard that little speech you gave them," said Frenka.

Victor raised an eyebrow at Frenka. "Well now that we know that the magistrate's story matches up with those maids upstairs, we now have a solid lead to go on."

"So, what now? We going to whore house?"

"Not yet. We've been invited to go hunting. You feel like joining me in a romp through the countryside?"

Frenka smiled, "I do so enjoy wasting time."

They arrived outside of the city, resting amongst a hill where Saffron was shooting an arrow into the distance.

The evening sun was shining down on the field as Victor watched the wind flow over the grass, creating a flowing wave amongst the greenery. On both sides of the field were rows of trees that stretched as far as the eye could see. And far off into the distance, Victor could see the cold mountain tops. He then looked over at Frenka.

I wonder which mountain clan she belongs to.

"It's always good to be out in the countryside," said Saffron gazing over the environment. "But tell me, Sir, Willow. Are you sure this is a good spot? I don't imagine any game here."

Willow walked up to the prince, handing him another quiver of arrows. "Oh yes your grace, ya see those woods over there. We can send a man or two in to rouse some game. And some will run out into that area over there. But we must be quick, or they'll be out of range. My pa used to do it with me all the time."

"Ah, yes, I see. So, we need someone vicious, vile, and all-around scary to startle the little beasts out, well I can think of no one better than—"

"Call my name, and I burn your hide clear across pasture," said Frenka.

"Dekol, my good man, be a sport and rouse up some game for us, would you?"

Dekol smiled at the prince as he strolled past him towards the wooded area.

"What did you want to talk about, prince?" asked Victor.

"Oh yes, I was interested in you, actually," said the prince as he remembered his words.

"Me?"

"I think you fail to realize what your name means in other kingdoms, Victor. The famous sixth general, the man who won outnumbered against the Kingdom of Dresha. And given the Starlight Queens current predicament, I'm surprised they haven't called for your return yet."

"I'm flattered that you've taken an interest in me," said Victor.

"Is that strange? You are quite famous, after all." The prince shook his head. "No, in truth, I didn't take much interest after our first meeting. But the setting now is quite odd. A famous general, a girl with a mysterious power vanishing into the night. Not once, but twice. I'd certainly have to be a fool not to take notice, given how things have progressed."

Victor stared at the prince.

"What? Did you assume me to be some kind of simpleton?" asked Saffron.

"Yes."

"Oh, you're not candid at all; are you, father told me you didn't play well with nobility."

"Tell me prince, why involve me in all this? I'd imagine this to be something to be handled by your own men. Not some outsider from a different kingdom."

"You'd have to ask father that. These past events have me perplexed as well. But tell me, Victor, what do you think of this whole situation?"

"I think the whole thing is shit. A little over a month ago, I was set to retire, find myself a lady friend, and call it a life. Now look at me, I'm in a foreign land, brown-nosing with an extravagant prince and his merry entourage of killers." Victor turned to the prince, "No offense, of course."

The prince chuckled, "Non-taken, at the very least, we both recognize the situation to be peculiar."

"Hey you two, stop woo'ing each other and come back. Dekol in position," said Frenka yelling from up the hill.

Victor turned back to see Frenka waving at them. He saw that the prince had a very peaceful smile on his face as he stared up at her.

"By the goddess, you really do love her. Don't you?"

The prince turned to Victor, "What, of course, I love all women."

"Prince I'm not some noble from a great house, I grew up in a little hut in the countryside. And the expression you just gave Frenka, is the same my father gave my mother every morning of my youth. That's not something you can fake."

The prince stared at Victor for a second, "Yes, well, you have a keen eye, I suppose. But it's not as if she'll ever notice. Well, come along then, no need to leave Dekol sulking in the brush."

They arrived back uphill as Saffron grabbed a bow. "Will you not be joining in the fun, Victor?"

"Sorry, I'm not much of a huntsman."

Frenka shot a wave of flame into the sky as the signal for Dekol. And soon, a dozen wild critters and birds were flushed out of the woods into the open. The men and few guardswomen all aimed and loosed their bows. But after the first volley, a large boar roared out of the brush.

"My goodness, where did that beast come from?" asked

the prince as he quickly nocked another arrow. "Anyone that bags that beast earns himself fifty gold pieces."

They all promptly reloaded their bows and let loose another volley of arrows.

One by one, the arrows landed into the dirt. But one arrow landed true, striking the beast in the neck.

"Spectacular shot. Whose arrow was that?" asked the prince as he looked around.

"I... I think it was mine, Your Grace," said Willow sheepishly.

The prince walked up patting Willow on the shoulder, "Good shot my man, the purse is yours. Tell me if you're ever wanting a job as an archer in the military, the job would certainly be yours." Willow rubbed his head shyly.

"Well there's Dekol; he's coming out of the brush now," said Frenka. "But who's that child with him?"

"Oh! That's me, apprentice, I'd wondered where he'd gotten off to."

Victor looked down to see Dekol making his way back up the hill, but he narrowed his eyes and stood slack-jawed as he saw Billy trailing behind. "Goddess help me, the vanishing bastards have joined together."

"Well done, Dekol," said the Saffron as the two rejoined the group, "Where did you ever find that boar?"

Dekol turned to Billy, "That was actually the kids doing; it was sleeping, so I didn't notice it in the brush. He sensed it and startled it right before I would have stepped on it."

Willow shook Billy's head in celebration, "Well done, lad, you just bagged us fifty gold pieces; I'll split it with ya, I swear it."

"That little bastard's right impressive," said Frenka as she turned to see Victor shaking his head. "What's wrong?"

"Nothing... I just suddenly seem to have grown quite weary."

"A feast we shall have tonight, men," yelled the prince.

Later on, that evening, they all returned to the magistrate's manor, enjoying a feast of roasted boar. Victor excused himself from the manor to take a step outside as Frenka walked up behind him.

"You not party person?" asked Frenka.

"Not especially no, just thinking about how I'm gonna find this girl."

"I don't think the prince expects you to find her."

"Perhaps not, but I'm not the type to give up unless I'm satisfied."

"Well, what's left besides following up on that Broderick fellow?"

"Not much, but that's our most likely bet at the moment," said Victor as he left for the city, "enjoy the party; I'll go check it out." Victor headed off into the city with Frenka following behind him.

"I'm not one for parties much myself."

Victor asked a few questions around town about Broderick, and they all pointed him to the tavern.

"You really think the whore house owner knows where she is?" asked Frenka.

"Probably not, but perhaps someone who frequents the place does."

The two walked inside and saw a few people eating or flirting with women as they themselves took a set at a table.

"Hey, darling, what can I get for you?" asked the lady.

"Just something to drink please," said Victor and Frenka nodded the same, "Excuse me, but who's in charge here, I was told to talk to him if I wanted to hire some maids."

"Oh, you be wanting Broderick then, that's him up at the bar. He handles all that business stuff."

"Thank you," said Victor as he glanced over to see the man working the counter. "Well, no need to waste time." Victor stood up. "Try to enjoy yourself while I'm away," he said to Frenka as he walked over to the bar taking a seat.

"What'll ya have," said Broderick.

"Ale, if ya would be so kind."

Broderick grabbed a mug and opened the tap on a barrel.

"I was told you were the owner of this place."

"Yeah that'd be me. If ya looking for cheaper prices for the girls. they make their own; I got no say in it."

"No, I heard you could help me as to the whereabouts of a brown-haired girl named Rana around the age of twelve or thirteen."

Broderick stiffened in front of the barrel of ale, "Oh yeah, by who."

"Just some people in town after asking around."

Broderick turned and placed the ale in front of Victor, "And why ya asking, who are you to her."

"I was sent by the crown to find her."

Broderick narrowed his eyes at Victor, "What, she some nobility or something?"

Victor just shrugged, "No idea, I was just told to find her."

"Yeah, well, I had her here for a while, but I gave her to the magistrate. She's his problem now. And her hair ain't brown; it's black."

Victor raised an eyebrow when Broderick said her hair was black. "Yeah, seems she was abducted from the magistrate's care not too long ago. So, I'm off to find her."

A smirk came across Broderick's face, "Well that's too bad, but as I've said. She's not my problem anymore."

"Any idea who might have taken her, perhaps someone in town who fancied her or something?"

"Hell if I know, I just train 'em and sell 'em. What they do after that ain't my concern."

Victor sighed and raised his mug to Broderick, "Well, thanks anyway. I guess I'll continue to ask around." Victor turned to walk back to the table and on the way, noticed a woman sitting down on Frenka's lap. "Well, don't you look comfy."

Frenka rubbed the woman's face, "I am. You say to enjoy myself while you were away, did you not?"

"I didn't take you for a lover of your own feminine joys."

Frenka gave the lady a coin and slapped her on the ass, sending her away. "Oh, I like good cock like any other lady, but ain't no harm in having bit of girl fun is there. Also, that boy Jacob, Rana was sposed to be hanging around. Seems he's second in command of Black Jewel Mercenaries."

Victor just stared at Frenka with an eyebrow raised.

"What? Ya think I just magic and pretty face? I told you that prince used to get us in all kinds of odd shit. Getting information part of it. Remember, me and Dekol here to help. You might want to start using us more."

Victor raised his hands in submission, "Point taken; I shall rely on you more."

"Right, well, let's be off then, unless you be needing a night's romp with one of tavern girls," said Frenka.

The two headed out of the tavern.

"So, what's next step, Royal Investigator?"

"We track down where the Black Jewels went. If we find them, then chances are we'll find the girl," said Victor scratching at the side of his neck.

"Leave that bit to me then, shouldn't be much trouble."

"What would I ever do without you?" asked Victor, placing his hands behind his head as they walked forward.

"Oh, you'd still do same. Just bungle it more, I'd guess."

CHAPTER 22

Rana awoke on the ground, looking face up into a hole in the tent as the morning sunlight shone down upon her. The previous night seemed like a bad dream. But on each side of her were two sakari girls sleeping with their hands and legs wrapped around her. Jomo nuzzled her face against

Rana's, getting more comfortable in her slumber. Rana would lay there with them for another hour thinking about all the events that led her to where she was. She then raised herself and saw the dead man's body. It still had the knife that she and Oscar had driven into the back of his neck.

Why did all this have to happen? Did he really need to die?

Slowly, she released herself from the embrace of the sakari girls and crawled over to the body and sat before it on her knees; it was still covered in dirt from where the girls had trapped him. Rana just stayed there for a while, looking at the man's dirt cover face. His skin had gone a purplish pale, and his mouth was open. She noticed the presence of a small amount of mud by his eyes as it seemed he was crying as he died. Reaching her hand out, she began rubbing the man's head, feeling the unnatural coldness of his body as she began to run her fingers through his hair. *I'm sorry,* she thought to herself before she pulled her hand back, feeling the lingering coldness of the man's death slowly leave her fingertips.

Rana heard some shuffling behind her and turned to see the sakari girls staring at her.

"Sister sad. First kill is always hard. Jomo's first kill, she cried like baby," said Momo.

Jomo pushed Momo, "Me not cry that much, and sides, you cry too. Sides, new sister did good on first kill."

Rana just stared at the two girls as they bickered with one another. "Why... why do you call me that, sister?"

The girls stared at Rana confused.

"Because you are new sister, we share blood, same blood," said Momo as she continued to tussle with Jomo.

The flap of the tent opened, and the sakari woman Gregga from the night before appeared, followed by Oscar who now had a bruise on his left eye and his right arm in a sling. The woman shook her head at girls who were all covered in blood and dirt.

"You're all a mess, go get yourselves cleaned. And take

her with you," said Gregga.

"Wait," said Oscar as he walked over and stood over Rana and the dead body of the man. "Take that blade with you; it's yours now."

"I..." Rana glowered up at Oscar with furrowed brows and hate in her eyes, "I don't want it."

Oscar smiled, "Nice to see that fires still there, but it's not about what you want. It's about what you will do. You wanted to become a killer; well, a killer is what I plan to make you."

"I wanted to learn to fight, not kill people."

Oscar gave a chuckle, "I don't know what you think fighting is," then pointed to the body of the dead man before them. "But that's what the result of fighting will usually end up like. Either you die, or they die."

"I won't do it," said Rana as she clenched her fists.

"Oh, this one's quite stubborn, are you sure you're up for this Oscar?" asked Gregga.

Oscar reached over, grabbing a turned over chair and sat down on it in front of Rana. "Until you take that blade, neither you nor your new friends there will bathe, you won't eat, you won't drink. You might be brave by yourself, but ya willing to make them suffer with you on ya little holy quest? And I don't think either of ya has had anything to eat since yesterday. We'll see how long you last before survival sets in."

Rana looked over at Jomo and Momo, all covered in blood and dirt as they stared back at her. Then, she turned back to Oscar, "That... that's not fair."

"Life's not fair, make a decision."

"I hate you."

"Good, hate keeps you alive. Make a decision."

Rana looked to the girls again before reaching over, grabbing the dagger by the hilt. She gripped it tightly and snatched the blade out of the man's neck. The blade was coated in dried blood as a few drops fell back down upon the back of the man's neck. She turned back to Oscar once again, holding the blade in her hands, glowering up at him.

"Now there's the look that's going to keep you alive," said Oscar as he grinned down at the girl, "Now go get the sheath too and get yourself cleaned up with them."

Rana scowled at Oscar before turning and starting to scan around the room. She noticed that Jomo and Momo also started to search around for the sheath.

"Oh! Here it be," said Momo as she lifted the sheath from under some cloth and brought it over to Rana.

"Okay, girls, let's go get you cleaned up," said Gregga as Jomo and Momo walked over to her. Rana stood up to her feet, glaring at Oscar, before making her way over to join up with the girls.

"Oh, one more thing, girl," said Oscar.

Rana turned to Oscar, still staring daggers at him.

"Welcome to the family. You can start calling me father now."

Rana's face turned from hate to confusion, to utter disgust as she watched a twisted grin come over Oscar's face.

"All right, you two, she's your responsibility now, see to it that she's cleaned properly and taken back to Dessi. Apparently, she's becoming a little knife thrower," said Gregga to Jomo and Momo.

"Oh, she good, she showed us," said Jomo as she grabbed Rana's hand, leading her out of the tent and off into the encampment.

After a while of walking, they entered another tent where sakari women with buckets of water were cleaning themselves. Jomo and Momo hurriedly took off their clothes and grabbed a nearby bucket of water. Rana stared at the other naked sakari women.

Jomo stared at Rana, "You must clean too; come we clean you." The two girls walked back and stripped Rana guiding and sitting her on a stool.

"Oh, what's this here. Momo, what you two doing over there with that kingdom girl," said a sakari woman.

The other ladies in the tent turned to stare at Rana.

Momo turned to the lady, "She new sister; we taking care of her before she go back."

The woman raised a brow and pressed her lips tight, "This kingdom girl be your new sister, now that can't be true. What your mother say to that?"

"She was there during first blood, she knows."

The woman gave the girl a suspicious eye as Momo dumped a bucket of water over Rana's head. "Oh, I heard about balance rites last night with the old man. It seems now we know the reason."

Rana shivered from the cold water being dumped on her.

The woman stood up, wrapped her body in a white cloth, and walked over to Rana, inspecting her. "Well, I guess one kingdom girl is as good as another. Her golden hair is pretty though."

Jomo shook the water from her head and started rubbing her nose at the woman in confusion, "What you mean, her hair is black like ours."

Rana wiped water from her eyes and looked over to Jomo, "My hair is brown, your hair is darker than mine."

The woman touched Rana's hair, "I not from the kingdom, but this looks gold to me. Jomo, what makes you say her hair dark like ours?"

"It is dark; you have gotten bad eyes," said Jomo.

The sakari woman made a knowing face before speaking in another language that Rana didn't understand. Suddenly all the women of the tent came over, and Rana was surrounded by a dozen naked ebony ladies, each touching her hair and saying out different colors. Rana closed her eyes and tried to think of anything else while she felt her hair being tugged from different directions.

Suddenly Rana heard Momo's voice yelling in a different

language. She opened her eyes to see Momo slapping all the ladies' hands away and standing in front of the women.

"Oh sorry, I guess we get a little carried away there," the sakari lady said to Rana, "but did you girls make art trick? Everyone here is claiming that girls' hair and eyes are different color."

Rana scratched her head, confused by the ladies' words. Every time she'd ever seen her reflection, her hair and eyes had never changed.

"It no matter, Rana is sister," said Momo.

"That be true," said the woman. "It be odd. But that be true," and turned around with the other woman to continue bathing.

Rana turned to Momo, "What is that way you were speaking before?"

"That how sakari speak."

"Oh, I never heard sakari before." Rana glanced around the tent, "are all the women here warriors too?"

Jomo laughed and turned around, gesturing around the tent, "Of course, all sakari are warriors. Even all lady here, they have killed many man."

Rana took a look around the tent again at the ladies bathing each other but noticed large markings over the back of Momo.

"Momo, what is that on your back?"

Momo turned around, trying to look over her own shoulder, "What is what?"

"Those markings on your back."

Momo thought for a second, "That is my... how do kingdom people say... my talent. Jomo has markings too."

Rana turned to Jomo and saw that she also had the same markings on her back.

"Oh, I didn't know people with magic had markings."

Jomo and Momo laughed as they continued to wash each other.

After washing their clothes Jomo and Momo wrapped

themselves in white cloth. Jomo picked up Rana's ragged tunic, but it ripped as it latched to something on the floor of the tent. Jomo inspected the beaten and torn tunic, shaking it as two gold coins fell out.

"Sister Rana, you should wear other clothes. These bad."

"I... don't have any other clothes."

Momo picked up the two gold coins. "We have clothes; you wear ours."

The two girls helped wrap Rana in white cloth and strolled out of the tent back into the camp with her. This time, they arrived at another bigger tent with a carriage outside of it. The girls went inside the tent, and Rana noticed that this was a much nicer tent than the others. It had rugs on the ground and beautiful silks hanging from the top. Jomo and Momo ran over to a corner and pulled out two trunks.

"Sister Rana, come to see."

Rana walked over, noticing what seemed to be weapons and weird armour hanging up on poles. After reaching the girls, she glanced down to the trunk and saw a large number of clothes of different fabrics messed together.

"What, where did you get all this."

"We have lots of clothes, mother and old man give us different stuff. You put some on. Some will fit."

Rana knelt, looking at the girls, and they nodded for her to go ahead. She plucked out random clothes noticing how different they all were. She even pulled out what she thought was a ballroom gown.

"Oh, that's the big fluffy one, we don't know how to put that on. Too many straps and ties and ribbons," said Jomo.

Rana found herself speaking before even realizing it. "Oh! I know how. I can show you if you'd like."

"Oh yes, we want to know, but not even mother knew," said Jomo.

And soon, the girls had stripped down and started trying on random items in the trunks. Jomo had left to get them some food and returned to witness her sister in a huge peach dress with an even more impressively large peach bow on her head that matched it. It appeared so ridiculous to Rana, that despite herself, she couldn't help but start laughing as Momo jumped and strutted around the tent in the absurd attire.

"I'm the princess of the kingdom people," shouted Momo as she danced around, kicking her legs out in a silly dance. Momo reached out her hand to Rana. "Come, you dance to and feel better." Rana slowly allowed herself to be lifted as they began to dance around the tent, each one in silly clothes.

After eating and trying on more outfits, Jomo and Momo decided to put on more skirts with ragged tops that exposed their stomachs. Rana decided on a long blue tunic.

"Now, it's time for you to go to Dessi, training time they said."

"Oh! That's right. I forgot, and Dessi is probably waiting on me," said Rana as she started to leave.

"Oh, new sister, wait," said Jomo as she grabbed the dagger and sheath from the floor, walking up to Rana. She tied the sheath around Rana's waist, letting the dagger hang off her hip. "Old man said you must keep."

Rana wanted to throw the dagger on the ground, but glancing down at Jomo, she decided to give up on those thoughts. "Can I... am I allowed to come back?"

The girls looked at each other, confused before they turned back to her.

"Of course, you sister now. You belong with us," said Jomo.

Rana smiled back and left the tent; she soon realized that she needed to get her blades that Holland had made for her. So, leaving the sakari part of the encampment, she wandered around asking for directions to Oscar's tent until she finally made her way there. When she opened her tent, she took a deep breath and steeled herself to go inside. She then opened the flaps to see Jacob and Oscar standing over the table, talking about something.

"Have we received any word back from Jasper?" asked Oscar.

"None as of yet, but it should be soon, he left last night."

"Knowing him, that jackass is probably telling his stores in a tavern somewhere, we'll give him till tomorrow to report in, no need to think much of it yet. He's always late."

"Perhaps, but I'm still worried if..." said Jacob as he noticed Rana peeking her head through the flaps of the tent. "Well, it seems we have a guest, what have you been up to since yesterday. I hand you off to Dessi, and you disappear."

Rana scowled at Oscar, "Is uncle Jasper, okay?"

Jacob tilted his head at Rana, "Uncle? Well, that's a new development."

"Oh that young one's been very busy, haven't you? She only been here a day and already decided to join our merry band of killers," said Oscar, still sporting his black eye and sheltered arm that Rana smirked at when she saw it again.

" I need the knives to practice with Dessi."

Oscar reached over and grabbed her satchel, holding it up for her to see. "You mean these things."

Rana stepped closer, holding out her hand, "Yes that."

"Not so fast little one, if you want these, you're going to have to ask the right way."

Jacob noticed the dagger on Rana's hip, "Where'd you get that?"

Rana glanced down at her waist.

"Oh that's a present from a fellow we were acquainted with, shame he died just recently. That daggers kind of a memento. Isn't that right... daughter," said Oscar with a grin on his face as he placed the satchel on the desk in front of Rana with his hands pressed firmly on top of it.

Jacob looked to Rana and then to Oscar with a raised brow. "Daughter?"

Rana gritted her teeth staring at the satchel.

"Remember you're responsible for those sakari girls now, so you'd best behave," said Oscar.

Rana grabbed the satchel, snatching it free from Oscar's hand and clutching it to her chest. "Yes... Father."

Jacob looked back down at Rana in shock, "Father?"

Rana ran out of the tent, leaving Oscar with a grin on his face and Jacob with a dumbfounded expression of his.

After making sure Jacob didn't follow her, Rana slowed her steps and started making her way to where she and Dessi had trained beforehand. But she began to wander a bit as she couldn't remember exactly which part of the camp it was. After wandering for a few minutes, she heard someone call out to her.

"Hey there, little one, ya looking for me?"

Rana turned around to see the large man Molan who was fighting the day before. "No, I'm trying to find Dessi."

"Now what ya got there?" Molan reached down and pulled out the blade from Rana's sheath. "Oh fancy, it even got little jewels and everything. You plan on being fancy killer then? One who decorates the body of fallen in shiny trinkets?"

"No, Oscar is making me keep it."

Molan rubbed his chin eyeing the blade, "The old man, huh? He must have taken some liking to you. Tell me, little one, have you ever killed a man."

"No, I... yes I did?" said Rana as she dropped her head in shame.

Molan pursed his lips and clapped his hand, "Wooo! That's good, then tell me what it felt like to you."

Rana thought for a second, "I was scared. It was wet. He... he made noises. And his blood was warm..." Rana saw Molan staring down at her. "What? Did I say something bad?"

"Tell me, child, has a man claimed you yet?"

"Claimed me, I don't... what does that mean?"

"It means you have picked a man to serve."

317

"Ah, no, I don't think so. I mean, don't I serve Oscar now?"

"Then I'll get Oscar to give you to me, you will be my war wife, and I'll teach you to kill properly."

"Hey, Molan, what you doing over there? We're about to head off to scout," yelled a man off in the distance.

Molan turned around, "Alright, quit your babying." He knelt back down, placing the sword back in its sheath at her hip. "Ah well, Dessi trains over that way," Molan pointed to the south of the camp, "Let me know if you ever wanna get broken in, I'll turn ya into a proper war wife." He pulled Rana close and kissed her on the cheek. "Be well."

Rana felt a shiver come over here as she watched as the burly man stroll off toward some men in the distance on mounted horses. She rubbed the cheek that he had kissed with the sleeve of her tunic before walking off towards the direction Molan had gestured towards. Eventually, she found Dessi sitting on a log reading a book and ran up to her.

Dessi noticed Rana coming, "Oh, there you are, I thought you'd run away after yesterday's training, figured I'd have to go on a hunt for you." Dessi looked Rana up and down, "I see you found yourself some new clothes and a right fancy blade there."

"Ah, yeah. Oscar... he... he gave them to me," said Rana gripping the blade and turn her face away, trying to hide any emotions that might show on her face from Dessi.

Dessi put down the book and stood up. "Seems someone's been busy. Well come along, then, the day's still early, so we can still get a decent amount of your training in." Rana nodded and placed the satchel on the ground unrolling it, revealing the blades that Holland had made for her. "Oh, ya found them did ya. Good! Best to practice with what you're gonna be using, rather than mine." Dessi slipped out a few of Rana's blades, inspecting them. "Humm, they're smaller than mine, good for your size, I guess. And what's with

318

these four with the little holes in 'em. Looks a bit odd to be throwing 'em with how they're curved."

Rana picked up one of the holed blades and gripped it how Holland had told her and began slashing at the air. "He said to use them like this."

Dessi watched Rana's demonstration as she danced around with the little blade, "Holland always did like trying out his new toys on people, just try not to let those things get ya killed."

Rana once again started her training with the small knives as Dessi instructed her through the routine. After another day of throwing blades, Rana laid on the ground, breathing heavily and cursing the fact that she even had arms.

"I guess that's good enough for today; you got more blades to stick than yesterday. So at least its progress. Your aim is still terrible, though." Dessi said as she inspected the piece of wood that had a few blades scattered about it. But past the piece of wood, she saw Oscar headed in her direction.

"You coming to check on how your baby is doing?" asked Dessi.

Oscar scanned over the jumbled mess of blades in and around the piece of wood. Then down at Rana, who was sprawled out on the ground. "I can make a guess on how it's going. You enjoying your training, then I take it?"

Rana just laid on the ground, "I'll get better."

"Oh, I expect you will. But I'm here to discuss another part of your training."

"What you got in that head of yours Oscar?" asked Dessi.

"Jasper hasn't contacted us yet; he was supposed to provide daily updates on what's happening in the city and find out why people kept disappearing. So, it's simple. Go to the city, find Jasper and report back. Take the girl with you to show her how it's done."

"And if I can't find him?"

"Then come back anyway, and I'll send Molan and his men in if there's fighting to be done. For now, all I want is information. You leave tomorrow if Jasper doesn't return tonight. The town's only an hour or so away from here."

Oscar glanced down at Rana, "And you, try not to cause any trouble while you're out there. I don't want to send men off to rescue you again."

Rana made a sour face at Oscar as he turned and walked off back into the camp.

"Well then, seems we got our first mission together," said Dessi. "Don't suppose you know how to ride a horse."

"I know how to ride. I used to go riding with Papa all the time."

Dessi stood up, grabbing her book, "Then come on, let's get you a saddle ready."

CHAPTER 23

The next morning Dessi and Rana arrived at the city of Nyril as they crossed a bridge on horseback. Rana looked over to the side of the bridge, watching as people in white robes splashed about in the river that ran through the town. The town had a wall of cut off moss-covered trees that encased it, where the only way inside was the bridges at each end of the village.

"Why are they playing in the water?" asked Rana.

Dessi laughed, "They're worshipping. That's how some of the goddesses worshipers show their dedication."

"By splashing in the water?"

"Well some people throw salt on the ground at the birth of a child; some kill animals to worship gods. Even the sakari mark their bodies for their beliefs. Who's to say, that splashing about in the water won't get you in the goddess's favor."

"Well it looks silly."

"I think you just wanna go play in the water."

Rana turned back to see Dessi giving her a knowing smile.

They entered the city, leaving their horses at a stable. Rana glanced around, noticing that all the houses were either log cabins or a few stone buildings scattered throughout the town. There were a lot of people walking through the streets carrying random things and talking to one another. And every now and then, she'd see one or two of those people that were down by the river splashing, who had on the white tunics as they wandered through the streets.

"Why are so many of them wearing the white robes?"

Dessi glanced ahead at the robbed people, "That's what the faithful wear in some cities." She spotted a vendor ahead of them and patted Rana on the back, "Come on, let's grab something to eat."

They made their way through the streets over to a vendor.

"Excuse me, Sir, I'd like two pieces of fish, please."

The man turned around smiling, "Sure thing." and threw two pieces of fish on some stone blocks, flipping them over as they began to sizzle.

"Me and my sister are new here, on our way to

Passala. You know where we could stay the night that's not dangerous?"

The man turned back to the girls and looked down at Rana. "Ahh, you don't have to worry about people messing with ya here. Nyril is a safe city. You can stay at damn near any tavern here and be fine. But if ya wanting for a view over the river, then you can stay at lady Deinne's place over there." The man gestured to a tavern over by the water. "She mostly handles the ladies that come into town, and I ain't never heard about any girls getting roughed up in there."

"Thank you, we were worried because of the rumors about people disappearing round here," said Dessi.

"Bah, just people telling lies. I've been here for years and I've still been seeing the same people every day," said the man as he finished up the fish. He reached into a bucket of water and pulled out two big leaves, wrapping the fish in them before handing it to the girls. "You girls enjoy yourselves in town and take care of that little cutey. The men are going to be after her one day," he winked at Rana.

"Thank you," Rana said, walking off with Dessi and munching on the fish.

"Seems like you already have an admirer in the city, you little cutey," said Dessi in a teasing manner.

Rana bit into her fish again, frowning up at Dessi.

They made their way to other parts of the city, where Dessi introduced herself and Rana as different types of people. To one person, they were a mother and daughter trying to join the church of the goddess. To another, Dessi was a flirtatious woman seeking to have a good time in the city. The story changed every time, but each time she repeatedly mentioned the story about people disappearing in the town. They ended up walking around the city for hours before finally stopping at a tavern and taking a seat.

"Woo! I'm feeling tired."

"I don't understand. How are we going to find uncle Jasper?"

"Jasper's not the type of man to hide. If he's around, we'll hear about him. And when did you start calling him uncle Jasper?"

Rana thought back to that night in the stable where she cried into Jasper's chest, "He told me to call him uncle before he came and got me."

Dessi twisted her lips while looking down at Rana.

"What?" asked Rana.

"You like him, don't you?"

Rana thought for a second about Jasper and nodded, "He's not bad, he's nice and funny and—"

"Oh, sweet goddess, he's got his hooks into you too. What do people see in that annoying buffoon? First Keltre and Prinja, and now you. I'm starting to wonder if he might have that mind control magic that Jacob has." Dessi shook her head in disappointment. "The world has no justice." She looked back at Rana, making a face at her and just waved her hand dismissively. "Well, either way, we gotta gather as much information as we can before we go back to the old man." Dessi waved her finger at Rana, "Now, did you pay attention to what all we did today?"

Rana pressed her lips together, thinking, "We pretended to be other people?"

Dessi laughed, "Yes! but why did we do that?" Rana shrugged her shoulders, and Dessi pointed to a man in a white rob across the room. "To the religious people, we pretended to want to join the church, and to the horny men, I pretended to like them."

"So, you didn't like them?"

"Goddess no, the men here smell like fish and desperation. I did that to get them to talk to me and make myself seem vulnerable. Most men love vulnerable women who depend on them."

"Does Jacob like women like that, do you depend on him?"

"What? No, I mean... I don't think Jacob, well, maybe I

do depend on him a little." Dessi thought for a second before shaking the thought from her mind, "That's not important now, and why'd you bring up Jacob anyway."

Now it was Rana's turn to give Dessi a knowing smile.

"Why you little minx," said Dessi, frowning her face. "You did that on purpose, trying to rile me up."

A woman walked over to their table, "Can I get you girls anything?"

"Just some water for the both of us, and can I get a room for the night here?"

"Oh sure, just go talk to Milly at the front, and she'll get you two squared away," said the woman as she began to turn away.

"Wait, has anything strange been happening in town, recently?"

The lady thought to herself, "Nah, not recently. The chapel guards burned a man for killing his brother a few moons back. But nothing much else since the new guards showed up."

"New guards?" asked Dessi.

"Yeah, they came in and started rebuilding parts of that old chapel. Saying it was falling apart. Ain't nobody been able to get in to worship for a moon or so, except them saved ones in the white robes. Can't wait till they finish and make it safe again. We all been having to worship down by the river since they locked it up."

After the woman left the table, Dessi turned to Rana, "Still feel like you wanna play in that river?"

Rana watched as Dessi walked over to the counter and bought a room key before coming back to the table. "Okay, now that I've got us a place to stay for the night, let's be on our way then." They walked down to the riverfront as Dessi spoke with a few more people about the things that may have been happening in the town.

After they reached the waterfront, they saw that there were still plenty of people in the water dunking themselves.

"Hello there, would you like to participate in today's cleansing?" asked a small boy around Rana's age. Rana shook her head.

"We're here to learn about it," said Dessi as she watched the people in white robes submerge themselves in the river, "We've never seen this ritual before. What does it mean?"

"Oh, every morning, the Kemlor prays over the river to cleanse it, and anyone that has felt themselves to be tainted could come and wash themselves clean."

"What is a Kemlor?" asked Rana.

"He's who the church of the goddess picked to be one of our leaders; there are Kemlors in a lot of kingdoms. They preach the words of the goddess and bless us with her mercy," said the boy excitedly.

Rana watched as another set of people in white robes dunked themselves into the river. "Isn't the water cold, though?"

"Oh, yes, it's very cold. But we bear it as a way to show our dedication."

Rana peered up the hill at a few men in white robes sitting down at tables playing some type of game. "What about them, are they going into the water?"

"Sometimes, the elders come down with us, but they mostly watch over us and inform us if we do something wrong in the ceremonies."

"Thank you, child, but we'll just watch for now," said Dessi.

The boy nodded and made his way down the hill near the water.

"You sure you don't wanna go play in the water?" asked Dessi as she smirked down at Rana, who kept her attention up the hill at the men playing the game. "What? You never played Four Queens before?"

"Four Queens?"

"It's an old game from way before I was born, I'm surprised you never learned," said Dessi as she looked around. "Why don't you run up there and ask one of the men to teach you while I go ask a few more questions." Rana gave Dessi an unsure glance, "It's fine; I'll be down here; you'll be able to see me from there."

"Okay," said Rana as she made her way up the hill towards the men in white robes sitting at the tables. Each of the men were focused on their game. As Rana came closer to them, she saw that each table had a board on it and a lot of stones of different colors. The men were moving them in all kinds of ways.

"Why hello there, you wanna go for a game?" asked an old man.

"Ah, how do you play?"

"Your granddaughter came to visit you Belvac?" asked another man a few tables down.

The old man turned and smiled, "Oh that would be something, wouldn't it?"

A young man with brown hair walked up beside Rana, "Hello there, you going up against Belvac next?" Before Rana could answer, the man turned to Belvac smiling, "Shame on you Belvac, picking on children at your age."

Belvac smiled, "Oh hello there Kemlor, you've come to entertain me with a game again, I hope."

"Then you hope right, old friend," said the man as he sat down in front of Belvac and arranged the stone pieces on the board. He looked over at Rana, "you wanted to learn how to play?"

"Ah, yes, Sir," said Rana.

"Okay, it's actually a simple game. On this board, there are sixty-four squares, and at each corner, we place twelve different color stones sets. Each stone set represents a different Queen and her armies."

Rana pointed to the center, "What's the black stone in the middle between the lines?"

"That's the Queen's tower, at the start of the game, the goal is to capture the Queen's tower. Each of us is allowed to move one piece, each turn. Each piece can either move up or down or diagonally as long as a piece of their own type isn't in the way. If there's a piece of another type in its way, then you must kill it to move forward. But you can't kill two in a row. If you kill a piece, then you flip the stone over to another color. And then that piece can move two spaces in any direction."

"But if you own two sets, what if one of your own sets is in the way?" asked Rana.

"Then you kill your own piece as a way to move forward. You sacrifice one as a way to try and win the game."

"The Kemlor is really good, we've been playing for the last two moons, and I haven't beaten him once," said Belvac.

"Ah, true, but you did come close quite a few times."

The Kemlor pointed to the Queen's tower on the board. "The trick is how you win the game. Every time a piece makes it to the Queen's tower, you remove it from the game and place it in this little bowl, and whoever has the most pieces in the bowl at the end of the game wins. But if you attack the Queen's tower too fast, then your opponent will have more pieces than you still on the board. So, he'll be able to stop you from entering the tower by killing your pieces since you won't have enough left to defend yourself, and he'll win the game. So, you must balance attacking the Queens tower and defending your pieces from your opponent at the same time."

"Why is there no king piece," asked Rana.

The old man laughed, "That's a question I've been asking since I was your age," said Belvac, "I think the common consensus is that the Queens ran him away."

The Kemlor picked up the Queen's tower piece from the board and held it in front of Rana. "Or, perhaps the king is inside the tower, and only his one true Queen can rescue him."

"That's a very romantic way to think of it, Kemlor," said Belvac.

The Kemlor smiled, "I like to think of myself as one of those hopeless romantics."

"No, for me it's hopeless, I'm too old. But you, you're still young enough to have children."

"Perhaps after my work is done, one day I'll find a woman for myself and—"

"Are you trying to steal my sister away from me?" asked Dessi from behind Rana.

The Kemlor looked up to see a beautiful woman with long dark hair and stood up, bumping the table, and sending the pieces to the ground. "Oh, ahh... sorry Belvac."

The old man started laughing, "No worries Kemlor. It's nice to see that a lovely lady can still make bumbling idiots of us all."

The Kemlor frowned at Belvac as he knelt to pick up the pieces." I'm sorry madam, I was just teaching her to play the game is all."

"It's alright. She told me she wanted to come up here and learn. Now, did you have fun, honey?"

Rana stared up to Dessi curiously before she caught on, "Oh... ah, yes, sister, I... he taught me how to play."

"Thank you, Mr... ah?" asked Dessi.

"Ah," The man stood up, offering his hand, "Retallia, Retallia Kolgin. But people round her just call me the Kemlor."

"Well Mr. Kemlor, me and my sister must get going. But we hope to see you around," said Dessi as she ushered Rana off with the Kemlor waving at them as they left.

Dessi and Rana walked back to the hotel and up to their room for the night and sat down on their beds and laid down until nightfall came.

Dessi peered out the window, "I'm gonna be leaving for a while Rana, but I'll be back before the morning."

"Okay, what should I do?"

"Nothing this time, just stay here. I'm gonna go check out that chapel that the woman was talking about."

Rana gave Dessi a nervous look.

"Don't worry. I won't get into trouble. I'm just going to have a look around." She reached down and pulled out two metal spikes from her legs, "Now turn around." She twirled Rana around and started twisting her hair into a small bun and stuck the two metal rods in on each side, "There, now you got your secret weapons, just use that if you feel scared." Dessi leaned down and kissed Rana on the forehead rubbing her cheeks. "Be back soon." And exited the window, sneaking away on the roof, disappearing into the night.

Dessi lowered herself from the roof of the building, dropping to the ground and headed off to the chapel, with Rana watching her from the window as she disappeared into the shadows of the night. She moved between the shadows of the buildings and was satisfied to see that at night there weren't many people out as most seemed to have settled in. Only the occasional guard that walked the streets on patrol was seen. After a few twists and turns down the streets of the small town, she arrived near the chapel. Two guards were standing at the door of the building. Dessi watched as a few white robe wearers came and went from the building. Some had buckets of water, while others only had large sacks.

"What are they hiding in there?" She whispered to herself.

Eventually, a man followed by two guards appeared from around a corner and started heading for the chapel. "Make sure everything is set up properly," he said.

"Yes, Sir," said the guard following behind.

Dessi saw another man in a white robe run up to the three guardsmen.

"Excuse me, Sir, but the leader requires your presence."

330

"Why? Has something happened?"

"Well, he said the men have died, but one was a success."

"What? Did you see it work?"

"No, Sir, the moment it fused, I was sent to come find you."

"Very well, then." The man turned to the soldiers behind him, "Ensure that all the supplies are brought in, I shall return soon." The two men bowed and walked off to the left, and the man who appeared to be in charge walked off to the right, following the man in the white robe.

Dessi watched the man in charge as he walked off. Glancing between him and the chapel doors, trying to make a decision. "Ah, goddess, help me if I'm wrong." She took off to follow the man that seemed to be in charge. After some time, she found herself in front of a small warehouse that she saw him enter. She started to sneak around the warehouse, trying to find a way inside. Eventually, she saw an opening in the building, but it was too high to reach. She scanned around the area, noticing a saddled horse in the distance. After grabbing the reins and walking the horse over to the side of the building, she stepped into stirrups and onto the saddle. Balancing herself up on the horse, she climbed inside the hole into the building.

This better be worth it.

The upper level of the warehouse had a balcony with sacks of grain and hay that stretched all the way around with the building. She looked down and saw several guards below her. But further ahead, Dessi spotted the man she followed standing next to another man in a white robe with brownish hair. They both stood over the body of a man lying on a table. The two men were talking, but she couldn't hear them. She slowly made her way around the balcony when a stench hit her nose.

Goddess, what is that smell?

Glancing down, she saw four dead bodies of grown men piled against each other in a corner. Dessi shook her head, narrowed her eyes, and held her breath, quickly trying to push forward towards the men. She did her best to stay out of sight, making it close enough to hear them.

"Excellent, how fast can you start making them?" asked the soldier.

"Now that I understand how it works, I just need to get more mages to start. It won't be easy, but the hard part is done. Now we just need to find more people," said the robed man.

"I'll start recruiting more people at once."

"No, not here. The people here have suffered their burden. For this prosperity, everyone must share equally in the sacrifice. But now that you've seen the miracle, I trust we can work together without any further complications."

"You've kept your word, and I'll do the same."

"Good, I shall take my leave then. I have an appointment in the morning, and I would like to keep it. In two days time, meet me in Frolock, and we will go from there," said the robed man as he placed his hand on the dead man's body. "Thank you for your sacrifice, Hector. I promise to follow through on this quest."

The two men left the body and began walking out of the warehouse. Dessi decided to creep closer to the body. She saw some red crystals laying on top of the body and looked around for anyone nearby before lowering herself to the ground beside the table. On the ground, she knelt after hearing the men speaking outside.

"What's wrong?"

"My horse, it's run off somewhere." The man yelled, "Suthala, come here Suthala."

Dessi frowned while closing her eyes. *Suthala? What the hell kinda name is that?*

She stood up and turned towards the table. Scanning over the body, she just stared at it amazement. The red crystals weren't on top of the body; they were actually in the body. The man had small crystals embedded in his face and neck, but there was a large jewel embedded into the man's right shoulder blade. She stared at the gem as she saw a light inside of it shimmer.

What the hell is that? She quickly made a decision and slapped the side of her leg, pulling out a blade. If this kills me, I swear I'm gonna haunt that old man.

She placed the blade against the dead man's skin and started cutting the crystal free. The sound of cutting skin and the oozing of blood made Dessi clench her teeth, but eventually, the crystal came free, and Dessi wiped off as much of the blood as she could before slipping the jewel down between her breasts. She then stepped on the table with the dead man and reached up to the balcony ledge of the warehouse to pull herself up.

"I'm not sure how you got in here, but I can't just let you leave with that," said a man's voice.

Dessi snapped her head around and saw the leader of the men narrowing his eyes directly at her.

Where the hell did he come from? "You don't plan on holding a woman hostage, do you?" asked Dessi, as she turned around, dropping her hands to her side.

"I'm assuming you're part of that group of rebels about half a day's ride from here."

Dessi raised a brow at the man. *Rebels?*

"No need to look like that. We caught one of your kind snooping around a few days ago. He took quite the beating before he finally broke. Trying to overthrow the king is one of the more foolish things I've heard."

Jasper and his tall tales again. Do they still have him? Is he still alive? Dessi glanced down at the dead man near her feet, "And what you're doing isn't just as unbelievable?"

The man shrugged, "Perhaps, but everyone must serve their purpose. Shame you'll never live to tell the tale." The man dashed forward, reaching for Dessi legs. She jumped over him, landing on her feet, pulling out a blade and throwing it at his head, he shielded himself with his hand as the blade pierced straight through getting stuck in his palm. Dessi slapped her sides again, pulling out four more blades, launching them at the man. The blades embedded themselves into his forearms as he tried to shield himself. Two more blades pierced his unprotected legs sending him dropping to one knee as he yelled in pain.

"Dammit, guards," the man yelled.

Dessi soon heard guards running toward her. She ran left, lifting herself over a wall into the next stall as the men came rushing in, seeing her fall to the other side.

"Get her, "shouted the man to the soldiers.

Dessi ran towards the door with guards chasing behind her. Two guards appeared from the door, but only to catch blades in their necks as she beamed past them. She neared the door, but another guard from a side stall grabbed her by the hair pulling her back.

"Got you."

Dessi grabbed at her hair while another guard ran up to them, trying to help. She kicked at the upcoming guard, but he caught her leg instead. She let go of her hair and threw her hand down, slapping the thigh of the leg that the man held, grabbing another blade, and stabbing the man holding her hair in the leg. He screamed in pain, and Dessi ripped the blade back out, flipping it over in her hand and bringing it back into the man's eye. He screamed again, letting go of her hair as Dessi fell, throwing the blade into the throat of the man that still had her leg. Both men collapsed to the ground by Dessi as she stood back up to her feet and ran forward out of the warehouse.

The captain hobbled his way out of the building into the night, glowering down at his dead men before him. He then stared off into the night, gritting his teeth as he saw even more dead bodies off in the distance.

"Get more men, she's still around here somewhere," said the captain while cradling his bleeding arm.

Over in a corner on the side of a building Dessi hid in

the shadows under a pile of wood, watching as the guards circled past her over and over again.

CHAPTER 24

Victor and Frenka were out in the forest, sitting on a log by a river in the middle of the night.

"You think we should have gone with him?"

Frenka threw a stone across the water, watching it skip a few times, "We're not exactly stealthy types, Victor. It's best to leave Dekol to do what he good at. If we with him, we'd slow him down or just bungle it up."

Victor leaned forward on the log, "Can't argue with that, I've never been good at sneaking around. A few days ago, I tried it to sneak up on some kids and almost got pelted by rocks."

Frenka reached down with a smirk on her face, picking up another stone and tossed it over to Victor. "And so, we wait."

Victor threw the stone across the water, "Frenka, you said that you were from one of the mountain clans, right?"

"Em-hum," moaned Frenka as she rubbed the side of her neck.

"You never thought about going back; you seem to be trying to escape the prince. I figured you would have run away by now."

Frenka sighed as she leaned back, surveying the stars up above her, "I thought about it before, but nothing left for me there. My sisters all have men and families now, and father takes grandkids hunting. If I go back now, father would just start searching for me a man, so that I could start popping out babies. Or so he says, 'strengthen the clan," she said in a pretend manly voice.

Victor chuckled, "How does marriage work in your clan anyway, is it like ours? With big stupid ceremonies like your Prince Saffron is about to have."

Frenka smirked, "Ha, thankfully no. Our coupling rituals vary. Sometimes the young boy and girl choose each other, or fathers give daughters to strong men for breeding strong offspring; other times, men claim children as war wives after battle. If all men of clan are killed in war, then Jalahe of clan forces the women to pick man from winning clan. That way, clan becomes bigger and stronger."

"That sounds like a fun time. But if that's the case, why did your father bring you to the kingdom then? Surely a mage would have added to the power of the clan."

"That is true, but I needed to be trained to become

strong. Father had promised me to War Leader Gresham and sent me to kingdom to become strong for him. But I did not like Gresham; he was good warrior, but terrible man. He had history of beating women."

Victor shook his head, "So when is this Gresham supposed to come get his wife."

"Oh, he did, two years ago. I killed him on castle steps."

Victor's eyes opened wide. "Wow, didn't expect that answer."

"In clans, when a girl is given, it can not be undone. Only in death is woman given her freedom. And I wanted my freedom, and it felt right, so I killed him."

"I guess that's not the life you envisioned for yourself."

"I have no vision for my life; I only live my life. The only truth I need is that it is indeed my life. What feels right, I will do, and what feels wrong, I simply will not. Gresham did not feel right."

"Well, I bet the prince was happy when he found out."

"That idiot prince is always happy, but he also does not feel right."

"The politics of your—" said Victor.

Suddenly, a stiff breeze blew through the air, making a whistling sound as the wind cut through the leaves of the trees. Soon slowly, all around them, little orange lights on the ground began to glow. Frenka and Victor began to gaze around themselves at the small orange lights as they began to float off the ground and started moving around them.

Frenka laughed at the tiny lights as they hovered in the air, "Look Victor, ember bugs. Oh, so many." She stood up from the log, extending her hand, trying to see if one of the bugs would land in her palm. Frenka slowly began to sway her hand through the air so soft and gentle that Victor was drawn to the movement of her fingers. And in that movement, her palm began to glow a pale orange as she tried to match the colors of the ember bugs.

Victor watched Frenka sway around as the little

creatures seemed to gather around her as if drawn in by the magical glow of her hands. And finally, two small embers bugs landed on her palm as Victor gazed upon her in a peaceful state of surprising bliss. He suddenly found himself not wanting to interrupt this moment. To him, it was as if the forest was alive and was determined to make Frenka the shining figure in a night of moonlit darkness and shadows. Everything just started to seem too perfect. Between the sound of the running stream, to the feel of the slight breeze around them. The sight of Frenka surrounded by the little lights was captivating. In an instant, it was as if the world decided to focus on her.

Frenka's lips gave a smile of genuine joy as the little embers danced around her. She turned to Victor with the ember bugs in her palms and noticed him staring at her oddly, "What is wrong, Victor? Do you not like ember bugs?"

Victor caught himself and blinked his eyes, trying to snap out of his gaze. He then took a deep breath, "Frenka, right now, at this very moment. You are probably the most beautiful creature in all the kingdoms."

Frenka's eyes opened wide at the remark, but soon a sly smile crept across her lips as she lowered her eyes at him. "Oh, my, is famous general trying to claim this Frenka for his own?"

Victor smiled back, "Out of fear of winding up like your last betrothed, I think that I will just admire you from afar."

Frenka chuckled and slowly walked over to Victor, kneeling on the ground before him. She held out her hands, showing him the ember bugs. "Look, they are dancing," Victor glanced down in Frenka's hand and saw the two little bugs moving around her palm in a circle. It did indeed seem as if the bugs were in a little dance. But he couldn't help himself but to focus Frenka's soft lips as she attempted to blow on the tiny lights. He felt the coolness of her breath as it flew over her hands and tickled the skin on his neck. She smiled as the little bugs lifted her hands and took off to join its brothers and sisters that were still circling around them.

Frenka's eyes opened wide as the creatures seemed to play in the air around them, some landing in her hair and on Victor's shoulders.

He and Frenka stood up, both watching in marvel at the sight. Dekol walked out of the night gazing at them in the spectacle of light.

"Well this is a sight," said Dekol.

Victor turned to Dekol, "Oh you're back, how did—"

Victor felt Frenka's hand on the side of his face as he was turned back to face her. His eyes opened wide with the feel of Frenka's lips on his. She stood on her toes to reach up to his face as she embraced the softness of their lips, pressing together. And as if in a flurry, the little ember bugs took off into the night sky above them as a small delicate wind blew them away. After a few seconds, Frenka removed her lips from his, lowering herself back down to her height and stepping back to smile at Victor.

Victor stared at her for a moment in shock before closing his eyes and taking in a long deep breath of air and slowly exhaling. He opened his eyes again and began to speak.

"Okay... why?"

Frenka tilted her head, "Because it felt right. Why? Did it not feel right to you?"

"Oh, it felt right. It probably wasn't right. But it most certainly did feel right."

"Good, I'm happy it felt right."

Victor quickly turned to Dekol, "Dekol my good man. Did you find those nasty diabolical mercenaries that we are searching for?"

Dekol raised an eyebrow at Victor with a small grin on his face, "Yes, they are set up around a few miles from here. But I think they sent the girl we are trying to find off into the town of Nyril."

"But why would they do that?" asked Victor.

Dekol shrugged, "I'm not sure. I saw a woman and a

girl leave their camp accompanied by a group of men on horseback headed in the direction of the city."

"Well, I guess that's our next destination then. It's not like we can just walk into their camp and demand the girl. So, at the very least, if some of their own are in the city, we can capture a few and try to propose a trade for the girl. How far is the city from here?"

"Less than a day's ride from here if we stick to the main road."

"Alright then, only a few hours till sunrise, so we might as well be on our way. It's not like I'll get any rest now, anyway."

Frenka walked by the men, "That's a shame; things were starting to get fun." The men watched as she strolled over to the horses preparing to mount up.

Victor bit his lip while shaking his head at her for a few seconds before turning to Dekol, "I don't suppose you can just omit tonight from your memory the next time you give your report to Prince Saffron about us?"

Dekol rubbed at his chin while giving Victor a knowing smile, before walking over to Frenka, preparing to mount his own horse.

Victor watched the two before rubbing his hand against his forehead. "Fuck."

CHAPTER 25

The next morning, Rana sat up, squinting her eyes at the light outside the window. She kept going in and out of sleep, waiting for Dessi to return, but she never did. So she laid there in the room, twirling the rod that Dessi had given her, wondering what to do. When she became anxious, she lifted herself from the bed and began to pace the room. But soon that wasn't enough.

Maybe she's in trouble, what do I do if she never comes back.

Rana made up her mind and walked outside of the tavern, then down the street searching for Dessi. After another hour of searching, she stopped back at the town center where people were playing Four Queens to rest. To her surprise, she noticed Dessi walking through a crowd of people and felt all her tension melt away, but she quickly noticed that Dessi seemed distracted, like she was looking over her shoulder. Her face was red, and her hair seemed to have stuff inside of it. Rana began to get up and run over to her when she saw a man step in front of Dessi. He had dark hair, and his right arm and hand were wrapped in cloth. Rana could see Dessi was making a mean face at him.

"Those blades of yours, you have a talent to be appreciated," said the man as he raised his hand in front of Dessi, showing her the bandages going up his arm and the wrap that he held around his hand.

"Well, it's nice to know that a man can appreciate a woman's work. We do go unnoticed so often," said Dessi.

"Oh, miss, I promise you have my full attention now. And I just can't wait to spend some time alone with you. But I can't waste this chance at a public execution. So, tell me, how will this happen? Will you come with us and probably die at the stake or am I going to have to cut you down in the street. Keep in mind; the second option is much more preferable to me."

"Well, it wouldn't be right for this girl to turn down your hospitality."

"A wise decision, although not the one that I would have preferred. Cutting you down here in the street would serve as a valuable lesson to the common people and the faithful. But alas, we can't always get what we want. Take her to the chapel and lock her up with the other one."

The guards grabbed Dessi and led her away as Rana tailed behind them. After following them throughout the city, they eventually lead her to the Church of the Goddess chapel where men were standing guard.

Rana struggled with what to do next. She would have to tell someone, but she didn't know who. Jacob was back in camp, and she didn't think she knew the way back even if she did try to make the trip. So, she just sat down on the ground with her back against the side of the building watching as people left and entered the chapel. After a few hours of watching people come and go, she noticed that sometimes the people in white robes who had been at the river when they entered the city would go into the building. Some of them were even children around her age. So she waited until the next child in white left the building and decided to follow her.

"Hey, excuse me," Rana called out to the other girl when there were few people around.

"Yes, what is it?"

"Can anyone get into the chapel, I wanna see the art inside," said Rana.

"Oh, they closed off the chapel to the public ever since the Kemlor arrived. Only the devoted can get in right now. We train for months to become one of the goddesses chosen ones. If you would like to join, I can ask—"

"Oh, no, I... my father is a merchant here. We just wanted to see the art and offer prayers before we left."

"Oh, I am sorry then, perhaps we will be accepting visitors on your next return."

"Yes, perhaps, but thank you anyway."

The girl bowed to Rana, turned, and walked away. Rana turned and ran down to the river, where there were still a few of the faith washing themselves. She noticed that the ladies didn't really watch their clothes as they hung them to dry and instead spent their time talking. It didn't take much effort for Rana to sneak up and snatch away one of the white robes when the ladies were preoccupied with their gossip.

On her way back, she noticed the sun had begun to set,

and as such, the streets were less crowded. Rana went into an alley and changed into the white robe before making her way to the chapel. She grabbed a bucket from a nearby house and turned the corner to the chapel. Seeing that the entrance still had two guards on duty, she took a deep breath for courage and walked towards the chapel doors. The guards noticed her coming, and when she reached doors, the one man smiled and stepped to the side.

"Go on, child."

Rana bowed her head, "Yes, Sir, I shan't be long."

Rana walked past the guards and into the building. The inside was alight with candles spread throughout the main hall. She glanced around the room at the paintings that were spaced out among the walls. While there were nine paintings, it was just the same three portraits over and over. And under each painting was a fragrance burner that made the room smell sweet. The sound of voices was heard coming from the back of the chapel. Rana began stepping closer to the voices and noticed shadows moving inside a hallway at the end of the chapel.

"The bitch was tough, but between the both of them, we got what we needed. I want you to send out a scouting party in the morning. Find out exactly where their camp is and how many there are. We don't need any more problems right now," said a man's voice.

"Are they really trying to overthrow the king?"

"What kinda name is that anyway? Mushroom Group, sounds ridiculous."

"I've heard of them, though to my knowledge, they only operated in the Kingdom of Ursjun. Why the hell are they out here?"

"Don't know, but they both sounded like their group was big. We ain't got enough men here for some big rebellion raid. If she's telling the truth, then we might be in big trouble."

"Then we'll kill them and escape before they find out, if

she's here alone, that means they don't know anything yet. We'll let the city guards deal with them. But only after we find out if she was telling the truth. I'm not giving up all my work because of some lies that bitch might be telling. Just go get some men ready to ride with you come the morning."

The man left the room and headed out. Hearing his footsteps, Rana hid behind a row of seats as the man passed her by. After being sure he was gone, she made her way back to where they were speaking before. The hallway had a lot of rooms inside. Peeking inside the first room, she saw the man from before who had taken Dessi away. He sat at a desk, looking at an odd red jewel over the parchment. Rana thought about the things Maggie had told her and started peering around the room, before noticing an empty bucket. She walked over and picked up the bucket before taking a breath and knocking on the door.

"Yes, what is it now," said the man glancing up and seeing a little girl in a tunic.

"Ah, Sir," Rana lowered her head, "I've come to ask if you needed your chamber pot changed, Sir," said Rana as she raised the bucket for him to see.

"Oh! No, I use the house out back, sorry about my tone. I'm quite tired this evening."

"My pardons then, Sir," said Rana as she turned to leave.

"Girl, wait."

Rana turned back to the man, "Yes, Sir?"

"I'm out of wine, bring me another and some bread."

Rana nodded her head, "At once, Sir," and left the room walking down the hall. She noticed a few guards as well as other men in robes sleeping in cots in the rooms as she passed by and made her way to the end of the hall. At the end were the steps into a basement, and next to it was a kitchen where Rana could see a bottle of wine on a table surrounded by three men talking to each other and throwing dice next to a window.

"You better not be cheating us Gordon."

A male soldier laughed as he picked up some money from the table, "Who me? You boys need some trust; I'm just lucky tonight."

"The fuck you are, you seem lucky most nights."

"Yeah, you tried that shit with the captain last time, and he kicked your ass for it."

"You boys are just bitter is all, you both need to learn to dice better. I can teach ya for a price."

"Oh fuck off with your teachings. Roll again, before I have a mind to finish what the captain started."

Rana silently stepped past the door with her bucket and went down the steps into the cellar. Where she saw a guard posted outside of a room. The guard noticed her but didn't speak. Rana stepped forward, seeing a room with scrolls that had a fragrance burner inside along with a table and a few stools. She could see the flame inside of it, but there was no smell coming out. She looked over to another room with barrels inside of it, and then one more room that housed water buckets and clothes. Rana walked into the one with the water buckets and dropped her empty bucket, picking up one with water and a cloth, then making her way back out of the room and over to the guard before dropping the bucket at his feet, spilling some water on his boots.

The guard grimaced down at Rana. "What!"

"I... I... well, that is."

"Spit it out."

"I was told to clean them before they started up again tomorrow, and ah... empty any chamber pots if you have one."

The guard frowned while observing the state of the cellar. He sniffed the air around them before shaking his head. He pulled a key from his side and unlocked the door. "Right, well, be quick with it then, but they ain't much to look at now."

The guard opened the door, and Rana saw Dessi's body hanging up the air by her arms along with another man.

347

Rana froze, and the guard shook his head at the image of the two strung up in the air.

"Told ya, they ain't much to look at. Now go on and finish up. If ya want out, knock on the door. I'm not supposed to keep it open."

Rana stepped forward as the guard closed the door behind her. She glanced around the room and saw some blades and other cutting tools on a table along with a large red crystal. She continued to inspect the room for anything that could help, but she couldn't see anything of use. She dropped her bucket of water and knocked on the door. The guard made a groaning noise from outside, and the door opened again.

"What now?" asked the guard.

"I... I'm too small."

"What?"

"I can't reach their faces."

"What do you expect me to do, pick you up so you can clean them?"

"Just a second," said Rana as she ran back down the hall into the room with the scrolls and came out with a large stool clutched to her chest and walked back with it to the guard.

"Are we all ready now for their cleaning?" asked the guard in a sarcastic tone. Rana nodded, and once again, the guard closed the door behind her, mumbling something about how he hated children.

Rana placed the stool before Dessi, soaked the cloth in water, and climbed atop the stool began to clean her face. Dessi flinched from her the cold rag against her skin and started mumbling.

"Are we... em... going again?" asked Dessi in a daze.

"Dessi, it's me Rana, Dessi... Dessi..." whispered Rana.

Dessi opened her eyes. Rana could see the damage that was done to her face was something brutal as her eyes were red with blood from getting hit in the face repeatedly.

"Ra... na, wha... wha are you?"

Rana placed the rag against Dessi's mouth, trying to wipe the blood from her lips. "I wanna get you out, but I don't know what to do. You have to tell me what to do."

Dessi tried to nod her head and smile, but all the effort of which allowed for was a shaking of her head a bit. "You... really are a little minx, but... I don't... think there's a way out of this one for me. Unless you got some magic, I don't know about or a way to get Oscar here before morning."

Rana pointed over to the man beside Dessi, "Who's he?"

"That's Jasper, hard to tell now, isn't it, though I couldn't tell either from how much they cut his face."

And instantly, Rana lost her ability to speak. His face was so swollen and cut that she couldn't even tell who he was anymore. Rana wanted to reach over and touch his face, but where could she touch, everywhere was cut. She thought back to the night in the stables and him coming to rescue her from the captain on the road. After all of that and he was here hanging like this, it didn't seem fair.

"Is... is he... dead?"

"Not yet, but close to it, I'd wager."

"Can you still stand?"

"Don't know, everything... feels broken. Hurts a lot."

"Okay... ah... okay," Rana looked at Dessi with unsure eyes, "Tell me what to do, and I'll do it. You have to tell me what to do."

"Run... you silly girl, nothing can be done for me now."

Rana just stared at Dessi, and then to Jasper. She stepped down from the stool and watched Dessi hang from her arms for a while. "No, I'm going to get you out," and walked over to Jasper, touching him on his legs, "Uncle Jasper hold on a little bit longer. I promise I'll get you out of here." She thought she could see one of his blue eyes notice her, but she wasn't sure.

Rana walked over and banged on the door, glancing back to Dessi and Jasper. Soon the turning of a key was heard, and the door swung open. Rana dragged out the stool and placed it in an open room and went back in to get the water bucket and cloth. The guard closed the door behind her and turned around to see Rana staring at the key.

"What now, girl?"

Rana looked up, "Do you have a chamber pot that needs to be emptied?"

"No, I do my business upstairs if need be, not down here in this filth. Be off with ya now."

Rana walked off down the cellar hall back to the room with the buckets and grabbed her empty one before heading back upstairs. She heard the men in the kitchen still talking and tried to sneak past again.

"Hey you there," said one of the men from before, "What are you doing over there? Come here."

Rana walked inside the kitchen up to the table, dropping her bucket on the floor.

"Your one of them chosen brats aye, tell me what does the goddess say about lying and cheating."

Rana dropped her head, "She punishes the wicked for lying because they are not clean."

The man slapped his knee, "That's right, she does," and pointed his finger at another man. "You hear that Gordon, you ain't clean, and neither is how you play dice. So, tell me, little lady, how should this bastard be punished?"

Gordon started laughing, "Oh piss off, I played fair, you just got bad luck," downing a cup of wine.

"Besides, the only goddess I'm interested in is the one of big tits and fucking." Gordon reached forward, grabbing Rana by the robe. And pulling her to him rubbing his hand across her chest. "What about you little one, them tits start coming in yet." Rana began trying to break free, but the man's grip was firm. She bit his hand, but it didn't stop him. "Oh, we got a biter. Them tits small, but what about down below." He lifted Rana into the air and reached down grabbing the bottom of her robe, beginning to lift it up over her.

"What's going on here?" asked a man as his voice sounded throughout the room.

The men all froze as the man who had taken Dessi entered the room. He walked forward and twisted his lips in disgust as he noticed the man holding Rana. "I sent this girl to fetch me some wine. So, I of course thought, she didn't do as I asked of her. But instead, I find that she is being held up by you idiots."

Gordon dropped Rana on the floor, and she ran away and hid behind the man who had just entered the room.

"It seems you didn't learn your lesson the first time, Gordon. Instead of burning the bitch downstairs, perhaps I should have your head tomorrow instead."

"Ah, my apologies, I didn't realize ya sent her. Me and the boys were just having a bit of fun is all."

"Hey don't drag us in this; you're the one that grabbed her," said the other man.

"Girl, get the wine," said the man as he stared at Gordon.

"Ah, that was the last one," said Gordon

"Good, perhaps, you three will stop acting like imbeciles if you're forced to not drink for a while."

Rana walked up and grabbed the half-empty bottle of wine from the table before walking back behind the man as they left the kitchen and headed back into his office. Rana walked up to a table, grabbing a goblet from a tray, and placed it on his desk as he sat down. She noticed a lot more of the red crystals scattered across the man's office.

"I'm sorry, Sir, but I think they ate all the bread," said Rana as she poured the wine.

The man rubbed his forehead, "Of course they did." He then turned his attention over to Rana and saw that the neck area of her white robe had been ripped. "I'm sorry for how they treated you, but what really can you expect from the savages out here. Sorry, no offense if you're from this area. They didn't hurt you, did they? I saw them trying to lift your skirts."

"No... No, Sir, you arrived before they did anything." She turned back to the man before looking away, "It's just, no, never mind."

"No, say it; you have a question."

"The man who held me, he... he said that he was going to break me in. What... what does that mean?"

The man's mouth began to twitch as he grinded his teeth. "It means that maybe I was right to think that I should have him burned right alongside the two downstairs." He waved his hand towards Rana, "Go home, girl, you're done here for today."

Rana turned to place the wine back on the table.

"No I'll take that; this night has proven that I'll need it."

Rana handed the man the wine, "Thank you, Sir, enjoy your night." and walked out of the room then out of the chapel into the cold empty night of the city. She wandered the street for a while, seeing a few soldiers before finding a ladder and climbing up to the top of a stone building, where she sat with her hands cradled around her knees gazing over the city. She tried to think of how she could help Dessi and uncle Jasper, who were locked in the cellar. Throughout the night, hundreds of different ideas ran through her mind: from hoping that Jacob would come and save them all to one of the giant reptiles from the fairy tales swooping in and carrying them all away. But she knew that none of that would happen and that every minute that passed led her closer to the time for them to be burned in the town square.

Time did not slow down for Rana; instead, as the sun began to rise on another day, it was as if the sound of people leaving their homes was the alarm to tell her that her time was running out. No solid plan came to Rana during the night, only ideas that all had no true end. Rana stood up, climbed down the ladder, and headed down the street, stopping by a few shops asking for directions. Eventually ending up at a herb shop where she reached into her pocket and pulled out the two gold coins that Jacob had given her so long ago. She walked into the shop and walked out with a big bag filled with pink flowers.

After hoisting the bag into her arms, she set off towards the chapel. Rana reached the front doors and saw another set of guards at the entrance. Rana walked up to the door.

"What are you doing here so early, shouldn't you be down at the lake with the rest of 'em, getting all holy-like in the river? And why's ya clothes all ripped?" asked one of the guards.

"It got caught on a nail, but I was told to change the fragrance burners today," Rana dropped the bag on the ground and showed the flowers to the guards. "It takes a while to grind them, so I have to start early."

The guards looked down at the flowers, and then he turned to the other. "Is that how they make those smelly smoke thingies? By grinding up them flowers."

"What ya asking me for, I don't know," said the guard before he looked back down at Rana. "Hey can you make them thingies smell like lemons then?"

Rana pretended to think, "I can, but I'd need to buy some lemons to mix in with a different grounded flower. Lemons smell sweet, so it's harder to make."

"Right, Right. That does make sense." The guard stepped aside, "alright, get on with it then."

Rana walked ahead, hearing the two guards who were beginning to argue about lemons as they closed the door behind her. Once inside, she smelled the flowery scent from the fragrance burners as they puffed smoke on each side of the building. Taking her time and walking up to each of them, she reached into the bag, pulling out some type of herb and placed a few into each of the burners before making her way back to the chapel. She noticed that this time, the man's room door was closed.

Okay, so far, so good.

Rana walked down the hall peeking into the kitchen to

see that it was empty. She then made her way downstairs into the cellar, where another guard was at the door to the chamber where Dessi and Jasper were. She lifted her bag up, displaying it to the guard as he nodded back at her. Rana walked into the room with the scrolls where the other fragrance burner was. She lifted herself on top of a table and plucked down the burner, hopping back down, placing it on the floor. Grabbing a bunch of parchment, she set them on the floor, before pulling out the pink flowers from the top of her bag and emptying out dozens of grey pieces of root on top of the parchment.

I hope this works.

She reached down into the bottom of the bag and pulled out another pouch that was tied at the top. Opening up the smaller pouch, she reached in pulling out orange sand and started spreading it in her hair, and rubbing some under her nose. It made her recoil as the sand made the inside of her nose feel as if it was on fire. Shaking off the burning feeling, she then opened the burner and set the parchment under the roots on fire. After the fire began to burn and take hold of the roots, Rana walked to the other side of the room, sitting on the floor, near the door with the small pouch of sand in her hand, staring at the fire as it burned.

Okay... okay... this will work... it has to work... oh papa help me, I hope this works.

After a few minutes, a small amount of smoke began to fill the cellar hall. The guard outside began sniffing the air and suddenly started to feel himself getting sleepy. He glanced down the hall and saw smoke coming out of the room with the parchment that the girl had entered. He pulled out his sword and made his way down the hall, blinking trying to stop the smoke from stinging his eyes. He peeked into the room to see a fire burning on the floor.

"What in the," said the guard as he looked down to see Rana bundled up on the floor with a pouch in her hand. "What've you done, you little brat." The man reached down, grabbing Rana's arm, trying to pull her up, but instead only found himself going down to the floor before the world turned black as he went fast asleep on the stones. Rana watched the man for a few seconds before jumping up and taking the keys from his belt. She ran into the next room, grabbing buckets of water and placing them in front of the door before going back once again for the stool.

"Please be awake, oh, please be awake," she mumbled to herself.

She fiddled with the keys in the lock until the door swung open, and she saw both Dessi and Jasper still hanging up in chains, not moving. She noticed Dessi's face had swollen some overnight. She grabbed a bucket of water and threw it in Dessi's face. Instantly she started shaking and coughing. She then threw water in Jasper's face and after a few seconds, saw his lips quiver a bit and blow out some of the water. She placed the stool back in front of them and reached into the pouch and started rubbing the sand in Dessi's face and hair. Dessi wriggled more as the dust stung her nose and made her eyes open.

"Wha... wha... wana, whoots happening?"

Rana reached over and smeared the dust into Jasper's face and nose, and over the cuts on his face. Soon, he also began to move his head slowly, trying to stop the pain in his nose. "I got the keys, everyone will be asleep, we have to go."

"Wha... yoo got whot?" Dessi looked down to see Rana fiddling with keys and realized what was happening. "Boot ... hoo did yoo?"

Rana cursed as several of the keys didn't work, but she finally heard a clicking sound and Dessi fell to the floor.

"Okay... okay... now it's your turn, uncle," she reached over to the lock that held Jasper up.

"Hey, what are you doing?" asked a man's voice from behind Rana.

Rana turned around and saw a man in the door with a

rag over his mouth and nose. Rana started looking around the room for anything and saw Dessi still wiggling on the floor. She then reached up in her hair and pulled out a metal rod. "Stay back."

The guard narrowed his eyes at the little girl holding the metal rod and stepped forward at her. Rana threw the metal rod at his leg, and it flew oddly, clinking off the stone floor near the man's feet. He eyed the spike at his feet before looking back at Rana with disgust in his eyes. He stepped forward quickly. Rana grabbed the other metal rod from her hair and launched it at the man's leg again. It flew straight and pierced the man's knee as he collapsed on the floor near her.

The man groaned in pain as he grabbed the stool and snatched it from under Rana, sending Rana falling to the stones below. She hit the ground on her back hard enough to knock the wind out of her and have her gasping for breath. The man wrapped his hands around Rana's neck and began to squeeze. Her mouth opened wide as she gasped for air with the man's hands tightening around her throat. Dessi crawled over to the man grabbing the metal spike in his knee and began twisting it inside of him. He quickly let go of Rana and started flailing in pain as Dessi ripped the metal rod out of his leg, then crawled on top of him and slammed the metal spike down into his throat. The man clawed at his neck as Dessi clenched her teeth and tightened her grip on the spike, pulling back on it while still inside of the man's neck. Blood began to pool out of the man's throat until he finally stopped moving.

Rana rose up, sitting on her knees and clutching at her throat, coughing, and gasping for breath. She stared down at Dessi, lying on top of the man as his dead eyes stared at her. After a few seconds, Rana forced herself back up. She grabbed the keys again and picked up the stool, setting it up in front of Jasper and climbed on top of it. Reaching up to the lock, she fiddled with the key until she heard the clicking sound, and Jasper fell to the floor.

"Oka..." Rana coughed, rubbing at her throat. "okay, we have to go."

Dessi struggled, trying to move her arms again as she lifted herself on top of the man. The strain on her arms seemed painful, but she willed herself up to her knees. She took a deep breath and crawled her way over to Jasper, trying to lift him.

"Joosper booby, I... I knoo it hoorts, bot we gottoh go."

Jasper moaned in pain, but his right eye opened just enough where Rana could make out the blue inside. He cracked what Rana thought was a smile, then struggled on wobbled knees, he lifted himself with support from Dessi as she placed one of his arms over her shoulders.

"Coom on, foony mon, time to go hoom. Rana, grab that red crystal from the table."

Rana ran over, taking the crystal from the table and placing it in her pocket. She then ran forward and started watching the way ahead. The group slowly made their way back up the smoky cellar stairwell. Up top, Rana could hear shouts from outside. She led the two into the kitchen, lifted herself up on the table, and kicked open the window.

"We gotta go through here."

Dessi brought Jasper to the window and helped lift him over, where he fell to the ground with a thud landing on his shoulder. He moaned in pain but dragged himself to the side of the wall sitting up. Dessi then hopped down, trying to land on her feet but fell to her knees, grabbing her side.

People in the streets were gathering as the smoke from the building attracted them. They saw the group fall from the window and started pointing and talking. Rana hoped down next and went to Jasper, trying to pull him up. Dessi joined in Rana's attempt, and they lifted Jasper to his feet once again. They struggled to carry each other down the street while Rana glanced around for a place to hide. A house, a corner, anything would do. But there were too many people around; everyone was just staring at them and pointing.

"Keep going," said Rana, "maybe we can leave the city."

Rana frantically looked around the city, and suddenly she saw Dessi falling away from them. And then came a wet sticky sound, and the group fell back down to the ground. Jasper's legs had given out from under him, and his weight came crashing down on the girls as he landed with his arms across them.

Rana lifted herself to her knees, "Come on, get up, just a little more uncle..." and Rana froze as she saw an arrow sticking out of Jasper's neck.

Jasper's blue eyes stared at her, "Muf..." and just like that, his last breath was gone.

Rana just stared for a second before seeing Dessi clawing at the dirt trying to lift herself, but it seemed like all her strength was gone as she fell back down to the earth face-first into the dirt. Rana reached her hand out to grab Dessi, but before she could grab her, she felt a sharp pain from below. She turned back to see an arrow sticking out of her leg. Rana howled in agony as the fire inside her leg consumed her mind, and her eyes began to water.

"Well, what do we have here," said a familiar man's voice.

Rana felt the back of her head being grabbed right before her face was smashed into the dirt and held there.

"If it isn't the little kitchen girl. Who'd have thought you brave enough to do all this, and to help the prisoners escape," said the voice of Gordon from the night before as he pressed his knee into Rana's back. "Ya know, when the captain gets back, I'm gonna show him your corpse and have him apologize to me personally." The man lifted Rana's head and slammed it into the dirt again.

The impact made Rana's world go dark for a few seconds as the pain from having her head reared back again, brought her back to reality. Rana pleaded to the crowd of people staring at her through tear-soaked eyes.

"Please... Please... someone, please help me."

Rana heard someone in the crowd of people yell and then felt the man above her release her hair as his head went rolling across the ground in front of her.

CHAPTER 26

"What in the goddesses name is happening over there," said Victor as he pointed to a large amount of smoke coming from the chapel. They all began walking over towards a building as a large crowd had gathered around.

Frenka pointed to the chapel, "Looks like your house of goddess is burning down, I wonder if that's a sign?"

"I take it you're not a believer then," said Victor

sarcastically.

Suddenly a loud yell pierced the sound of the crowd from nearby. Victor walked forward, shuffling his way through the crowd towards where he had heard the sound and was stunned to see a male soldier atop a girl. Victor looked closer, and his eyes opened wide.

"That's her, that's the girl," said Victor as his body began to move forward unconsciously, but Frenka grabbed his arm.

"Careful Victor, soldiers, lots of soldiers."

Victor glanced around, seeing dozens of guards mixed in with the people. He noticed that Dekol seemed ready to strike as his hand hovered over his blade. Victor turned back to Frenka, "Anyone got a plan then?"

"We wait and—" said Frenka just before the man smashed Rana's head into the ground.

Victor saw Frenka clench her teeth as her eyes began to show something else entirely from what she had just said. They just watched as Rana's arrowed pierced leg wormed under the man's weight as he slammed her head against the ground again. Victor's heart and sanity broke watching the girl struggle, and then came the most heart-wrenching sound he'd ever heard.

"Please... please... somebody, please help me."

"Dekol!" yelled Victor, and in a flash, the man atop Rana had his head severed from his body. People screamed and ran as chaos and flames erupted on the side of the chapel. Victor ran to Rana, pushing the man's body off of her and picking her up. "It's okay; I got you, I got you."

Rana's trembling face looked into Victor's eyes, "Dessi, don't... leave Dessi." Victor stared down at the man with an arrow in his neck, and the swollen faced woman. "Hey, you still alive down there. Hey."

Dessi reached out her hand, grabbing Victor's boot and lifted herself. Victor hoisted Rana into one arm and placed his arm under Dessi's shoulder while trying to carry them through the crowd. He saw two guards coming at him, but before they could get close, they were engulfed in flames. Victor turned to see Frenka blasting fire from both hands as her long black hair hovered above her head. He didn't see Dekol, but he heard the screams of the guards.

"Get him."

"Where'd he go?"

"Argh!" a man screamed in pain.

Victor kept pushing through the crowd before he finally saw hope. A horse and hay carriage were tied to a post outside of a building. He hoisted Rana into the carriage.

"Sorry dear, this is gonna hurt," He grimaced at the sight of the blood leaking out of her leg, but grabbed the arrow and snapped the tail end off. Rana didn't move; she seemed to have passed out from the pain. Dessi released Victor's shoulder and lifted herself onto the wagon, crawling in beside Rana.

"Hood sooth... Bloock Joowls dare," said Dessi.

Victor shook his head, focusing back on the moment. But as he untied the horse, a dark-haired man with a scar on his cheek came running up from the chaos of people.

"Hey, that's mine, you can't..."

Victor pulled out a blade, "Your horse or your life, pick one." The man threw his hands up, backing away as Victor stepped into the carriage seats and snapped the straps for the horses to move. Frenka had caught up to them and hopped on the carriage front seat with Victor.

"Where's Dekol?"

"Back where they be screaming would be my guess."

"Sorry about dragging you into this," said Victor as a few arrows whizzed past their heads. "Shit." Victor and Frenka ducked their heads as the wagon turned towards the gate.

"You kidding, never had so many men come after me before. Maybe I get married after all," said Frenka as she started laughing before turning around to see who was behind them "Ah, fuck spirits."

362

"What?" asked Victor.

"They got horses."

Victor turned his head to see men trying to mount up as they went to nearby stables. "Have any ideas on how to slow 'em down?" asked Victor as they headed under the gate.

Frenka smiled at Victor and jumped off the carriage, rolling on the ground as they headed out of the gate. Victor turned back only to see a wall of flames envelope the gate and Frenka disappearing inside of them. He turned back and faced forward, gritting his teeth, and snapping the reins of the horses as they barreled up the countryside, leaving a burning and smoking city behind them.

Victor turned around to see the woman with her arms over Rana, along with an arrow embedded into the wood of the wagon beside her head. She held Rana tightly in her arms as the carriage bounced along the uneven dirt road going up the hill. Only after they had escaped a decent length from the city, where it was off in the distance, did Victor finally slow the horses down a bit.

Dessi turned her half-swollen face to him, "Who... who yooo?"

Victor shook his head, "An idiot sent to find the girl. I would ask you the same question, but you seem not to be speaking well at the moment. But you did say, head south towards Milak didn't you?"

Dessi nodded her head.

Victor turned, "then we should be there soon if we—"

"Gawds," muffled Dessi.

"I'm sorry, what's that?"

"Gawds!" Dessi yelled as loud as her injured face would allow her.

Victor turned to see at least a dozen guards leaving the city all on horseback and starting up the hill, heading in their direction.

"Oh, for the fucking goddess's tits," said Victor as he snapped the reins once again, sending the horses galloping forth. Victor pushed the horses as hard as he could, cursing along the way, trying to think of ways to avoid the men chasing them. But he knew that the carriage slowed them down immensely, and it would only be a matter of time before they caught up. Still, he continued to push the horses as they barreled into the forest down its winding roads. A few minutes into the forest trail, the wagon hit something and bounced into the air, coming down hard and leaning to one side as it slid along the ground. When they came to a stop, Victor hopped down and saw the wheel of the carriage had broken from the impact. He cursed once again, as he heard the sound of horses far off into the distance.

Victor reached into the wagon, lifting Rana into his arms again and supported Dessi as she lifted herself. "Come on, can't quit now," he said as the group limped into the forest. Once they got deeper into the green forest, Victor sat Dessi down at the base of a tree and placed Rana into her arms.

Dessi looked up at Victor, "Dod... good."

"I'm gonna try to do even better and get us outta this."

Victor took off his cloak and searched through the belt of pockets across his chest. He opened them, searching for anything that he thought could help. "Come on, come on, something in here has to be worth a dam." He took out a large ball with a hole in it and placed it in Dessi's hand, lifting it to her face. "Listen, if you see someone, you throw this at them and close your eyes, okay."

Dessi stared at the ball, "Lottool... rook?" asked Dessi with one eye half open and tired.

"Yes little rock, throw it at anyone who shows up and close your eyes. Do you understand?" asked Victor, focusing on Dessi's eye. Dessi sighed, staring back at him, and tiredly nodded her head. "Good, I'll be nearby." Victor opened up another pouch and grabbed some grey balls with yarn sticking out of them along with two odd-looking stones and two balls that had a wire attached to them, sliding them into his back pocket, then sprinted off into the woods leaving Dessi and Rana with each other.

Minutes later, Victor was crouched on the ground by an overturned tree, focusing his attention over at the broken wagon as the men on horseback arrived.

"Search the area, they haven't gone far," said one man dropping from his horse.

Victor held out one of the balls and squeezed the yarn between the two rocks, rubbing them together until the yarn caught fire. The ball started smoking, and Victor threw it into the forest. He moved around the area, repeating the process several times, and watched as each little ball put out large amounts of smoke.

"What the hell is this?" Shouted one of the guards.

"The fools might've started a fire, find them quickly, or it'll be our heads when the captain gets back."

Victor threw out the last ball and watched as the guards spread out in the forest, getting confused by the smoke. Pulling out his short sword, he began stalking one of the guards closest to him. He stayed low to the ground and close to a tree as a soldier came closer to him, wandering in the smoke. As he passed, Victor placed his hands over the man's mouth and slit his throat in a smooth motion. The man's eyes went wide as the blood gushed from his neck. Victor held the man tightly, supporting his weight and slowly and silently lowered him to the ground, before slinking off to through the woods again.

Take that you little bastard, you're not the only ones who can sneak.

Dessi laid against the tree with Rana in her arms. Her arms hurt, her chest hurt, even breathing hurt. The cuts on her face from before had reopened from all the movement and blood was now leaking into her left eye. She chuckled as she thought about the words Holland had told her the last time she saw him. *Seems the old man might have been right. Why did I go to see Holland? Oh, my blades. That's what it was.* Dessi glanced down at Rana lying against her chest. *You were there too. You wanted to be a warrior.* She noticed the tip of the arrow that still pierced Rana's leg. *You really should have run, you silly child.* She looked up. *No, maybe I should have run, then we wouldn't be in this mess.* She placed her left hand on Rana's head stroking her hair. *Now here we are, two girls in the woods waiting to die.*

A man appeared from around a tree holding a sword. He noticed them and checked around for anyone else before putting his sword back to his side.

"Well what do we have here, seems like we found ourselves some runaways. You both are coming with me." The man yelled out, "Hey, I found two of 'em, they're here." as he began to make his way towards them.

Dessi, with as much strength, as she could muster threw the rock that Victor had given her at the man. It hit the man's armour and made a clinking sound, before plopping to the ground beneath his feet. She chuckled and struggled not to tear up. *And that's how it ends, with a stupid rock. Goddess I'm tired.* And she just closed her eyes.

"Ha! What was that?" asked the man laughing as he leaned down to grab the girls, but stopped with his fingers inches away from Rana's face as he heard a hissing sound from beneath him.

Victor slowly moved between the trees, staying as low to the ground as he could as he approached another guard. The lingering smoke in the air was keeping the men distracted enough for him to get in close to a second man sneaking up behind him. Victor reached forward.

"Hey, I found two of 'em, they're here," yelled the voice of a man nearby. All the soldiers turned in the direction of the voice as Victor clenched his teeth and stabbed the man in the back of the neck. The man gave a loud gasp, and a gurgling sound as Victor then kicked his body forward, sending it crashing to the ground. The men nearby turned to the man's body as he hit the ground, and Victor dodged back behind a tree.

"What the... what happened?" asked another guard.

Then came a loud popping sound off into the distance and the sounds of a man screaming in pain. The men paused at the sound of the man screaming.

"What the hell's happening," asked a guard in a panic.

Victor reached into one of his pouches and grabbed all the rocks with holes in them. But soon, the ground began to rumble as the sound of horses charging was heard. Victor made a face. *Now what!* And soon out of the smoke, a dozen shirtless men emerged on horseback, waving their swords, and hacking away at the guards. *Fucking barbarians? Now?*

Victor placed some rocks back inside his pouch and took off running towards where Rana and Dessi were. One of the barbarians saw him and tried to turn his horse in order to give chase. But the moment he did, a series of bright flashes of light blinded him as both he, and his horse fell to the ground. Victor continued through the smoke towards where Dessi and Rana were.

Come one; please be safe. We might have a way out.

He finally made it to them and saw a soldier laid out on the ground a few feet away from them. Victor stepped forward with his short sword in front of him, looking for anyone else but didn't see anyone. He knelt in front of Dessi, "Hey, time to go." He tried to shake her, "Come on, we got a chance to." Suddenly Victor heard footsteps quickly approaching and jumped back out of the way before a sword would have pierced the side of his head. He landed on his feet with his short sword in front of him and pointed the blade at a blonde-haired soldier holding a sword, who was now standing between him and the girls.

Victor took a breath. "Right then, I don't have time for

this shit, so come on."

The men rushed each other as Victor sidestepped the first sword swing. He swung his short sword at the man's head, but the man dodged and headbutted Victor in the face sending him reeling back. The man thrust his blade at Victor's head, but Victor parried with his short sword palming the man in the face and kicking him back, forcing him to roll over, but he completely rolled back onto his feet still holding his guard.

Why must this one be such a pain in my ass?

Victor reached down, grabbing a small stick from the ground, holding it in his left hand. The two men squared off again as Victor rushed in and started attacking the man, dodging his strikes, and fending him off with his stick. After another parry with his blade, Victor swung the stick at the man's head, but he ducked under the attack and thrust his shoulder into Victor's chest.

Victor was lifted off the ground by the man's force but managed to bring the stick down on the back of the man's neck as they went rolling over in the grass, landing by the body of the other soldier. He gasped for air clutching his chest with the stick hand. Gritting his teeth, Victor looked over to see the man before him who was already starting to get up. *Okay, he's good, but I'm not such an—* Victor's thoughts ended, and all his hope of escaping the fight instantly vanished as he saw three more barbarians ride up on their horses.

"Ohhh, looks like we got ourselves a show," said the large shirtless man.

"Shouldn't we help him out, Molan?" asked a smaller man.

"And miss chance to see Pretty Boy get his ass kicked? You interfere and I kill you myself."

Victor stood to his feet staring past the blonde-man before him to the three me behind him. Molan noticed Victor staring and smiled back.

"He's all yours. If ya kill him, I promise I'll kill ya quick myself," said the large man as he laughed.

Victor turned his attention back to the man soldier on the ground beneath him and the soldier before him. *Okay, here I am at the ass end of a foreign kingdom.* Victor dodged an attack from the man and hoped back and began poking at him with the stick, trying to keep a distance. *Fighting to my death for the enjoyment of barbarian spectators.*

"Gather round boys; we got us a good ol' fight here. Place your bets, I put fifty silver on new guy," said Molan.

"Against Jacob? I'll take that bet," said another man as well as a host of other voices that joined in on the bet taking.

Victor looked around again, seeing almost a dozen men. *So, escape definitely isn't happening. Well fuck.* Victor focused back on the man in front of him. *Apparently, his name's Jacob. Well, Jacob, I'm gonna kick your ass.*

Victor leaned forward, swinging with his short sword at Jacob, but he deflected the blade off his gauntlet and tried to head-butt Victor. Victor lowered his knees, leaning back and spit in Jacob's eye and struck him in the face with the stick. Jacob recoiled back as Victor leaped forward only to be caught on the side of the head by Jacob's elbow as he released one hand from his blade and thrust it forward.

Victor gritted his teeth as the blow rattled his senses. Jacob pushed forward, planting his boot into Victor's chest, sending him flying back. Victor dropped his stick as he went sprawling out on the ground, sliding over by the body of the other soldier with Jacob following behind, bringing his sword down towards him. Victor rolled over the man's body barely evading Jacobs blade as it sliced through the other soldier's arm, embedding itself into the ground.

I'll take this if you don't mind.

Victor pushed himself up off the soldier's body,

ripping the helmet from the man's head and tossing it at Jacob's face. Jacob raised his hand just in time as the metal whacked his hand against his head, sending him stumbling back. Jacob gritted his teeth as Victor leaped forward and thrust his sword at Jacob's face. Jacob ducked under the blade and swung his sword, only to be whacked in the face with something soft and wet that sprayed across his face before he caught a foot to the chest and wet rolling across the ground. Jacob quickly stood up, wiping his face, and staring at blood on his gloves. Jacob looked up to see Victor holding a sword in one hand and the arm of the dead soldier he killed earlier in the other.

Are you fucking kidding me.

Victor held the dead man's hand as the severed end of the arm dripped blood down onto the ground. He then rushed at Jacob, swinging the severed arm at Jacob's head and, sending blood flying in his direction. Jacob leaped forward allowing the blood to strike him in the face and clashed blades with Victor once again. Jacob thrust his knee at Victor's stomach, but Victor turned to the side to dodge and used the leverage to thrust his shoulder into his push and force Jacob back. Jacob braced himself, planting his feet into the dirt and tried to push forward.

Victor allowed himself to be forced back so that he could respond by smashing the wet end of the severed arm into Jacobs face. Jacob groaned as the severed flesh and bone grinded against his nose, teeth, and lips. He could smell the man's blood and taste it as it entered his mouth. Jacob bit down on the severed arm and leaped forward with all his might sending Victor falling backward from the force and himself stumbling forward but managing to keep his balance. Through blood-soaked eyes Jacob saw Victor lying on the ground and tried to stab the sword through him.

"Die, damn you," said Jacob coughing out blood that

wasn't his own.

Shit, he's a tough bastard.

Victor saw the blade falling towards him and leaned on his side as the sword pierced the ground. Grabbing Jacob's leg, Victor pulled forward with all his might, tripping Jacob into the air and on his back as he fell to the ground. Victor dived at Jacob with the short sword in a flurry of dust and leaves, but Jacob rolled out of the way, he jumped again, and Jacob rolled away again, lifting himself to his knees, and grabbed Victor's arm as he tried to dive once more and twisted it, forcing Victor to drop his blade.

Victor groaned in pain before throwing himself forward, headbutting Jacob violently, making him loosen his grip as Victor fell forward. Victor smashed to the ground, unable to catch himself with his wrenched arm, but Jacob rotated around after the blow, grabbing Victor's short sword. Victor grabbed Jacob's blade and quickly lifted himself off the ground, only to see his own blade being pointed at his face as Jacob slowly stood up. Victor, with blood dripping down his face, stared back up at a shattered Jacob and realized that he had broken his glasses.

"That was not a fight, I... I don't know what that was. But it seems... like ... I win. Anything to say?"

Victor shook his head and released Jacob's sword as he clenched his fist into the dirt in frustration. He then raised his head and stared up into Jacob's eyes, "Fuck off."

Jacob frowned, "Not the words I would have chosen, but," and thrust the blade at Victor's head.

Victor threw himself backward, barely missing the blade as it cut through the side of his cheek. And while falling backward, he threw the dirt, dust, and leaves in his hand into Jacob's face, kicking his knee out from under him as he came forward. Jacob tripped, falling to the ground with Victor jumping onto his back and pulling out two balls with a wire attached between them from his back pocket. He quickly wrapped the wire around Jacob's neck and stood to his feet, pulling Jacob up to his knees with his force. Victor planted his knee into Jacob's back, gritted his teeth again, and pulled with all the might he had left. Jacob quickly dropped the short sword and started clawing at his neck. But no matter how hard he dug into his own flesh; he couldn't grab hold of the wire. Jacob's dirt ridden face started to turn purple as everything started to go black for him. His movements slowed as his hands finally dropped to his side. Victor let go of the rope, kicking Jacob's body to the ground as silence took over the forest. He stared at the crowd of barbarians as they all just stared at the bloody faced, broken glasses man standing tall over Jacob in the smoke as sunlight that shone down on them through the trees.

The large man dismounted his horse and walked over to Victor until they stood inches apart. "Before you die, I want you to know, you have earned the respect of every man here. We will remember this day."

Victor smiled, "Guess... you're not... the prisoner taking type, with your bunch, huh."

The man nodded down at Jacob's body. "We could, but you killed boss's son. If I take you back, you would have wished you died here."

"Oh, well... he's not dead yet," said Victor as he raised his leg, then stomped on Jacob's back. Molan was surprised to see Jacob start twitching and coughing. He was barely breathing, but the wheezing of his breath could be heard. "If you massage the throat, the airways will open back up." Victor looked down at Jacob and smiled, "Eventually."

Molan bellowed a great laugh and patted Victor on the shoulder before turning around to his men, "All right, boys, we keep this one. Bound him up and bring him back." He walked back and mounted onto his horse, looking back down at Jacob on the ground and grinned. "Put the good fighter on the now, not so pretty boy's horse and have him hauled back. He deserves ride after putting on a show like that."

"Hey!" Victor yelled out.

Molan raised an eyebrow at Victor.

"I can't leave without them, I need them," said Victor as he pointed to Dessi and Rana, who were still passed out against the tree.

Molan smiled and laughed, "Them? Of course, we take them, they who we came for. And that little one now belongs to me, thanks to you."

The men picked up Rana and hoisted her up into the big man's arms. Victor watched them and noticed how small she seemed next to Molan's oversized physique. The men then sat Dessi up behind another rider and tied her to the man with rope so that she wouldn't fall.

"Hey, any of you find funny man?" asked Molan.

"No, Sir, we couldn't find 'em."

"Knowing funny man, he probably off doing something stupid again. Take few men and continue search; we heading back. We got what we came for. Time to get out of this damned smoke."

And together, the group headed back to the main path and set off down the road.

CHAPTER 27

Victor and company rode into the camp as people stared at him. He began to scan over the crowd and was shocked as he saw sakari in the camp.

" I have come back the hero," said Molan as he raised his arm at the people as he passed.

"I must admit, this is a larger group than I expected to

be here," said Victor.

"We are strong here and have fought many battles to victory. We could fight an army and maybe not lose a man. That is the strength of the Black Jewels clan."

They made their way up to a large tent with an old man waiting outside. The large man stopped the horse in front of the old man with a grin on his face.

"You missed fun time, old man."

"I would assume so," said Oscar as he watched the unconscious Rana bobble up and down in Molan's arms. "Alright, get the girl down," he ordered as men went and took Rana from Molan. He walked over and grabbed Rana's face. "Beaten up pretty bad." Oscar inspected the arrow wound in her leg, where the tip was still poking out. "Went clean through, missed the bone, good. Take her to a healer." The men took Rana off into the camp. Oscar saw Dessi staring at him while tied to another man. He walked up to her, looking at Jacob strapped over the back of a horse as he passed him. "Seems like you had a lot of fun this time to Dessi, did you find out anything?"

Dessi nodded, "I... dood."

"Alright, cut her down and take her away too," said Oscar as he turned around, walking back up to Jacob. He grabbed his son's face and listened to his breathing. "Boy took a pretty bad beating," moving his head and inspecting the marks around his neck, "Worse than usual." He then looked up at Victor and noticed the bindings on his wrists and turned back to Molan. "You brought a prisoner, why?"

"Because he's one that did beating," said Molan with a great smile on his face.

Oscar turned back to Victor with a skeptical look on his face while rubbing his beard. "What, by himself?"

"It was beautiful," said Molan with his arms out stretched wide, "He gave your boy the best ass whopping I ever saw."

"I imagine it was," said Oscar as he raised a brow at Victor and started walking forward. "Alright, bring him into the tent, and take my more worse for wear son to the healer's tent with the women. I imagine when he wakes, he's going to be feeling like one anyway."

Molan laughed at Oscar's words, "I expect payment for this old man."

"You'll get your due in time, like you always—"

Molan leaned over his horse, placing his elbow on its head, "I want the girl as my payment."

Oscar shook his head back at Molan, "My daughter is not for sale, you should know that. Go find yourself another thing to ruin."

"I did what you asked and brought back two of the three. Maybe the third if my men can find him. I want the girl, and your little pretend family shouldn't deny me what I am owed."

Oscar turned around and walked back to Molan and stood before him and horse. He spoke in a much harsher tone than before, "I tolerate you because you're strong and a leader of men, that alone deserves respect. But if you mention disrespect against my family again, I'll have you and your men cut down in this very spot. Do you understand me?"

Molan looked around as men placed their hands on their blades, waiting for a command. He nodded at Victor, "Fine, take him. But I will get what I'm owed," and turned his horse around galloping back down into the camp, followed by his men.

Victor was helped to dismount the horse and was led inside the tent behind Oscar and another soldier.

"Leave us, Amos," said Oscar to the soldier.

"Yes, Sir," said the soldier as he nodded and walked out as Oscar walked over to a table, grabbing a bottle of wine and began pouring drinks into two mugs. "So, you did that to my son?"

"He didn't really give me much of a choice."

"No, I imagine not, but still, you didn't kill him. Why?"

"What makes you so sure I didn't try?"

Oscar pointed to his neck while still pouring the wine, "I assume the finale was whatever that marking was around his neck, and how I know you didn't try to kill him is because the man that brought you in would kill my son himself if he didn't think I'd find out about it and burn his whole world down. No, I assume he was hoping you would and save him the trouble." Oscar brought over the mug of wine and placed it in Victor's still tied hands before taking a seat in front of him, "So that brings me back to my first question of, why didn't you kill my boy?"

Victor rotated the wine cup in his hand, "Didn't seem right at the time. He fought well enough, and when his friends arrived, he didn't ask for help. He just planted his feet and came at me. Your boy's a talented fighter. I respect him for that. Seemed like a waste to kill him if I was going to die anyway."

"I appreciate the sentiment, seeing as I'm the one who trained him." Oscar sipped from his cup. "But that brings us back to you, who was victorious and is still amongst the living. So that makes me wonder, who are you?"

Victor smiled, "You probably wouldn't believe me if I told you."

"Try me; I've seen many things in my life. Not much surprises me nowadays."

"My name is Victor Krill, former sixth general of the Imperial Army of Mari."

Oscar just stared at Victor for a few seconds, "Okay, you win, that is hard to believe. Why would the sixth general be out in a foreign country, near the backwoods of a border, that isn't even his own."

"Looking for Fairline Hasher or the girl that you just so recently called daughter."

Oscar raised an eyebrow while swirling the wine in his cup, "Why, what's so special about her?"

Victor shook his head, "Don't know, orders were just to

find her."

"Whose orders, your Queen Clarissa?"

"The one and only, she sent me here to negotiate with King Nevander, and part of that negotiation was for me to find the girl for him."

Oscar tilted his head back in contemplation, "Okay, say I believe you. You gave my son back his life, so I'm inclined to give you back yours, but I won't let you have the girl."

"I figured as much, but you've no need to worry. I have no intention of taking her now. But allow me to be bold here and ask, what do you intend to do with the girl, now that you have her back here?"

Oscar rubbed his beard, "I don't know yet, I picked her up because my man Jasper asked me to take her in. But seeing as she's valuable to someone, I figure I'll hold onto her until I'm able to gather more information on why the king wants her. Until then, I'll let her do as she pleases here. Within reason, of course."

Victor nodded his head, "Given the situation, that's a fairly reasonable response."

Oscar pulled out a dagger from behind his back and cut the ropes over Victor's hand. "You may also move around the camp as you like, but you will not be allowed to leave it until we have finished up here. You said the king wanted her; does he know where we are?"

Victor sipped from the cup, "The king probably doesn't know anything. But I had two companions with me. They most certainly know where you are."

"Then you will be released to your own devices, only after we have left this kingdom. Latrusa is only three days travel from here, and we will leave in a day or so."

Victor rubbed at the rope marks along his wrists, "I appreciate the hospitality. Although I'm surprised, you're being so generous with me."

Oscar smirked, "Oh, I could have you chained and gagged if needed. But you sat here and answered my questions truthfully, as I detected no trace of lying in you. That tells me you're a man who fully understands the situation he's in." Oscar then pointed to Victor's rope burned wrists, "Not all chains need to be physical."

Victor smirked, "Well spoken."

"Guards," shouted Oscar as the previous soldier re-entered the tent. "Take Victor here to a bucket of water so that he may wash the blood off his face. After which, you are to accompany him everywhere." Oscar stood up from his seat. "I'll have my men set you up in a tent."

Victor stood, "Much appreciated," and was ushered out of the tent, through the camp to a water hole, where he sat down before a bucket of water and began to clean himself.

"What's your name," said Victor to the soldier.

"Amos, Sir."

"Amos, may I borrow the use of your dagger?"

"Ah! I don't think I'm allowed—"

"I just need it to check my reflection soldier, I will return it shortly, or you can hold it up in front of me."

"Oh, I guess that's okay."

Amos handed Victor the blade, and he placed it in front of his face seeing that the left side of his face was covered with blood, and he had a welt under his eye. "Well, ain't I a pretty fellow?" He noticed a large gash above his left eye and a cut on his cheek. "Probably gonna need stitches for that one." Victor handed the blade back to Amos, grabbed a wet rag, and started washing his face.

"How old are you, boy?"

Amos stiffened "Almost seventeen, Sir."

"You've been with this group long?"

"Since I was twelve, my lord."

"I'm not a lord," said Victor as he surveyed the camp and started rubbing his shoulder and popping his neck. "I saw sakari when I entered the camp, are there many here?"

"Ah, yes, Sir, they have their own part of the camp just downhill there."

Victor's gaze followed where the boy's hand pointed down a hill where he could just barely make out a few ebony-skinned men moving about. "How in the goddess's name did he get sakari to join his merry bunch?"

"Oh, the commander knows their leader. Ah, Gregga, I think that's her name. I heard the commanders known her all her life. Some even say she's his lover."

Victor chuckled, "Him? With a sakari lover, and he's still alive. The world really is filled with magic."

After cleaning the dirt off his face and poking his wounds to ensure the bleeding didn't persist, Victor stood. "Okay, where's the medical tent?"

Soon Victor was led to another tent where he saw a sakari woman inspecting Rana's leg and two men applying ointments to Dessi and Jacob's faces. Victor walked over to the men. He saw that they had stripped Dessi and Jacob out of their clothes and covered them in sheets. He noticed a lot of scars on the woman's shoulders, even just seeing the top of her. "What's the damage on these two?"

One man looked up, "Who are you?"

"It's okay, he's with the commander," said Amos.

The man gave Victor a bothered look. "Dessi took the worst of it, it seems. Repeated impacts on the face had her right eye completely swollen shut. A broken finger and two broken ribs, it's amazing she was still awake when she got here."

"And him?" Victor nodded to Jacob.

"Loosened jaw, bruised ribs, and multiple impacts to the face. He's got bruises all over, but it's the strangulation that's the main concern. The windpipe was partially crushed by some type of rope or strong wire," The doctor shook his head. "I know Jacob; he's a good fighter. The poor bastard must have been fighting like six men to do him in this bad."

Victor smirked. *It's nice to know someone appreciates my work; I tried really hard on that one.* He then walked over to Rana as the Sakari woman hovered over her. Victor was taken aback to see the woman using healing magic on Rana's leg.

"Ah, do you speak our language?" asked Victor.

"Yes, I heard you over there with them. I assume you wish to know of any issues with her."

Victor pulled back in surprise by the woman's grasp of the kingdom's language, "Ah, yes, that's right."

"The arrow didn't break the bone. And I've already cleaned the wound, so there shouldn't be any risk of infection. I'm currently using healing arts on the leg. When she wakes, her leg will still cause pain, but with crutches, she should be able to manage."

Victor nodded, watching as the magic flowed from the sakari woman's fingers down into the wound. It made him think of Nahtalli. *I wonder where that bastard went after he got off the ship.* He saw that the sakari woman's hands and arms were covered in black markings. "Do all the sakari have those markings like you have there? Usually, only pirates and thieves have stuff like that here."

"No, some do not. Some warriors have them, some wives. For me, they help to focus my arts."

"And by arts, does that mean magic?"

"Yes and no, I do not fully understand what your kingdom people do, but the flow of our gift is different in many ways, but sometimes they feel similar. It is hard to describe where the separation begins."

Victor nodded and turned around about to leave before he remembered the magistrate's words. He then turned back to the Sakari woman, "If you use healing arts, tell me. Do you notice anything odd about this girl when you look at her?"

The sakari woman raised a brow to Victor in surprise. "Ah, so you see it also, her art is different. It does not flow as it should. It is like the art inside is fighting itself. And there is something else, some type of aura around her, I think it affects people that are near here. But I can't understand what it does."

"That last part is new to me. Is this aura dangerous?"

"It does not seem that way. It seems very subtle. Only the main art that is attacking itself is easy for me to see."

"Yeah, I was told about that part. How long will she be out for?"

"A day, most certainly. After that, I cannot be sure; the june dust is still in their system. We washed it out of their hair, but they were exposed to a large amount of it and given their recent exhaustion and this one's tiny figure. It will take some time." The woman nodded over to Jacob, "He, on the other hand, will be fine after I begin work on his throat."

Victor took a deep breath leaning back, pushing his hands into his spine, creating an audible cracking sound. "I guess that's it for me then." He received some gauze from the kingdom doctors for his facial wounds and walked out of the tent with Amos following behind him. "Tell me, Amos, where would that man be who brought me here?"

"Ahh, that'd be the mess or the training area," said Amos.

Victor glanced ahead to see two small sakari girls running towards him. He just stared at them as the two girls ran past him into the tent. "What the? They even have children here?" Victor turned around, looking at the tent. "What kind of camp is this?"

"Did you hear me, Sir?"

"Huh, what's that?"

"Molan, Sir, the man you asked about, he'll be in either in the mess or the training area."

Victor turned back around, "Ah, yeah, take me to him then."

They found Molan in the training area, eating on a piece of meat while watching the men train.

Victor walked up behind Molan, "Greetings once again, my captor, been enjoying yourself?"

Molan turned around and smiled, "Hey, boys, it seems bastard missed our company. Seeing that he is back so soon,

I guess old man decide to let him go."

"As gratitude for sparing his son, it would seem, so I came to offer my gratitude to you for not killing me when you could have."

Molan leaned his back against a wooden pole crossing his arms. "You did not have fight left in you; any man could see killing you then would be boring." He waved a hand over his face rubbing his beard. "Plus, that just means I can kill you myself later. I will not lie. Watching you and pretty boy fight. I was jealous. Been a while since I got in a brawl that good. Makes me wonder how I would have done."

Victor looked Molan up and down as he walked up beside him, staring ahead as the men trained. "Well you're a much bigger man than he is."

"Aye, and Pretty Boy had a bigger sword, yet you beat him off with a stick."

Victor smirked, "You know, you seem more perceptive than most big men I know."

"Ha," Molan laughed as he began cracking his fingers. "I just go after what I want, and what I want is entertainment. A good fight to get the blood boiling."

Victor turned to Molan, "Tell me, your fight with your commander, why do you want the girl so bad."

"She's young and will grow to be beautiful. If you want a war wife, it's best to take control of them young and train them as they grow. She is tough and feisty; will make a good war wife after I break her in."

"Doesn't seem like your commander is willing to give her up, though."

"Bah." Molan spat on the ground. "The old fool has gone mad since he lost family. But I will get girl; he owes me debt now. I gave him back son thanks to you, so I will get his daughter as payment." Molan smiled as he patted Victor on the back, while Victor began to have thoughts on how he could arrange for the oversized man to fall victim to a terrible accident.

Victor stepped back, "Well, I'm having Amos show me around the camp, I'm sorry I wasn't able to provide you with the entertainment that you desired."

Molan rubbed at his chin while giving a grin, "Oh! I don't know about that; I think you still provide plenty of entertainment."

Victor spent the rest of the day walking around the camp with Amos asking questions until the sun had set, before returning to a tent they set up for him that had two guards standing outside of it. *Well, don't I feel special.* Victor noticed that one guard had an odd smile on his face as he walked past. He stepped inside the tent and saw two beautiful ladies lying beside each other on the floor together.

"Oh the guest has returned," said one woman.

"Okay, now I really do feel special," said Victor as a smile stretched across his face. "So, to whom do I owe this pleasure."

One lady stood up smiling, Victor's eyes immediately glanced to her nipples that showed through the thin fabric that barely covered them.

"We heard that you're the strong warrior that beat up poor Jacob."

Suddenly Victor's instinct to run started to trigger, "Ah, it was a fair fight, I didn't—"

The lady laughed, "We don't care about Jacob. It was Molan, who was so happy to send us here. Said you deserved some relaxation after your hard fight," said the woman as she wrapped her arms around Victor, kissing him on his neck.

Goddess, she smells good. "Ladies, I am very grateful for this, but I don't think I have the energy left to do what you want me to do."

The ladies giggled as the woman on the floor sat up to her knees and reached her hand out to Victor. "Then let us do all the work for you, just enjoy yourself."

"And what would you ladies' names be, if I may ask?"

"I'm Prinja" said the woman around Victor's neck.

"I'm Keltre," said the woman on the floor.

Prinja pulled Victor down and laid his head to rest between Keltre's legs. Unbuckling his belt, Prinja pulled down his pants, revealing his small clothes. Rubbing her hands across his legs, she mounted herself atop him. Pulling her hands to her waist, she grabbed the transparent cloth, pulling it over her head before reaching down to find Victor's fingers and lifting his hand to her breast.

"I'm not sure I deserve you ladies."

Prinja leaned forward, sliding her breasts across Victor's mouth and nose. "Oh, there's only one man who deserves us."

And while Victor felt her nipple on his lips, he also felt a blade across his throat. *And there it is. Proof that I'm an idiot.*

Prinja lifted herself back up, staying mounted on top of Victor, "And we'd very much appreciate it if you'd tell us where he is."

Victor closed his eyes and took a deep breath, "Ladies, I assure you that I will assist you in any way possible. So, how can I help?"

"We want to know what happened to Jaspie," said Keltre in a more desperate tone than before as she held a dagger to his neck.

"Jaspie?" asked Victor confused, "I don't know—"

Prinja grinded her ass on top of Victor and tapped his balls with her blade. "Oh that's not the answer we want, is it Keltre." Prinja reached down between her legs, grabbing Victor's cock in her hand, and squeezed it. "Jasper Flannigan, a brown-haired, blue-eyed man that should have been with Dessi and Rana in the city. Molan said he caught you trying to escape with Rana and Dessi. So that leaves the question," She placed the blade against the side of his cock. "Where's our man?"

Victor silently cursed Molan while looking at Keltre's breasts above him, Prinja breasts before him, and feeling the constant motion of her on top of him with his cock in her hand. *Goddess! I don't have enough blood to think myself out of this.* "Ladies, please, if you would be so kind, this absurdly sexy and dangerous situation has got me at a loss for words. Can I ask that you cover yourselves before the interrogation continues?"

The women looked at each other before Prinja nodded to Keltre. Victor's head suddenly fell to the floor as Keltre opened her legs and slid over to cover herself with garments held over her chest. She then pointed her shaking blade back at Victor.

Victor winced from the impact of his head hitting the floor, still focusing his attention upwards as Prinja sat atop him.

"Oh, I'm fine where I am dear," she tugged on Victor's cock a bit, "And judging by this right here, you're fine as well."

Victor took a breath. "Okay, first things first. I did not capture Dessi and Rana. I rescued them from the city with guards chasing after me. I fought and killed a lot of men to ensure their safety."

The women glanced at each other before Prinja turned back to Victor. "That's a lie, Molan said—"

"I can assure you that's the truth. If you doubt me, then bind me until those women wake, and I guarantee they will tell you the same."

"But why would Molan lie?" asked Keltre.

Prinja bit her lip, "Because he's a fucking bastard, that's why."

"On that, we both are in agreement," said Victor before Prinja turned back to him with narrowed eyes. Soon Victor slowly felt the blade remove itself from the side of his cock. And with that release came a feeling a new feeling that he didn't know even existed as Prinja released his cock from her grip.

Prinja waved the blade around nonchalantly in her

hand. "Well, ah, sorry about all of this, we thought you tried to... well we assumed."

"Oh... No worries. Outside of the danger of having my manhood chopped off. The sight of you two ladies has really been a gift from the goddess herself. But as for news of you, man, I'm afraid I might have information on him." Victor raised himself up on his elbows. "When I assisted in the rescue of Rana and Dessi, there was a man on the ground with them. But he was already dead from an arrow wound to the neck. I cannot be sure who he was, but he did have brown hair. Of that, I am certain."

Both women paused at the news.

"Did... did he have blue eyes?" asked Prinja.

"His face was badly bruised, I couldn't tell."

Prinja slid off Victor and just sat to his side, staring at the fabric of the tent.

"There's no guarantee it was him, you'll need to get the information from the other two when they wake," said Victor trying to be considerate.

"It was him; you said it was three of them you found, right. There were three that went in. I won't cling to a hope that's not there," said Prinja as she cradled her knees in front of her.

Victor watched her trying and very much succeeding to hold back her tears as her lips began to quiver. He then heard the sound of muffled crying as he turned his head to see Keltre with tears in her eyes. She dropped her blade and went to cry into the arms on Prinja. Victor stared up at the roof of the tent and began to think to himself. *Here I am, in a tent with two beautiful naked ladies, with my cock out. Wishing that I were as lucky as a fallen man.* Victor then closed his eyes and listened to the sounds of a crying woman and the whispers of her partner as she tried to soothe her.

CHAPTER 28

Victor awoke to the sounds of the camp waking. He glanced over at the two naked women straddled to each side of him. *Ah! So, the cock teasing continues.* Victor shook the arm that Prinja was on a little until she began to stir. When the sleep began to fade from her eyes, he closed his eyes and pretended he was still asleep.

Prinja awoke, rubbing at her eyes before she realized where she was. She looked down at Victor and then over to Keltre. She woke Keltre and handed her some clothes as they both tried to silently get dressed. Once clothed, Prinja led Keltre out of the tent and turned back to Victor, "I know you're awake. Thank you for letting us—"

Victor cut her off, "Go on and see if Dessi's awake, I pray that it wasn't your man that I saw."

Prinja nodded and disappeared out of the tent.

"I wonder if the goddess created women as a giant jest to test the stupidity of men, said the Poet Hilago," Victor muttered the lines to himself as he laid on the floor with his pants down to his feet, until his stomach started to grumble. He then stood, pulling his pants back up and buckling his belt. After putting on his jerkin, he walked out of the tent into the fresh morning sunlight.

"You're a lucky man, Sir," said Amos.

Victor turned to his side. "Oh, joining me for another day, I take it. But how's that?"

"They were pretty ladies just left here, and they were mages. I'm right jealous of you." Amos said with a knowing smile.

Victor squinted his eyes as he tried to adjust to the sunlight, "Yeah, it's easy to be jealous when you don't have to suffer the other end of it."

"What's that, Sir?"

"Nothing. Just come and show me where breakfast is," said Victor as he followed Amos through the camp.

Victor sat with Amos in the morning sun, eating meat and drinking ale as they watched as the camp bustled with energy in the morning sun. "Tell me, Amos, how many men are in the militia?"

"Well, now it's only around one and ten. But the largest I have seen was at Mordred's Tower. Then we had two and fifty."

"That's quite the size for a militia. One that's hard to

maintain, even my old unit was barely over fifty men at a given time."

Amos bite into his meat, "The commander keeps us pretty spread out. Most of the men here have families back home and only fight when called. Oh, there's Mr. Jacob."

Victor raised a brow at the sight of the man who was walking towards them. A man that he had just a day ago, fought, and strangled half to death. "I wonder if the goddess has gotten tired of me cursing her name, these last few days."

Amos gave Victor a puzzled face as Jacob walked up and stood before them.

"It seems like I owe you thanks and apologies, Sir," said Jacob in a deeper voice than usual.

"Between you and me, I think I've had enough of the people in this camp trying to thank me. Between that big fella and the ladies here, I'm wondering if I'd have been safer with your sword at my throat."

Now it was Jacob that gave a confused look.

Victor waved it off, "Just forget it," and pointed to his throat. "How long until it's back to normal?"

Jacob gestured beside Victor, and Victor nodded his acceptance as Jacob sat beside him.

"Healers say a few days, maybe a week's time."

"Good, be a shame to have you talking like that the rest of your life."

"That fighting style you have, it was very—"

"Brillant, I know. I'm a warrior of the goddess herself," said Victor while flicking his hand into the air.

"Em... I was going to say dirty, underhanded, and disgusting."

"Perhaps, but it kept me alive. Being chivalrous was beaten out of me, my first year in the military. Only survival was left after that."

Jacob laughed while rubbing his hair in frustration, "And here I thought I was the hero coming to save the damsel in distress; instead, I wound up on my knees, getting the life choked out of me."

"Keep your girl. If you would have shown up a little earlier and saved my ass, then I would have happily been your damsel in distress."

Jacob coughed while trying to laugh. "You... have an odd humor about you."

"Perhaps. But I prefer to think that I just have a different view of the world than most."

Jacob reached his hand over, "Jacob Highland of the Black Jewel Militia, and you?"

Victor shook Jacob's hand, "Victor Krill, current captive of the Black Jewel Militia."

Jacob stood up with a smirk on his face. "Well then, I only wanted to offer my apologies and thanks, which I have now done. I'll see you around Mr. Captive; I wish to head back and check if the damsels have awoken yet."

In the healers' tent, Rana lay sleeping in her cot as Dessi sat over her rubbing her hair, with Oscar standing behind her.

"Let me know if you remember anything else," said Oscar as he began to leave, but bumped into Jacob as he entered the room.

"Excuse me, Father," said Jacob to Oscar. He then glanced over at Dessi and Rana. "Are they okay?"

"Go have a look for yourself," said Oscar as he walked out of the tent.

Jacob walked over to Dessi, sitting down on the other side of Rana, "How you two holding up?"

Dessi glanced at Jacob's black eye and the claw marks around his neck. "Oh, I imagine we've both seen better days."

Jacob reached over, rubbing Dessi's swollen face. "Sorry,

I didn't get there in time."

Dessi grabbed Jacob's hand, rubbing it against her face to feel his warmth, breathing in the smell of his skin. "It's okay. You're here now."

"They really did a number on you two, though," said Jacob staring down at the bruises on Rana's face. Half her face was scared; she had a deep cut on the top of her forehead and black spots around her eyes.

"She's a lot stronger than she seems, I'd be dead now if not for her." Dessi dropped her head, "But Jasper, he... he didn't make it."

Jacob grimaced at the thought of the man, "He was a good man, do Prinja and Keltre know?"

Dessi nodded, "They were here earlier. I told them what happened. Prinja seemed to already know, but Keltre, she... she took it hard." Dessi bit down on her lip so hard that blood began to drip as her eyes began to water.

"Hey, hey, what's wrong?" asked Jacob as he stood and reached over Rana's cot placing his hands on her shoulder.

"I'm a coward," said Dessi as she gripped her trousers around the knees. "Jasper... he... he died saving me. He pushed me out of the way and took an arrow that was meant for me. I saw him; he was smiling when the arrow went through his neck." Dessi shook her head, "And I didn't have the courage even to tell the girls how he died."

Jacob took a deep breath and let the silence fill the room, giving Dessi time to collect herself, "Listen to me, Jasper died doing what he wanted. If he were here now and if we could ask him. I'm sure he'd make a joke about it and tell us not to worry about him. We've all lost people before, it's our job to keep moving."

Dessi shook her head, frowned, and wiped at her tears. "I'm sorry, you know I usually don't cry this much. It's just... It's just... I bad-mouthed him so much and," she looked over at Rana, "she kept calling out Uncle Jasper in her sleep." Dessi placed her hands over her face trying not to let Jacob see the next flow of tears she felt coming.

Jacob stood up and walked over to Dessi, wrapping his arms around her, and allowing her to cry into him as she clenched his shirt and whelped on his shoulder. He held her until she finally calmed back down. After finally letting Dessi go, he spotted a wooden horse above Rana's blades on a stool next to Rana's bed that he hadn't noticed before. He reached over, picking it up and held it in front of Desi as she began wiping her eyes again. "Where'd this come from?"

Dessi took a deep breath to gather herself before, wiping the last tear from her eye, "Oscar... he... he brought it, I think he made it for her."

Jacob stared back at Dessi as he made his way back around to the stool, "The old man? Really? You've got to be kidding."

"Yeah, remember recently, when you'd sometimes catch him carving some wood, I think he was making that for Rana."

Jacob examined the little toy horse, "I never got a horse; all I ever got was sword training and beatings."

Dessi gave a small chuckle at Jacob, "So you want a toy horse now?"

Slowly Rana began to stir from her slumber and opened her eyes to see Jacob and Dessi smiling back down at her.

Jacob placed the toy back down on the blades.

"Hey there, welcome back, little hero," said Dessi.

Rana recognized Dessi's voice as her eyes opened wide, and she started to panic. Quickly she began flailing in her cot, "Wha... we got... huh... escape."

Jacob grabbed Rana holding her down, "Hey, hey, it's okay. We're safe; you're safe." He repeated the words out loud again, and in her mind, until she finally began to calm down. He let her go, and Rana stared at them, confused.

"We're back at camp now. Everything's okay. Jacob came and saved us," said Dessi.

Jacob felt a ping of pain in his chest at Dessi's words.

But he decided to keep the feelings to himself and let the lie comfort Rana for a while. Dessi rubbed Rana's head, "See, there's Jacob."

Rana stared up at Jacob with confusion in her eyes, but she began to slowly calm down, "What... what happened to your face?"

Jacob laughed, "The same thing I suspect happened to yours."

Rana stared up at him, confused.

"You took an arrow in the leg honey and got beat up real bad," said Dessi as she held Rana's hand. "The healer said, you'll be fine after a moon or so, but you'll need a crutch until then."

Momo and Jomo entered the tent and saw Rana was awake and ran over to her, smiling and talking. Rana smiled back at them, and for the next few hours, she listened to Jacob and Dessi recount the events that lead to them all coming back together.

CHAPTER 29

That night, Victor laid in his tent before Amos stuck his head inside, "Excuse me, Sir, but the commander would like to see you." Victor raised off the floor, scratching his head and followed behind Amos to the commander's tent. He walked in to see Jacob along with Oscar.

"Hello again, how can I help?"

Jacob waved, "Come in."

Oscar walked over and waved a red crystal in front of Victor. "Don't suppose you know what this is."

Victor inspected the gem. It seemed reasonable enough but thought he saw something inside of it and squinted his eyes, trying to get a better view, "Now would be a good time to have my glasses. What's that light moving around inside of it?"

"That's what we're trying to figure out," said Jacob. "Our Sakari healer said that it has power in it, but we don't know what kind of power. According to Dessi, they were putting these crystals into people's bodies."

"In people's bodies?" asked Victor.

"Seems so, she herself said that she cut this one out of a fresh corpse."

Victor grimaced, thinking about it.

Oscar pulled out a small book. "Jasper might have known something about it, but his notes ain't clear. All it says is that, 'Red gems float for magic transfer.' "

Jacob glanced at the book, "Where'd you get that? Isn't it Jasper's?"

"Prinja dropped it off earlier; apparently she and Keltre were meeting up with him outside of town. He gave it to them; she didn't know what to do with it."

"Anything else useful inside?"

"It's Jasper's book, it has everything in it from rumors of the return of the shadow king, to hidden treasure, to building a magic catapult. It even mentions a magic rock people called the Bremlok. And none of it makes sense. It's no wonder he told so many tales, judging by this thing." Oscar slapped the book in his hand and placed it into a pocket. He then walked over and placed the crystal on a table. "All of those are a mystery for another time." He turned back to Victor. "We'll be picking up camp tomorrow and start heading for Latrusa. The trip should only take three days, and we'll leave you at the border or your welcome to travel with us into Jalenworth, where you could probably charter an airship home."

"I appreciate the consideration. In truth, I look forward to this whole mess being over and done with."

In the healer's tent, Rana lay in her cot sleeping when someone entered the tent under cover of darkness. The person crept over to Rana, covering her mouth with their hand. Rana's eyes opened in shock, but her voice was muffled by the hand.

"Well now, looks like it's finally time to break you in."

In the dim light, Rana saw Molan's smiling face in front of her. He ripped off the sheet that was over her and lifted her into his big arms. Rana tried to struggle, but all her muscles were still tired and weak. She tried biting the man's fingers; they felt like chewing on leather. Molan sat with her on his lap as she groaned, trying to pull his hand away from her mouth.

"Tonight, I will claim you as my own."

CHAPTER 30

Jacob fell to the floor of the tent in pain, grabbing his head. "What the hell."

Oscar turned to Jacob, concerned, "What's wrong with you, boy?"

The sound of rattling came from behind them as Victor pointed to the table. "Is it supposed to move like that?"

Oscar turned around, "Is what..." and saw the red crystal shaking on the table. "Now, why would it be..." Suddenly the night sky lit up outside of the tent. Victor opened the flap of the tent as a beam of white light appeared in the night.

Oscar walked forward, staring up at the beam of light, "What in the goddess's name is happening?" The crystal behind them continued to shake, but now it started to emit a loud humming noise. Victor and Oscar turned back to it as the humming noise grew louder and louder. Suddenly the crystal lifted itself from the table and started to glow a brighter crimson that shone through the tent. The red crystal hovered in the air for a few seconds as white light started swirling around inside of it. Oscar narrowed his eyes at the floating gem, and suddenly it exploded, destroying the table it was above and sending the two men tumbling to the floor with Jacob.

"The fuck is happening," shouted Oscar as debris from the explosion flew around the tent, cutting holes in the fabric. He stood back up, looking at a hole in the back of the tent where the table used to be.

Amos ran up to the tent. "Sir... Sir, I think you need to come quick. It's the girl who was in the healer's tent."

Victor and Oscar turned to each other and knew it was Rana again. Oscar grabbed a lantern off a post and headed back outside to where the previous beam of light had now vanished. Victor followed behind Oscar as he made his way through the camp down towards the healer's tent. They both entered, but it was completely dark inside.

Oscar raised the lantern to see as he moved in slowly inside, wary of the shadows. It seemed empty until he spotted a burned and charred cot where Rana was supposed to be. He furrowed his brows and grit his teeth, thinking that someone had snuck in for the girl until he moved a few steps further inside and saw Rana's face off in a corner.

"Girl, girl! Are you okay?" asked Oscar as he stepped forward, shining the lantern light at her. Rana seemed okay to him, although she did not answer to his calls. He stepped past the charred cot getting closer to her, only to see her fully naked and covered in blood. It only took another second to see that Rana sat mounted atop a naked, severely burned, and large dead man.

"What in the goddesses name happened," said Victor as he stared down at Rana, who twisted her neck and began to slowly turn and look back at them.

For a few seconds, Oscar was speechless as he stared at the sight of the girl. He swallowed and took a breath before he regained his composure. "Girl, what happened here?"

Rana stood up and turned to the two men and smiled at them, a smile that sent shivers down their spines. "He... he hurt me."

The two men noticed the blade in her hand as she started to walk towards them with her arrow wounded leg sliding its foot across the burned ground beneath her. The air around her began to swirl with heat. And slowly, a few white lights started to appear around her. The image made it seem as if her upper body was bending out of proportion.

Dessi appeared behind the two men and saw Rana covered in blood. She immediately ran forward, dropping to her knees and wrapped her arms around the girl. "Oh, baby, it's okay now. It's okay now." Dessi felt her skin start to burn for a second. But then suddenly the air around Rana spread out as the small lights vanished. The gust of wind made the light of the lantern in Oscar's hand flicker as Dessi kept repeating, "It's okay now, it's okay now."

Rana dropped the knife and wrapped her hands around Dessi, "I don't... I don't... I don't know anymore."

Oscar stared down where Rana dropped the blade and saw the little toy horse he had carved, now half-burned and covered in blood.

"I have no idea what to make of this, but I'm pretty sure we both almost just died," said Victor.

Oscar watched Dessi, as she and Rana embraced each

other, then took a deep breath. "Dessi, take the girl to get cleaned up. We'll handle things here."

Dessi lifted herself to her feet, grabbing a half-burned cloth from the floor and wrapping it around Rana. "Come on, Rana, let's go back to my tent and get you cleaned up." She held Rana's hand and slowly led her out of the tent as Rana hobbled on her leg on the way out.

Oscar walked forward, picking up the toy horse and the blade, noticing that both were soaked in blood.

Victor examined the cot and noticed that even the ground beneath it had been burned. He then turned to Oscar, "You ever seen anything like that before?"

"No."

"The girl obviously has talent, but with Jacob collapsing on the floor and the crystal exploding, all around the same time. That's not just some happenstance."

Oscar rubbed at the blood and soot beneath him on the ground, grinding it between his fingers. "Perhaps not, but that's something to figure out later. We're leaving first thing in the morning." He glanced over at the dead body of Molan. His skin seemed as if it had been put through a furnace, and his eyes were gone; only empty burned dark sockets remained. Oscar grimaced at the sight, then and placed the wooden horse back into his cloak. He then stood up and began walking out of the tent. After exiting, he saw that a crowd of people had gathered outside, "Alright everyone, go back to your tents. It's over. We pack everything up first thing in the morning." A few soldiers parroted his words as he made his way back to his tent with Victor behind him.

"That light that we saw, I'm pretty sure that thing could be seen from leagues away," said Victor.

"Aye, and I'm sure people will come snooping around for the cause of it soon enough, but if we panic and try to leave now, only confusion and chaos will follow. Best to let the people's minds settle in the night before we move."

Amos ran back up to them, "Commander, I have more

news."

Oscar shook his head while not breaking his stride, "What now, can't it wait?"

"Sir, it seems like whatever happened affected all the mages in camp. Most of them were on the ground, passed out, or throwing up. I ain't even seen one of 'em that could even stand up."

"All of them?" asked Victor.

"I done been through the main camp; it appears like it's all of 'em."

Oscar stopped and began to think before he turned to Amos, "Fine, take me to see some of the other mages, I've already seen what it's done to my son. There are still a few things that must be handled tonight. None of which sounds pleasant." Oscar nodded to his tent. "Victor, go and ensure my son isn't dead from whatever that was, and I'll try to ensure that I still have a camp before the morning rises."

A little while later, over in Dessi's tent, she was keeling over a bucket of bloody water and with a wet rag in her hand. She dunked the cloth into the water and squeezed it as the dark crimson water slid back down into the bucket. She reached over and began to wipe off a covered in blood Rana as the girl sat there on the floor with her arms around her knees.

"Why... why did he..."

"Some men try to take what they want; it's not your fault Rana. It's..."

"His hand... He put his hand inside... I... I felt it."

Dessi stopped washing Rana and slid around in front of her. She reached up to her doublet and began unbuttoning her top. She finished and removed it from her body then lifted her small clothes above her head, tossing it to the floor, exposing her body for Rana to see.

"I guess you haven't seen these yet since you were out when they brought us back."

Rana stared at the markings and wounds over Dessi's body. There were small slash wounds all over her body, across her shoulders and breasts.

"Twice... 'I've been... I've been raped twice. The first was... well it was my..." Dessi looked down and started rubbing at the scars over her body. "These scars are from all the missions I've done over the last five years."

"Angela..." said Rana.

Dessi looked at her, confused.

"There... There was a girl named Angela, she... she was in the tavern. She said it happened to her too. The men did the scars to her."

"I know Angela, Broderick, has her work in the kitchen." Dessi reached out her hand to Rana. "Come here, Rana." Dessi waited for Rana to feel comfortable enough to crawl over to her, and she wrapped her arms around the girl's still bloody body. "It's not easy; it won't be easy being with us here."

"I don't... I don't have anywhere else to go."

"Most of the people here don't, to us this is the only home we've ever known. Did you know that I was homeless when Oscar found me? Pickpocketing on the streets of Kirkwald. I tried to steal from Oscar when I saw him in town once. He caught me, spanked me, and then sent me off to train with Addison." Dessi raised her head, glancing around her tent. "And I've been with the group ever since. Everything I own is in this little tent." Dessi squeezed Rana in her arms "I wonder what would have happened to me if I'd stayed a pickpocket. It's a shit life I know, but it's a life I'm choosing for myself and if—"

The flap to the tent opened as Oscar walked in to see a half-naked Dessi and a fully naked and blood-covered Rana. Walking in, he stood before them as they stared up at him.

"She's not clean yet," said Oscar.

"We were having a talk," said Dessi with an annoyed tone on her lips. "And we're not exactly ready to have guests yet."

Oscar rubbed at his chin and smirked, "I wonder if you'd say that if it was my son that walked in here. Oh, he's passed out on the floor, by the way."

"What! What happened," asked Dessi.

Oscar gestured to Rana, "Whatever that little one did, damn near knocked out every mage in the camp. And speaking of what you did, I was told that you managed to free Dessi before she could get herself killed."

Rana looked up to Oscar and opened her mouth before closing it not knowing what to say.

"She did, and she was very brave," said Dessi.

"Be that as it may, the girl has been with less than a week, and she's killed two men, rescued you from death, and crippled every mage in my camp. I think she should now understand what life will be like here. You wanted to become a warrior, tell me what do you want to be now."

"Oscar, this is hardly the time," said Dessi, shaking her head.

"This is the perfect time. Right now, when everything is fresh in her mind, she will need to understand exactly what happens here."

Rana scowled up at Oscar, "Did you... did you send him and make him do that to me?"

Oscar looked into Rana's eyes as they began to once again fill with hate and took a deep breath. "No, I'm a lot of things, but I'm not the type to send a man to rape a child. That is one thing I shall never be. You killed him, and that was probably for the best, because after that, I would have had him killed myself and forced you to watch."

"Oscar, I think that's enough, you should let her rest now," said Dessi.

"Fine, I've just come to give and return something." Oscar reached into his cloak and pulled out the jewel-encrusted blade he told Rana to keep after they had used it to kill the man in the tent. He knelt and placed it before Rana. "Staying with us means that in the future I may send you to the bed of a man whom I wish you to kill. But I promise that I'll never send a man to your bed." Oscar nodded to Dessi. "The one holding you now is proof of my words on that." He then reached at his other side and pulled out a small book. This was Jasper's book; Rana's eyes focused on the book as she remembered Jasper scribbling in it that night in the stables, and unconsciously she reached out her hand for it.

"Go on, take it," Oscar allowed the girl to take the book as Rana held it against her chest. He closed his eyes and sighed before standing back up and leaving the blade of the floor in front of Rana. He turned around and began to leave the tent.

Rana slowly reached out for the blade taking it in her hand, "The horse."

Oscar turned back around, "What's that?"

Rana lifted herself from Dessi's arms and hobbled over to Oscar, holding the blade and the book. "You made me a horse. Can I have it back?"

Oscar and Dessi turned to each other with equal surprise in her eyes before. But Dessi just shrugged her shoulders in confusion. Oscar returned his gaze back to the naked and bloody Rana before him and reached into his cloak, pulling out the burned and blood-soaked small wooden horse. Rana took the horse and hobbled her way back to the bucket of water with her items. She knelt, placing the bloody toy, blade, and book beside her as she grabbed the wet towel, dunking it in the bucket, and began cleaning herself. Oscar just stared at her for a moment, before turning his back to her and leaving the tent.

A few seconds later, Dessi began to hear Rana start crying. She turned around. "Rana, what's..." Dessi looked down to see Jasper's book open, and on the last page, she saw a crude drawing of bread, next to the words, *Save the muffin.*

CHAPTER 31

The following morning Victor watched as the camp was broken down and loaded into wagons. He walked up the hill to see Jacob sitting outside his father's tent, sharpening his sword with a whetstone.

Victor waved at Jacob, "How's the head?"

"Still hurts like hell, but better than last night, I can assure you."

"You remember anything, from when it happened?"

Jacob stared up at the blue sky above the camping grounds, "I remember hearing voices in my head, and when I tried to push them away, everything went dark."

"That sounds like a pain in the ass, honestly," said Victor as he leaned against the support beam on the tent. "They said what happened last night only affected mages. I didn't realize you were one."

"I guess it never came up," said Jacob, and he slid the whetstone across his blade.

"It didn't come up in our fight either," said Victor with a suspicious look on his face.

"Oh! I tried, especially when you had that string around my neck. But my magic doesn't work unless I touch you, and I had gloves on at the time, so I figure it was useless either way, really."

Two soldiers left the tent behind them, with Oscar himself stepping outside into the morning sun.

"You find out anything good?" asked Victor.

"Still nothing on that damned crystal. And seeing as it's gone and blown up, I don't think I'll learn anything anyway. But as for that incident with the mages last night. Apparently, all the sakari mages were fine. Whatever that was didn't affect them at all."

"So, only kingdom mages, then?" asked Victor.

"Seems like it."

Amos ran up to the tent, "Sorry, Sir, but I bring bad news."

Oscar dropped his head and sighed before turning to the boy, "Amos you really are the bringer of bad tidings. I swear during the next war, I'll surrender you to our enemy, just to ensure our victory."

Both Victor and Jacob chuckled at Oscar's jest.

Oscar waved his hand at Amos. "Well you're here now, go on, spit it out."

"A group of people have come out of the woods and would like to speak with you. One is even claiming to be

Prince Saffron of Burlus."

"Shit," said Victor.

Oscar narrowing his eyes at Victor, then turned back to Amos rubbing his eyebrows, "You said it was a group of them. About how many?"

"Ah, about a dozen or so, I think," said Amos.

"Well, no need to drag it out, let's go and see his highness."

They walked down the hill to the edge of the camp, and Victor could see Prince Saffron as he approached. Getting closer, he saw Frenka and Dekol, who now had his arm in a sling. They all approached and stood before the prince.

"Greetings and salutations, I am Prince Saffron of the Kingdom of Burlus."

"And I'm Oscar Highland, commander of this here group of happy folk. What can I do for ya, your highness?"

Dessi walked up behind the crowd that had formed behind Oscar, with Rana beside her with her arm on a stick to support her injured leg.

"I am under the impression that you have the kingdom's property in your group. A small girl named Fairline Hasher; she might also be going under the name Rana."

"Aye, she's here," said Oscar scratching his head.

"Good, then if you'd be so kind as to—"

"Ya can't have her, she's mine now," said Oscar so quickly that the prince began choking on his own words.

"I... I'm sorry, Sir. But that wasn't a request; we're taking the girl."

"Well as far as I see it, you're not my prince, and Nevander's not my king, and no matter how powerful you are. Not even you're stupid enough to start a fight here. Not when I have plenty mages of my own."

The prince peered over the increasing amount of people that were gathering around them and performed a double-take when he noticed that even sakari were among their ranks. "You... you can't just assume you'll get away with this. Perhaps we could negotiate a trade. You're a mercenary, after all. Perhaps if I were to offer some sort of monetary arrangement."

"Oh a negotiation is it. Okay, you're right, that girl you've been searching for is special. Both you and I know it. So how about you either go back where you came from or fight here and lose, and I'll take that girl straight to Queen Floranna. I'm sure that magic academy of hers will have a big interest in what's so special about her."

The prince twisted his mouth, "That's not a negotiation, that's blackmail."

"And blackmails the best type of negotiation. I taught your father that some years back. But why not let the girl decide." Oscar turned around and saw Dessi with Rana in front of her. "Rana, come here, girl," he said as he waved at Rana to come forth.

Rana planted her wooden crutch into the ground and slowly hoped her way forward with Dessi behind her.

"Now girl, this here be Prince Saffron, he says you should go with him. And seeing how you saved Dessi's life. I'll let you decide what you want to do with yours. You can stay with your family here, or you can go with that prince over there."

Rana looked over at Prince Saffron as he smiled back at her.

"Come here, Fairline; I'll take you to a big castle where you'll be safe. Don't you wanna live in a castle?"

Rana looked up at Oscar, "And you'll let me go if I want?"

Oscar nodded, "As I said, you've earned the right to choose. This is your decision to make. It's not mine anymore."

Rana stared at the prince for a few seconds, "I... I think I'd rather stay with you... Father."

Oscar turned back towards Prince Saffron with the wickedest smile the prince had ever seen. "It seems like the decision has been made. So, if you'll excuse me, your highness, I must get going. But if you still feel I am being unfair, tell your father that Oscar Highland says hello, and that he's keeping the girl. That should do well enough."

The prince frowned as Oscar began to walk away, then he turned to Victor. "Don't suppose you'll be able to talk some sense into them."

Victor just shrugged as he walked forward over to Frenka and Dekol. "Glad to see you two survived."

"You look like you almost didn't," said Frenka as she rubbed at the cuts on the side of Victor's face. Victor quickly glanced over at Saffron to see if he noticed her attention to him. But his back was turned as he watched Rana wander back off into the crowd.

"How many did you get after you jumped off the cart?" asked Victor.

"I think I got six or seven before I made run for it," said Frenka. "Prince appeared soon after, got things under control. Did you get any after you left? I saw some mount and head through gates after I ran."

"I only got two," Victor thought about his fight with Jacob, "Well two and a half. What about you, Dekol?"

"Twenty-one before I got an arrow in the shoulder."

"Goddess protect me; I don't know whether to be surprised or terrified."

Victor glanced over at the prince, who was shaking his head while talking to his guards. "I'm pleased he's not going to do anything fancy."

Frenka whispered, "Not sure he could. We pass out last night from something strange. He not look it, but prince feeling pretty weak now."

CHAPTER 32

Days later, Rana was sitting on the back of a cart of supplies being pulled by horses as The Black Jewels approached the border to the kingdom of Latrusa. Her leg was still wrapped as she had trouble walking.

Victor rode up beside her on a horse. "We finally made it; you gonna be okay?"

Rana looked up at him, "I... I think so; what are you gonna do now?"

Victor glanced over at the gate to the mountains as they passed it. "Well, there's no need for me to stop here. I figured I'd follow you all till you got to a town with a port for airships, and I'll try to find a ride back to Mari." Victor stared at Rana oddly for a second, "Why does your hair and eyes do that?"

"Do what?" asked Rana.

"When I'm away from you, you have blonde hair. But when I get close to you, it changes back to brown."

"I don't know; whenever I see myself in a mirror, I always have brown hair."

"Another mystery for another day, I guess, but it's not like you aren't' filled with enough mystery about you already," said Victor shaking his head.

"Oh, thank you for saving me. Dessi told me what happened in the city."

Victor smiled down at her, "That just means I'm one up on you, next time you're going to have to save me."

Rana smiled back, "I'll remember that."

Victor reached his hand out to Rana's face. "Your face is still pretty scared on one side, you should probably..." But at the sight of his hand, Rana flinched and placed her hands over her head to protect herself while closing her eyes. Victor quickly snatched his hand back, "Sorry, I didn't mean to scare you."

Rana realized what she was doing and opened her eyes, pulled her arms down from her head, and noticed her hands were trembling. She looked up at Victor, "I'm sorry... I didn't mean... I don't know why I did that."

Victor looked back down at her, concerned, "Don't worry. I guess it's to be expected after everything you've been through."

Rana looked at Victor's hand again as he gripped the reins of his horse and took a deep breath, "Can I... can I hold your hand for a bit?"

Victor narrowed his eyes, "You sure, there's no need to force—"

"I'm sure, can I please."

Victor frowned, but sighed his consent, and extended his arm out for Rana to inspect.

She reached her small hands over and placed them on Victor's fingers, rubbing at his palm. His hands seemed so rough and hard to her; his fingers had small cuts all across them from gripping things tightly. *Why are his fingers so much bigger than mine? These are a man's fingers, like his fingers. I wanna be strong too. If i were strong, then... then...*

Victor glanced ahead to see Gregga talking to Oscar, before she broke away from him leading a horde of her sakari warriors with her back into Burlus. They were followed by Keltre and Prinja.

"Where do you think they're headed?" asked Victor to Rana before he noticed the tears in her eyes and quickly pulled his hand back. "Hey, are you okay?"

"Huh?" asked Rana as she looked up at a blurry Victor. She quickly realized that she had started crying and started to wipe at her eyes. "I'm sorry, I didn't mean to..."

"It's okay... just take your time. No need to try and force yourself."

Rana dropped her head with a frown while closing her eyes, "Okay."

Victor shook his head and looked up ahead at Oscar on his horse, "Tell me something; you don't really think of Oscar like a father do you?"

Rana turned her head back trying to blink away the last drops of tears from her eyes as she watched Oscar bounce along on his horse, "He's... he's not like my real Papa, but he treats me nice... sometimes and says that he'd teach me things. But he said that I would have to change my name from now on, to make sure the king and other people don't find me."

Victor nodded, "A smart plan, I doubt you'd want to get taken away after everything you've been through. How did you come up with Rana anyway?"

"Papa used to tell me stories about Rana and her sister Isha, when they went on a quest to save the Kingdom of Jillian."

"Now there's a tale I haven't heard before," said Victor as he looked ahead towards the sky. "So, no more Rana the Bold or Fairline Hasher? Have you decided what you want to be called in your new life?"

"No... not yet. I haven't really thought about it much."

"Well, you still have plenty of time to decide. And your new family up there seems like they plan to keep you around."

"I guess so... I mean, Dessi treats me real good and tries to take care of me."

"Well, a wise man once said, 'the family you make is often stronger than the one that made you.'"

"Who said that?"

"I did, just now. And I'm quite wise if I do say so myself. But will you be learning magic? That show you put on a few days ago was impressive."

"Oscar... I mean, father said he knew someone named Soulden who would teach me."

Victor's eyes opened wide, "Soulden... as in Soulden Fegmont of the floating city?"

Rana tilted her head in confusion, "What floating city?" Victor pointed to the horizon, and Rana turned around to see off in the distance this huge thing floating in the sky. "What is that?"

"That, little Rana, is Sceana, the Magic Academy of Latrusa. The school where the best mages in the world go to train."

Rana stared at it in amazement but noticed something large and red at the bottom of the floating island. "Victor, what's that red thing, under the city?"

"Oh, that's the magic crystal that keeps the city in the sky, airships run off the same thing. But the one under the city is said to be the largest in the world and..." Suddenly Victor remembered the red crystal that blew up in Oscar's tent and watched as Rana stared in amazement at the large one underneath the school.

"It seems I have something to talk with Oscar about," said Victor as he reached out his hand to rub Rana's head, but stopped himself and instead extended his finger to her.

Rana smiled and grabbed his finger for a second, before Victor smiled back and rode off ahead to speak with Oscar. Rana then turned back to the giant red crystal beneath the city. She began to think that she could feel the power inside of it, like it was calling to her. Rana reached down beside her, pulling up the small wooden horse that Oscar had made for her. It was still burned at the bottom side and still had traces of blood on the other side. She began rubbing the blood-stained side of the wooden horse with her thumb as she held it up and gazed at the toy's image beside her vision of the Magic Academy of Latrusa.

Teddy Baire

Thank you for taking the time to read this novel. More info on any upcoming novels from Teddy Baire can be found at:

www.afantasybook.com
https://twitter.com/afantasybook

www.ingramcontent.com/pod-product-compliance
Lightning Source LLC
Chambersburg PA
CBHW020346220726
48290CB00014B/1197